JACK JACKSON'S
AMERICAN HISTORY
VOLUME I

J. SEGUÍN

J. W. HARDIN

LOS TEJANOS

AND

LOST CAUSE

Fantagraphics Books
7563 Lake City Way NE
Seattle, Washington 98115

Editor: Gary Groth
Associate Editor: J. Michael Catron
Designer: Emory Liu
Production: Paul Baresh
Associate Publisher: Eric Reynolds
Publishers: Gary Groth and Kim Thompson

To receive a free catalog of comics, graphic novels,
prose novels, artist monographs, and other fine
works of artistry, call 1-800-657-1100, or visit
www.fantagraphics.com.

ISBN: 978-1-60699-504-4

First Fantagraphics Books printing: December, 2012

Printed in China

TABLE OF CONTENTS

⊷ LOS TEJANOS ⊷

⊷ LOST CAUSE ⊷

⊷ EXTRAS ⊷

LOS TEJANOS

THE TRUE STORY OF JUAN N. SEGUIN AND THE TEXAS-MEXICANS DURING THE RISING OF THE LONE STAR

BY JACK JACKSON

INTRODUCTION TO LOS TEJANOS by Ron Hansen

Texas History Movies ©1970 Graphic Ideas, Inc., and ©1974 by T.S.H.A., Austin, TX.

American cartoonist Jack Jackson was born in tiny Pandora, Texas in 1941, the great-great-grandchild of one of the first settlers in the post-revolutionary Republic of Texas. Jackson once noted that as a schoolboy in a town just south of Seguin, he read the "nasty, racist little comic book" *Texas History Movies* that, in spite of its repellent nature, "launched my career as a distinguished Texas historian, recognized for my attention to the Latino contribution."

That career would hang fire while he majored in accounting at the University of Texas and contributed to its irreverent humor magazine *The Texas Ranger*. After being fired from the magazine for what he called "a petty censorship violation," Jackson, under the pen name "Jaxon," self-published and peddled around Austin, in 1964, the satirical pamphlet *God Nose*, since identified as one of the very first underground comic books.

In San Francisco, in the psychedelic '60s, he found work as an art director for posters announcing Avalon Ballroom concerts. In 1969, Jackson, with other Texas expatriates Fred Todd, Dave Moriaty, and Gilbert Shelton, co-founded Rip Off Press, one of the first independent publishers of underground comix.

But by the mid-'70s Jackson was back in Austin, getting by as an accountant, and concentrating on retelling Texas history through pageantry, sarcasm, caricature, and an ever impish wit. In 1979 he published *Comanche Moon*, a graphic biography of Quanah Parker, through Last Gasp, another publisher of comix. In 1981 he submitted the 125 captivating pages of *Los Tejanos* to Fantagraphics Books.

Jackson's creative method involved extensive, loving, and almost obsessive research. He first mapped out the full book, distilling the history and jotting out the high and low points. Then, he fractionalized chapters into likely pages and panels. Finally, he wrote the complete narrative before beginning the exciting, all-important drawings.

He executed his artwork on 10-inch by 15-inch sheets of paper, in pen and ink, with little else beyond his highly organized imagination. All decisions in terms of the size and shape of the panels, their sequencing, visual rhythm, and emotional and narrative content were Jackson's, not an editor's.

The regularity of the lettering above and inside the panels might suggest that an eccentric font was used, but in fact each character was hand drawn, itself an arduous and painstaking task that permitted no smears or misspellings. Each page was then hung and dried, then stacked. Finally, the gigantic pile of paper containing hundreds of drawings was submitted to Fantagraphics.

Jackson ultimately would sell all his original art to make extra income, but because he was so meticulous, he made pristine, full-size, Xerox copies of all his work. This book is based on those.

The choice of topic was completely Jackson's. Historical novelists such as Jackson have in common a fetching and bewitching wonder about the origins of things: Where did this come from? Why do we say that? Who is the person named there — and how come I've never heard of him or her?

At the core of all historical novelists is the quest for finality, truth, and justice. They accumulate books, scour footnotes, visit locations, and assiduously research an enormous variety of musty historical documents to

This sequence is from Jack Jackson's *God Nose*

From *Los Tejanos*

determine what was left out in the retellings, or how much was fact and how much was bias in what has been handed down.

Such was the case with Jack Jackson, whose fascination with and profound respect for the history of the Lone Star State compelled him to seek out sources. Jackson acutely felt the marginalization of most artists — particularly those who focus on the graphic novel — so he was primed to look for those historical personalities who themselves had been overlooked or misunderstood.

Writing on the general theme of *Los Tejanos*, Jackson noted:

> When we "Remember the Alamo," it is usually a vision of a small, grim band of Anglo-Saxon martyrs being overwhelmed by a screaming horde of maniacal Mexicans, their bayonets glistening with the blood of patriots as they trample in endless waves into the sanctuary of Texas liberty.
>
> What we don't remember is that *inside* the walls of the Alamo, amongst its defenders, there were also Mexicans who fought and died, except they called themselves "Tejanos" — Texans! Nor do we remember that at the battle of San Jacinto, where in eighteen minutes the fate of a vast land was decided, there was also a company of Tejano volunteers fighting beside Sam Houston and the Anglo conquerors.

And so Jackson focused his considerable talents, time, and energy on Juan N. Seguín, a Mexican "Tejano" who so opposed the anti-federalist dictator Antonio Santa Anna that he became a cavalry officer under Stephen F. Austin, helped rout the Mexican army in the conclusive battle of San Jacinto, and was elected to a senate seat in the new Republic of Texas in 1839.

Two years later, Seguín became mayor of a racially divided San Antonio, but soon resigned due to extreme financial difficulties and fraudulent charges that he was

in favor of the "reconquest" of Texas.

With numerous threats on his life, he in vain sought peace and exile in Laredo, where he was arrested and forced to serve as a captain under the hated "Napoleon of the West," Santa Anna. Riding against his former Tejano and Anglo friends on the land that he loved in the Mexican-American War, Seguín seemed to confirm for others that he was a turncoat and traitor. Still, he somehow managed to reconstruct his life in Texas, establishing a ranch, penning a memoir, and finding such new respectability that he was became a county judge in his old age.

Jack Jackson soon realized that Seguín had, for the most part, been erased from Texas history.

Jackson wrote of *Los Tejanos* and Juan Seguín, "Had he been Anglo, his name would be remembered among the lists of the great — beside Travis, Crockett, Bowie, and the rest. But being Tejano, his contribution has been ignored, for his exploits did not conveniently fit into the myth of Anglo-Saxon prowess that historians have seen fit to fashion from the events of our revolution."

Jackson took on the job of illustrating Seguín's life and restoring the reputation of a highly influential Latino whom he felt had been badly misjudged. He did this out of a deep sympathy — and possibly from a sense of kinship with a man of conviction and purpose whom others would have ostracized and silenced.

In *Los Tejanos*, Jackson makes his case with a stately presentation of facts that are freshened and enlivened by the opinionated wit, surprise, verve, and melodrama

From *Los Tejanos*

From *Los Tejanos*

of his wonderfully drawn depictions. It is the nature and appeal of graphic novels to be as histrionic, fervent, and damning as televangelists, and so readers of *Los Tejanos* can be entertained by the grotesque features and defects that one instantly recognizes as the given aspect of a villain, while noting the tenderly limned, governor's mansion portraits of those whom Jackson considered heroes. Often, he populates his scenes with background figures that represent all those who have been silenced and forgotten — the peons, the underlings, the wives and children, the unskilled and seemingly unimportant.

Recognizing that he had hundreds of illustrations to create, we realize that there could only be so much attention devoted to detail, even for one who never hurried his labors of love. Yet there is an expressive clarity of line in Jackson's art, especially in his pastoral and architectural views. Working in the hard-edged medium of pen and ink, he employs old school crosshatching to evoke softer tones. A fierce Comanche warrior can only manage a "GAKK!" in one frame as Jim Bowie's "thirsty knife drinks its fill," while in another panel there may be a ceremonial view with all the serenity and mannerly poise of a festive wedding picture.

The range of tone, the irony, and the seriousness of his subject matter created a market resistance to Jackson's art that he never overcame. Over twenty years, *Los Tejanos* sold only 4,000 copies. As Fantagraphics publisher Gary Groth told me, "Selling Jack has always been tough. [*Los Tejanos*] was published at a time when there was no bookstore distribution for comics or graphic novels, so it was only available in comic book stores (which want superhero comics, not stories about American history) and old underground venues like head shops.... Jack always struggled financially and my impression was that he lived a very Spartan life.... Since he was paid royalties based on the sale of his books, he was always paid a pittance. The original *Los Tejanos* book retailed for $7.95 in 1981 and if we in fact sold 4,000 copies over twenty years, he would've been paid a grand total of $2,544."

But there are other forms of compensation. The first and most lasting is the sheer artistic satisfaction in having produced, *ex nihilo*, a good thing. Another is the critical recognition that too often arrives after one has gone. Jack Jackson died in 2006, but not before he was made a Lifetime Fellow of the Texas State Historical Association and was inducted into the Texas Institute of Letters. In 2011 he was posthumously inducted into the Will Eisner Award Hall of Fame, an honor bestowed upon cartoonists for a lifetime of meritorious work.

And what did he call that work? As Jackson humbly said in a 1998 interview, "I wanted to do at least a couple of books to show that you could teach Texas history in a picture form. And that you could put enough research into it to get you a doctorate... and at the same time make that information accessible to somebody that doesn't have a high school education. And to me, that's a challenging and interesting trick."

With *Los Tejanos*, we can consider that trick honorably, deftly, and beautifully accomplished.

———

RON HANSEN'S most recent novel is *A Wild Surge of Guilty Passion*. His other novels include *The Assassination of Jesse James by the Coward Robert Ford* and *Desperadoes*. He is the Gerard Manley Hopkins, S.J. Professor in the Arts and Humanities at Santa Clara University, where he teaches courses in writing and literature.

From *Lost Cause*

LOS TEJANOS IS DEDICATED TO MY CHILDHOOD CHUM, JESÚS "JESSE" CONTRERAS, AND TO OUR LOST INNOCENCE, WHICH DIDN'T SEE ANY DIFFERENCE BETWEEN BROWN AND WHITE.

FOR MEXICANS — AS MUCH BECAUSE OF OUR INDIAN ORIGINS AS OUR SPANISH ORIGINS — RESPECT IS AN IMPORTANT THING. WE LINK IT VERY MUCH WITH OUR DIGNITY. FEELING THAT WE ARE BEING TREATED WITH RESPECT, WE CAN DO ANYTHING.

JOSÉ LÓPEZ PORTILLO
PRESIDENT OF MEXICO, 1981

THE REAL, UNDERLYING CAUSE OF THE TEXAS REVOLUTION WAS EXTREME ETHNIC DIFFERENCE BETWEEN TWO SETS OF MEN, NEITHER OF WHOM, BECAUSE OF DIFFERENT IDEAS OF GOVERNMENT, RELIGION, AND SOCIETY, HAD ANY RESPECT FOR THE OTHER. ADDED TO THIS WAS THE INHERENT DISTASTE OF ANGLO-AMERICANS FOR THE RACIAL COMPOSITION OF THE MEXICAN NATION.

T.R. FEHRENBACH
"LONE STAR", 1968

OF THE MEXICAN CHARACTER I NEVER ENTERTAINED A HIGH REGARD. I LOOKED UPON THE MEXICANS AS BEING AN INFERIOR RACE, DOMINEERING, LAZY, VINDICTIVE, AND TREACHEROUS, AND OFTEN TOLD MY COMRADES THAT THERE WAS NO MORE HARM IN KILLING A 'GREASER' THAN THERE WAS IN SLAYING A COMANCHE.

CREED TAYLOR
"REMINISCENCES", 1901

THE MEXICAN CITIZENS OF TEXAS WHO WERE LOYAL TO THE REPUBLIC OFTEN HAD THEIR LOYALTY SEVERELY TRIED BY THE ILLIBERAL SUSPICIONS AND ROUGH BEARING OF THE LOWER ORDER OF THE ANGLO-AMERICAN ELEMENT; AND IT WAS *THIS*, MORE THAN ANY NORMAL TENDENCY TO DISAFFECTION, WHICH DROVE SEGUIN FROM THE FLAG UNDER WHICH HE FOUGHT SO GALLANTLY. IN NO PEOPLE ARE RACE ANTIPATHIES LIABLE TO BE MORE BIGOTED AND MEAN THAN IN THOSE OF ANGLO-SAXON BLOOD; AND OF THE UNDER STRATA OF THAT BREED THE LOW AMERICAN IS PERHAPS THE WORST EXAMPLE.

REUBEN M. POTTER
"THE TEXAS REVOLUTION", 1878

SAN ANTONIO CLAIMED THEN, AS IT CLAIMS NOW, TO BE THE FIRST CITY OF TEXAS; IT WAS ALSO THE RECEPTACLE OF THE SCUM OF SOCIETY. MY POLITICAL AND SOCIAL SITUATION BROUGHT ME INTO CONTINUAL CONTACT WITH THAT CLASS OF PEOPLE. AT EVERY HOUR OF THE DAY AND NIGHT, MY COUNTRYMEN RAN TO ME FOR PROTECTION AGAINST THE ASSAULTS AND EXTRACTIONS OF THOSE ADVENTURERS. SOMETIMES BY PERSUASION I PREVAILED ON THEM TO DESIST; SOMETIMES ALSO, FORCE HAD TO BE RESORTED TO.

HOW COULD I HAVE DONE OTHERWISE? WERE NOT THE VICTIMS MY OWN COUNTRYMEN, FRIENDS, AND ASSOCIATES? COULD I LEAVE THEM DEFENSELESS, EXPOSED TO THE ASSAULTS OF FOREIGNERS, WHO, ON THE PRETEXT THAT THEY WERE MEXICAN, TREATED THEM WORSE THAN BRUTES?

JUAN N. SEGUIN
"MEMOIRS", 1858

Juan Nep.no Seguin

TEXAS HISTORY IS FILLED WITH TRAGIC FIGURES, BUT NONE MORE TRAGIC — OR CONTROVERSIAL — THAN JUAN NEPOMUCENO SEGUIN.

BY SIDING WITH THE REBELLIOUS "TEXIANS" AND HELPING TO WIN INDE-PENDENCE, HE AND HIS FELLOW "TEJANOS" EARNED FOR THEMSELVES LASTING DAMNATION FROM MEXICO, THEIR CULTURAL HOMELAND, AND THE STIGMA OF TRAITORS. BUT EVENTS IN THE TUMULTOUS REPUBLIC OF TEXAS WERE SOON TO PLACE MEN LIKE SEGUIN, CAUGHT IN THE MIDDLE OF AN ANGLO/MEXICAN CONTINENTAL STRUGGLE, IN AN EQUALLY UNENVIABLE POSITION. THUS, HE BECAME A "TRAITOR" TWICE — FIRST TO MEXICO, THEN TO TEXAS — AND BOTH SIDES HAVE BEEN DISOWNING HIM EVER SINCE.

SEGUIN WAS THE FIRST AND MOST INFLUENTIAL TEJANO TO EXPERIENCE THE IDENTITY CRISIS OF STANDING ASTRIDE THE TWO OPPOSING CULTURES. HIS STORY IS UNIQUE BUT AT THE SAME TIME TYPICAL, JUST AS HIS PER-SONAL MISFORTUNES SPEAK ELOQUENTLY OF THE LARGER TRAGEDY OF HIS PEOPLE. "AMERICAN", BUT STILL "MEXICAN", NEITHER COUNTRY KNEW WHAT TO DO WITH THEM AND NEITHER, IN A SENSE, WANTED THEM. "LOS TEJANOS" — INDEED, ALL THE MEXICANS LEFT STRANDED ON U.S. SOIL AFTER 1848— WERE PAINFUL REMINDERS. TO MEXICO, THEY WERE REMINDERS OF ITS WORST NATIONAL DISGRACE; TO THE UNITED STATES, OF ITS MOST GRASPING ACT OF IMPERIALISM.

WIN OR LOSE, WE USUALLY TRY TO FORGET OUR PAINFUL REMINDERS. AND SO, JUAN SEGUIN'S SHADE WAS CAST INTO OBLIVION, FORCED TO WANDER RESTLESSLY BACK AND FORTH ACROSS AN INTERNATIONAL "TWILIGHT ZONE", KNOWN AS THE RIO GRANDE BORDER. HIS DESCEND-ANTS — THE PEOPLE HE CAME TO SYMBOLIZE — HAVE BEEN LEFT ADRIFT IN THIS SAME LIMBO FOR A CENTURY AND A HALF. IGNORED OR DISPARAGED, THEY HAVE RECEIVED LITTLE CREDIT FOR THEIR CON-TRIBUTION TO THE SHAPING OF OUR SOUTHWEST. *BASTA!*

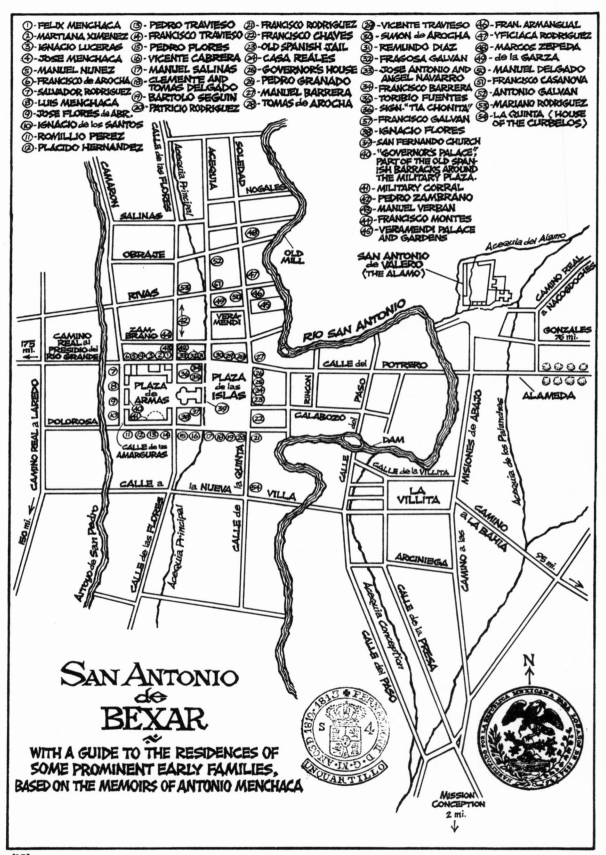

1 - FELIX MENCHACA
2 - MARTIANA XIMENEZ
3 - IGNACIO LUCERAS
4 - JOSE MENCHACA
5 - MANUEL NUNEZ
6 - FRANCISCO de AROCHA
7 - SALVADOR RODRIGUEZ
8 - LUIS MENCHACA
9 - JOSE FLORES de ABR.
10 - IGNACIO de los SANTOS
11 - ROMILLIO PEREZ
12 - PLACIDO HERNANDEZ
13 - PEDRO TRAVIESO
14 - FRANCISCO TRAVIESO
15 - PEDRO FLORES
16 - VICENTE CABRERA
17 - MANUEL SALINAS
18 - CLEMENTE AND TOMAS DELGADO
19 - BARTOLO SEGUIN
20 - PATRICIO RODRIGUEZ
21 - FRANCISCO RODRIGUEZ
22 - FRANCISCO CHAVES
23 - OLD SPANISH JAIL
24 - CASA REALES
25 - GOVERNOR'S HOUSE
26 - PEDRO GRANADO
27 - MANUEL BARRERA
28 - TOMAS de AROCHA
29 - VICENTE TRAVIESO
30 - SIMON de AROCHA
31 - REMUNDO DIAZ
32 - FRAGOSA GALVAN
33 - JOSE ANTONIO AND ANGEL NAVARRO
34 - FRANCISCO BARRERA
35 - TORIBIO FUENTES
36 - SIGN." TIA CHONITA"
37 - FRANCISCO GALVAN
38 - IGNACIO FLORES
39 - SAN FERNANDO CHURCH
40 - "GOVERNOR'S PALACE", PART OF THE OLD SPANISH BARRACKS AROUND THE MILITARY PLAZA.
41 - MILITARY CORRAL
42 - PEDRO ZAMBRANO
43 - MANUEL VERBAN
44 - FRANCISCO MONTES
45 - VERAMENDI PALACE AND GARDENS
46 - FRAN. ARMANGUAL
47 - YFICIACA RODRIGUEZ
48 - MARCOS ZEPEDA
49 - de la GARZA
50 - MANUEL DELGADO
51 - FRANCISCO CASANOVA
52 - ANTONIO GALVAN
53 - MARIANO RODRIGUEZ
54 - LA QUINTA (HOUSE OF THE CURBELOS)

SAN ANTONIO de BEXAR

WITH A GUIDE TO THE RESIDENCES OF SOME PROMINENT EARLY FAMILIES, BASED ON THE MEMOIRS OF ANTONIO MENCHACA

San Antonio de Béxar, 1835

DON ERASMO SEGUIN TURNS FROM THE STACK OF LETTERS ON HIS DESK TO STARE OUT AT THE SCENE ON MILITARY PLAZA. HIS MIND IS DEEP IN REFLECTION, TROUBLED ABOUT THE FUTURE OF TEXAS.

IT IS JUST PAST SIESTA TIME, AND THE PEOPLE ARE SLOWLY COMING TO LIFE AS THE SCORCHING HEAT OF MIDDAY GRADUALLY GIVES WAY TO GENTLE AFTERNOON BREEZES.

(SEGUIN PRONOUNCED "SAY-GEEN")

⟨11⟩

AROUND THE CORNER THE MAIN PLAZA, DOMINATED BY THE SAN FERNANDO CATHEDRAL, ALSO IS STIRRING. CARTWHEELS CREAK AS THEIR DRIVERS URGE PROTESTING OXEN DOWN THE DUSTY SIDESTREETS.

ALONG "ZAMBRANO ROW" WHERE THE WELL-TO-DO FAMILIES LIVE — INCLUDING HIS OWN — THE WOMENFOLK FAN THEMSELVES AND TALK QUIETLY OF SMALL MATTERS AS THEIR BOISTEROUS CHILDREN SWARM ABOUT THEM.

SOME, DOUBTLESS, ARE DOWN BY THE RIVER, SPLASHING AND CHATTERING AT THE PUBLIC BATHING AREA, SERENADED BY THE DRONE OF SUMMER LOCUSTS IN THE TREES ABOVE.

FURTHER DOWN THE RIVER LIE THE PROUD MISSIONS — ONCE A MAJOR INSTRUMENT IN SPREADING SPANISH CULTURE, IN CIVILIZING THE LOCAL INDIAN TRIBES.

NOW THEY ARE ABANDONED AND RAPIDLY FALLING INTO RUIN, HOME ONLY TO MYRIAD BATS AND SMALL SCURRYING CREATURES

BUT A FEW HUMAN RESIDENTS, MOSTLY DESCENDANTS OF THE EARLY INDIAN NEOPHYTES, STILL REMAIN, AS IF CLINGING TO THE TATTERED SKIRTS OF THE GRAND DREAM THAT THE PAPAL FATHERS LEFT BEHIND...

ONE OF THEM — THE ALAMO — IS STILL USED AS A BARRACKS AND ARMORY FOR TROOPS STATIONED AT BEXAR.

NEARBY IS LA VILLITA, A *BARRIO* WHERE MOSTLY POOR PEOPLE LIVE — THE "SALT OF THE EARTH" — BUT NEVERTHELESS A CASTE APART FROM PEOPLE LIKE DON ERASMO.

ALL TOLD, BEXAR CONTAINS A RESPECTABLE 2,000-ODD SOULS, THE MOST POPULOUS TOWN IN ALL OF TEXAS.

BEYOND, IN THE SOUTHERN DEPARTMENT, THERE IS ONLY *LA BAHIA* — GOLIAD — A POOR LITTLE HAMLET, BUT BIGGER THAN VICTORIA, REFUGIO, OR SAN PATRICIO. BETWEEN THEM AND THE RIO GRANDE, THERE IS NOTHING BUT A FEW RANCHOS.

ERASMO SIGHS... AFTER OVER A HUNDRED YEARS SINCE ITS FOUNDING, A MERE 2,000 SOULS! IN THE REST OF TEXAS, MAYBE ANOTHER 3,000. NOT MUCH TO SHOW FOR ALL THOSE YEARS OF SUFFERING AND HARDSHIP BORNE SINCE OUR ANCESTORS FIRST TREKKED INTO BEXAR, BRINGING CATTLE, CATHOLICISM, AND HOPE FOR A BETTER LIFE.

YES, IT'S A PEACEFUL ENOUGH SCENE HERE *ON THE SURFACE*, BUT *UNDERNEATH*, ALL IS TURMOIL AND UNCERTAINTY— LIKE A KETTLE ON THE VERGE OF BOILING OVER! AND WHO SHOULD KNOW BETTER THAN ERASMO SEGUIN, POSTMASTER OF BEXAR, THROUGH WHOSE HANDS ALL OUTSIDE COMMUNICATION MUST PASS?

LIKE THIS LETTER FROM AN OUTLYING FAMILY, COMPLAINING THAT THEIR CHILDREN HAVE NO EDUCATION. AFTER THE MISSION SCHOOLS WERE SHUT DOWN, HE AND GOV. SAUCEDO HAD FINALLY HELPED ORGANIZE THE FIRST MUNICIPAL SCHOOL— NOT MUCH OF A SCHOOL, BUT BETTER THAN NOTHING. STILL, FOR CHILDREN ON THE RANCHOS, IT IS MORE DIFFICULT...

〈15〉

IN COMMERCE, THERE HAS BEEN SOME IMPROVEMENT— LIKE THE COTTON HE IS EXPERIMENTING WITH, AND THE NEW STRAINS OF SHEEP AND CATTLE BEING INTRODUCED AND DEVELOPED WITH THE HELP OF ANGLOS LIKE ERASTUS SMITH OVER ON THE CIBOLO.

CROSS THESE MULEYS WITH THE LONGHORN, DON ERAS-MO, AND WE'LL GET MORE BEEF!

BUT THEN HOW CAN ONE EXPECT MUCH FROM A TOWN THAT HAS SUFFERED LIKE BEXAR HAS? ONLY 20 YEARS AGO, ARREDONDO PRACTICALLY EMPTIED IT WITH HIS PURGE OF REPUBLICANISM.

OBSERVE, LIEUTENANT ANTONIO LOPEZ de SANTA ANNA, AND LEARN FROM THE MASTER HOW TO DEAL WITH ALL TRAITORS!

SINCE THEN THE PROVINCE HAS BEEN REPEATEDLY MAULED BY VARIOUS FILIBUSTER AND MEXICAN ARMIES OF RETRIBUTION ALIKE

DOWN WITH TYRANNY!

REDMEN AND WHITE UNITED! LONG LIVE THE REPUBLIC OF FREDONIA!

INDEPENDENCE
FREEDOM AND JUSTICE

⟨16⟩   (Long Expedition - 1819)   (Fredonian Rebellion - 1827)

WHAT THEY DIDN'T FINISH, EPIDEMICS AND HOSTILE INDIANS ALMOST HAVE. THE FRONTIER IS A SHAMBLES. THIS LETTER, FROM A FRIEND ALONG THE RIO GRANDE, TELLS HOW PRACTICALLY ALL THE LOWER RANCHOS HAVE BEEN BROKEN UP BY RECENT INDIAN ATTACKS.

NOTHING IS SAFE FROM THE *DREADED COMANCHES*. BEFORE THEM, IT WAS APACHES. THE MISSIONS HAD DONE MUCH WITH THE WEAKER TRIBES BUT NEVER TOUCHED THESE FIERCE MONGOLS OF THE PLAINS. FOR GENERATIONS THEY HAVE DEVASTATED THE NORTHERN PROVINCES AND FORMED A BARRIER TO SPANISH EXPANSION IN TEXAS.

EVEN AROUND THE TOWN HERE, WITH ITS PRESIDIO, ONE MUST CONSTANTLY BE ON THE LOOKOUT, OR SUFFER DIRE CONSEQUENCES.

BUT IT HAD BEEN *WORSE*, IN THE OLD DAYS. THEN THE CONTEMPTUOUS SAVAGES EVEN DARED TO RIDE OPENLY IN THE STREETS, FORCING US TO HOLD THEIR HORSES WHILE THEY LOOTED THE TOWN AND CARRIED OFF OUR WOMEN AND CHILDREN.

THIS, COMANCHE LAND... YOU STAY, YOU PAY!! COMPRENDE ?!?

⟨17⟩

AND THESE "SOLDIERS" THAT THEY SEND US — SCUM, RIFFRAFF FROM MEXICAN PRISONS, FIT ONLY TO LOLL ABOUT, DRINK PULQUE, AND MOLEST THE LOCAL GIRLS!

HEY SUGAR, YOU LIKE 'UM HEFTY, EH?!

YUK YUK

DROOL

AHH, THERE GOES SAMUEL MAVERICK, ONE OF THE FEW ANGLOS LIVING AMONG US HERE AT BEXAR. A PROMISING GENTLEMAN, A LAWYER, EVEN — WE NEED MORE LIKE HIM.

LOOK HOW THOSE LOW-LIFE SOLDIERS SCOWL AT HIM. WHAT MUST HE THINK OF US?

TOO GOOD TO DRINK WITH US, EH YANQUI?

HUERO!!

YES, THE ANGLOS — WHAT ABOUT THEM? THERE SEEMS TO BE NO END TO THE PROBLEMS THEIR PRESENCE INVOKES! AND HE, DON ERASMO, AS ALCALDE, HAD BEEN AMONG THE FIRST TO WELCOME THEM TO TEXAS.

¡BIENVENIDO A TEXAS, SEÑOR AUSTIN!

⟨18⟩ ("Huero"- "Whitey"; güero)

HE HAD BEEN SENT TO NACOGDOCHES BY GOV. MARTINEZ TO ESCORT AUSTIN TO BEXAR. DESPITE THE LANGUAGE BARRIER, THEY HAD BECOME FAST FRIENDS ON THE JOURNEY.

THIS SURE IS BEAUTIFUL COUNTRY, DON ERASMO.

¡SI, SEÑOR! ES UN PAÍS MUY GRANDE— E VACANTE!

IN THE FOLLOWING YEARS HE HAD ALWAYS BEEN A SUPPORTER OF THE ANGLO COLONY, WORKING FOR THEIR INTERESTS EVEN IN THE NATIONAL CONGRESS IN MEXICO CITY.

UNLESS WE ALLOW THEM TO BRING IN SLAVES, THE MORE PROSPEROUS CLASS, THE PLANTERS, THE SOLID PEOPLE, WILL NOT BE ATTRACTED TO OUR PROVINCE!

AND HOW THEY HAD PROSPERED, THOSE INDUSTRIOUS YANQUIS! IN A MERE 15 YEARS THEY HAVE ACCOMPLISHED MORE THAN OUR PEOPLE HAVE IN 150 YEARS! ALREADY THEY OUTNUMBER US SIX TO ONE, AND CONTINUE TO SWARM INTO OUR EASTERN DEPARTMENT FROM THE UNITED STATES. WHO KNOWS WHAT IS IN THEIR MIND?

CERTAINLY DON ESTEVAN IS A MAN OF GOOD INTENTIONS — DECENT, UPSTANDING, RECEPTIVE TO SPANISH CULTURE, AND LOYAL TO OUR GOVERNMENT. BUT HIS EFFORTS AT STATEHOOD, LOCAL AUTONOMY WITHIN THE MEXICAN FEDERATION — WHICH ALL "FEDERALISTS" DESIRE — HAD BEEN MISUNDERSTOOD BY THE AUTHORITIES, FOR THEY FEAR THE RISING POWER OF THIS ALIEN MINORITY AND THE SPREAD OF THEIR LIBERAL IDEAS.

THOSE ANGLOS ARE GETTING TOO STRONG!

IF WE'RE NOT CAREFUL, THEY'LL TAKE TEXAS AWAY FROM US!!

HUMPH!! WE'LL SEE ABOUT THAT!

DAMN OUR LOCAL AYUNTAMIENTO, SENDING AUSTIN'S LETTER, WRITTEN IN A MOMENT OF ILL-CONSIDERED HASTE, BACK TO MEXICO CITY MARKED AS TREASONOUS! WHY EVEN HE, ERASMO SEGUIN, HAD ONCE BEEN ACCUSED OF TREASON. WHAT INFLUENTIAL CITIZEN HAS NOT??

!

AHH, SEÑOR AUSTIN, SO NICE OF YOU TO STOP IN! I HAVE HERE ORDERS FOR YOUR ARREST!!

NOW HE, THE STAUNCHEST ANGLO FRIEND OF MEXICO, IS LANGUISHING IN PRISON, HIS COLONISTS DANGEROUSLY ADRIFT WITHOUT THEIR MODERATE LEADER.

HOW CAN TEXAS LIVE UNDER A SYSTEM SUCH AS THIS??

YES, AUSTIN HAD WORKED DILIGENTLY FOR PEACE, BUT *NOW*, AFTER TWO YEARS IN A DUNGEON, WHO KNOWS HOW HE FEELS? IF HE SPEAKS FOR WAR, WHERE WOULD THAT LEAVE OTHER FEDERALISTS— LIKE *MYSELF!* PERILOUS TIMES...

AND *THIS* LETTER—THE WORST OF ALL—FROM A FRIEND IN COAHUILA, TELLING OF SANTA ANNA'S BRUTAL SUPPRESSION OF THE ZACATECAN MOVEMENT, OF COS MARCHING TO PACIFY COAHUILA, AND THEN, MAYBE TEXAS! THEY WANT ZAVALA...

AH, THE WOES OF A MAN WHO LOVES HIS COUNTRY, YET LOVES FREEDOM AS STRONGLY. SO MUCH EASIER FOR THE YOUNG ONES LIKE MY SON JUAN. HE IS TROUBLED BY NO SUCH NAGGING DOUBTS, HE AND HIS IMPETUOUS YOUNG CABALLERO FRIENDS.

WHAT WE NEED AROUND HERE ARE SOME CHANGES.

THE QUICKER, THE BETTER!

WHY JUST LAST YEAR JUAN, THE ACTING *JEFE POLITICO*— "POLITICAL CHIEF"— HAD EVEN DARED TO ISSUE A CIRCULAR, CALLING FOR A MEETING TO ESTABLISH A LOCAL GOVERNMENT OF OUR OWN. UNHEARD OF, TO DO SUCH A THING!!

...DUE TO THE CENTRAL GOVERNMENT'S INDIFFERENCE TO OUR PREVIOUS PETITIONS AND TO THE STATE OF ANARCHY EXISTING IN TEXAS...

OF COURSE THE ARMY HAD MARCHED UP FROM MATAMOROS TO PREVENT IT, BUT A DARING GESTURE ANYWAY...

YOU'D BETTER WATCH YOURSELF, SEGUIN. YOU, OF ALL PEOPLE, SHOULD KNOW THAT POLITICAL ASSEMBLIES ARE AGAINST THE LAW! GEN. COS IS IN NO MOOD FOR ANY FUNNY STUFF!!

THIS PAST APRIL, ONLY TWO MONTHS AGO, JUAN HAD COMMANDED A COMPANY OF NATIONAL GUARDS SENT FROM BEXAR TO MONCLOVA IN ANSWER TO THE GOVERNOR'S CALL FOR HELP. THAT WAS MORE THAN A GESTURE — THAT WAS INSURRECTION AGAINST CENTRALIST AUTHORITY!

SANTA ANNA HAD PUT THE LID ON THE MONCLOVA-SALTILLO DISPUTE, AND NOW JUAN WAS BACK, SOMEWHERE ON THE RANCHOS SOUTH OF TOWN. BUT HE WAS ON THEIR LIST AND HIS MOVEMENTS PROBABLY BEING WATCHED...

KEEP AN EYE ON SEGUIN — LET ME KNOW WHERE HE GOES, AND WHAT HE DOES...

AS DARKNESS FALLS ON "SLEEPY" LITTLE SAN ANTONIO DE BEXAR, DON ERASMO WALKS ACROSS THE PLAZA TO HIS HOUSE, FEELING ALL THE WEIGHT OF THE WORLD UPON HIS TIRED SHOULDERS.

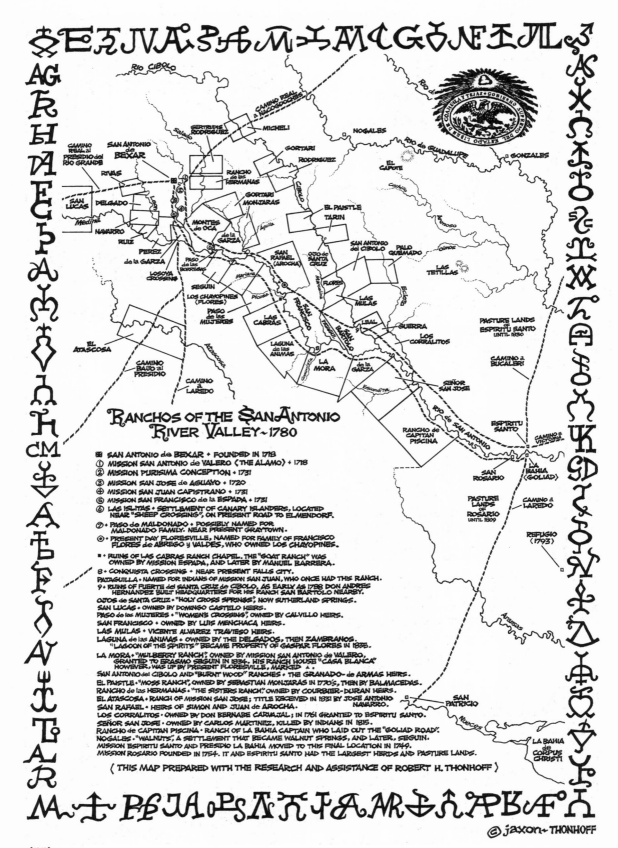

THE GATHERING STORM

STRUNG OUT ALONG THE SAN ANTONIO RIVER, SOUTH AND EAST OF BEXAR, ARE VARIOUS RANCHOS. THEY ARE LARGELY SELF-SUFFICIENT, BUILT ALONG THE LINES TO BEST REPEL INDIAN ATTACKS AND PROTECT THEIR LIVESTOCK.

ONE OF THE GRANDEST BELONGS TO ERASMO SEGUIN. MANY OF HIS FRIENDS AND PART-TIME RESIDENTS OF BEXAR OWN NEIGHBORING RANCHOS, FOR THIS RICH VALLEY IS THE CRADLE OF SPANISH RANCHING IN THE PROVINCE OF TEXAS.

SINCE TRAVELLERS GOING TO AND FROM GOLIAD ON THE OLD CART ROAD MUST PASS ALONG THE RIVER, THE RANCHOS PROVIDE STOPPING PLACES — WELCOME RELIEF FOR BOTH THEM AND THE ISOLATED RANCHEROS.

HOWDY, FOLKS, WHAT'S ALL THE NEWS IN THE *BIG CITY?*

SOUTHWARD TO THE RIO GRANDE IS NOTHING BUT VAST TRACTS OF SCRUBBY, SEMI-ARID GRAZING LAND, INHABITED ONLY BY INNUMERABLE WILD HERDS OF BONY LONGHORNS, WIRY MUSTANGS — AND MARAUDING BANDS OF HOSTILE INDIANS!

INTO THIS WASTELAND OCCASIONLY VENTURE PARTIES OF HARDY VAQUEROS, TO FLUSH THE CATTLE LOOSE FROM THEIR MESQUITE THICKETS, BRAND AND CARRY THEM BACK TO THE RANCHOS.

THEY ARE A TOUGH BREED, RAISED ON THE FRONTIER AMID CONSTANT DANGER AND DEPRIVATION, A MATCH FOR THE LONGHORN AND INDIAN ALIKE. THEY ARE PROUD MEN, CALLING THEMSELVES NOT MEXICANS, BUT "TEJANOS"— TEXANS. THEY ARE THE FIRST COWBOYS

FROM THEM, LATER GENERATIONS OF COWBOYS AND TRAIL DRIVERS WILL TAKE ALL THEIR EXPERTISE — EVEN THEIR TERMINOLOGY. WORDS LIKE "MUSTANG," "LARIAT," "CHAPS", AND "RODEO" WILL PASS INTO THE ENGLISH LANGUAGE.

IT IS FROM THEIR PRACTICE OF CULLING OUT THE UNDESIRABLE BEASTS, TAKING THE HIDES FOR LEATHER AND BOILING DOWN THE CARCASSES FOR TALLOW, THAT ANOTHER, LESS-FLATTERING WORD IS COINED FOR THESE TEJANO FRONTIERSMEN. "GREASER." IT IS INDEED A NASTY JOB, AND SOAP IS STILL A LUXURY...

A BATH?? HELL, THEN I'D JUST GET DIRTY AGAIN!

BUT IT IS ALSO THESE VAQUEROS THAT MAKE UP THE FRONTIER'S ONLY EFFECTIVE FIGHTING FORCE, AND IT IS TO THEM MEN LIKE JUAN SEGUIN COME WHEN THEY NEED CAVALRYMEN.

FIGHTIN' IS ABOUT TH' CLOSEST THING TO RECREATION WE GET OUT HERE!

⟨25⟩

BY JUAN'S SIDE RIDES DON SANTIAGO BOWIE — JAMES BOWIE, ANOTHER MAN MARKED AS "SEDITIOUS"— BUT THAT WAS NOT ALWAYS SO. BOWIE IS SOBER TODAY, BUT THAT TOO IS A NEW CONDITION TO HIM LATELY.

ONLY A FEW YEARS AGO, BOWIE WAS AN HONORED MEMBER OF BEXAR SOCIETY — RICH, MARRIED TO THE BEAUTIFUL URSULA VERAMENDI, DAUGHTER OF THE VICE-GOVERNOR OF COAHUILA AND TEXAS — WITH A BRIGHT FUTURE AHEAD OF HIM IN HIS ADOPTED HOMELAND. AN "HOMBRE, MUY SIMPATICO"...

BUT THEN, ALL WAS SWEPT AWAY IN A CHOLERA EPIDEMIC, AND BOWIE FELL INTO RUIN, WHISKEY HIS ONLY COMPANION. HIS HAGGARD FACE BEARS THE SCARS, BUT JUAN KNOWS THAT THIS MAN POSSESSES DEEP RESERVOIRS OF STRENGTH. YES, IN A FIGHT, DON SANTIAGO IS STILL THE BEST MAN IN TEXAS TO HAVE AT YOUR SIDE — SOBER OR NOT!

AND THE SELF-RELIANT VAQUEROS, THEY TOO ARE FIGHTERS — A FAR DIFFERENT SORT FROM THE DOCILE PEON CLASS THAT CLINGS TO THE FRINGES OF BEXAR AND LOCKS THEIR DOORS WHEN THE FULL MOON BRINGS COMANCHES PROWLING.

AMONG THEM ARE MANY RELATIVES AND FRIENDS OF JUAN'S, LIKE ANTONIO MENCHACA, THE FLORES BROTHERS AND OTHER YOUNG MEN FROM THE RANCHOS ALONG THE RIVER. SOME HE RECOGNIZES AS VOLUNTEERS THAT RODE WITH HIM TO MONCLOVA.

WORK IS STOPPED, A BOTTLE BROKEN OUT AND LIES SWAPPED. BUT ALL IS NOT FUN, FOR THESE MEN, LIKE SEGUIN, ARE AVOWED FEDERALISTS, AND THEY CRAVE NEWS OF HOW THINGS STAND.

BE READY.. THE TIME DRAWS NEAR!

THE NEXT MORNING, WHILE SCOUTING FOR LONGHORNS, THE VAQUEROS SPOT A BAND OF INDIANS, WARILY MAKING THEIR WAY THROUGH THE BRASADA.

THE FEARLESS RIDERS CHARGE HEAD ON INTO THE INDIANS, FORCING THEM TO ABANDON THEIR BOOTY AND BEAT A HASTY RETREAT.

GAKK

THE TEJANO HORSEMEN ARE EXPERT WITH THE LARIAT, AND IN THEIR HANDS IT IS A LETHAL WEAPON.

AIIIEEEEEE!!!

IN ADDITION TO THE COMANCHE PLUNDER, THREE CAPTIVES ARE RECOVERED—2 CHILDREN AND A YOUNG WOMAN, INTENDED FOR A LIFE OF *SLAVERY* IN THE CAMPS OF THE COMANCHES.

THE WOMAN, DAUGHTER OF A WEALTHY RANCHERO NEAR CAMARGO, CAN SCARCELY BELIEVE HER GOOD FORTUNE, FOR HER FATE AS AN INDIAN CHATTEL WOULD HAVE BEEN CRUEL.

BRAVE CABALLERO!

DON'T WASTE YOUR THANKS ON HIM, SENORITA! HE'S AN OLD MARRIED MAN!!

BUT I'M NOT! HA

HA HA

JUAN AND SEVERAL CABALLEROS TAKE HER TO SAN ANTONIO, WHERE HER APPEARANCE GIVES CAUSE FOR GREAT REJOICING. IT IS NOT OFTEN THAT THE COMANCHES ARE CHASTISED AND THEIR CAPTIVES RETURNED TO CHRISTIAN WAYS.

THE GRATEFUL CITIZENS GIVE A FANDANGO TO CELEBRATE THE OCCASION. THE YOUNG MEN RIDE THROUGH THE STREETS, BECKONING ALL THE FAIR SEÑORITAS TO COME TO THE GALA BAILE.

BY MIDNIGHT THE FLORES HOME IS JUMPING.

(29)

IN THE REAR, THE OLDER MEN GATHER TO DRINK, SMOKE AND TALK— THEIR PLEASURE HEIGHTENED BY THE SOUNDS OF THE MUSIC AND DANCE. BUT IT IS NOT LONG BEFORE THE TALK DRIFTS TO POLITICS.

YOU'VE HEARD? COS IS COMING..

AHH NAVARRO, THEY'VE BEEN HERE BEFORE... AND, AS USUAL, CITIZENS LOYAL TO THE SUPREME GOVERNMENT HAVE NOTHING TO FEAR.

FOLD...

RAISE YOU TWENTY!

I'M NOT SO SURE. SANTA ANNA SEEMS BENT ON BRINGING US TO OUR KNEES THIS TIME!!

YES, AND IT'LL BE WORSE THAN EVER! WORD HAS IT THAT THE STATE LEGISLATURE HAS BEEN PACKED UP AND SENT HOME.

AND WHY NOT?! SQUABBLING BACK-BITERS, SLY OPPORTUNISTS, AND BRAZEN LAND SPECULATORS. WHY, IT'S A NATIONAL DISGRACE!

NEVERTHELESS, IT WAS OUR ONLY VOICE, AND NOW IT IS SILENT!

YOU'RE CLOSE TO THIS THING, JUAN— WHAT DO YOU THINK ABOUT IT ALL?

GENTLEMEN, YOU ALREADY KNOW MY SENTIMENTS, FOR I HAVE ALWAYS BEEN OUT-SPOKEN ON THE SUBJECT OF FREEDOM. WHAT HAS THE CENTRAL SYSTEM DONE FOR US? NOTHING! ALL THE FUNCTIONS OF GOVERNMENT— EDUCATION, PUBLIC WORKS, EVEN DEFENSE— WE MUST PERFORM ON OUR OWN. WE GET NO HELP FROM MEXICO CITY, ONLY TAXES TO PAY AND WORTHLESS SOLDIERS TO FEED! AFTER ALL, WE ARE BUT A POOR AND DISTANT PROVINCE, REMOTE FROM THE GILDED HALLS OF OUR OPPRESSORS.

I SAY IF WE MUST GOVERN OURSELVES IN FACT, WHY NOT IN NAME AS WELL? WE SHOULD FORM OUR OWN STATE GOVERNMENT HERE, SEPARATE FROM THE MUDDLED AFFAIRS OF COAHUILA, CLOSE TO OUR OWN NEEDS!

GASP! JUAN, THIS IS TOO MUCH! NEXT YOU'LL BE SAYING WE SHOULD SEPARATE FROM MEXICO ALTOGETHER!

THE IDEA *HAS* OCCURRED TO ME — WHY NOT?! ALREADY THE ANGLO SETTLE-MENTS TO THE EAST ARE ON THE VERGE OF OUT-RIGHT INSURRECTION. THEY CAN BE COUNT-ED ON TO HELP US IN THE STRUGGLE!

TREASON! TREASON!!

TREASON, IS IT?! WAR IS COMING, WHETHER YOU LIKE IT OR NOT! WHEN IT DOES, NOT JUST THE ANGLOS WILL SUFFER. ALL FEDERALISTS WILL BEAR THE SAME YOKE!!

I AGREE WITH JUAN! THE HUNGRY MOUTHS OF MARCHING SOLDIERS MUST BE FED, REGARD-LESS OF THEIR BANNER.. IT IS *OUR* CATTLE, *OUR* CORN THEY WILL TAKE. WE WILL BE RUINED EITHER WAY! BETTER WE TAKE THE LEAD, THAN BE FORCED TO FOLLOW!!

YOU ARE WRONG, JUAN, TO TAKE THE SIDE OF THE AMERICANS. THEY CARE NO-THING FOR OUR LAWS, OUR CUSTOMS, OUR RELIGION — FOR US! GREED IS THEIR MOTIVE — TO TAKE EVERYTHING THEY CAST THEIR EYES UPON!!

SOME, PERHAPS, BUT THERE ARE GREEDY MEN AMONG ALL PEOPLES. OTHERS I RESPECT — AND VALUE AS FRIENDS — LIKE DON ESTEVAN AUSTIN..

BUT HE'S IN JAIL!!

..AND BOWIE, WHOM YOU ALL KNOW!

(31)

YES, BUT HE'S NOT LIKE THE OTHERS! DON SANTIAGO UNDERSTANDS US — MARRIES AMONG US! THE NEW ONES THAT FLOCK IN KNOW NOTHING BUT GREED! THEY WANT TO TAKE OUR COUNTRY FROM US!!

I WARN YOU, SEGUIN — STAY CLEAR OF THOSE YANQUIS. IF YOU TAKE THEIR SIDE AGAINST MEXICO, YOU WILL BE A RUINED MAN — WORSE THAN THAT — A TRAITOR TO YOUR PEOPLE, AND A CURSE UPON YOUR ANCESTORS!!

AND WHAT WILL YOU BE?! A COWARD-LY SCUM, BOOTLICKER TO A TYRANT!!

HEAR, HEAR, GENTLEMEN! PLEASE CONTROL YOURSELVES. WE ARE ALL FRIENDS HERE!!

BUT SEVERAL MEN IN THE ROOM ARE *NOT FRIENDS*. THEY ARE *AGENTS*, WHOSE SECRET PURPOSE IS TO SPY ON JUAN SEGUIN, AND THEIR EVENING HAS BEEN RICHLY REWARDED.

AT EARLY MASS, TEMPERS HAVE COOLED AND CONFESS-IONS ARE MADE, BUT DEEP CONVICTIONS LIE UNSHAKEN.

AS THE SUMMER MONTHS PASS, RELATIONS BETWEEN MEXICO AND TEXAS DETERIORATE. THEN, A LETTER IS INTERCEPTED..

WHUT DO IT SAY, JED?

BOYS, WE GOT US A HOT ONE — COS IS COMING...

WOOOEEE.. THAT MEANS A FIGHT FOR SURE!

A SHORT TIME LATER, CITIZENS OF ANAHUAC — LED BY THE FIREBRAND, WILLIAM BARRET TRAVIS — REBEL OVER TAX ENFORCEMENT, DISARM THE MEXICAN GARRISON, AND FORCE IT TO EVACUATE. THE SHOWDOWN DRAWS CLOSER.

AWARE THAT HE IS UNDER SURVEILLANCE, JUAN QUIETLY GATHERS MEN WHO SUPPORT REVOLUTION. MEETINGS ARE HELD AT THE RIVER RANCHOS, LIKE THAT OF SALVADOR FLORES.

MEANWHILE, AUSTIN HAS BEEN RELEASED AND MADE HIS WAY HOME, HIS FAITH IN THE MEXICAN SYSTEM UTTERLY DESTROYED.

A RIDER FROM THE RIO GRANDE BRINGS WORD TO JUAN THAT COS' ARMY IS CROSSING INTO TEXAS, VIA COPANO BAY. ANOTHER, THAT GONZALES HAS REFUSED TO SURRENDER THEIR CANNON TO A MILITARY DETACHMENT FROM BEXAR!

REVOLUTION!

COME AND TAKE IT

JUAN SEGUIN AND HIS NEIGHBORS VIEW THE UPRIVER MARCH TOWARD BEXAR OF THE MEXICAN ARMY UNDER GEN. MARTIN de COS, BROTHER-IN-LAW OF THE DICTATOR SANTA ANNA.

THEIR STANDARDS SAY "MEXICO", BUT THEY STILL LOOK LIKE INVADERS.

COS MAKES THE MISTAKE OF INSULTING JUAN'S FATHER, ERASMO, FORCING HIM TO WALK THE 33 MILES TO HIS RANCHO.

JUAN TAKES HIS TEJANO VOLUNTEERS AND JOINS THE RAG-TAG REBELS MARCHING ON BEXAR FROM GONZALES.

HE FIGHTS BESIDE BOWIE WHEN THEIR 90 MEN PUT 400 MEXICAN CAVALRY TO FLIGHT NEAR MISSION CONCEPTION.

TAKE THAT RUBBLE INSIDE THE CHAPEL AND BUILD A CANNON RAMP. PUT BREASTWORKS OVER THERE...

San Antonio ½ mi.

THE REBELLIOUS "TEXIANS" SETTLE DOWN TO A SIEGE, LASHED BY BITTER WINTER WINDS.

NOT MUCH OF A WAY TO SPEND THANKSGIVING.

BBBRRRR... WONDER HOW TH' LITTLE WOMAN'S DOIN' AT HOME...

AMONG THE LOCAL RANCHEROS OFFERING PROVISIONS TO THE REBEL ENCAMPMENT IS THE OFFENDED ERASMO SEGUIN, NO LONGER UNCERTAIN OF WHAT COURSE HE MUST TAKE....

BLESS YOU, DON ERASMO. THESE SERVICES TO THE CAUSE WILL NOT BE FORGOTTEN!!

REMEMBER, GENERAL BURLESON, THAT I HELPED FRAME THE CONSTITUTION OF 1824 AND AM HONOR-BOUND TO DEFEND ITS PRINCIPLES AGAINST DESPOTISM.

JUAN'S MEN ARE JOINED BY OTHER TEJANOS, LIKE PLACIDO BENAVIDES, SILVESTRE DE LEON, AND 25 MEN FROM VICTORIA.

HIS REGIMENT OF VOLUNTEERS TAKE ON SCOUTING CHORES AND FORAGING EXPEDITIONS. THEY ALSO HELP PROMOTE DESERTION AMONG THE HOMESICK SOLDIERS OF GEN. COS.

WHY ARE YOU HERE? THIS IS A FIGHT AGAINST TYRANNY—YOU DON'T LOOK LIKE A TYRANT.

I'M NOT—I'M A FARMER! THEY DRAFTED ME.

ME TOO. I SURE MISS MY OLD LADY AND KIDS..

JUST AS THE TEXIAN SIEGE IS CRUMBLING AND THE MEN PACKING UP TO LEAVE, A MEXICAN OFFICER DEFECTS TO THE REBELS.

HE SAYS THEIR MORALE IS REALLY BAD— THAT WE CAN TAKE BEXAR EASY.

YOU HEAR THAT, BOYS ??! UNPACK THOSE MULES !!

BENJAMIN MILAM, AN UNSUCCESSFUL LAND SPECULATOR WHO HAD BARELY ESCAPED THE WRATH OF COS IN COAHUILA, CALLS FOR VOLUNTEERS TO ASSAULT THE TOWN.

WHO'LL GO WITH OL' BEN MILAM INTO SAN ANTONE!

NOW YOU'RE TALKING!

THREE HUNDRED MEN GATHER ABOUT MILAM. THE HOUSE-TO-HOUSE, STREET-TO-STREET FIGHTING IS NOT TO COS' LIKING. HIS NERVE BEGINS TO SNAP.

ON DEC. 7TH MILAM IS KILLED OUTSIDE THE VERAMENDI HOUSE, BUT THE TEXIANS PUSH ON WITHOUT HIM, UNTIL THEY HAVE CLEARED THE PLAZA AND DRIVEN COS BACK INTO THE ALAMO.

SIX OFFICERS AND 179 MEN DESERT COS AND FLEE TOWARD THE RIO GRANDE. NOT EVEN THE ARRIVAL OF 600 REINFORCEMENTS CAN REPAIR THE DAMAGE DONE TO THE DEFENDERS' MORALE.

FOR MY PAY, IT AIN'T WORTH IT!

AFTER THREE DAYS OF BITTER GUERRILLA WARFARE, GEN. COS SURRENDERS HIS THIRTEEN-HUNDRED MEN, PLEDGING NEVER AGAIN TO FIGHT AGAINST TEXAS. HE IS GIVEN RATIONS AND ALLOWED TO MARCH SOUTH, BUT 200 OF HIS SOLDIERS ELECT TO STAY BEHIND.

SANTA ANNA ISN'T GOING TO LIKE THIS..

SEGUIN AND TRAVIS ARE DETAILED TO FOLLOW THE WITHDRAWING ARMY AND TAKE AS MANY OF THEIR HORSES AS POSSIBLE.

OKAY.. WE'LL GET THEM AT PARRITA!

THEIR COMPANIES HIT THE DISPIRITED MEXICAN TROOPS ON THE LAREDO ROAD, DRIVING OFF A REMUDA OF 100 MOUNTS THAT THEY TURN OVER FOR THE BENEFIT OF THE REBEL CAUSE.

BASTARDOS! CABRONES!!

THE FOLLOWING MONTH JUAN RECEIVES THE COMMISSION OF CAPTAIN OF CAVALRY FROM THE PROVISIONAL GOVERNMENT. HE JOINS BOWIE AND TRAVIS, WHO HAVE DECIDED THAT THE ALAMO IS THE *KEY* TO THE DEFENSE OF TEXAS IN REVOLT.

THERE'S SOMETHING MAGICAL ABOUT THIS PLACE, DON'T YOU THINK ??

ONE OF JUAN'S SCOUTS, HIS NEPHEW BLAS HERRERA, BRINGS NEWS OF SANTA ANNA'S RAPID MARCH NORTHWARD WITH AN ARMY TO PUNISH THE REBELS.

I'LL TEACH THEM TO MESS WITH THE NAPOLEON OF THE WEST!

TRAVIS, DISPLAYING THE ARROGANCE THAT HAS ALREADY ALIENATED BOWIE AND THE TEJANO VOLUNTEERS, DIS- MISSES HERRERA'S REPORT AS EXAGGERATED HEARSAY.

IMPOSSIBLE! NO MEXICAN COULD MOVE THAT MANY MEN SO FAST OVER DESERT TERRAIN IN THE MIDDLE OF WINTER!

YO-YO..

NOT SO THE RESIDENTS OF BEXAR. THEY BELIEVE, AND HASTILY DEPART THE EYE OF THE COMING STORM.

GOING FARMING? THIS TIME OF THE YEAR ?!

AS SANTA ANNA'S TROOPS SWARM INTO TEXAS, MANY TEJANOS BEGIN TO REASSESS THEIR POSITION.

WE STARTED OUT TO FIGHT FOR THE LIBERAL CONSTITUTION OF 1824.

NOW IT'S EITHER MEXICO OR OUTRIGHT INDEPENDENCE...

AND THE GRINGOS OUTNUMBER US SIX TO ONE! I TELL YOU I DON'T LIKE IT.

SOME FAMILIES, LIKE THE DE LA GARZAS OF GOLIAD, ARE DIVIDED IN THEIR SYMPATHIES.

BUT JOSÉ MARIA, MEXICO IS OUR COUNTRY AND IT'S OUR COUNTRY, RIGHT OR WRONG!

MAYBE FOR YOU, CARLOS, BUT NOT FOR ME. I'M GOING TO JOIN DON PLACIDO AND HIS VOLUNTEERS!

WHEN MEXICAN SOLDIERS UNDER GEN. URREA REACH GOLIAD, THEY ARE ACTIVELY SUPPORTED BY "LOYALIST" TEJANOS LIKE DON CARLOS DE LA GARZA...

WELCOME TO OUR RANKS, LOYAL CITIZENS. YOU ARE WISE TO UPHOLD THE SUPREME GOVERNMENT!

VIVA MEXICO!

I SURE HOPE WE DON'T RUN INTO MY BROTHER AND HIS CAVALRY!

AT BEXAR THERE IS ALSO INDECISION AS TO LOYALTIES, BUT THE ARRIVAL OF SANTA ANNA WITH 6,000 MEN SEALS THE MATTER FOR MANY...

MAYBE IF WE KEEP QUIET AND LAY LOW, THIS WHOLE THING WILL BLOW OVER.

GOD HELP THE ONES ALREADY INSIDE THE ALAMO!

THIS "NEUTRALITY" IN THE FACE OF OVERWHELMING ODDS REINFORCES TRAVIS' CONVICTION THAT ALL THE TEJANOS OPPOSE INDEPENDENCE.

THEY'RE ALL AGAINST US...WE SHOULD TREAT THE WHOLE BUNCH AS ENEMIES!!

AFTER SANTA ANNA OCCUPIES THE TOWN AND SURROUNDS THE ALAMO, JUAN IS SELECTED TO CARRY THE THIRD APPEAL FOR HELP TO FANNIN AT GOLIAD.

WE NEED SOME-BODY THAT CAN GET PAST THEIR PICKETS ......

SEGUÍN'S THE MAN!

BEFORE LEAVING, HE ADDRESSES THE SEVEN MEN OF HIS COMPANY WHO REMAIN BEHIND AMONG THE ALAMO DEFENDERS.

COMPAÑEROS— NEVER SURRENDER TO TYRANNY!

ON BOWIE'S FAST HORSE, JUAN — ALONG WITH HIS ORDERLY, YOUNG ANTONIO CRUZ Y AROCHA — MAKE THEIR WAY TOWARD THE MEXICAN PICKET LINE.

HALT! WHO GOES THERE?!

WE ARE FELLOW COUNTRYMEN, GOOD MEXICANS!

AW, IT'S JUST SOME LOCAL VAQUEROS.

THE RUSE WORKS JUST LONG ENOUGH FOR JUAN TO REACH THE PICKETS. AFTER THAT, BOWIE'S HORSE DOES THE REST!

HEY, YOU! COME BACK HERE!!

⟨42⟩ (This "dashing escape" is the mythical version. Juan later said he crept through the Mexican lines on foot, often on all fours, bombs bursting all around.)

THE NEXT DAY, AT THE RANCHO SAN BARTOLO ON THE CIBOLO, JUAN MEETS ONE OF FANNIN'S OFFICERS, WHO GIVES HIM *BAD NEWS.*

WE'VE GOT PROBLEMS AT GOLIAD. GO LOOK FOR GEN. HOUSTON. MAYBE HE'LL SEND SOME HELP...

AT HOUSTON'S HEADQUARTERS NEAR GONZALES, JUAN FINDS A SCENE OF CHAOS. MANY OF JUAN'S TEJANO VOLUNTEERS ARE ALREADY THERE. SALVADOR FLORES IS ORDERED TO TAKE A DETAIL TO PROTECT THE RANCHOS FROM INDIAN ATTACK AND SANTA ANNA'S PILLAGERS. JUAN KEEPS THE REMAINDER ON SCOUTING DUTY.

HOUSTON'S DUE ANY DAY NOW. WE'RE JUST TRYING TO HOLD THE ARMY TOGETHER TILL HE GETS HERE.

FINALLY, ON THE 6TH OF MARCH, HE IS ORDERED TO GO TO SAN ANTONIO WITH HIS COMPANY, CARRYING PROVISIONS TO THE BELEAGUERED DEFENDERS. THEY MAKE IT AS FAR AS THE CIBOLO.

DON'T GO THERE JUAN. IT'S ALL OVER—TERRIBLE! THE ALAMO HAS FALLEN! ALL DEAD!

THUS, JUAN SEGUIN IS SPARED DEATH AT THE ALAMO, BUT 7* OF HIS VOLUNTEERS SHARE THE MARTYRDOM OF THEIR ANGLO COMRADES, FIGHTING BENEATH THE FLAG OF THE 1824 CONSTITUTION, A BANNER FASHIONED FOR THEM BY ERASMO SEGUIN.

IN THE AFTERMATH, ALCALDE FRANCISCO RUIZ — WHOSE FATHER FRANCISCO SR. AND COUSIN JOSE ANTONIO NAVARRO ARE AT THAT VERY MOMENT AMONG THE SIGNERS OF THE DECLARATION OF TEXAN INDEPENDENCE — PLEADS WITH SANTA ANNA TO GIVE THE FALLEN TEJANOS A CHRISTIAN BURIAL.

JUAN HURRIES BACK TO HEADQUARTERS WITH THE NEWS. LATER, TWO OF HIS MEN, LEFT TO GATHER INTELLIGENCE, CONFIRM THE SAD TIDINGS — WHICH HOUSTON QUICKLY STIFLES TO AVOID PANIC AMONG HIS THREADBARE TROOPS.

⟨44⟩ * *The precise number of Tejanos in the Alamo — and of those who fought in the Revolution — is the subject of unending debate, but the total undoubtedly surpasses what has been traditionally allowed.*

BUT HOUSTON KNOWS THEY BEAR THE TRUTH, AND SO DOES THE REST OF GONZALES! THEY HAVE ALREADY BEGUN TO JOIN THE STREAM OF REFUGEES FROM BEXAR, HASTENING AWAY FROM THE APPROACH OF SANTA ANNA'S ARMY!!

WHERE'S EVERYBODY GOIN'?

AIN'T YOU HEARD? THE MEXICANS ARE COMIN' TO KILL US ALL!

MOMMA, WHEN'S DADDY COMIN' BACK?

HUSH CHILD, AND TRY TO KEEP UP!

AMONG THEM IS ERASMO SEGUIN, HIS FAMILY, AND THE FAMILIES OF THEIR NEIGHBORS WHO HAVE CAST THEIR LOT IN WITH THE TEXIANS. THEY BRING WITH THEM WHAT LITTLE THEY CAN CARRY. THE REST IS LEFT BEHIND...

GEN. HOUSTON ORDERS JUAN AND HIS MEN TO FORM A REAR GUARD FOR THE FLEEING SETTLERS.

THEN COMES THE NEWS THAT FANNIN, INDECISIVE TO THE END, HAS BEEN CAPTURED AT GOLIAD AND HIS ENTIRE FORCE OF 400 MEN EXECUTED BY ORDER OF SANTA ANNA.

THE TEJANOS IN THE GOLIAD-VICTORIA AREA KNOWN TO SYMPATHIZE WITH THE REBELS ARE DEALT WITH HARSHLY BY THE CONQUERORS.

WELL, De LEON, LOOKS LIKE YOU PICKED THE WRONG SIDE! NOW YOU'LL HAVE TO PAY THE PRICE...

THEIR POSSESSIONS, AND THE ABANDONED HOMES OF THEIR TEXIAN NEIGHBORS, ARE LOOTED UNDER THE DIRECTION OF MEXICAN OFFICERS.

CAREFUL, YOU CLUMSY OAFS! THAT STUFF HAS A LONG WAY TO GO BEFORE IT REACHES MY HACIENDA IN TAMAULIPAS!!

SANTA ANNA, FLUSH WITH VICTORY AND THINKING THE WAR NOW OVER, PROCEEDS TO DRIVE THE LAST HOLDOUTS FROM THE BLEEDING PROVINCE.

I DETEST THESE MOPPING-UP OPERATIONS...

EXCELLENCY, PERHAPS THIS ROSE WILL BRIGHTEN UP THE REST OF YOUR TEDIOUS CAMPAIGN.

Note: This "rose" was Emily, a beautiful slave girl whose light, "high yellow" coloration gave her immortality as "The Yellow Rose of Texas".

BUT MOSELY BAKER AND THE TEXIANS, AIDED BY JUAN'S TEJANOS, MOUNT A STIFF RESISTANCE, PREVENTING SANTA ANNA FROM CROSSING THE BRAZOS NEAR SAN FELIPE AND GIVING HOUSTON'S RETREAT PRECIOUS TIME.

DID ANYBODY REMEMBER TO BRING OUR FLAG?

HELL, THEY DON'T NEED A FLAG TO KNOW WHICH SIDE WE'RE ON.

JUAN AND HIS COMPANY REJOIN HOUSTON NEAR SAN JACINTO. AS THE BATTLE NEARS, THE GENERAL — AFRAID THAT SOME OF THE "MEXICANS" UNDER SEGUIN MIGHT BE SHOT IN THE MELEE BY MISTAKE — ORDERS THEM TO STAY BEHIND.

TELL THEM TO GUARD THE HORSES AND BAGGAGE..

BUT THE TEJANOS ARE INSULTED BY THE ORDER. ANTONIO MENCHACA, INTERPRETER FOR THE GROUP, FACES HOUSTON.

WE JOINED UP TO FIGHT, AND WANT TO DIE FACING THE ENEMY! IF HORSE-HERDING IS ALL WE CAN DO, THEN WE'LL GO HELP OUR FAMILIES, WHO ARE UN-PROTECTED AND IN FLIGHT TO LOUISIANA!!

GEN. HOUSTON CHANGES HIS ORDER...

GENTLEMEN.. I LIKE YOUR KIND OF GRIT. IT'S SANTY ANNA'S SIESTA TIME..... LET'S RIDE!!

(4.7)

SEGUIN'S MEN — THE 2ND REGIMENT OF TEXAS VOLUNTEERS, 9TH CAVALRY — FIGHT VALIANTLY AT SAN JACINTO. THEIR BATTLE CRY ECHOS THAT OF THEIR ANGLO-SAXON COMPATRIOTS!

IT IS A CRY THAT FLASHES DOWN THE TEXIAN LINE LIKE A *LIT FUSE*, A CRY THAT STRIKES TERROR INTO THE HEARTS OF THE MEXICAN SOLDIERS!

NOTHING CAN STAND BEFORE THEIR TERRIBLE ONSLAUGHT, AND THE "BATTLE" RAPIDLY TURNS INTO A ROUT. IN ONE VIOLENT SPASM, TEXAS IS RIPPED FROM THE BLOODY GRASP OF DICTATORSHIP!!

GEN. CASTRILLÓN TRIES IN VAIN TO RALLY A DEFENSIVE STAND AROUND THE 12-POUNDER, BUT HE IS SWEPT OVER BY THE AVENGING TEXIANS.

ALL IS LOST! SAVE YOURSELF, DON MANUEL!

I'VE NEVER SHOWED MY BACK, AND I'M TOO OLD TO START NOW!

SANTA ANNA, AROUSED TOO LATE FROM A "SIESTA" WITH THE YELLOW ROSE OF TEXAS, TAKES ONE LOOK AT THE CARNAGE AND DECIDES TO ABANDON THE BATTLEFIELD.

GOD!! TRY TO RELAX FOR A MINUTE AND EVERYTHING FALLS APART!

EXCELLENCY! DON'T LEAVE US!

IN TRYING TO ESCAPE BACK TO HIS MAIN ARMY, THE DICTATOR FINDS THAT DEAF SMITH HAS DESTROYED THE ONLY BRIDGE!

◎✳✸✲!!

A DEATHLY FEAR OF WATER CAUSES HIM TO SPEND THE NIGHT HIDING IN BULLRUSHES.

SKRONNKK

WHAT WAS THAT?!? AN ALLIGATOR, MAYBE... WONDER HOW BIG THE MONSTERS GROW IN THIS DREADFUL PLACE? AIEE, THERE IT GOES AGAIN!!

AFTER THE TEXIANS HAVE SATIATED THEIR BLOODLUST, THE SHATTERED REMNANTS OF THE MEXICAN VANGUARD ARE ROUNDED UP AND PUT IN A COMPOUND, RINGED BY THEIR MENACING CAPTORS.

THE SHOE IS ON THE OTHER FOOT NOW, YOU MURDERIN' SCUM.

¿QUÉ DICEN?

REMEMBER GOLIAD? YOU'RE GONNA' PAY FOR THAT WITH YOUR HIDES!

SAM HOUSTON, SUFFERING FROM A GUNSHOT WOUND IN HIS ANKLE, ALSO SPENDS AN UNEASY NIGHT, FEARFUL THAT HIS PREY HAS ELUDED HIM.

BOYS, WE'VE GOT TO CATCH SANTA ANNA OR FACE ANOTHER FIGHT!

THE NEXT MORNING A VERY DISORIENTED "NAPOLEON OF THE WEST" SNACKS ON A BOX OF CHOCOLATES AND DISCARDS HIS SILK PAJAMAS FOR SLAVE CLOTHING IN A DESERTED CABIN.

I'M SAFE IN THIS RIDICULOUS GET-UP.. NOW IF I CAN JUST REACH FILISOLA'S COMMAND — WHEREVER THAT IS..

BY MERE CHANCE HE IS FOUND BY A TEXIAN PATROL MORE INTERESTED IN HUNTING DEER THAN MEXICAN SOLDIERS. UNAWARE OF THE IDENTITY OF THEIR CATCH, THEY TAKE HIM BACK TO CAMP WHERE HIS OWN MEN SPILL THE BEANS.

EL PRESIDENTE! EL PRESIDENTE!

SHUT UP, YOU FOOLS!

I KNEW IT WAS TOO GOOD TO LAST..

DO "PRESIDENTE" MEAN TH' SAME IN MESKIN TALK AS IT DO IN 'MERICAN, JOEL?

GAWD..

MAJ. LORENZO de ZAVALA, JR. — SON OF THE MEXICAN EXILE AND NEW VICE-PRESIDENT OF THE REPUBLIC — SERVES AS HOUSTON'S INTERPRETER WHEN THE TWO COMMANDERS MEET. SANTA ANNA, FEARING FOR HIS LIFE, AGREES TO ALL THE REBEL DEMANDS.

HE SAYS HE NEEDS SOME OPIUM TO HELP CALM HIS NERVES..

JUAN AND HENRY KARNES ARE SENT TO WATCH THE RETREATING LEGIONS OF MEXICO, FOLLOWING AS FAR AS VICTORIA.

ON THE WAY TO SAN ANTONIO, HE STOPS BY HIS FAMILY'S RUINED RANCHO.

WE'LL HAVE TO START OVER, BUT AT LEAST WE HAVE OUR FREEDOM!!

(51)

WHAT PRICE,

THEY SURE TRASHED OUT THE PLACE!

AFTER THE BATTLE OF SAN JACINTO, JUAN SEGUIN IS SENT TO SAN ANTONIO TO RECEIVE THE SURRENDER OF THE OLD PROVINCIAL CAPITAL. HE FINDS HIS HOMETOWN ALMOST DESERTED OF FRIEND AND FOE ALIKE.

SOME OF ITS INHABITANTS LEAVE WITH THE RETREATING MEXICAN SOLDIERS.

WE'LL BE BACK WITH THE ARMY OF RECONQUEST!

FREQUENT THREATS OF INVASION DURING THE SUMMER OF 1836 CAUSE UNSETTLED CONDITIONS. IN JUNE, JUAN IS ORDERED TO TAKE HIS MEN AND RETURN TO HEADQUARTERS, NEAR VICTORIA...

CITIZENS! YOUR CONDUCT ON THIS DAY IS GOING TO DECIDE YOUR FATE BEFORE THE GOVERNMENT OF TEXAS!

FREEDOM?

YOU CAN HAVE IT, WHAT'S LEFT OF IT, AND I HOPE YOU AND YOUR GRINGO PALS *ROT IN HELL!*

...HE ADVISES THE CITIZENS OF THEIR PRECARIOUS SITUATION, URGING THEM TO EVACUATE WITH HIS TROOPS.

BUT THE RE-INVASION THREATS FAIL TO MATERIALIZE. MEXICO'S MILITARY LEADERS HAVE MIRED THEMSELVES IN AN ENDLESS HARANGUE TO PINPOINT RESPONSIBILITY FOR THE DISASTROUS TEXAS CAMPAIGN.

IF THEY'D BEEN WHERE THEY WERE *SUPPOSED* TO BE...

YOU CAN'T HANG THIS THING ON ME! IT WASN'T MY FAULT!!

DON'T BLAME ME!

GRADUALLY FAMILIES BEGIN TO RECLAIM THEIR WRECKED HOMES, TO REBUILD AND CARRY ON AS BEFORE. THE FLAG MAY BE DIFFERENT, BUT THE *LAND* IS UNCHANGED. LIFE HAS NEVER BEEN A CERTAIN THING IN TEXAS.

FOR HIS EXCEPTIONAL SERVICE IN THE STRUGGLE FOR INDEPENDENCE, JUAN IS PROMOTED TO LT-COL. AND ORDERED TO TAKE OVER THE MILITARY GOVERNMENT OF BEXAR UNTIL CIVIL RULE CAN BE RESTORED.

HE IS GRANTED A LEAVE OF ABSENCE TO SEE ABOUT HIS FAMILY IN EAST TEXAS. HE FINDS THEM DESTITUTE, ALL SICK WITH FEVER, AND BECOMES SICK HIMSELF.

AFTER SEVERAL DEATHS, THE FAMILY DECIDES TO LEAVE THE PESTILENTIAL CLIMATE AND TRIES TO MAKE ITS WAY HOME. IT IS A PITIFUL SPECTACLE. ANTONIO MENCHACA, ALSO THERE TO SEE TO HIS FAMILY'S SAFETY, IS THE ONLY ONE STRONG ENOUGH TO DRIVE AND CARE FOR THE SICK.

IT IS OCTOBER BEFORE JUAN IS WELL ENOUGH TO TAKE CONTROL OF BEXAR. HIS APPEARANCE DOES MUCH TO RESTORE ORDER AND CONFIDENCE AMONG THE OLD-TIME TEJANO RESIDENTS, UNCERTAIN OF THEIR FATE IN THE NEW ORDER OF THINGS.

HE GATHERS THE ASHES OF THE ALAMO MARTYRS, AND AFTER A SOLEMN CEREMONY, INTERS THEM IN AN OLD PEACH ORCHARD ONCE USED AS A MILITARY CEMETERY.

A SMALL PORTION OF THE ASHES ARE QUIETLY PLACED IN AN URN AND BURIED IN THE SAN FERNANDO CATHEDRAL OUT OF RESPECT FOR THE CATHOLICS AMONG THOSE FALLEN.

REQUIEM AETERNAM DONA EIS, DOMINE..

BUT HIS JOB IS AN IMPOSSIBLE ONE. PROVIDED WITH NEITHER MONEY NOR SUPPLIES BY THE FLEDGLING REPUBLIC, HE MUST MAKE REQUISITIONS ON THE CITIZENS. DISSATISFACTION IS INEVITABLE.

WHO DOES HE THINK HE IS, GOD ALMIGHTY?!! TAKING MY CORN AND CATTLE LIKE THAT!

AND MY HORSES! WHAT GOOD IS A SCRAP OF PAPER?? IT'S AN OUTRAGE!

I.O.U.

PART OF HIS JOB AS JEFE IS THE FERRETING OUT OF "ENEMY" SYMPATHIZERS AND OUTRIGHT SPIES — NOT A PLEASANT TASK, FOR MANY OF HIS OLD ACQUAINTANCES FALL INTO THIS CATEGORY.

YOU'RE ENTITLED TO YOUR POLITICAL OPINIONS, BUT I'M ENTITLED TO MINE!

TREAD GENTLY, JUAN, LEST THE FIRM GROUND NOW UNDER YOUR FEET TURN TO QUICKSAND!

TO ADD TO JUAN'S PROBLEMS AMONG HIS OWN PEOPLE, THERE IS AN INFLUX OF ANGLO NEWCOMERS, MOST OF WHOM ARRIVED TOO LATE TO EVEN FIRE A GUN IN THE REVOLUTION. NOW, THEY ARE PENNILESS, ADRIFT, AND PRONE TO MISCHIEF.

WAHL, HERE IT IS LEM — PICTURESK OL' SAN ANTONE!

LET'S GO LOOK AT TH' ALAMO, AND THEN KNOCK SOME HEADS!

HE MUST CONTROL THE LAWLESS ELEMENT AMONG THEM — WHICH IS WIDESPREAD — AND THEY DO NOT TAKE KINDLY TO ORDERS FROM A "MEXICAN".

GIVE HIM BACK HIS BURRO..

?

YOU'RE IN CHARGE? HELL, I THOUGHT YOU PEOPLE LOST TH' WAR!

SEGUIN AND HIS FELLOW TEJANOS FAIL TO GRASP THE *INTENSITY*, THE DEEP NEED FOR VENGEANCE, THAT MOTIVATED THESE RECRUITS TO RUSH TO THE DEFENSE OF TEXAS. BACK IN THE STATES, LURID ACCOUNTS OF THE MEXICAN ATROCITIES AT THE ALAMO AND GOLIAD, EMOTIONAL PUBLIC RALLIES ON THE FATE FACED BY THEIR KINSMEN IN TEXAS — COUPLED WITH PERSONAL FAMILY LOSSES — ALL WORKED TO CREATE A FRENZY OF HATRED AGAINST THE "MONSTER MEXICO".

...AFTER THEY SUR-RENDERED, THEY WERE MARCHED OUT AND SHOT DOWN LIKE DOGS!!

OH LORD, I HOPE THOMAS WASN'T AMONG THEM...

THE SENSELESS BUTCHERY OF THE GOLIAD VICTIMS AND THE DEATH OF POPULAR FOLK HEROES LIKE CROCKETT AND BOWIE *CRIED OUT* TO THE AMERICAN PEOPLE FOR ATONEMENT.

YEP, FROM WHAT I HEAR, OL' DAVY DIDN'T HAVE A MEAN BONE IN HIS BODY.

FRIENDS OF TEXAS

DAMN VERMIN!! TO THINK THAT SUCH COWARDLY SCUM SHOULD SHED THE BLOOD OF MEN LIKE BOWIE!

MANY SONS OF LIBERTY, LIKE YOUNG WILLIAM A.A. WALLACE (LATER TO BE KNOWN AS "BIGFOOT"), FELT IT WAS THEIR SACRED DUTY TO TEACH THE "TREACHEROUS" MEXICANS THAT THEY COULD NOT SLAUGHTER FREE MEN WITH IMPUNITY.

PA, I'M GOING TO TEX-AS TO SET THINGS RIGHT FOR THE WALLACES.

IF I WUZ A LITTLE YOUNGER, SON, RECKON I'D BE GOIN' WITH YOU..

AND SO THEY CAME, FROM ALL SECTIONS OF THE YOUNG, ENERGETIC NATION, ARMED WITH LONG RIFLES AND THE CONSUMING PASSION, THE SELF-RIGHTEOUS INJUNCTION — *MAKE THE MEXICANS PAY !!*

THE PITY IS THAT THESE CHAMPIONS OF DEMOCRACY NEITHER KNOW NOR CARE TO UNDERSTAND THE DIFFERENCE BETWEEN MEN LIKE JUAN SEGUIN AND ANTONIO LOPEZ de SANTA ANNA. TO THEM, "TEJANO" IS JUST ANOTHER FANCY WORD FOR "MEXICAN"!

⟨57⟩

THESE FRUSTRATED EMIGREES FLOCK TO THE BANNER OF FELIX HUSTON, A TURBULENT AND OVER-BEARING SOLDIER OF FORTUNE WHO ALSO ARRIVED IN TEXAS AFTER SAN JACINTO, TOO LATE FOR GLORY — AND THE SPOILS OF WAR.

WAR? AIN'T YOU HEARD, STRANGER? THE WAR'S ALREADY OVER!

A DAY LATE AND A DOLLAR SHORT...

CRAP!

NOW, HUSTON — HOT BECAUSE HE HAD MISSED KILLING ANY MEXICAN TYRANTS — IS HEAD OF AN "ARMY" *THREE TIMES* AS BIG AS THE ONE THAT HAD WON INDEPENDENCE, AND WANTS TO USE IT. HE REFUSES TO RECOGNIZE LAMAR, THE AUTHORIZED COMMANDER OF THE TEXIAN ARMY.

I'VE GOT THE TROOPS, SO I'LL BE THE BOSS!

HOUSTON!

HOUSTON!

GOD, THESE TURKEYS DON'T EVEN KNOW WHICH "HOUSTON" THEY'RE ROOTIN' FOR!!

WHEN HE IS PASSED OVER AGAIN AND ALBERT SIDNEY JOHNSTON GIVEN COMMAND OF "HIS" ARMY, HUSTON WOUNDS JOHNSTON IN A DUEL TO KEEP HIM FROM TAKING COMMAND.

THAT SETTLES THAT!

HEH HEH

HUSTON HAD SPENT $40,000 BACK IN MISSISSIPPI, RAISING AND EQUIPPING 500 VOLUNTEERS TO COME FIGHT IN TEXAS, AND HE DOESN'T PLAN TO LOSE HIS INVESTMENT!

ALL THOSE RICH MEXICANS DOWN AT BEXAR— WE OUGHT TO PUT THEM IN THEIR PLACE!!

YEAH, WHAT RIGHT DO THEY HAVE TO KEEP ALL THOSE BIG LAND GRANTS? WHAT WAS THE DANG WAR FOUGHT FOR, ANYWAY?!

HUSTON AND HIS CRONIES DEVISE A PLAN TO MOVE ALL THE TEJANO POPULATION OUT OF BEXAR SO THEY CAN RAVAGE THE AREA AT THEIR CONVENIENCE.

TELL 'UM THEY'VE GOT TO EVACUATE TO THE EAST SIDE OF THE GUADALUPE, CAUSE THEY'RE TOO EXPOSED DOWN THERE TO ATTACK FROM MEXICO!

CHUCKLE CHUCKLE

WHEN SEGUIN IS HANDED THE ORDERS TO SCUTTLE AND ABANDON SAN ANTONIO, HE REFUSES TO CARRY THEM OUT AND APPEALS DIRECTLY TO PRESIDENT SAM HOUSTON.

I'M IN CHARGE HERE..I'LL DECIDE WHEN WE STAY AND WHEN WE GO!

YOU'LL BE SORRY FOR THIS, HOTSHOT. WE'VE GOT POWERFUL FRIENDS AND THE ARMY BEHIND US.

THE PRESIDENT TAKES JUAN'S SIDE AND PREVAILS UPON HUSTON TO DESIST.

SEGUIN IS A PROVEN PATRIOT— HIS JUDGEMENT I TRUST. WHO THE HELL IS THIS FELIX "HUSTON" CHARACTER ANYWAY? I'VE GOT A FEELING HE'S IN THIS FOR SOMETHING BESIDES THE WELFARE OF TEXAS!

SO JUAN SAVES HIS TOWN FROM DESTRUCTION, BUT HE HAS MADE A BITTER ENEMY IN FELIX HUSTON.

SOONER OR LATER I'LL GET THAT UPPITY SEGUIN!

(59)

THESE HERE LOOK LIKE MESKIN' COWS TO ME..

YEAH— SPOILS OF WAR! HA HA

ENCOUNTERS BETWEEN TEJANOS, LIKE YOUNG AGAPITO de LEON, AND THE FORAGING ANGLOS, LIKE "MUSTANG" GRAY, SOMETIMES TURN UGLY.

THOSE ARE MY FATHER'S CATTLE! AS YOU CAN PLAINLY SEE, THEY BEAR THE DE LEON BRAND.

IZZAT RIGHT?? WELL, I FIGHT FOR TEXAS SONNYBOY, AND EVERY-THING IN TEXAS BE-LONGS TO ME—

NOT TO THE LIKES OF YOU !!!

THROUGH THE ABUSES OF THESE "TEXAS VOLUNTEERS", MANY OF THE OLD-TIME TEJANO RESIDENTS BECOME HOSTILE TO THE ANGLOS AND OUTWARDLY SYMPATHETIC TO MEXICO.

THIS WHOLE IDEA OF INDEPENDENCE WAS A MISTAKE! I THOUGHT SO FROM THE BEGINNING...

I DIDN'T FIGHT FOR THE TEXIANS, BUT I DIDN'T FIGHT AGAINST THEM, EITHER... NOW THEY COME IN HERE + TREAT US LIKE TRASH!

THE SCOUT AND LONG-TIME TEXIAN, ERASTUS "DEAF" SMITH, RETURNING TO BEXAR FROM A SKIRMISH NEAR LAREDO IN THE SPRING OF 1837, NOTICES THAT THE SENTIMENTS OF THE TEJANOS ARE SWINGING TOWARD THE ENEMY.

LET'S HEAR IT FOR TEXAS!

GRUMBLE..

GRUMBLE..

THE PRACTICE OF STEALING STOCK FROM THE TEJANOS BECOMES AN ESTABLISHED FEATURE OF THE "GUERRILLA WARFARE AGAINST MEXICO". THE NAME "COW BOYS" IS GIVEN TO THE ANGLO BANDS THAT RAID RANCHOS WITHOUT BOTHERING TO ASK THE POLITICAL SYMPATHIES OF THEIR OWNERS.

SOON THE FAR-FLUNG COUNTIES ARE VIRTUALLY UNDER THE CONTROL OF THIS WILD "COW BOY" ELEMENT, AND THE DESERTED FRONTIER TOWNS ARE LITTLE MORE THAN DEPOTS FOR THEIR "LIBERATED" CATTLE HERDS.

AT FIRST THEY RESTRICT THEIR OPERATIONS MOSTLY TO RAIDS BELOW THE NUECES, PLUNDERING "LOYALIST" RANCHOS, BUT SOON DISCOVER THE RICH POSSIBILITIES CLOSER TO HOME.

HELL, WHY GO ALL THE WAY TO THE BORDER? THERE'S PLENTY OF MESKIN' COWS RIGHT AROUND HERE!

YOUNG HENRY WAX KARNES, HEAD OF TEXAN CAVALRY FORCES ON THE FRONTIER, TENDERS HIS RESIGNATION IN DISGUST BECAUSE OF THE REPUBLIC'S LICENSING OF THESE "COWBOYS"— WHO ARE IN FACT ONLY OUTLAWS.

HOW AM I SUP- POSED TO KEEP ORDER DOWN HERE WITH ALL THESE TROUBLEMAKERS RUNNING WILD??

TO SURVIVE, THE RANCHEROS MUST FIGHT FIRE WITH FIRE. SOON ALL THE AREA OF "WEST" TEXAS IS AFLAME WITH TERRORISM.

OTHER TEJANOS, LIKE AGATÓN QUIÑONES, TURN TO A LIFE OF BANDITRY, FORMING CATTLE RAIDS OF THEIR OWN AND PREYING UPON TRADERS WHO DARE TO VENTURE ACROSS THE "NUECES STRIP" WHICH RAPIDLY BECOMES A NO-MAN'S LAND.

BUT MY WIFE IS MEXICAN..

OH, THAT'S OKAY. WE ROB MEXICANS TOO!

YEAH, WE'RE VERY OPEN-MINDED.

JUAN AND ERASMO SEGUIN'S PROPERTY— DEVASTATED BY THE REVOLUTION— IS NOW SUBJECTED TO SIMILAR TREATMENT BY "COWBOYS" AND "BANDIDOS" ALIKE.

...AT THE CONQUISTA CROSSING!

VAQUEROS! TO YOUR HORSES!!

SOME HIGH-PLACED ANGLOS PARTICIPATE IN THE TRADE OF STOLEN CATTLE, EVEN BACKING RAIDS ON THE HERDS OF LEADING TEJANO RANCHEROS AND FORMER FREEDOM-FIGHTERS.

GOT THIS BUNCH OVER AT ALDRETE'S RANCH JUDGE..

IF WE DON'T, SOMEBODY ELSE WILL. ANYWAY, TIMES ARE TOUGH!

LET ME WORRY ABOUT TH' DETAILS. YOU BOYS JUST KEEP TH' COWS COMING.

MOST OF THE TEJANOS AT GOLIAD RETREAT TO CARLOS RANCHO AND BAND TOGETHER FOR SELF-PROTECTION.

DE LA GARZA, YOU'RE UNDER ARREST FOR TREASON!

..AND ALL YOUR PROPERTY IS HEREBY CONFISCATED!

GO TO HELL, GRINGO!

AT VICTORIA, WHERE THE VOLUNTEERS HAVE THEIR HEAD-QUARTERS, THE TEJANOS SUFFER WORST. INDIGNITIES ARE HEAPED UPON THEM, AND MANY OF THE PROMINENT FAMILIES, LIKE THE DE LEONS, THE CARVAJALS, AND PLACIDO BENAVIDES'— ALL EARLY PARTICIPANTS IN THE STRUGGLE FOR INDEPENDENCE — ARE FORCED TO FLEE THE COUNTRY.

WE CAN'T GO TO MEXICO. MAYBE WE CAN FIND REFUGE IN NEW ORLEANS..

ONCE THEY ARE GONE, THEIR VAST CATTLE HERDS AND EXTENSIVE LAND HOLDINGS BECOME EASY PICKINGS FOR THE RAPACIOUS NEWCOMERS.

BOY, THESE WILD COWS SURE ARE THICK AROUND HERE!

THINK I'LL FILE MY HEADRIGHT CLAIM OVER ON PLACIDO CREEK. NEVER SAW SUCH TALL GRASS!

A BRISK BUSINESS IN HEADRIGHT CERTIFICATES DEVELOPS AROUND SAN ANTONIO. ALMOST OVERNIGHT, POTENTIAL OWNERSHIP OF THE LAND PASSES FROM THE HANDS OF TEJANOS TO A FEW ANGLO SPECULATORS.

ALSO ENGAGING IN THIS BUSINESS ARE SOME TEJANOS, INCLUDING JUAN SEGUIN — WHO NOT ONLY BUY FOR THEMSELVES, BUT ACT AS GO-BETWEENS FOR THEIR ILLITERATE TOWNSMEN WHO WANT TO CASH IN ON THE REPUBLIC'S GENEROUS LAND POLICY. ⟨SEE NOTE⟩

WHAT DO YOU NEED 4,000 ACRES FOR, PEDRO? YOU'VE NEVER BEEN OUT OF TOWN IN YOUR LIFE! I'LL GIVE YOU $700 — AND THAT'S TOP DOLLAR!!

GEE, $700! I NEVER SAW SO MUCH MONEY!!

TAKE IT.. TAKE IT.

ARE YOU SURE YOU WANT TO SELL, BLAS?

WHY NOT? AFTER ALL, IT'S FREE MONEY — AND YOU NEVER KNOW WHEN SANTA ANNA WILL BE BACK!

WHILE NO ONE GETS RICH QUICK THROUGH LAND SPECULATION, THE FOUNDATIONS ARE LAID FOR FUTURE FORTUNES BY THE TRAFFIC IN HEADRIGHT CERTIFICATES.

WELL MR. MAVERICK, THIS LATEST SURVEY BRINGS YOU UP TO AROUND 50,000 ACRES OF THE FINEST RANCH LAND IN TEXAS!

YEAH, NOW ALL I NEED IS SOME CUSTOMERS.

BUT FOR THE TEJANOS WHO SELL, THEY LOSE NOT ONLY THEIR CHANCE TO PARTICIPATE IN THE "JEFFERSONIAN DREAM", THEY ALSO BARGAIN AWAY THEIR STAKE IN THE NEW REPUBLIC.

EARLY IN 1838 JUAN GOES TO CONGRESS TO SERVE AS SENATOR FROM BEXAR. HE TRIES TO PROMOTE UNDERSTANDING AND BETTER RELATIONS BETWEEN THE ANGLOS AND HIS PEOPLE.

THINK OF IT, 'SEFA. WITH ALL THIS MONEY, I CAN FINALLY SET MYSELF UP AS A SHOEMAKER!

YEAH, BUT THERE GOES OUR CHANCE TO BE SOMEBODY — LANDOWNERS, NOT JUST PEONS LIKE WE'VE ALWAYS BEEN.

IF NEW LAWS WERE ALSO PUBLISHED IN SPANISH, THEN THE TEJANOS WOULD KNOW BETTER THEIR RIGHTS AND RESPONSIBILITIES TO OUR REPUBLIC IN THIS DIFFICULT TIME.

⟨NOTE: UNDER THE REPUBLIC, EVERY HEAD OF A HOUSEHOLD WAS ENTITLED TO A "LEAGUE AND LABOR" — 4,605½ ACRES.⟩ ⟨65⟩

DESPITE HIS EFFORTS, THINGS AROUND BEXAR GROW WORSE. EVENTUALLY, TRADE ACROSS THE ENTIRE SOUTHWESTERN FRONTIER COMES ALMOST TO A STANDSTILL BECAUSE OF THE DEPREDATIONS OF THE RIVAL GANGS, ANGLO AND MEXICAN.

GETTING TO WHERE IT'S NOT SAFE TO WALK THE STREETS AT NIGHT...

NIGHT, HELL. I AVOID IT IN THE DAYTIME!

ERASMO SEGUIN, AS JUSTICE OF THE PEACE IN BEXAR COUNTY, ORDERS THE SHERIFF TO ARREST ONE NOTORIOUS GROUP OF ANGLOS WHO HAVE BEEN ROBBING AND MURDERING TRADERS PLYING THE BORDER ROUTE. TESTIFYING IN THE CASE IS ONE OF THE EARLIEST RECRUITS IN JUAN'S COMPANY, BUT JUSTICE IS HARD TO COME BY FOR MEXICANS IN THESE TROUBLED TIMES.

YOUR HONOR, SINCE WE DON'T GOT A JAIL, WE VOTE TO RELEASE THEM ON BAIL...

WITH THE OPENING OF THE LAND OFFICE, SAN ANTONIO SINKS INTO A PITHOLE, OVERRUN BY THE DREGS OF SOCIETY.

YEE HAW

WAHWHOO

IF THIS KEEPS UP MUCH LONGER, I'M TAKING THE CHILDREN AND GOING BACK TO ALABAMA!

A "VOLUNTEER" NAMED TINSLEY PROVOKES A QUARREL WITH AND KILLS A YOUNGER BROTHER OF JOSE ANTONIO NAVARRO—BUT NOT BEFORE EUGENIO PUTS A KNIFE INTO HIS ASSASSIN.

ONLY THE FACT THAT BOTH MEN PERISH KEEPS THE TWO SIDES FROM DEEPENING THE FLOW OF BLOOD.

IF IT HAD TO HAPPEN, IT'S BEST THAT IT END LIKE THIS...

NEVERTHELESS, JUAN REMAINS STEADFAST IN HIS CONVICTION THAT JUSTICE WILL PREVAIL. SERVING ON THE SENATE'S COMMITTEE OF MILITARY AFFAIRS, HE ACCOMPANIES LAMAR ON THE "BUFFALO HUNT" THAT VIEWS THE SPOT LATER TO BE SELECTED FOR THE NEW CAPITAL OF TEXAS.

WHAT DO YOU CALL THIS SCENIC SPOT, FRIEND?

WATERLOO, IF YOU GET WHAT I MEAN.. HEHE

HMM... MAYBE LOCATING THIS DEEP IN INDIAN TERRITORY WOULD HELP US BRING PEACE TO THE FRONTIER—AND BEXAR!

REZIN BOWIE EMPOWERS HIM TO ADMINISTER THE ESTATE OF HIS FAMOUS BROTHER, MARTYRED IN THE ALAMO.

JIM THOUGHT A LOT OF YOU, MR. SEGUIN. ACCEPT THIS MEMENTO. IT WAS ONE OF HIS FAVORITES.

YOU DO ME A GREAT HONOR, SIR..

(Exactly how Juan came by this knife is another of those mysteries...)

JUAN'S SERVICES TO THE REPUBLIC ARE NOT FORGOTTEN BY THE OLD, "HOME-GROWN" TEXIAN FREEDOM-FIGHTERS.

SAY WHAT YOU WILL ABOUT MEXICANS YOUNG FELLER, BUT I'D STAKE MY LIFE ON JUAN SEGUIN!

YEP, HE'S A GOOD MAN, ALRIGHT. I'LL NEVER FORGET HIS CHARGE AT SAN JACINTO.

WHILE HE IS VISITING THE RANCHO OF HIS BROTHER-IN-LAW MANUEL FLORES* ON THE GUADALUPE, THE RESIDENTS OF NEARBY WALNUT SPRINGS — MOSTLY EARLY RANGERS — RENAME THEIR SETTLEMENT IN HIS HONOR.

HURRAY SEGUIN!

THANKS FOR GETTING US A POSTAL OFFICE, SENATOR. WE NEEDED IT!!

BUT NOT LONG AFTER OCCURS AN INCIDENT THAT DOES MUCH TO INTENSIFY SUSPICION OF *ALL* THE TEXAS-MEXICANS. A GROUP OF RANGERS CATCH SOME FOLLOWERS OF VICENTE CÓRDOVA WITH PAPERS FROM THE MEXICAN GOVERNMENT, INCITING THE EAST TEXAS INDIANS TO *RISE UP* AGAINST THE ANGLOS.

JUST LIKE WE FIGURED. THE MESKINS AND INJUNS ARE TEAMING UP ON US.

THAT PREVIOUS FALL AT NACOGDOCHES, CÓRDOVA AND OTHER TEJANOS STILL LOYAL TO MEXICO — ALONG WITH A FEW ANGLO MALCONTENTS — HAD DISCLAIMED ALLEGIANCE TO TEXAS, AND AFTER CAUSING A MINOR FUSS, HAD DISPERSED TO THEIR FRIENDS AMONG THE INDIANS.

WE'VE HAD ALL WE CAN STAND OF *THIS* SO-CALLED "FREE" COUNTRY!

⟨68⟩ ★ Note: This is an entirely different "Manuel Flores" than the one supposedly killed in the next panel.

THE CHEROKEES AND OTHER EAST TEXAS TRIBES WERE NONE TOO HAPPY WITH THE REPUBLIC EITHER. CONGRESS HAD REFUSED TO HONOR HOUSTON'S TREATY, IN WHICH THEY WERE FINALLY TO GET TITLE TO THE RICH LANDS THEY OCCUPIED.

LOOKS LIKE THE TEXIANS ARE GONNA' TRY TO GIVE US THE SAME TREATMENT "OLD HICKORY" DID — THE BOOT!

IF WE UNITE, WE CAN DRIVE THE ANGLOS OUT, AND A GRATEFUL MEXICO WILL RESTORE OUR LANDS!

THE RESULT OF THE SHORT-LIVED "CÓRDOVA REBELLION" WAS THAT MOST OF THE ENCLAVE OF EAST TEXAS TEJANOS WERE FORCED TO ABANDON THEIR HOMES AND FLEE SOUTHWARD.*

THEY HAVEN'T HEARD THE LAST OF ME!

ALL OVER TEXAS THE WORD SPREADS: THE MEXICANS ARE IN LEAGUE WITH THE INDIANS, AND TEJANOS ARE ACTING AS AGENTS TO STIR THEM UP.

TRUST ANY OF THEM AND YOU'LL WIND UP MURDERED IN YOUR SLEEP!

YOU CAN'T TELL THE GOOD ONES FROM THE BAD ONES...

WE OUGHT TO CLEAN 'UM ALL OUT OF TEXAS!

THEY ALL HATE US ANYWAY.

TO HELP COUNTER THE RISING HOSTILITY AGAINST THEM, JUAN AND OTHER TEJANO VOLUNTEERS RIDE WITH CAPT. JACK HAYS' RANGERS WHILE CONGRESS IS IN RECESS.

PEOPLE ARE BEGINNING TO THINK THAT WE TEJANOS ARE IN THE SAME BAG AS TORY MEXICANS AND RENEGADE INDIANS.

* (Or to Louisiana where they settled around "Spanish Lake".)

DESPITE THE UNCERTAIN TIMES, THE TEJANOS STILL FIND TIME FOR FESTIVITIES. MEXICAN INDEPENDENCE DAY, SEPT. 16TH, IS CELEBRATED IN SAN ANTONIO. THE PROCESSION ENDS AMID MUCH GAIETY AT THE HOUSE OF JOSE FLORES, JUAN'S FATHER-IN-LAW.

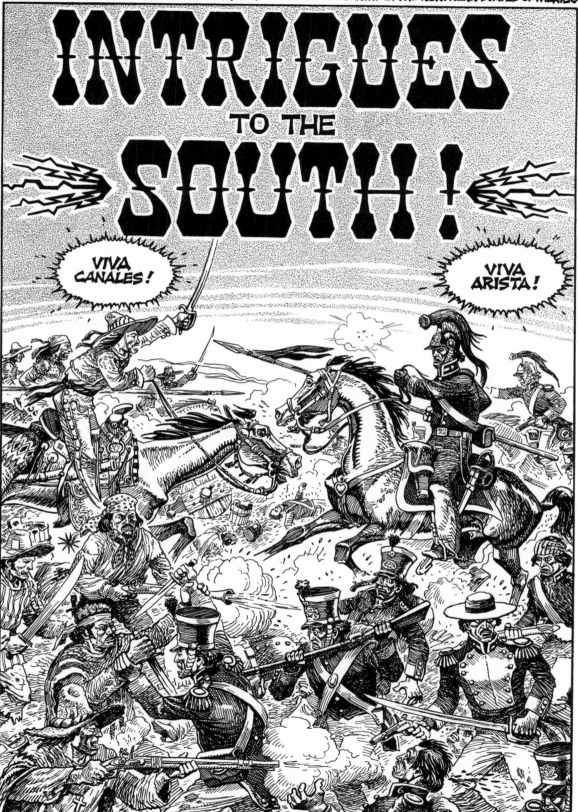

MANY INFLUENTIAL LEADERS IN THE FEDERALIST WARS ARE FORMER TEJANOS WHO HAVE BECOME DISILLUSIONED WITH THE COURSE OF THE TEXAS REPUBLIC. THEY INCLUDE RAMON MUSQUIZ, FORMER POLITICAL CHIEF OF BEXAR; JOSE ANTONIO MEJIA, "PROFESSIONAL" LIBERAL LEADER AND LAND SPECULATOR; ANTONIO ZAPATA, A LARGE RANCHERO EAST OF THE RIO GRANDE; JOSE M. J. CARVAJAL, FORMER RESIDENT OF VICTORIA, AND SON-IN-LAW OF THE COLONIZER MARTIN de LEON; ANTONIO CANALES, A CAMARGO LAWYER AND LONGTIME FOMENTOR OF BORDER POLITICS; AND OTHER MEN THAT ONCE HAD A HAND IN GUIDING THE AFFAIRS OF TEXAS — BUT A TEXAS UNDER *MEXICAN* RULE.

SAN ANTONIO BECOMES A HAVEN FOR THEM, AND MANY OF ITS TEJANO RESIDENTS FOLLOW WITH INTEREST THEIR EFFORTS TO SET UP A "FREE STATE" WITHIN MEXICO.

JOSE ANTONIO NAVARRO, WHO HAD REPRESENTED BEXAR COUNTY IN THE HOUSE OF THE THIRD CONGRESS AND RESIGNED HIS SEAT IN THE FOURTH BECAUSE OF ILLNESS, IS OFFERED A JOB AS AGENT BETWEEN THE FEDERALISTS AND THE REPUBLIC.

BUT THEY DO MANAGE TO ATTRACT TO THEIR RANKS A NUMBER OF TEXIAN VOLUNTEERS UNDER SUCH MEN AS COL. SAMUEL JORDAN, A FORMER RANGER CAPTAIN; COL. REUBEN ROSS, ONE OF GEN. FELIX HUSTON'S AIDES; AND EWEN CAMERON, LEADER OF THE VICTORIA "COWBOYS." EVEN JACK HAYS MARCHES SOUTH TO BRIEFLY FIGHT FOR THE FEDERALIST CAUSE.

WELCOME, COMPAÑEROS! YOU COME TO HELP US WIN OUR FREEDOM, NO?? HEH HEH

SI, SI, AMIGO, YOU BETCHA.. HEH HEH..

BEFORE LONG, THE TEXIAN VOLUNTEERS HAVE TROUBLE WITH CANALES.

THIS IS *MEXICAN* TERRITORY.. GET RID OF THAT FLAG!

THE BOYS ARE MIGHTILY FOND OF *THAT* FLAG, GENERAL..

AFTER A PROMISING START, THE FEDERALISTS SUFFER SOME SERIOUS SETBACKS. ZAPATA, THE MOST CAPABLE REBEL FIGHTER, IS CAPTURED AND EXECUTED. CANALES IS DEFEATED AND BARELY ESCAPES, LIMPING INTO SAN ANTONIO.

HE OFFERS JUAN, STILL A SENATOR FROM BEXAR, A HIGH POSITION IN THE ARMY OF THE "REPUBLIC OF THE RIO GRANDE" AND ASKS HIS HELP IN RECRUITING MEN FOR ANOTHER TRY.

THERE'S GOT TO BE A BETTER WAY TO MAKE A LIVING!!

IF YOU THROW IN WITH ME, THE MEXICANS HERE WILL JOIN FOR SURE, AND MAYBE A FEW HUEROS TOO!

⟨73⟩

CANALES, BEARING A LETTER OF INTRODUCTION FROM SEGUIN, GOES TO SEE PRESIDENT LAMAR. NEITHER ONE TAKES TO THE OTHER VERY MUCH...

WELL, WHAT DO YOU THINK OF OUR NEW SEAT OF GOVERNMENT, GEN. CANALIS?

ANOTHER BORDER BANDIT..

MARVELOUS, MR. PRESIDENT.

SMUG GRINGO.. HOPE HE'LL SELL ME SOME GUNS — ON CREDIT!

A MAJOR PROBLEM IS THE STRIP OF LAND BETWEEN THE NUECES AND THE RIO GRANDE, WHICH BOTH TEXAS AND THE FEDERALISTS CLAIM.

SAN ANTONIO de BEXAR • | SEGUIN • | • GONZALES
SEGUIN'S RANCHO | • CUERO
Rio San Antonio | • VICTORIA
• GOLIAD
• REFUGIO
PRESIDIO del RIO GRANDE | LIPAN-TITLAN • | • SAN PATRICIO
KING'S RANCHO | • CORPUS CHRISTI
Rio Grande | Rio Nueces | GULF OF MEXICO
• LAREDO
COAHUILA
TAMAULIPAS
• MONCLOVA
• GUERRERO
NUEVO LEON | • MIER
• CAMARGO
□ MONTERREY | REYNOSA •
• MATAMOROS

WHAT ABOUT THE NUECES STRIP?

LET'S TALK ABOUT THAT LATER, AFTER YOU HELP ME WIN..

MEXICO

U.S.A

TEXAS

HOWEVER, SOME VOLUNTEERS ARE AGAIN RAISED IN TEXAS, UNDER MEN LIKE THE FORMER SEC. OF WAR OF HOUSTON'S ADMINISTRATION, WILLIAM FISHER. THE FEDERALISTS SET UP THEIR BASE OF OPERATIONS AT LIPANTITLAN, ON THE NUECES.

ANYTHING THAT WEAKENS THOSE CENTRALIST DICTATORS IS GOOD FOR TEXAS.

⟨74⟩

DEEP IN MEXICO, THE TEXIANS FIND THAT *NEITHER* THE FEDERALISTS NOR THE CENTRALISTS CARE MUCH FOR THEM.

LOOKS LIKE WE'LL HAVE TO FIGHT OUR WAY TO THE BORDER, BOYS. THEY'RE *BOTH* SHOOTIN' AT US!

JUAN, UNAWARE OF THESE DEVELOPMENTS, RESIGNS HIS SEAT IN THE ADJOURNED FOURTH CONGRESS AND MARCHES AT THE HEAD OF 200 MEN TO JOIN THE FRAY.

PRESIDENT LAMAR IS SYMPATHETIC TO THIS MOVEMENT, BUT WON'T OFFICIALLY SANCTION IT...

AT THE RIO GRANDE, HE IS MET BY SOME OF THE TEXIANS RETURNING FROM THEIR BETRAYAL BY THE FEDERALISTS.

IT'S GETTING STICKY DOWN THERE JUAN. CANALES HAS SOLD OUT TO ARISTA'S BUNCH!

WE WERE DURN LUCKY TO GET BACK WITH OUR SKINS!

JUAN DECIDES TO VISIT CANALES AND SEE ABOUT COLLECTING SOME OF THE PAY HIS VOLUNTEERS WERE PROMISED, INCLUDING THE #4,000 HE HAD PERSONALLY SPENT OUTFITTING HIS COMPANY FOR FEDERALIST SERVICE.

YOU'RE CRAZY TO GO NEAR THAT SCUMBAG, JUAN.

HE'LL THROW YOU IN JAIL, OR WORSE!

WHILE IN MIER, JUAN NOTICES THAT PREPARATIONS ARE UNDERWAY FOR SOMETHING BIG...

HE SOON HEARS FROM GEN. REYES AND GEN. VASQUEZ ABOUT THE FEDERALISTS' CHANGE OF PLANS.

THAT'S THE NOTORIOUS TEJANO, JUAN SEGUIN...A GRINGO LOVER!

ARISTA AND CANALES ARE BUDDIES NOW! WE SHOULDN'T FIGHT EACH OTHER. AFTER ALL, WE'RE MEXICANS. BETTER TO FIGHT THE USURPERS IN TEXAS THAT TOOK OUR LAND, NO?

WE COULD USE A MAN LIKE YOU, SEGUIN. WHEN ARE YOU GONNA WISE UP AND QUIT FIGHTING FOR LOST CAUSES?

TEE HEE

HOPING TO LEARN SOMETHING DEFINITE ABOUT THEIR INVASION PLANS, HE PROCEEDS TO MONTERREY WHERE HE MEETS ARISTA. HE ENCOURAGES THE GENERALS TO TALK BY FEIGNING DISSATISFACTION WITH TEXAS.

OH SURE, OUR PEOPLE ARE DISGRUNTLED. GIVEN THE RIGHT LEADER, THEY MIGHT RISE UP.

WONDERFUL! WONDERFUL!!

IT IS SOON BEING SAID LOCALLY THAT SEGUIN'S SENTIMENTS ARE ONCE AGAIN WITH MEXICO..

I HEARD IT FROM RAUL, WHO GOT IT STRAIGHT FROM GEN. ARISTA'S PERSONAL FOOD TASTER!

FOR THE COMING CAMPAIGN, I'VE GOT 6,000 MEN, CANNON, AND LOTSA' MONEY..

BUT WHEN HE LEAVES, IT IS WITHOUT THE MONEY THAT CANALES HAD PROMISED FOR JOINING THE FEDERALIST CAUSE — A DEBT THAT THEIR NEW CENTRALIST "ALLIES" HAD GUARANTEED TO HONOR.

GUESS I'LL HAVE TO MORTGAGE SOME LAND...

HE BRINGS WORD OF THE IMPENDING CAMPAIGN BACK TO ACTING-PRESIDENT BURNET AND THE TEXAS GOVERNMENT.

I'VE NEVER SEEN EVERYONE SO WORKED UP DOWN THERE.

HMM.. SOUNDS LIKE ALL THE FACTIONS ARE PUTTING ASIDE THEIR DIFFERENCES TO UNITE AND DRIVE US OUT.

UPON HIS RETURN TO SAN ANTONIO, JUAN — HAVING RESIGNED HIS SENATE SEAT — IS PROMPTLY ELECTED MAYOR.

THE TOWN IS RAPIDLY BECOMING ANGLICIZED. SOME OF THE NEWCOMERS, JEALOUS OF HIS POSITION AND INFLUENCE, BEGIN TO DEVELOP INTRIGUES AGAINST HIM.

THAT SAGEEN HAS TOO MUCH POWER FOR A MEXICAN!

YEAH — ESPECIALLY ONE THAT HOB-NOBS WITH THOSE S.O.B.'s DOWN SOUTH!

J. GOODMAN

⟨77⟩

JUAN'S JOB BRINGS HIM INTO DAILY CONTACT WITH THE MORE UNDESIRABLE ELEMENTS OF BEXAR— MANY OF THEM OUT TO EXPLOIT THE COMMON PEOPLE. EACH TIME HE THWARTS THEIR PLANS, HIS ENEMIES INCREASE.

WHAT WE NEED IS A MAYOR THAT REPRESENTS TEXICANS, NOT MEXICANS!

WHAT WE NEED IS A MAYOR THAT'S NOT SO FRIENDLY TO THE *HUEROS*.

THE DEFENSE OF THE FRONTIER FALLS MOSTLY TO MEN LIKE CAPT. JACK HAYS AND HIS STALWART BAND OF RANGERS, OFTEN AIDED BY TEJANOS RIDING UNDER ANTONIO PEREZ.

CATTLE RAIDING AROUND THE AREA BECOMES WORSE. SOMEONE IS OBVIOUSLY TIPPING OFF THE MEXICAN RAIDERS AS TO RANGER MOVEMENTS, MAKING IT HARDER TO CATCH THE THIEVES.

SAN ANTONIO TIGHTENS ITS SECURITY.

THERE'S WAY TOO MUCH TRAFFIC IN AND OUT OF HERE. TOTAL STRANGERS SHOW UP EVERY MONTH OR SO.

NOT TO MENTION OUR SEMI-PERMANENT CROWD OF VAGRANTS, THUGS, DRUNKS AND SUSPICIOUS CHARACTERS!

TOWN HALL
CABILDO

LET'S MAKE ALL OUTSIDERS REGISTER WHEN THEY GET TO TOWN. THAT'LL PUT THE OL' SCREWS TO 'UM!

I DON'T KNOW, SMITHERS. MIGHT BE BAD FOR THE TOURIST TRADE..

TOURIST TRADE! WHAT TOURIST TRADE ?!?

THE COUNCIL ALSO VOTES TO EXPELL JAMES GOODMAN, A NEWCOMER WHO HAS SQUATTED ON MILITARY PLAZA. JUAN, AS MAYOR, HAS TO EVICT GOODMAN, WHO IS SOMETHING OF A LEADER AMONG THE ROWDY CLASS.

DAMN YOU SAGEEN! THE REPUBLIC OWES ME THIS PROPERTY! I BEEN SHOEING TEXIAN HOSSES WITHOUT PAY, AND BY GOD, THIS IS TH' THANKS I GIT!

THIS PLACE HAS BELONGED TO THE CITY SINCE INDEPENDENCE! YOU HAD NO BUSINESS TAKING IT OVER LIKE YOU DID, SEÑOR.

J. GOODMAN BLACKSMITH GUNSMITH

IN THE SUMMER OF 1841 PRESIDENT LAMAR COMES TO VISIT SAN ANTONIO AND IS LAVISHLY ENTERTAINED. BUT HIS *REAL PURPOSE* IS TO GATHER SUPPORT FOR AN EXPEDITION TO SANTA FE, AND THUS STRENGTHEN TEXAN CLAIMS TO PART OF NEW MEXICO.

HE'S A FANCY TALKER, BUT DOESN'T CUT THE MUSTARD ON THE DANCE FLOOR!

BE SURE TO TAKE THE SHUCKS OFF HIS TAMALES JUST IN CASE..

HE PICKS NAVARRO AS ONE OF THE MEN TO HEAD HIS GRANDIOSE SCHEME.

I HAVE RESERVATIONS ABOUT THIS, MR. PRESIDENT..

NONSENSE!! YOU'RE THE ONLY MAN QUALIFIED FOR THE JOB. IT'S YOUR PATRIOTIC DUTY TO TEXAS!

CONVINCED THAT THE PEOPLE OF NEW MEXICO WOULD WELCOME THE OPPORTUNITY FOR INDEPENDENCE, *TEXAS-STYLE*, LAMAR MAKES NO SECRET OF HIS INTENTIONS — EVEN SENDING AHEAD AN OPEN LETTER TO THE CITIZENS OF SANTA FE!

WE TORE DOWN ALL WE FOUND IN THE PLAZA..

HMPH! LET THEM COME. WE'LL GIVE 'UM A HOT RECEPTION!

SANTA FE

WHILE PREPARATIONS ARE BEING MADE FOR THE SANTA FE EXPEDITION, AN ENVOY SENT BY GEN. ARISTA PASSES THROUGH SAN ANTONIO, ON HIS WAY TO SEE LAMAR AND TALK ABOUT THE BORDER SITUATION.

HMM.. LOOKS LIKE THESE TEXIANS ARE PLANNING A LITTLE INVASION OF THEIR OWN.

GIVE 'UM HELL IN SANTA FE!

BOWIE'S BAR

JUAN IS THE ENVOY'S CONTACT AND TO RECOUP HIS EARLIER LOSSES WITH THE FEDERALISTS, HE AGREES TO DO A LITTLE SMUGGLING.

EVERYBODY DOES IT ANYWAY, BUT WITH MY HELP, IT'LL BE A CINCH!!

I'LL DRINK TO THAT!

BUT WHEN JUAN GETS TO THE BORDER, HE IS NOT ALLOWED TO CONTINUE WITH THE COMMISSIONERS AND HIS TRADE GOODS ARE CONFISCATED.

NO PROBLEM. WE'LL SELL EVERYTHING FOR YOU, AMIGO, AND SEND THE MONEY! TRUST US! HEH HEH

SO JUAN, HAVING BORROWED YET ANOTHER £3,000 FOR THIS VENTURE, IS PLUNGED DEEPER IN DEBT.

AT THIS RATE, MY FAMILY WILL END UP IN THE POORHOUSE.

EVEN MORE DAMNING TO HIS FORTUNES, HOWEVER, IS THE REPORT THAT THE ENVOY, URIBE, CARRIES BACK TO ARISTA — INFORMATION THAT JUAN, BY ASSOCIATION, WILL SOON BE ACCUSED OF GIVING TO THE ENEMY.

THEY'RE ON THEIR WAY TO SANTA FE WITH AN ARMY — TO TAKE NEW MEXICO LIKE THEY DID TEXAS!!

THE TYRANNICAL RULER IN SANTA FE, MANUEL ARMIJO, LAUNCHES AN ABUSIVE PROPAGANDA CAMPAIGN TO AROUSE HIS SUBJECTS AGAINST THE TEXIANS.

CITIZENS, BE NOT DECEIVED BY THE SMOOTH WORDS OF THESE GODLESS FREEBOOTERS! THEY MEAN TO DESECRATE THE HOLY CHURCH, RAVISH OUR WOMEN, AND PILLAGE OUR FAIR PROVINCE!

RALLY AROUND YOUR ILLUSTRIOUS GOVERNOR, OR WE WILL ALL PERISH.

PERCEIVED BY THE MEXICANS AS A MILITARY INVASION RATHER THAN A COMMERCIAL VENTURE, THE TEXIAN "PIONEERS" MEET WITH DISASTER WHEN THEY STRAGGLE INTO NEW MEXICO.

TRADE COMMISSION, EH? SINCE WHEN DO TRADERS WEAR THE UNIFORM OF THE TEXAS ARMY?! DO NOT TAKE ME FOR A FOOL, SEÑORES!!

THE REAL BETRAYER OF THE SANTA FE FIASCO TURNS OUT TO BE THE MAN WHO ORIGINALLY SOLD PRES. LAMAR ON THE IDEA AND GUIDED IT TO DESTRUCTION, CAPT. WILLIAM P. LEWIS.

BELIEVE ME BOYS, GIVING UP YOUR GUNS IS ONLY A FORMALITY.. CUSTOMARY PROCEDURE FOR THE SANTA FE TRADE!

?!

WHILE LEWIS PARADES AROUND ON A MULE, ACTING AS GOV. ARMIJO'S PERSONAL INTERPRETER, NAVARRO AND THE OTHER TEXIANS ARE MARCHED OFF TO A MEXICAN PRISON.

YOUR AMIGOS DO NOT LIKE OUR LITTLE JOKE, EH SR. LEWIS?

DAMN YOU, LEWIS! YOU BROKE YOUR WORD— VIOLATED YOUR MASONIC OATH!! LIAR! LOW DOWN TRAITOR!

ALL OF THE TEXIANS ENDURE GREAT SUFFERING, BUT NAVARRO — HATED BY SANTA ANNA FOR HIS ROLE IN THE TEXAS REVOLUTION — SUFFERS WORST OF ALL.

I HAVE SWORN TO BE A TEXAN, AND I WILL NOT FORSWEAR!

WHEN THE FULL EXTENT OF THE EXPEDITION'S ABJECT FAILURE BECOMES KNOWN IN TEXAS, THERE IS WIDESPREAD FRUSTRATION AND GREAT NEED FOR A SCAPEGOAT. MANY FIND IT CONVENIENT TO WHISPER AND POINT AN ACCUSING FINGER AT SEGUIN.

I'LL BET HE SPILLED THE BEANS TO ARISTA'S SPY LAST SUMMER...

YEAH, HE'S BUDDY-BUDDY WITH ALL THOSE BIG MEXICAN GENERALS!

I HEARD THAT LEWIS WAS HIS INTERPRETER IN CONGRESS FOR AWHILE!

JUAN, WHEN APPRISED OF THE VICIOUS RUMORS, INDIGNANTLY DENIES THEM, BUT THE LOOSE TALK PERSISTS.

IF YOU REALLY WANT TO KNOW HOW THEY FOUND OUT WE WERE COMING, ASK PRESIDENT LAMAR. HE SENT THIS LETTER A YEAR AGO!

TO THE CITIZENS OF SANTA FE

IN A DESPERATE LAST ATTEMPT TO PAY OFF HIS NOTES, JUAN PLANS TO BUY AND BRING BACK SOME SHEEP FROM MEXICO.

MY DAD KNOWS MORE ABOUT SHEEP THAN ANYBODY IN TEXAS!

CORRESPONDENCE WITH GEN. VASQUEZ CONCERNING PERMITS FOR THE PURCHASE CONVINCES HIM THAT THE LONG-ANTICIPATED INVASION OF TEXAS IS NOW IMMINENT.

HMM..THIS SOUNDS BAD! I'D BETTER GET WORD TO PRESIDENT HOUSTON...*

POST OFFICE

★ SAM HOUSTON TOOK OFFICE FOR THE SECOND TIME IN DEC. 1841.

I THINK IT'S FOR REAL THIS TIME.. WHATEVER'S NOT NAILED DOWN, BETTER BE THINKING OF A SAFE PLACE TO HIDE IT!

BUT SEC. OF WAR HOCKLEY INFORMS JUAN THAT THE GOVERNMENT IS *BROKE,* AND BEXAR WILL HAVE TO RELY ON ITS OWN DEFENSES.

THIS IS THE LAST STRAW!

JUAN, DISGUSTED AT THE REPUBLIC'S INABILITY TO RESPOND TO HIS WARNING, CALLS THE CITY OFFICIALS TOGETHER ONE LAST TIME.

DREAM TURNS TO NIGHTMARE

THE TOWN CAN'T BE DEFENDED WITHOUT AID FROM THE REST OF TEXAS, AND THEIR ATTITUDE IS SINK OR SWIM. TO HELL WITH IT ALL — I'M GOING TO MY RANCH! AT LEAST I CAN TRY TO KEEP THEM FROM CARRYING OFF MY PROPERTY AGAIN, AND I'D ADVISE YOU TO DO THE SAME...

HIS DECISION TO ABANDON THE DEFENSE OF BEXAR MAKES PEOPLE MORE SUSPICIOUS. MALICIOUS GOSSIP HAS ALREADY LAID THE "BETRAYAL" OF THE SANTA FE AFFAIR AT HIS DOOR.

HMM... JUAN'S NEVER BEEN ONE TO RUN WHEN THE GOIN' GETS TOUGH..

MAYBE HE'S SWITCHED SIDES ON US, LIKE ALL THE OTHER MEXICANS IN TOWN!

JACK HAYS IS CHOSEN BY THE ANGLOS TO ORGANIZE A DEFENSE GROUP UNDER MARTIAL LAW— INCLUDING A CONTINGENT OF LOCAL TEJANOS UNDER SALVADOR FLORES.

SALVADOR — ALERT YOUR MILITIAMEN! CHEVALLIE — YOU AND DUNN RIDE OUT FOR A LOOK-SEE!

BUT WHEN VASQUEZ AND HIS ARMY SUDDENLY APPEAR ON THE OUTSKIRTS OF TOWN, THE SURPRISED TEXIANS HASTILY FALL BACK AND BEAT THE DUST TOWARD THE LITTLE SETTLEMENT RENAMED IN HONOR OF JUAN SEGUIN.

LET'S MEET ON THE GUADALUPE, AT FLORES' RANCHO!

ONE OF VASQUEZ' FIRST ACTS IS TO SEND A BUNDLE OF PROCLAMATIONS TO JUAN'S RANCH IN HOPES THAT HE WILL BREAK WITH TEXAS.

IN THE NAME OF HIS EXCELLENCY, GEN. RAFAEL VASQUEZ — GREETINGS TO ALL LOYAL MEXICANS SUFFERING UNDER THE YOKE OF FOREIGN OPPRESSION!

PLOP

VASQUEZ TELLS THE CITIZENS OF BEXAR THAT SEGUIN BACKS HIM AND HIS "RECONQUEST" OF TEXAS...

OH SURE, HE'S ONE OF OUR BIGGEST BOOSTERS. I'VE GOT A LETTER OF HIS HERE THAT PROVES IT!

LET ME SEE THAT. I KNOW JUAN'S HANDWRITING!

SORRY, YOU'LL HAVE TO TAKE MY WORD ON IT..

THEY DIDN'T WASTE ANY TIME...

VASQUEZ' RETREATING CARAVAN IS PURSUED TO THE NUECES BY CAPT. HAYS AND THE TEXIANS, ACCOMPANIED BY JUAN SEGUIN AND A GROUP OF TEJANO MILITIAMEN.

BUT WHEN JUAN RETURNS TO BEXAR, HE FINDS THE PLACE AGAINST HIM...

YOU GOT A LOT OF NERVE, COMING BACK HERE, SEGUIN!

WHY DIDN'T YOU JUST KEEP RIDING SOUTH, WITH THE REST OF YOUR BUDDIES?!

WE'RE WISE TO YOU! YOU'VE BEEN WORKING WITH THEM ALL ALONG- VASQUEZ EVEN ADMITTED IT!

YOUR LITTLE JIG IS OVER!

?!

ONE OF HIS FRIENDS, AND A SAN JACINTO VETERAN, MATIAS COURBIER, IS BEATEN SENSELESS BY GOODMAN AND SOME OF HIS BULLIES.

THAT'S NOTHING COMPARED TO WHAT WE GOT PLANNED FOR YOUR COMPADRE SAGEEN!

JUAN, HIS LIFE NOW IN DANGER, MOVES ABOUT THE STREETS IN DISGUISE.

JUAN, YOU KNOW I'M YOUR FRIEND. TAKE MY ADVICE AND OPEN YOUR EYES BEFORE IT'S TOO LATE...

MORE VIOLENCE IS AVERTED BY THE TIMELY ARRIVAL OF GEN. ED BURLESON AND A COMPANY OF ARMY REGULARS.

WHAT'S GOIN' ON HERE!?

SEGUIN'S GONE OVER TO THE ENEMY!!

HE'S A TRAITOR!

JUAN DEMANDS A PUBLIC HEARING TO CLEAR HIMSELF OF MISDOING, BUT BURLESON REFUSES TO CALL A COURT OF INQUIRY.

BUT JUAN'S ENEMIES, SOME WHO HAVE NURSED PETTY GRIEVANCES AGAINST HIM FOR YEARS, CONTINUE TO AGITATE THE MOB.

THESE CHARGES ARE RIDICULOUS! I WON'T DIGNIFY SUCH SLANDER BY GIVING IT FORMAL TRAPPINGS. SEGUIN HAS SUPPORTED US SINCE DAY ONE!

IF HE'S SUCH A NOBLE PATRIOT, THEN WHY DIDN'T HE HAVE ALL THOSE PEOPLE, WHO OPENLY CONSORTED WITH OL' VASQUEZ, ARRESTED?

I'LL TELL YOU WHY—'CAUSE HE'S ONE OF 'UM HISSELF!!

ONE OF THE MAIN RABBLE-ROUSERS IS JAMES GOODMAN, THE RECENTLY EVICTED GUNSMITH, AND HE RELISHES THE OPPORTUNITY TO TAKE VENGEANCE AGAINST JUAN.

BOYS, THIS IS OUR CHANCE TO MAKE THINGS *RIGHT* AROUND HERE! EITHER THIS PLACE IS TEXAS, OR IT'S MEXICO — WHICH IS IT GONNA' BE?!!

GET SEGUIN!

THROW TH' MESKINS OUT!!

BURLESON, REALIZING THE PUBLIC MOOD IS TURNING UGLY, COMMISSIONS JUAN TO "FORAGE FOR PROVISIONS IN THE LOWER RANCHOS"— REALLY AN EXCUSE TO GET HIM BEYOND THE GRASP OF HIS TORMENTERS.

PEOPLE ARE PRETTY HOT RIGHT NOW, BUT THEY'LL SIMMER DOWN AND COME TO THEIR SENSES. JUST LAY LOW FOR AWHILE...

BESIDES, YOU WON'T GET A FAIR TRIAL HERE ANYWAY, OLD FRIEND..

BUT A VOLUNTEER LYNCHING MOB LEARNS OF HIS "ESCAPE" AND GOES AFTER HIM. THEY STRING UP SENOR CALAVERAS, ONE OF JUAN'S NEIGHBORS.

WHERE'S HE HIDING AT, YOU OLD BUZZARD?

TALK, OR WE'LL MAKE IT ROUGH ON YOU!

SENOR CALAVERAS DOES NOT TALK, AND JUAN MAKES HIS GETAWAY. HE GOES INTO HIDING FOR SEVERAL WEEKS, RUNNING FROM RANCHO TO RANCHO.

FINALLY, UNWILLING TO FURTHER ENDANGER THE LIVES AND FAMILIES OF HIS FRIENDS, HE DETERMINES TO FORTIFY HIS OWN RANCHO.

SO IT'S FINALLY COME TO *THIS* — A PRISONER IN MY OWN HOME...

NEAR DESPAIR, HE PENS HIS RESIGNATION AS MAYOR OF SAN ANTONIO de BEXÁR.

..DUE TO THE DISORDERLY STATE IN WHICH THIS UNHAPPY COUNTY FINDS ITSELF AT THE PRESENT.. ..TIME...

THE WORDS ECHO BACK TO HAUNT HIM, FOR THEY SOUND MUCH LIKE THE WORDS HE HAD WRITTEN ON ANOTHER, MORE HOPEFUL OCCASION — WORDS THAT HE HAD USED BACK IN 1834, TO CALL FREE-THINKING TEXANS TOGETHER TO CONSIDER FREEDOM FROM MEXICO!

...DUE TO THE CENTRAL GOVERNMENT'S INDIFFERENCE TO OUR PREVIOUS PETITIONS AND TO THE STATE OF ANARCHY EXISTING IN TEXAS...

HIS ENEMIES GLOAT. BUT THE MOB WANTS MORE THAN JUST JUAN'S PERSONAL CAPITULATION. THEY WANT TO DESTROY THE POWER OF THE TEJANOS AS WELL. CAPT. JAMES SCOTT BRINGS A COMPANY DOWN THE SAN ANTONIO RIVER VALLEY, LOOTING AND BURNING THE RANCHOS IN HIS PATH.

JUAN'S NEIGHBORS FLOCK TO HIM FOR PROTECTION.

I AM A LOYAL TEXAN. AS YOU KNOW, MY SONS FOUGHT IN THE REVOLUTION. NOW, TO BE TREATED THIS WAY.. IT'S TERRIBLE!

THEY'VE GONE CRAZY. ONLY YOU, JEFE, STAND BE-TWEEN THEM AND US!

HE HASTILY PUTS TOGETHER 100 VAQUEROS, JUST LIKE IN THE DAYS OF OLD...

EXCEPT NOW HIS FOES ARE NOT LIPAN OR COMANCHE MARAUDERS. THEY ARE OTHER *TEXANS*, MEN THAT RIDE UNDER THE FLAG OF THE REPUBLIC— *HIS FLAG!!* CAPT. SCOTT, FACED WITH THIS UNEXPECTED RESISTANCE, PULLS HIS "VOLUNTEERS" BACK AND CHOOSES TO BE CONTENT WITH HIS CHEAPLY-WON SPOILS.

WE'LL FINISH THIS JOB ANOTHER DAY, BOYS...

JUAN LOOKS INTO THE FUTURE AND SEES NO HOPE. HE DECIDES TO LEAVE HIS FAMILY, HIS RUINED RANCHO, HIS UNGRATEFUL COUNTRY, AND SEEK ASYLUM IN MEXICO— THE SAME MOTHERLAND THAT HE HAS RAISED HIS HAND AGAINST SO OFTEN IN THE PAST.

WHAT'S TO BECOME OF US, JUAN?

..FOREIGNERS IN OUR NATIVE LAND...

(89)

BITTER EXILE

IN LAREDO, HE IS PUT BEHIND BARS UNTIL GEN. ARISTA CAN DECIDE WHAT TO DO WITH HIM.

WELL, WELL— YOU DON'T LOOK SO HIGH AND MIGHTY NOW, MR. JUAN SEGUIN, *YOU DIRTY TRAITOR!*

WHAT'S THE MATTER? YOUR HUERO FRIENDS DON'T NEED YOU ANYMORE, EH?

SO YOU COME RUNNING, HAT IN HAND TO EL PRESIDENTE— A GOOD JOKE, NO?? HA HA HA HA

HAHA

SANTA ANNA DECIDES TO MAKE AN EXAMPLE OF JUAN TO THE OTHER TEJANOS. HE GIVES HIM A CHOICE: JOIN THE INVASION FORCE OF GEN. ADRIAN WOLL, OR *ROT IN PRISON!*

FINALLY I'VE GOT THAT STINKING TURN-COAT WHERE I WANT HIM— *HEH!!*

SO JUAN SEGUIN, ONE OF THE FIRST NATIVE TEXANS TO SIDE WITH THE ANGLOS IN REVOLT, FINDS HIMSELF IN THE UNHAPPY SITUATION OF HAVING TO RIDE AGAINST HIS FORMER COMRADES..

YOU MIGHT AS WELL FACE IT, SEGUIN. ALL YOUR OLD TEXIAN FRIENDS ARE GONE. YOU'LL BE FIGHTING AGAINST THE *NEWCOMERS*, AND THEY'RE YOUR ENEMIES, VERDAD?

WE'RE CAUGHT BETWEEN A ROCK AND A HARD PLACE !!

THEY ARE BRIEFLY RESISTED BY SOME CITIZENS OF BEXAR, WHO THINK THEY ARE JUST ANOTHER BANDIT GANG, COME TO
PLUNDER THE TOWN. ANTONIO MENCHACA, WOUNDED IN THE FIGHTING, IS AGHAST WHEN HE FINDS WHO THE ENEMY REALLY IS.

JUAN..??? WHAT'S — WHAT ARE YOU DOING IN A MEXICAN UNIFORM?!

THE APPEARANCE OF JUAN SEGUIN IN THE RANKS OF THE INVASION FORCE SPREADS CONSTERNATION AMONG THE
TEJANOS THAT HAD PLANNED TO HELP DEFEND THEIR TOWN. NOW, THEY DO NOT KNOW WHICH SIDE TO JOIN..

I'LL STILL FIGHT MEXICO, BUT NOT JUAN SEGUIN! HE'S LIKE A BROTHER TO ME!

LOOK! THERE'S ANTONIO AND MANUEL WITH HIM.

OTHERS, NOW FED-UP WITH ANGLO RULE AND THE ABUSES OF THE ROWDY ELEMENT, SOON SWELL THE RANKS OF GEN. WOLL'S ARMY.

WHEN WOLL'S OCCUPATION OF BEXAR IS COMPLETE, MANY OF JUAN'S FORMER ENEMIES ANXIOUSLY COURT HIS FAVOR.

WELL SAM, LOOKS LIKE THE TIDE HAS FINALLY TURN-ED AGAINST US.

WITH JUAN GONE OVER TO THE ENEMY, NOT ONE MEXICAN IN THIS TOWN WILL HELP US!

I DIDN'T MEAN TO SPREAD ALL THOSE LIES ABOUT YOU, MR. SAGEEN. HOPE YOU DON'T HOLD A GRUDGE..

SEGUIN IS SENT BY WOLL TO RECONNOITER ALONG THE GONZALES ROAD. SOME OF HIS TROOPS ENCOUNTER AND KILL THREE ANGLOS BATHING AT THE SULPHUR SPRINGS ON THE CIBOLO. ONE IS A FORMER COUNCILMAN, FRIEND OF JUAN'S.

WHAT COULD WE DO, JEFE? THEY WERE GOING FOR THEIR GUNS!

SMITHERS, YOU STUBBORN OLD GOAT! NOW I'LL CARRY THE BLAME FOR THIS TO MY GRAVE..

WHEN A FORCE OF TEXIANS APPEARS ON THE SALADO CREEK, WOLL ORDERS JUAN TO ATTACK "AT ALL HAZARD".

WE'LL SOON SEE WHICH SIDE SEGUIN IS REALLY ON...

HE AND THE BEXAR DEFENDERS ARE PLACED IN THE FOREFRONT OF BATTLE SO THAT *JUAN*, BY SHEDDING HIS BLOOD, MIGHT VINDICATE HIMSELF FOR PAST OFFENSES AGAINST MEXICO.

JUAN'S COMPANY ATTACKS *TWICE* AND IS HURLED BACK IN GREAT CONFUSION BY THE TEXIANS' DEADLY FIRE — JUST AS HE KNEW THEY WOULD BE.

TEXIANS THAT HAD ONCE FOUGHT BESIDE JUAN — LIKE JACK HAYS, HENRY McCULLOCH, CREED TAYLOR, "BIGFOOT" WALLACE, AND OTHERS — ARE NOW ASTOUNDED TO SEE HIM LEADING THE ENEMY!!

GEN. WOLL, SATISFIED THAT JUAN IS NOW LOYAL TO MEX-
ICO, RELIEVES HIM AS A THIRD CHARGE IS READIED.

MAYBE HE *HAS* HAD
A CHANGE OF HEART—
AT LEAST NOW EVERYBODY
WILL THINK SO, THAT'S
FOR SURE !!

IN THE LULL, MATHEW "OLD PAINT" CALDWELL —
ONE OF MANY IN THE TEXIAN RANKS THAT HAD SPENT
TIME IN A MEXICAN PRISON— ADDRESSES HIS SMALL ARMY.

NOW MY BOYS, YOU KNOW
WHAT'S IN STORE FOR US GRINGOS
IF EVEN MEN LIKE JUAN SEGUIN TURN
THEIR BACKS ON TEXAS! KEEP COOL
AND REMEMBER — WE FIGHT FOR
LIBERTY AND OUR INSULTED
COUNTRY!

BUT IN *THIS* TEXIAN ARMY, THERE ARE PITIFULLY FEW TEJANOS: THE ANGLO-SAXON SONS OF KENTUCKY AND TENNESSEE
STAND FACING THE HISPANO SONS OF CASTILE AND MEXICO.... AT LAST THE *UGLY LINE* HAS BEEN DRAWN FOR TEXAS.

AT SUNSET, AFTER A DAY OF BITTER FIGHTING
AND HEAVY LOSSES ON BOTH SIDES, WOLL WITH-
DRAWS FROM THE FIELD TO LICK HIS WOUNDS. *

HAVING OCCUPIED BEXAR FOR A BRIEF TEN
DAYS, WOLL — CONCLUDING THAT HIS MISSION
IS COMPLETE — HEADS BACK TOWARD MEXICO.

⟨94⟩ * Vicente Cordova and some of his Cherokees were killed at this battle.

UNLIKE VASQUEZ, HE DOES NOT ALLOW HIS TROOPS TO PILLAGE THE CITY, BUT HE SENDS AHEAD 53 "PRISONERS OF WAR" — INCLUDING SAM MAVERICK AND ALL OF SAN ANTONIO'S CIVIL OFFICIALS AND IMPORTANT ANGLO CITIZENS.

SOME 200 PROMINENT TEJANO FAMILIES OF BEXAR GO WITH HIM, FEARING REPRISAL IF THEY REMAIN BEHIND. AMONG THEM ARE THE WIFE AND CHILDREN OF JUAN SEGUIN.

WE MUST LEAVE NIÑO. IT'S NO LONG-ER SAFE FOR US IN THIS PLACE..

ERASMO FOLLOWS, HOPING TO PERSUADE HIS LOVED ONES TO REMAIN IN THEIR HOMELAND.

SON, LISTEN TO ME — THIS IS A MISTAKE! WE STILL HAVE A FEW INFLU-ENTIAL FRIENDS LEFT. THEY WILL HELP US THROUGH THIS THING!!

FRIENDS, FATHER? YES, WE HAD FRIENDS HERE ONCE.. AUSTIN, BOWIE, DEAF SMITH, ZAVALA.. BUT NOW THEY ARE DEAD. ONLY OUR ENEMIES LIVE ON!

BUT JUAN KNOWS THAT TEXAS WILL NO LONGER EMBRACE HIM AFTER HE HAS BORNE ARMS AGAINST HER. HE HAS NO CHOICE BUT TO LEAVE THE LAND AND ALL THAT HE HAS FOUGHT FOR AND SUSTAINED THROUGH SO MUCH TRIBULATION.

NO PAPA... WHAT IS DONE, CANNOT BE UNDONE! ··I MUST GO···

NEAR THE MEDINA RIVER, TEXIAN TROOPS IN PURSUIT OF THE RETREATING CAVALCADE, ENCOUNTER ERASMO—WORN, HAGGARD AND RENDERED DESOLATE BY HIS SON'S FLIGHT. THE OLD MAN, EVER LOYAL TO TEXAS, IS ALLOWED TO PASS UNMOLESTED.

ARE WE JUST GONNA LET THAT OLD MESKIN' GO?!

SHOW SOME RESPECT, YOU KNUCKLEHEAD. THAT'S DON ERASMO SEGUIN, AND HE WAS A TEXAS PATRIOT BEFORE YOU WUZ EVEN BORN!

BUT FOR JUAN SEGUIN— ONCE THE PROUDEST NATIVE SON THAT TEXAS HAD TO OFFER— THERE IS NO CONSOLATION. AS HE RIDES TOWARD THE BORDER AND AN UNCERTAIN FUTURE, ALL HIS HOPES AND DREAMS REMAIN BEHIND, IN THE LAND THAT HE STILL LOVES — *TEXAS!!*

IN THE WAKE OF THE WOLL INVASION, TEXIAN MILITIAMEN SWARM ON SAN ANTONIO, MAD AS HORNETS.

IT'S ABOUT TIME WE CLEANED OUT THIS DEN OF THIEVES AND TRAITORS!

FROM THE RAMPARTS OF THE ALAMO, ED BURLESON — VICE-PRESIDENT OF THE REPUBLIC — MAKES A ROUSING SPEECH, CALLING FOR A MASSIVE STRIKE AT MEXICO THE FOLLOWING MONTH...

THIS WAR AND CONSTANT STATE OF INSECURITY WILL NOT END UNTIL WE TEACH THE MEXICANS A LESSON THEY WON'T FORGET!!

THE ANGLOS TAKE THEIR FRUSTRATION OUT ON THE TEJANO RESIDENTS, CONFISCATING STOCK AND ANYTHING ELSE OF VALUE.

SOY AMIGO!

AMIGO, HELL!! YOU SHOULDA LEFT WHEN YOU HAD THE CHANCE, GREASER.

OINK?

THE TEJANA WIDOW OF DEAF SMITH HAS HER HOUSE BROKEN INTO AND LOOTED BY TEXIAN VOLUNTEERS.

THIS 'UN IS REALLY SQUAWKIN' AIN'T SHE?

POR FAVOR, SEÑORES, NO SE LLEVEN LAS COLCHAS DE MIS HUERFANOS!! POR FAVOR..

ALTHO CAPT. BOGART ORDERS WIDOW SMITH'S THINGS RETURNED, THE ASSEMBLING ARMY CONTINUES TO "LIVE OFF THE MEXICANS."

BUT HOW'S WE SUPPOSED TO KNOW SHE WUZ MR. DEAF SMITH'S WIFE?

HELL, CAPT'N, SHE LOOKED PLAIN MESKIN' TO ME..

WITH THE WAR CRY CIRCULATING ALL OVER TEXAS, IT IS NOT LONG BEFORE JUAN SEGUIN IS PUBLICALLY DENOUNCED AS A TRAITOR TO THE REVOLUTION AND A FOUL MURDERER.

SEZ HERE HE KILLED POOR OL' SMITHERS AND THEM OTHERS IN COLD BLOOD!

IF OLD PAINT SEZ SO, IT MUST BE TRUE.

IT'S TRUE ALRIGHT. I SAW HIM IN A MEXICAN UNIFORM WITH MY OWN EYES!!

TELEGRAPH & TEXAS REGISTER

THE FACT THAT HE WAS THE MOST RESPECTED, POLITICALLY POWERFUL TEJANO IN THE REPUBLIC ONLY MAKES PEOPLE MORE BITTER AGAINST HIM — AND HIS FELLOW TEJANOS!

IF WE CAN'T TRUST A MAN LIKE SEGUIN, WE SURE CAN'T TRUST THE REST OF THESE PELADOS..

AFTER SEGUIN IT IS VIRTUALLY IMPOSSIBLE FOR A TEJANO TO GAIN HIGH PUBLIC OFFICE.

FOR US "MESKINS", DOG CATCHER IS ABOUT IT THESE DAYS...

THE WHITE RACE, MY FRIENDS, WAS PLACED ON THIS EARTH TO BLA BLA BLA

JUAN'S DEFECTION IS A SOURCE OF DISAPPOINTMENT — AND EMBARASSMENT — TO FORMER FRIENDS OF HIS LIKE SAM HOUSTON.

WITHOUT JUAN THINGS LOOK PRETTY BLEAK ON OUR WESTERN FRONTIER..

I FEAR, RUSK, THAT TEXAS HAS LOST THE SERVICES OF A TRUE PATRIOT..

THE FAILURE OF THE SOMERVELL EXPEDITION IN THE WINTER OF 1842, MEANT TO PUNISH THE MEXICANS FOR THEIR RECENT INVASIONS, ONLY ADDS FUEL TO THE FLAMES OF RACISM.

WE'RE IN FOR IT NOW, BOYS.

AN ESCAPE ATTEMPT LED BY EWEN CAMERON RESULTS IN THE "BLACK BEAN EPISODE" AND THE DEATH BY FIRING SQUAD OF 17 TEXIANS.

EVEN THOUGH CAMERON DRAWS A WHITE BEAN HE IS EXECUTED AT THE INSTIGATION OF GEN. ANTONIO CANALES, A FORMER COMRADE IN THE FEDERALIST WARS WHO FEARS HIS INFLUENCE ON THE WESTERN FRONTIER.

NO BLINDFOLD... FOR THE LIBERTY OF TEXAS, I CAN LOOK DEATH IN THE FACE.

(99)

IF I EVER GIT OUTTA HERE, MESKINS IS GONNA' PAY !!

McCUTCHAN'S GOT THE *VOMITO,* POOR DEVIL..

GAKKKK..

WHEN PRESIDENT HOUSTON CRITICIZES THE MEN WHO SPLIT OFF FROM SOMERVELL'S COMMAND AND WERE CAPTURED AT MIER, HE INCURS THE WRATH OF MANY WAR-MINDED TEXIANS.

SAM SAYS THEY WENT ACROSS THE RIVER FOR SPOILS AND LOOT AND THE TEXAS FLAG SHOULDN'T SHELTER BANDITTI...

BANDITTI, HELL! THEY'RE *TEXIANS*—AND THEY'RE ROTTING IN A MEXICAN DUNGEON !!

THE FEW MEN WHO MANAGE TO ESCAPE FROM PRISON, LIKE SAMUEL WALKER AND T.J. GREEN, RETURN HOME FILLED WITH BITTERNESS, CONVINCED THAT HE ABANDONED THEM IN THEIR HOUR OF NEED.

NO, HOUSTON.. I WILL NOT SHAKE THE HAND THAT'S RESPONSIBLE FOR THE DECIMATION OF MY COMRADES !!

SORRY YOU FEEL THAT WAY, MR. WALKER..

SOME OF HOUSTON'S ENEMIES TRY TO LINK HIM TO JUAN'S "TREASON".

SAM ALWAYS BACKED THAT LOUSY TRAITOR SEGUIN.

IF WE COULD JUST PROVE THEY WERE IN IT TOGETHER, WE COULD PULL THAT OL' DRUNK CUR OFF HIS THRONE!

HOSTILITY AGAINST THE TEJANOS REMAINING IN TEXAS AT LAST GAINS RESPECTABILITY AND COMES OPENLY TO THE SURFACE.

WONDER WHICH SIDE THAT THERE GREASER'S ON?

WHO CARES? HE'S A GREASER, AIN'T HE?!

UH-OH. HERE COMES TROUBLE AGAIN..

EVEN *ANGLOS* WHO MUST DEAL WITH BOTH MEXICO AND THE REPUBLIC COME UNDER SUSPICION. HENRY KINNEY, OPERATOR OF A TRADING POST ON CORPUS CHRISTI BAY, HAS TO DEFEND HIMSELF ON CHARGES OF TREASON.

DON'T DENY IT — YOU BEEN SEEN DRINKING COFFEE WITH MEXICAN OFFICERS!

SENATOR, IT'S EASY FOR YOU TO SIT UP HERE IN JUDGEMENT, BUT DOWN ON THE FRONTIER, WE HAVE TO COMPROMISE SIMPLY TO SURVIVE!

THE PROVISION IN THE TEXAS CONSTITUTION THAT LANDS MAY BE STRIPPED FROM THEIR OWNERS FOR "TREASONOUS ACTIVITIES" BEGINS TO TAKE ON OMINOUS IMPLICATIONS FOR TEJANO GRANTEES.

WE LEFT FOR MEXICO. IF *THAT* AIN'T TREASON, I DON'T KNOW WHAT IS!

THE MORE VALUABLE THE PROPERTY, THE MORE A TEJANO'S PATRIOTISM COMES UNDER SCRUTINY.

THIS XIMINEZ HAS GOT FOUR LEAGUES OF MIGHTY FINE LAND DOWN ON TH' LAVACA.

I'LL BET HE AIDED AND ABETTED TH' ENEMY, LIKE TH' REST OF 'UM DID!!

DEED RECORD A

FORTUNATELY, CONGRESS AND THE JUDICIARY NEGLECT TO SET UP ORGANIZED PROCEDURES FOR ACTIVATING THIS CONSTITUTIONAL BASIS FOR DEPRIVING TEJANOS OF THEIR LAND.

THIS IS A HOT POTATO! TOO MANY OF OUR PEOPLE TOOK THE "SABINE CHUTE" TO AVOID FIGHTING.

IF WE CRACK DOWN ON THE MEXICANS, WE'LL HAVE TO DISPOSSESS THEM TOO!

AGAINST THE SMALL TEJANO LANDOWNERS OR "SQUATTERS"— THE ONES THAT NEVER FORMALLY DOCUMENTED THEIR TITLES— THREATS AND OUTRIGHT FORCE SOMETIMES ACCOMPLISH THE SAME END.

LET 'UM GO.. THEY'RE PROBABLY HALF-WAY DOWN TO MEXICO BY NOW!!

HAHA

MANY PROMINENT RANCHERO FAMILIES FIND IT TOO DANGEROUS TO REMAIN ON THEIR GRANTS, ESPECIALLY THOSE IN THE NUECES STRIP. THEY GO TO THE RIO GRANDE TOWNS FOR REFUGE.

THOSE WHO REFUSE TO BE BULLIED OFF THEIR LAND, ESPECIALLY THOSE WITH KNOWN "TORY" SYMPATHIES, ARE BRAVE MEN INDEED.

THE De la GARZAS FROM GENERATIONS BACK WATERED THIS GROUND WITH THEIR SWEAT AND BLOOD, AND I AIN'T LEAVING!

OCCASIONALLY THEY MUST DEFEND THEIR SPANISH AND MEXICAN TITLES AGAINST ANGLOS WHO HAVE "LOCATED" ON DESIRABLE PARTS OF THEIR GRANTS. IT IS AN EXPENSIVE PROCESS...

DIOS..

WELL 'NACIO, YOUR TITLE IS GOOD NOW, BUT YOU OWE ME A THIRD OF YOUR LAND FOR LEGAL FEES..

DESPITE THEIR DETERMINATION TO STAY, THE TEJANO RANCHEROS FIND THAT THEIR HERDS GRADUALLY DIMINISH THROUGH THE OPERATIONS OF ROVING FRONTIER "COW BOYS".

I'M SORRY BOYS, BUT I'VE GOT TO LET YOU GO. NOT ENOUGH STOCK LEFT TO FOOL WITH..

RANCHING BEGINS TO PASS INTO THE HANDS OF ENTERPRISING ANGLOS. SINCE THE RANGE REMAINS OPEN, IT IS NOT EVEN NECESSARY TO BE A LANDOWNER TO RUN LARGE HERDS OF "RECENTLY BRANDED" STOCK.

SON, WITH ALL THOSE LOOSE COWS SOUTH OF THE NUECES, ANYONE WITH A ROPE, A BRANDING IRON, AND A LITTLE GUTS CAN BECOME A CATTLEMAN!

WELL, WHAT WE WAITING FOR?!

WHERE SELDOM IS HEARD, A DISCOURAGING WORD ♫

⟨103⟩

IRONICALLY, THE COMMON VAQUEROS, WHO ONCE WORKED IN AN ALMOST FEUDAL-LIKE SYSTEM FOR LARGE TEJANO "PATRONS", NOW FIND EMPLOYMENT WITH THE NEW, UP-AND-COMING ANGLOS.

THEIR JOB IS OFTEN THE SAME — ROUNDING UP MESTEÑAS — EXCEPT THE BRANDS APPLIED ARE NOW OF BOLD, SIMPLE ANGLO DESIGN RATHER THAN THE ELABORATE "QUIEN SABE?" MARKS OF OLD.

YEAH, I'M RIDING FOR SEÑOR HOWARD NOW. HE'S A JEFE MUY FUERTE!

PUT IN A GOOD WORD FOR ME, EH DIEGO?

ME TOO

BUT WHEN THE LAND CHANGES HANDS, IT IS USUALLY FROM OLD FAMILIES TO NEW. TEJANO LANDHOLDINGS BEGIN TO RETREAT SOUTHWARD, TOWARD THE NUECES STRIP.

OLD SEÑOR PEREZ DOWN AT CAMARGO DECIDED HE'D BETTER GIT SOMETHING FOR THIS SPREAD WHILE THE GITTIN' WAS GOOD!

HAW HAW

THE FACT IS, WE GOT 'UM OVER A BARREL.

IN 1844 DUNCAN OGDEN AND GEORGE HOWARD FORECLOSE ON THE MORTGAGE COVERING THE $3,000 JUAN HAD BORROWED FOR HIS SMUGGLING VENTURE BACK IN 1841. ALL THE PLEDGED LAND, TOWN HOUSES, AND LOTS ARE PUT UP FOR PUBLIC SALE.

..GOING.. ..GOING.. GONE!!

HOWARD, THE SHERIFF OF BEXAR COUNTY, AND HIS BUSINESS PARTNER OGDEN ARE THE HIGH BIDDERS ON SEVERAL CHOICE PIECES OF SEGUIN'S REAL ESTATE.

4,600 ACRES FOR 10¢ AN ACRE..THAT'S NOT A BAD IN-VESTMENT, PARTNER.

AND HIS HOUSE WENT CHEAP, TOO.

WHEN THE THREE PARCELS SECURING THE LOAN ARE SOLD, OGDEN AND HOWARD LOOK FOR MORE OF SEGUIN'S PROPERTY TO SATISFY THEIR SEEMINGLY-BOTTOMLESS JUDGEMENT.

LET'S SEE.. THAT'S EVERY-THING LISTED IN THE MORT-GAGE AND HE STILL OWES US $1,926!

WHAT ABOUT THIS "LAS MULAS" LEAGUE HE GOT FROM ALL THE TRAVIESO HEIRS?

THUS, JUAN'S WEALTH IS WHITTLED AWAY DURING HIS ABSENCE.*

I'LL BID ON THIS TOWN LOT. IT FRONTS ON THE PLAZA.

FINE, SAM. GEORGE, YOU TAKE THE TRAVIESO LEAGUE. IT'S GOT AN EXCELLENT CROSS-ING ON THE CIBOLO...

MEANWHILE, HE AND HIS DISPOSSESSED FOLLOWERS, STILL CONNECTED TO THE MEXICAN ARMY AS "IRREGULARS", VENT THEIR FRUSTRATIONS IN THE RIO GRANDE SETTLEMENTS.

OH LORD, HERE COMES THOSE WILD NORTEÑOS AGAIN!

BECAUSE OF THEIR PREVIOUS SERVICE TO TEXAS, IN MEXICO THEY ARE MEN WITHOUT A COUNTRY. THEY GAIN A REPUTATION AS ROUGH AND ROWDY, AND JUAN SEGUIN BECOMES KNOWN AS THE RAGING TEJANO WITH THE "CUCHILLO GRANDE"— BIG KNIFE!

BOWIE WAS THE LAST GRINGO I KNEW THAT WAS WORTH A DAMN..

I'LL DRINK TO THAT, JEFE ..HIC..

* Seguin was not the only Tejano to be so victimized, nor were the gentlemen named the only perpetrators. Indeed, hardly a single Anglo family of Bexar emerges without some questionable land "transaction" blemishing its claim to prominence, so common was the practice.

SOME TEXIANS SUSPECT THAT SEGUIN AND OTHERS LIKE HIM ARE INVOLVED IN RAIDS INTO TEXAS, USING THAT AS A PRE-TEXT FOR FURTHER ANIMOSITY TOWARD TEJANO RANCHEROS.

THEY COME AND GO AT WILL, AND THEIR KINFOLKS' RANCHOS ARE A BREEDING GROUND FOR RUSTLING.

NOTHIN' TH' TORCH CAN'T CURE!

RANCHO LA MORA

SUGGESTIONS ARE MADE THAT THE TOWN OF SEGUIN CHANGE ITS NAME. A PAGE IS MYSTERIOUSLY RIPPED FROM THE TOWN'S MINUTE BOOK...

NOW THEY'LL NEVER PROVE IT WAS NAMED FOR A TRAITOR!

ON JULY 4, 1845, THE TEXAS CONVENTION MEETS TO CONSIDER ANNEXATION TO THE UNITED STATES AND TO FORM A CONSTITUTION. JOSE ANTONIO NAVARRO, RECENTLY OUT OF PRISON, IS THE SOLE TEJANO DELEGATE.

SO, I'M THE ONLY ONE LEFT...

HE SPEAKS AGAINST THE USE OF THE WORD "WHITE" AS A VOTER QUALIFICATION, FEARING IT MIGHT BE USED AGAINST MANY DARK-SKINNED TEJANOS.

THE TERM IS ODIOUS, AND MAY BE USED BY ARBITRARY JUDGES TO KEEP PEOPLE FROM VOTING THAT THEY DON'T CONSIDER "WHITE".

THE SUBJECT OF LAND FORFEITURE AGAINST THOSE WHO "AIDED AND ABETTED" THE ENEMY IS HOTLY DEBATED.

IT WOULDN'T HAVE BEEN PUT INTO THE 1836 CONSTITUTION UNLESS IT WAS INTENDED TO BE USED. LET'S USE IT!

JUAN SEGUIN IS MENTIONED AS ONE TYPICAL OF THOSE WHOSE RIGHTS TO HOLD LAND IN TEXAS SHOULD BE TAKEN AWAY.

THIS CELEBRATED GENTLEMAN HAS NOT ONLY ABANDONED US BUT ACTUALLY TURNED OUT WITH A FORCE BENT ON DESTROYING THE GOOD PEOPLE OF TEXAS!

DELEGATES FROM THE WAR-TORN COUNTIES, LIKE H.L. KINNEY AND A.C. HORTON, SPEAK CANDIDLY IN DEFENSE OF THE TEJANOS' LAND AND CITIZENSHIP RIGHTS.

AGAINST WHOM HAVE THESE "MEXICANS" TAKEN UP ARMS? NOT AGAINST TEXAS, SIR, BUT AGAINST A SET OF ROBBERS! WHO, IN THEIR SITUATION, CAN BLAME THEM?

THEY ARE JOINED BY THE PRESIDENT OF THE CONVENTION, THOMAS J. RUSK, IN ADVOCATING LENIENCY TO THE FRONTIER TEJANOS, VICTIMIZED IN THE STRUGGLE BY BOTH SIDES.

WILL THIS CONVENTION, NOW IN A TIME OF PEACE AND QUIET, DESCEND FROM ITS NOBLE TASK TO WREAK VENGEANCE UPON THESE POOR PEOPLE? GENTLEMEN, LET US PUT AN END TO THIS EVIL MATTER AND BIND THE WOUNDS OF TEXAS!

JUAN, IN TOUCH WITH OPINION SOUTH OF THE BORDER, KNOWS THAT THE NATIONAL HONOR OF MEXICO WILL NOT PERMIT THE LOSS OF TEXAS TO ITS CONTINENTAL RIVAL.

IF THEY'D JUST REMAIN AN INDEPENDENT REPUBLIC, MEXICO WOULD EVENTUALLY GIVE THEM RECOGNITION.

FEARING THAT THE CONVENTION WILL RESULT IN ANNEXATION, HE WRITES THE PRESIDENT OF THE REPUBLIC, INFORMING HIM THAT SUCH A COURSE WOULD INEVITABLY MEAN WAR.

THEY SAY YOU'RE A TRAITOR TO TEXAS, SEGUIN, BUT I'LL NEVER BELIEVE IT...

JUAN'S FEARS SOON BECOME REALIZED. THE CONVENTION DECIDES FOR ANNEXATION, AND ON FEB. 19, 1846, ANSON JONES PROCLAIMS THAT THE REPUBLIC OF TEXAS IS NO MORE.

UNITED STATES TROOPS UNDER GEN. ZACHARY TAYLOR, "OLD ROUGH AND READY" MOVE SOUTH FROM THEIR BASE AT CORPUS CHRISTI, ANTICIPATING MEXICO'S RESPONSE.

STUCK A FEATHER IN HIS CAP AND CALLED IT MONTE-ZUMA ♪♫

THE RESPONSE COMES QUICKLY AT PALO ALTO AND RESACA de la PALMA, JUST ABOVE MATA-MOROS, BUT TAYLOR'S TROOPS PUT ARISTA AND THE MEXICAN ARMY TO PRECIPITOUS FLIGHT.

PRESIDENT POLK SENDS A WAR MESSAGE TO CONGRESS, BUT MEXICO IS ALREADY IN A STATE OF WAR — NOT JUST BECAUSE OF TAYLOR'S ADVANCE, BUT BECAUSE THE UNITED STATES HAS DARED TO ANNEX TEXAS, TERRITORY WHICH NO MEXICAN POLITICIAN CAN ADMIT AS LOST.

AMERICAN BLOOD HAS BEEN SHED ON AMERICAN SOIL...

CRITICS OF "POLK'S WAR" ARE OUTSPOKEN FROM THE BEGINNING.

AMERICAN BLOOD HAS BEEN SHED IN A MEXICAN CORNFIELD!

THE DETERIORATING MILITARY SITUATION FORCES THE MEXICAN AUTHORITIES TO SET ASIDE COURT MARTIAL PROCEEDINGS AGAINST JUAN AND HIS HELL-RAISING TEJANOS. THEIR SERVICES ARE QUICKLY ENLISTED AS SPIES, SCOUTS, AND GUERRILLA FIGHTERS.

THESE FUNCTIONS THEY PERFORM SO WELL THAT THEY IRRITATE GEN. TAYLOR AND THEIR FORMER COMRADES, THE TEXAS RANGERS, WHO ARE SERVING THE U.S. ARMY IN A SIMILAR CAPACITY.

THESE GUERRILLA BANDS ARE CUTTING OUR COMMUNICATION LINES!!

RANGERS UNDER BEN McCULLOCH MAKE AN EFFORT TO CATCH SEGUIN, SAID TO BE OPERATING ON THE RUGGED CHINA ROUTE TO MONTERREY.

WE JUST MISSED HIM... HE LEFT LAST NIGHT FOR MANTECA.

OL' JUAN ALWAYS WUZ A CRAFTY ONE!

THE TEXANS SETTLE MANY OLD SCORES IN MEXICO, EARNING THE REPUTATION AS "LOS DIABLOS TEJANOS"—THE TEXAS DEVILS!

¿DONDE ESTÁ CANALES?! TALK, YOU DAMN' CARAJO!

DON'T WASTE YER BREATH ON 'EM, J.D.

SEGUIN AND HIS TEJANOS FIGHT AT THE BATTLE OF BUENA VISTA, THE LAST DECISIVE ENCOUNTER IN NORTHERN MEXICO.

THE CARNAGE ON BOTH SIDES IS AWESOME AND JUAN IS WOUNDED IN THE FIGHTING. WHEN SANTA ANNA'S SHATTERED ARMY ABANDONS THE FIELD UNDER COVER OF DARKNESS, "OLD ROUGH AND READY" IS MUCH RELIEVED.

A CARNIVAL OF HORRORS.

AGUA..

AGUA

YEARS of TURMOIL

AFTER THE TREATY OF GUADALUPE HIDALGO ENDS THE WAR, JUAN LEAVES THE MILITARY SERVICE AND DETERMINES TO BRING HIS FAMILY BACK TO TEXAS.

MY MOTHER IS DYING.. HOW I MISS THE OLD HOME PLACE ON THE RIVER...

HE APPEARS BEFORE THE AMERICAN MILITARY COMMANDER AT PRESIDIO *del* RIO GRANDE, J.A. VEATCH, ANNOUNCING HIS INTENTION TO "RISK THE CONSEQUENCES" OF HIS RETURN HOME.

HE SURE LOOKS LIKE HE'S BEEN THRU TH' MILL..

FROM SALTILLO HE WRITES SAM HOUSTON, NOW A UNITED STATES SENATOR, ASKING HIS HELP IN RESUMING LIFE AS AN ORDINARY TEXAS CITIZEN.

HE DOESN'T SOUND VERY CONTRITE, SAM.

NO NEED.. WE HAVE A LITTLE ..UH.. PRIVATE UNDERSTANDING..

..BURNED OUT RAN-CHES.. ROADS FULL OF MIGRANTS.... WHAT'S HAPPENING ??

HE FINDS HIS FATHER'S RANCH IN RUINS AND IS SHAKEN BY THE PITIFUL CONDITION OF HIS ONCE-PROSPEROUS NEIGHBORS.

MANY HAVE LEFT WILLINGLY. OTHERS HAVE NOT BEEN SO FORTUNATE...

DON ERASMO TELLS OF HOW EVEN HE AND HIS FAMILY WERE FORCIBLY EJECTED FROM THEIR HOME DURING THE WAR YEARS.

..TOSSED OUT, LIKE TRASH ON THE STREET...

GILBEAU— OF ALL PEOPLE! WHO WOULD HAVE THOUGHT ?!

DESPITE THE MOOD OF DOOM THAT HAS CAST ITS SHADOW OVER THE RIVER VALLEY, DON ERASMO HAS HUNG ON... BUT LITTLE REMAINS OF THE ONCE-GRAND "CASA BLANCA".

MY SON, TIMES HAVE BEEN HARD FOR US HERE..

LIKE SEGUIN, OTHER HOMESICK TEJANOS MAKE THEIR WAY BACK TO TEXAS NOW THAT THE WAR IS OVER. MANY FIND THEIR CATTLE GONE, THEIR LAND, AND EVEN THEIR HOMES, TAKEN BY THE ANGLOS.

BUT I USED TO LIVE IN THIS HOUSE. I WAS BORN—

TEXAS GIVE US THIS HERE PLACE FOR SERVICES RENDERED — FIGHTIN' TRAITORS LIKE YOU!

YOU BETTER GIT BACK TO MEXICO, IF YOU KNOW WHAT'S GOOD FOR YOU..

SOME, LIKE THE DE LEONS, TRY TO REGAIN TITLE TO THEIR LAND GRANTS BUT INSTEAD FIND THEMSELVES EMBROILED IN YEARS OF COSTLY LITIGATION.

..BLAH BLAH, ENEMY ALIEN BLA BLAA..

ARTICLE X OF THE TREATY OF GUADALUPE HIDALGO, VALIDATING ALL MEXICAN GRANTS IN THE SOUTHWEST, IS STRICKEN OUT BY THE U.S. SENATE FOR FEAR THESE OLD TITLES MIGHT IMPERIL MORE RECENT ACQUISITIONS BY AMERICAN SETTLERS IN TEXAS.

TO REVIVE DEAD TITLES AND ALLOW PRESENT OWNERS TO BE KICKED OUT WOULD BE CRUEL, UNJUST— AND PROBABLY CAUSE ANOTHER REVOLUTION IN TEXAS!

SO EVEN THOUGH THE TREATY GUARANTEES THE RIGHTS AND PROPERTY OF FORMER MEXICAN CITIZENS, THE UNIQUE STATUS OF TEXAS MAKES THE REALITY QUITE DIFFERENT.

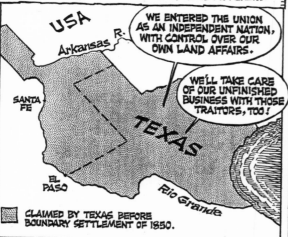

USA

Arkansas R.

WE ENTERED THE UNION AS AN INDEPENDENT NATION, WITH CONTROL OVER OUR OWN LAND AFFAIRS.

WE'LL TAKE CARE OF OUR UNFINISHED BUSINESS WITH THOSE TRAITORS, TOO!

SANTA FE

TEXAS

EL PASO

Rio Grande

CLAIMED BY TEXAS BEFORE BOUNDARY SETTLEMENT OF 1850.

FLUSH WITH THE CONQUEST OF MEXICO, THE SWELLING ANGLO POPULATION IS IN NO MOOD TO VIEW SYMPATHETICALLY THE OLD CLAIMS OF "MEXICANS" WHO LEFT DURING THE YEARS OF WARFARE.

THEY'RE LUCKY WE EVEN LET THEM COME BACK!

NEXT THING YOU KNOW, THEY'LL BE CLAIMIN' THEY WUZ HERE ALL ALONG!!

⟨113⟩

THE RETURNING TEJANOS JUSTIFIABLY FEEL BITTERNESS TOWARD THE TEXANS FOR THEIR IMPOVERISH-
MENT. THERE IS AN UNDERLYING FEELING THAT THE LAND WAS STOLEN — LEGAL OR OTHERWISE!

THEY DROVE US OUT, AND THEN CALL-ED US TRAITORS FOR LEAVING!

JUAN'S DEFECTION HAS LEFT HIM POWERLESS IN POLITICAL AF-FAIRS. HE CAN DO NOTHING TO RIGHT THE WRONGS OF HIS PEOPLE.

I'M SORRY CARVAJAL, BUT I CAN'T HELP YOU. I CAN'T EVEN SOLVE MY OWN MUDDLED LAND AFFAIRS.

AHHH, JUAN.. IF ONLY DON ESTEVAN WERE STILL ALIVE, EH? INSTEAD OF THIS WORLD, TURN-ED UPSIDE DOWN!

IN TIME COMES THE REALIZATION THAT THIS IS PERHAPS WHY HE HAS BEEN ALLOWED TO RETURN HOME: WITHOUT INFLUENCE AND HIS POLITICAL ASPIRATIONS BLASTED, HE NO LONGER POSES A THREAT TO THE DOMINANT ANGLO POWER STRUCTURE.

JUANITO, IT'S LATE.. COME TO BED..??

JUAN SOON FINDS HIMSELF THE DEFENDANT IN MANY LAW-SUITS DIRECTED AT WHAT LITTLE REMAINS OF HIS WEALTH.

WE FIND FOR THE PLAINTIFF — $300 PLUS INTEREST SINCE 1840!

TO PUT HIMSELF BEYOND THE REACH OF HOSTILE "CREDITORS" JUAN IS OBLIGED TO DEED HOLDINGS TO HIS CHILDREN AND FILE A DECLARATION OF HIS WIFE'S SEPARATE PROPERTY. ALL FAMILY CATTLE BEAR BRANDS REGISTERED IN *THEIR* NAMES, NOT HIS.

!6*!! BLOOD-SUCKING LEECHES! SOME-TIMES I WONDER WHY I BOTHER TO STAY HERE.

THE POSTWAR YEARS DO NOT BRING AN END TO HOSTILITIES BETWEEN ANGLOS AND MEXICANS — ESPECIALLY IN THE NUECES STRIP. THE WIDE-OPEN BORDER DRAWS LAWLESS MEN OF ALL SHADES AND HUES LIKE A MAGNET.

TH' LAND OF GOLDEN OPPORTUN-ITY, EH ZEKE?

YES, BUT ONLY FOR THEM THAT *CARPE DIEM*, MY TRUSTED FRIEND.

MANY OF THESE RUFFIANS CLAIM TO BE "MUSTANGERS," LIVING OFF THE HERDS OF WILD HORSES AND ABANDONED CATTLE, BUT THEY ARE MORE ACCURATELY DESCRIBED AS CUT-THROATS AND PRAIRIE PIRATES.

WE'RE RIFF-RAFF AND PROUD OF IT!!

RAIDS ACROSS BOTH SIDES OF THE BORDER ARE FREQUENT AND THE PEACEFUL SETTLERS, ANGLO AND TEJANO, ARE THE ULTIMATE VICTIMS.

LEAVE THESE AROUND AND THEY'LL BLAME IT ON THE INJUNS..

EACH TIME A MEXICAN-BASED BAND ROBS AND PLUNDERS, ANGLO VIGILANTES RETALIATE AGAINST INNOCENT TEJANOS. WHEN "COW BOYS" STRIKE ACROSS THE RIO GRANDE, THE MEXICANS AVENGE THEMSELVES AGAINST ANGLO FAMILIES LIVING IN THE WARZONE.

ZING!

WE CAN'T KEEP LIVIN' LIKE THIS, MINERVA...

WITH THIS INTERNATIONAL BORDER SCUM HOLDING SWAY, IT IS NOT SAFE TO LIVE ON THE FRONTIER. THOSE WHO DO, FIND IT EXPEDIENT TO HIRE THEMSELVES PRIVATE ARMIES.

HAD ANY EXPERIENCE, BOY?

YOU'LL DO!

JUST KILLIN' GREASERS AND REDSKINS, SIR...

THE CHAOS CAUSES MANY TEXANS TO THINK THE UNITED STATES TOO GENEROUS WITH SETTLING FOR THE RIO GRANDE AS A BOUNDARY. THEY CONSIDER THE SIERRA MADRE A MORE LOGICAL — AND IMPOSING — NATURAL BARRIER.

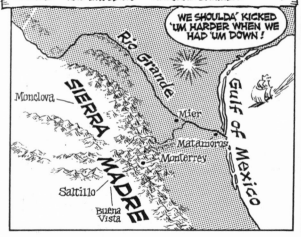

WE SHOULDA' KICKED 'UM HARDER WHEN WE HAD 'UM DOWN!

Rio Grande

Monclova

SIERRA MADRE

Mier

Matamoros

Monterrey

Gulf of Mexico

Saltillo

Buena Vista

WHEN JOSE M. J. CARVAJAL, THE FORMER TEJANO FEDERALIST LEADER, DECIDES TO SEPARATE TAMAULIPAS FROM MEXICO AND CALL IT THE "SIERRA MADRE REPUBLIC" HIS SCHEME IS AVIDLY PROMOTED BY MANY ENTREPRENEURS NORTH OF THE RIVER.

IF CARVAJAL WINS, WE'LL HAVE OUR WAY ON THE RIO GRAND!

HE RECEIVES SUPPORT FROM RICHARD KING AND MIFFLIN KENEDY, TWO OF THE "NEW BREED" OF TEXANS, WHO WILL SOON BECOME THE MOST POWERFUL RANCHERS SOUTH OF THE NUECES.

YOU SCRATCH OUR BACK, JOSE', AND WE'LL SCRATCH YOURS!

WITH THEIR BACKING, CARVAJAL'S CAUSE IS JOINED BY MANY HOT-BLOODED YOUNG ANGLOS WHOSE TASTE FOR TAME, "PEACEFUL" LIFE HAS BEEN SPOILED BY SERVICE IN THE MEXICAN WAR.

WHUT TH' HELL... I NEVER CARED MUCH FOR BEING A SHOE-CLERK NOHOW.

LET'S GIVE IT A WHIRL!

VOLUNTEERS!
RENDEZVOUS
Exciting Service in Tamaulipas!

ALTHO CARVAJAL IS AGAIN UNSUCCESSFUL IN DISMEMBERING THE NORTHERN PORTION OF MEXICO, HIS FILIBUSTERING BANDS DO MUCH TO KEEP BORDER RELATIONS INFLAMED.

A FURTHER CAUSE OF CONFLICT IS THE FLIGHT OF BLACK SLAVES ACROSS THE BORDER. MANY SLAVE OWNERS FEEL THAT THE MEXICAN ABHORRENCE OF THE INSTITUTION OF SLAVERY ENCOURAGES RUNAWAYS.

NUMEROUS RAIDS INTO MEXICO ARE MADE BY ANGLO TEXANS ON THE PRETEXT OF PUNISHING INDIAN RAIDERS, BUT THEY ARE REALLY "BOUNTY HUNTING" EXPEDITIONS TO CAPTURE FUGITIVE SLAVES.

STRANGELY ENOUGH, THE BORDER CAUSES A SIMILAR PROBLEM FOR MEXICO. PEONS, IN VIRTUAL LIFE-LONG SERVITUDE BECAUSE OF DEBTS, ARE CROSSING INTO TEXAS TO ESCAPE THEIR TASKMASTERS AND START A NEW LIFE.

JUAN SEGUIN, CAUGHT IN THE MIDDLE AS ALWAYS, IS APPOINTED BY THE GOVERNOR OF NUEVO LEON TO DISCUSS A TREATY WITH TEXAS' GOV. RUNNELS FOR THE EXTRADITION OF "FUGITIVE SLAVES, PEONS, ROBBERS, MURDERERS & INCENDIARIES." ⊛

WE NEED A TREATY LIKE THIS, AND SEGUIN COULD PROBABLY SWING IT...

YES, IT'S A PITY..

TOO BAD THE U.S. CONSTITUTION FORBIDS SUCH THINGS.

BUT SLAVES CONTINUE TO MAKE THEIR WAY TO FREEDOM, SOME WITH THE HELP OF SYMPATHETIC TEJANOS, A SITUATION WHICH CAUSES MANY TEXANS TO REGARD THEIR "LOWER CLASS OF MEXICANS" AS PUBLIC ENEMIES.

HOT DAMN! THAT'LL KEEP 'UM BUSY AWHILE!

MEXICO, HERE WE COME!

IN SOME COUNTIES TRANSIENTS ARE ARRESTED AND EJECTED, AND OTHER PLACES REQUIRE EVEN KNOWN TEJANOS TO HAVE PASSES TO USE THE PUBLIC ROADS.

BUT SEÑOR BEN, YOU KNOW ME.. ITS OL' JESSE, JESUS TREVIÑO!!

IN GOLIAD, PARTLY BECAUSE OF THE TEJANOS' SUSPECTED ANTI-SLAVERY SENTIMENTS, A RESOLUTION IS PASSED THAT "THE CONTINUATION OF THE GREASERS OR PEON MEXICANS AS CITIZENS AMONG US IS AN INTOLERABLE NUISANCE."

TEXAS FOR TEXANS!

⟨118⟩ ⊛ Note: This governor of Nuevo Leon, Don Santiago Vidaurri, later established warm (and lucrative) trade relations with the Confederacy but the event depicted was in January of 1859.

IT TAKES A FORMAL COMPLAINT FROM THE MEXICAN LEGATION FOR THE SITUATION TO GET THE ATTENTION OF TEXAN OFFICIALS.

BY THAT TIME, IT'LL BE ANCIENT HISTORY!

GOV. PEASE, RESPONDING TO PRESSURE FROM WASHINGTON, GOES TO BEXAR TO INVESTIGATE THE CHARGES. HE FINDS LOCAL AUTHORITIES INDIFFERENT TO THE ABUSES OF THE FREIGHTERS.

WHAT'S ALL THE FUSS? THEY'RE JUST HELPING KEEP TH' MESKINS IN LINE...

FINALLY, WHEN THE TEAMSTERS BEGIN TO UNLEASH THEIR VIOLENCE AGAINST *OTHER ANGLOS*, PEASE IS FORCED TO CLEAN UP THE MESSY SITUATION.

I WANT YOU MEN TO GO DOWN THERE AND BREAK UP THESE GANGS BEFORE WE HAVE A WAR ON OUR HANDS!

THE SAME YEAR THAT WITNESSES THE SPECTACLE OF THE CART WAR MARKS THE DEATH OF DON ERASMO, AT AGE 75. HE IS LAID QUIETLY TO REST BESIDE THE RIVER, NEAR THE HOME HE HAD CARVED FROM THE WILDERNESS.

DESPITE THE RACIAL TENSIONS OF THE PERIOD, ERASMO IS EULOGIZED AS "THAT TRUE HEARTED OLD MAN", WHO "IN THE INFANCY OF TEXAS — IN THE DAYS OF HER WEAKNESS AND HIS STRENGTH — WAS THE FAITHFUL FRIEND OF THE AMERICANS."

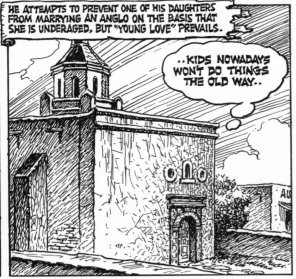

RATHER THAN CHANGE THE NAME OF THE TOWN, LET'S JUST SAY IT WAS NAMED AFTER THE OLD DON.

Seguin·2mi.

New Braunfels

JUAN'S ATTEMPT TO REINVOLVE HIMSELF IN COUNTY POLITICS BRINGS A RASH OF *HATE MAIL*, SOME OF WHICH IS CIRCULATED IN AREA NEWSPAPERS.

"MURDERER OF THE SALADO"— WHAT A PACK OF LIES!

VICTORIA ADVOCATE

HE ATTEMPTS TO PREVENT ONE OF HIS DAUGHTERS FROM MARRYING AN ANGLO ON THE BASIS THAT SHE IS UNDERAGED, BUT "YOUNG LOVE" PREVAILS.

..KIDS NOWADAYS WON'T DO THINGS THE OLD WAY..

JUAN BUILDS A STONE HOUSE ON HIS FATHER'S LAND, BUT FOR HIM THESE ARE RESTLESS YEARS. HE CONSTANTLY TRAVELS BACK AND FORTH TO MEXICO, ROOTLESS IN THE TURMOIL AROUND HIM.

IN 1858 HE PUBLISHES HIS MEMOIRS IN WHICH HE CITES HIS LONG SERVICE TO TEXAS AND OFFERS A VINDICATION FOR HIS CONDUCT IN THE FATEFUL YEAR OF '42.

> IF NOT NOW, MAYBE SOMEDAY PEOPLE WILL BE ABLE TO UNDERSTAND MY SIDE OF IT..

BUT THE TUMULTUOUS TIMES CALL FOR ANOTHER TYPE OF POPULAR HERO — EVEN AMONG THE TEJANOS THEMSELVES. THIS NEED FINDS EXPRESSION IN THE YOUNG, FLAMBOYANT JUAN "CHENO" CORTINA.

> LOOK AT ALL THIS CACA! WHEN I WAS A KID, THIS WAS JUST ANOTHER OF MAMA'S PASTURES..

BROWNSVILLE EXCHANGE

THE SCION OF AN OLD RANCHING FAMILY ON THE RIO GRANDE, CORTINA HAS WATCHED THE ANGLOS SLOWLY TAKE OVER SINCE THE WAR AND PUSH HIS PEOPLE ASIDE.

> HEY CHENO, AIN'T THAT OL' PANCHO VELA OUT THERE, GETTING PISTOL-WHIPPED?

> ?

> ISN'T HE A VAQUERO ON YOUR MOMMA'S RANCH?

CORTINA MAKES A DRAMATIC ENTRANCE INTO THE PUBLIC EYE, SHOOTING THE MARSHAL OF BROWNSVILLE AND HELPING A POOR MEXICAN DRUNK MAKE AN UNEXPECTED GETAWAY.

GRACIAS, MI PATRON, GRACIAS!

SHORTLY AFTERWARDS, HE RETURNS WITH A RAG-TAG ARMY AND TAKES POSSESSION OF THE TOWN.

DEATH TO LOS GRINGOS!

VIVA CORTINA!! VIVA MEJICO!!

OHMIGOD... Hide th' wimmen and children!

HE DEFEATS BOTH A MOTLEY GROUP OF LOCAL "RANGERS" AND SOME MEXICAN TROOPS FROM MATAMOROS, SENT OVER TO PUT A STOP TO HIS "RABBLE-ROUSING".

ALTHO VIEWED BY THE ANGLOS AS JUST ANOTHER PETTY BORDER BANDIT, TO HIS PEOPLE — FROM THE LEGALLY VICTIMIZED GRANDEES TO THE DOWN-TRODDEN PEONS — JUAN CORTINA IS REGARDED AS THE CHAMPION OF THEIR RACE.

THEY SAY I'M JUST A COWTHIEF, BUT I ONLY TAKE WHAT IS MINE — GRANDMA'S CATTLE!

HA HA

HE IS A SKILLFUL PROPAGANDIST AND THE EFFECTIVENESS OF HIS "PROCLAMATIONS" IS DOUBTLESS ROOTED IN THE MANY INJUSTICES WHICH HE ADDRESSES.

LISTEN AT THIS: "If the Gringos and their lawyers wish to rob us and possess our land, let them know that they must first fatten it with their own gore."

BOY, THAT CHENO IS ONE BAD HOMBRE!

PRONUNCIAMIENTO!
JUAN NEPOMUCENO CORTINA
A LOS VECINOS del ESTADO
de TEJAS, VILLA BROWNS..

A FEW OF THE VALLEY'S SLICK REAL ESTATE MEN AND CROOKED LAWYERS HAVE SECOND THOUGHTS ABOUT THEIR PROFESSIONS.

SUN BELT PROPERTIES

SAY, J.B., MAYBE WE'D BETTER DEPART FOR SAFER CLIMES.. THE NATIVES DON'T SEEM TO APPRECIATE US BRINGING CIVILIZATION TO THEM..

I HEAR JACK HAYS NEEDS HELP DEVELOPING OAKLAND!

AFTER A SIX-MONTHS REIGN — A SOURCE OF EMBARASSMENT TO BOTH GOVERNMENTS — CORTINA IS FORCED TO FLEE INTO THE INTERIOR OF MEXICO BY U.S. TROOPS AND RANGERS UNDER RIP FORD.

NOW, IF HE'LL JUST STAY THERE...

HIS THREATS OF AN ANGLO BLOODBATH SERVE ONLY TO DEEPEN FRUSTRATION AND ENTRENCH HOSTILITY BETWEEN THE TWO RACES. FOR DECADES TO COME, BORDER RELATIONS WILL BE DOMINATED BY THE GRIM SPECTERS RAISED IN SOUTH TEXAS BY JUAN N. CORTINA.

NO SON, WE DON'T COUNT INJUNS AND MESKINS — JUST WHITE MEN!

GOSH..

MEANWHILE, AN AGING SAM HOUSTON HAS TAKEN OFFICE AS GOVERNOR. AWARE THAT STORM CLOUDS ARE BREWING OVER THE UNION, SAM CONCEIVES A GRANDIOSE SCHEME TO UNIFY THE DIVIDED NATION.

..A PROTECTORATE OVER MEXICO, WITH ME AT THE HELM!

HOUSTON PLANS TO LAUNCH A WELL-ARMED EXPEDITIONARY FORCE AGAINST MEXICO, USING PROVEN RANGERS AS A NUCLEUS. HE ENLISTS BEN McCULLOCH AS HIS "BIG CAPTAIN" AND EVEN ATTEMPTS TO WOO LT-COL ROBERT E. LEE, SENT TO QUELL THE CORTINA DISTURBANCES.

IF WE HAD DONE IT AFTER THE MEXICAN WAR, WE WOULDN'T HAVE HAD A DECADE OF BORDER HEADACHES.

SAM BELIEVES THAT MANY MEXICAN FEDERALISTS WILL RUSH TO ENLIST. JUAN SEGUIN IS DOUBTLESS TAKEN INTO HIS OLD MENTOR'S CONFIDENCE.

THE NORTHERN STATES, TAMAULIPAS, NUEVO LEON, COAHUILA — THEY'LL ALL JUMP AT THE CHANCE.

WE CAN COUNT ON CARVAJAL FOR SURE, GOVERNOR — MAYBE EVEN CORTINA!

BUT BEFORE HOUSTON CAN GET HIS AMBITIOUS PLAN IN MOTION, THE UNION IS SPLIT ASUNDER AND PLUNGED INTO CIVIL WAR.

DANG! I COULD HAVE PULLED IT OFF!!

SAM HOUSTON! SAM HOUSTON!! COME UP!

THE CIVIL WAR BRINGS A SORT OF PROSPERITY TO THE BORDER AREA. THE CONFEDERACY NEEDS AN OUTLET FOR SOUTHERN COTTON, AND MATAMOROS BECOMES A BUSTLING CENTER OF ACTIVITY.

MILMO & MADERO

IN TOWNS ALL ALONG THE RIO GRANDE, COTTON TRAFFIC IS HEAVY AND THE WEALTH TRICKLES DOWN — EVEN TO THE TEJANOS.

CCREEAK..

I'M DREAMING OF A WHITE CHRISTMAS..

MANY RIVER TEJANOS JOIN THE CONFEDERATE FORCES AND SOME, LIKE SANTOS BENAVIDES, DISTINGUISH THEMSELVES IN AREA FIGHTING.

US ARISTOCRATS HAVE TO STICK TOGETHER!

OTHERS, LIKE JUAN CORTINA — NOW A BRIGADIER GENERAL IN THE MEXICAN ARMY — CALL THEMSELVES "YANKEES" AND CONTINUE RAIDING IN TEXAS FOR CATTLE TO SELL TO THE FEDERAL FORCES.

ANY EXCUSE TO PAY BACK THE *!@!! GRINGOS!

THE SITUATION IN MEXICO IS COMPLICATED BY THE CONFLICT BETWEEN THE *FRENCH INVADERS* AND THE *JUAREZ LIBERALS*, WHO ARE BACKED BY THE UNION.

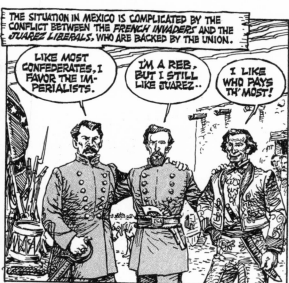

LIKE MOST CONFEDERATES, I FAVOR THE IMPERIALISTS.

I'M A REB, BUT I STILL LIKE JUAREZ...

I LIKE WHO PAYS TH' MOST!

MANY TEJANOS ARE SYMPATHETIC TO THE CAUSE OF BENITO JUAREZ. JUAN SEGUIN AND HIS COUSIN FROM LA BAHIA, IGNACIO ZARAGOZA, BOTH JOIN THE JUARISTAS TO HELP EXPEL THE FRENCH AND THEIR PUPPET EMPEROR, MAXIMILIAN.

IN THE TURNING POINT OF THE WAR, ZARAGOZA AND SEGUIN LEAD TATTERED RECRUITS TO VICTORY OVER SUPERBLY EQUIPPED FRENCH FORCES AT PUEBLA, GIVING RISE TO THE NATIONAL HOLIDAY, *CINCO de MAYO.*

✱ At the time of the May 5, 1862, battle, young Zaragoza was the Minister of War in Juarez's cabinet!

BETWEEN HIS ABSENCES IN MEXICO, JUAN TAKES AN ACTIVE PART IN THE AFFAIRS OF NEWLY-FORMED WILSON COUNTY. HIS HOUSE AT LODI IS A POLLING PLACE AND HE IS APPOINTED TO OVERSEE ELECTIONS.

DESPITE HIS CHECKERED CAREER, JUAN SEGUIN STILL COMMANDS RESPECT AMONG HIS NEIGHBORS, ANGLO OR TEJANO, FOR THEY RECOGNIZE THAT HE IS A MAN OF CONVICTIONS — AND WILLING TO STAND UP FOR THEM.

THAT'S JOHN SE-GUIN, SON — HE WUZ IN TH' ALAMO!

THEN HOW COME HE AIN'T DEAD, PA?

HIS SONS SANTIAGO, JOSE ERASMO AND JUAN JR., NOW GROWN AND MARRIED, CARRY ON THE FAMILY RANCHING TRADITION.

MANY OF THE OLD RIVER FAMILIES — LIKE THE TREVIÑOS, HERRERAS, CANTUS, YNDOS, DE LA ZERDAS, SOTOS, AND OTHERS — ARE ALSO ACTIVE IN RANCHING AND COUNTY POLITICS DURING THE CIVIL WAR AND RECONSTRUCTION YEARS.

WHEN THE SITE FOR THE COUNTY SEAT IS SELECTED, IT IS NAMED "FLORESVILLE" IN HONOR OF THIS OLD RANCHING DYNASTY.

TIMES MUST BE CHANGING, BUCK..

YEAH, 15 YEARS AGO, A MESKIN NAME WOULD OF NEVER BEEN CONSIDERED...

FUTURE SITE OF WILSON COUNTY COURTHOUSE

MAVERICK & KROEGER CONSTRUCTION CO.

IRONICALLY, JUAN — STILL HOLDING A COMMISSION IN THE MEXICAN ARMY — SERVES AS WILSON COUNTY JUDGE IN 1869.

..ONLY BECAUSE THE SCALAWAGS AND CARPETBAGGERS RUN THINGS NOW...

AND I'M ONE OF THE FEW MEN IN THE COUNTY WITHOUT A CONFEDERATE RECORD!

SHORTLY AFTER, WITH TEXAS IN THE THROES OF CARPETBAGGER RULE AND RAMPANT ANTI-MEXICAN PREJUDICE, JUAN RETURNS TO THE RIO GRANDE WHERE SOME OF HIS CHILDREN HAVE MOVED. IN 1871 HE RESIGNS HIS COLONELCY IN THE ARMY OF MEXICO.

SEGUIN? THERE'S NO "COL. SEGUIN" IN OUR RECORDS.

TRY THE WAR DEPARTMENT IN MEXICO CITY..

WE RODE AS IR-REGULAR CAVALRY MOST OF THE TIME.

BY LATE 1874 HE IS BACK IN TEXAS TO SETTLE HIS AFFAIRS. HE IS AWARDED A PENSION AS A SOLDIER OF THE REVOLUTION.

I'VE BEEN IN MEXICO ON BUSINESS A LOT, BUT THIS HAS ALWAYS BEEN MY HOME...

HE, ANTONIO MENCHACA, AND OTHER AGING TEXAS VETS PETITION THE STATE COMPTROLLER ON BEHALF OF THEIR FELLOW TEJANOS, WHOSE CLAIMS FOR MILITARY PENSIONS SEEM TO MOVE SLOWER THAN ANGLOS'.

THE WORD OF A TEJANO DOESN'T SEEM TO CARRY MUCH WEIGHT THESE DAYS, JUAN.

SO, WHAT'S NEW?

IN APRIL OF 1875 JUAN'S SON SANTIAGO, ACTING WITH A POWER OF ATTORNEY FROM OTHER FAMILY MEMBERS, SELLS THE "JUAN SEGUIN LEAGUE" IN WILSON COUNTY, CLOSING OUT A LONG CHAPTER IN TEXAS HISTORY.

.. LESS THAN 50¢ AN ACRE...

MY FATHER PAID MORE THAN YOU'LL EVER KNOW, SIR!

IT'S A LOT MORE THAN YOUR FATHER PAID FOR IT.

DOLLAR STORE
ONE PRICE EMPORIUM · D&A OPPENHEIM
D&A OPPENHE
SALOMON DEUTSCH
SCHRAM & CO.

THE DOCUMENTS ACCOMPANYING THE DEED OF TRANSFER LIST BOTH JUAN AND HIS WIFE GERTRUDIS FLORES AS RESIDENTS OF THE STATE OF NUEVO LEON. THEIR DAYS IN TEXAS ARE NOW BEHIND THEM..

REMEMBER THAT OLD MULBERRY TREE DOWN IN THE RIVERBOTTOM THAT WE CUT OUR INITIALS INTO?

MULBERRY? YOU SURE IT WAS-N'T A HACKBERRY TREE, JUAN?

IN 1887 JUAN APPLIES FOR A MILITARY PENSION FROM MEXICO, BUT IS DENIED BECAUSE HE HAD ONCE BEEN A TEXAS REBEL.

*!!© PENDEJOS! ALL MY LIFE I HAVE BEEN A SOLDIER AND THIS IS MY REWARD, IGNOMINY!!

THAT SAME YEAR A NEWSPAPER REPORTER FINDS HIM LIVING WITH SANTIAGO, WHO IS MAYOR OF NUEVO LAREDO. JUAN MAINTAINS THAT HE HOLDS NO RANCOR AGAINST TEXAS.

IT IS USELESS TO BE CONSUMED BY BITTERNESS. SO MANY OF THE OLD ONES ARE GONE...

IN HIS LAST YEARS JUAN BECOMES SOMETHING OF A CELEBRITY. ANGLO HISTORIANS WRITE HIM TO GET HIS RECOLLECTIONS OF THE REVOLUTION.

TRAVIS DIDN'T WANT ME TO GO FOR HELP, BUT THE OTHERS SAID I MUST..

WHAT THEN, PAPA?

AT THE RIPE OLD AGE OF 84 HE DIES AND IS BURIED AT NUEVO LAREDO — IF NOT EMBITTERED BY HIS "EXILE", CERTAINLY SADDENED BY THE UNGRATEFUL WAY TEXANS REWARDED HIS PATRIOTISM.

OTHERS, LIKE JUAN'S OLD FRIEND ANTONIO MENCHACA, NEVER LEAVE THEIR BIRTHPLACE — EVEN IN THE HARDEST OF TIMES. THEY STAY, WORKING TOWARD A BETTER DAY, STRIVING TO KEEP THEIR LANGUAGE, CUSTOMS, AND DIGNITY ALIVE.

THE SYMBOL OF ALL WE FOUGHT FOR..UNRECOGNIZABLE! TURNED INTO A GRINGO SIDESHOW!

SCHMELTZER

NOW JUAN SEGUIN'S BONES ARE HOME AGAIN, FINALLY RESTING IN TEXAS SOIL, AND IF YOU LOOK CLOSELY YOU CAN PERHAPS SEE HIS VISAGE IN THE FLEETING CLOUDS — LOOKING DOWN ON A *NEW* TEXAS, THE RESULT OF A CENTURY AND A HALF OF CLASH AND FUSION BETWEEN THE TWO CULTURES, ANGLO AND HISPANIC, A TEXAS WHERE EACH NEW GENERATION BRINGS US REBORN HOPE FOR YESTERDAY'S BROKEN DREAMS.

VIVA SEGUIN! MAY HIS IDEALS OF FREEDOM, JUSTICE, AND EQUALITY SHINE BRIGHTLY, LIKE A LONE STAR, AND MAY HIS MEMORY LIVE IN THE HEARTS OF ALL TEXANS — *FOREVER!*

END

SOURCES AND REFLECTIONS

SINCE NO MAJOR WORK HAS YET BEEN PUBLISHED ON JUAN N. SEGUIN — OR THE TEJANOS — IT WAS NECESSARY TO DIG AND PIECE TOGETHER THE SHARDS TO PRODUCE THIS BOOK. MORE THAN THAT WERE THE DIFFICULTIES IN PERSPECTIVE: SEGUIN LIVED IN A TIME OF RAMPANT RACISM, AND IT IS NOT EASY TO TRUTHFULLY DEPICT THOSE EVENTS IN A MANNER ACCEPTABLE TO MODERN-DAY, "ENLIGHTENED" MINDS.

AS WE IN TEXAS APPROACH OUR GLORIOUS SESQUICENTENNIAL, THE FACT THAT OVER THE PAST 150 YEARS SO FEW HAVE TRIED TO PUT THIS MALIGNED PATRIOT IN HISTORICAL PERSPECTIVE SHOULD INDICATE SOMETHING OF THE PITFALLS INVOLVED. THOSE RECKLESS ENOUGH TO ATTEMPT IT SHOULD REALIZE BEFOREHAND THAT FAILURE IS ALMOST A DEAD CERTAINTY. IT MAY WELL BORDER ON THE IMPOSSIBLE — EVEN NOW — TO TELL THE TRUTH ABOUT SEGUIN AND NOT OFFEND SOMEONE IN TEXAS. MORE LIKELY, EVERYONE WILL BE OFFENDED.

BUT THE STORY WAS NOT ALL AS UGLY AND GRIM AS I MAY HAVE LED THE READER TO SUSPECT. LIKE ANY OTHER CLASH OF CULTURES, THE HUMAN SPIRIT SOARED AS WELL AS STAGGERED DURING THE EXPERIENCE. THEN, AS NOW, MANY PEOPLE MAINTAINED THEIR RESPECT FOR EACH OTHER; THEY LIVED TOGETHER, WORKED TOGETHER, AND SOUGHT TO MAKE TEXAS A BETTER PLACE FOR ALL ITS CITIZENS. THEIR COURAGEOUS EXAMPLE SHOULD NOT BE OVERLOOKED AMIDST ALL THE BLOOD AND THUNDER, FOR IN THE END, IT WILL TRIUMPH.

I MUST ACKNOWLEDGE THE VARIOUS RESEARCH FACILITIES IN TEXAS WHERE THE TRUTH CAN STILL BE FOUND, IF ONE IS PATIENT AND AUDACIOUS ENOUGH TO SEEK IT, AND EXTEND MY THANKS TO THEIR CAPABLE STAFFS: THE BARKER TEXAS HISTORY CENTER AT UT; THE BEXAR COUNTY CLERK'S OFFICE; THE TEXAS STATE LIBRARY; THE GENERAL LAND OFFICE (SPANISH ARCHIVES); THE DRT LIBRARY (LOCATED AT THE ALAMO); AND THE WILSON COUNTY CLERK'S OFFICE IN FLORESVILLE. THE PORTRAIT OF SEGUIN, PAINTED BY THOMAS JEFFERSON WRIGHT IN 1838 AND NOW HANGING IN THE GOVERNOR'S OFFICE AT THE STATE CAPITOL, WAS REPRODUCED WITH PERMISSION OF THE STATE ARCHIVES.

ALSO, MY THANKS TO THOSE SCHOLARS (WHO SHALL REMAIN ANONYMOUS) FOR THEIR HELP AS I WORKED TO PUT TOGETHER THIS STORY AND MAINTAIN MY OBJECTIVITY. TO THEIR CREDIT, ON ALL FRONTS I FOUND ECHOED THE SENTIMENT: "IT'S HIGH TIME THE TRUTH ABOUT THE TEXAS-MEXICANS WERE TOLD." THIS COMFORTED ME GREATLY IN MOMENTS WHEN I WASN'T SO SURE MYSELF, FOR IT MUST BE ADMITTED THAT OUR HISTORY AT TIMES READS LIKE A CHRONICLE OF HORRORS — HORRORS THAT MOST TEXANS NOWADAYS HAD RATHER PUT BEHIND THEM.

MOST OF MY DOCUMENTATION IS TOO OBSCURE TO BENEFIT THE GENERAL READER. ITEMS, FOR INSTANCE, LIKE JACK BUTTERFIELD'S UNPUBLISHED

MANUSCRIPT, "JUAN N. SEGUIN: A VINDICATION", REUBEN LOZANO'S TEXAS CENTENNIAL PAMPHLET, "VIVA TEJAS", OR SEGUIN'S OWN "PERSONAL MEMOIRS" ARE SCARCE AS HEN'S TEETH — EVEN IN TEXAS. A FEW OF THE MORE READILY AVAILABLE SOURCES ARE LISTED BELOW.

"13 DAYS TO GLORY"- LON TINKLE ; "A TIME TO STAND"- WALTER LORD ; "DAY OF SAN JACINTO"- FRANK X. TOLBERT. The Alamo and San Jacinto battles in rip-snorting detail. Next to nothing on the Tejano role; mostly Divine Intervention on behalf of White-Anglo-Saxon-Protestants.

"LONE STAR"- T. R. FEHRENBACH. Good historical overview, altho some Chicano authors think his writing reflects an unconscious racism. I don't (but I ain't from Aztlán).

"THE TEXAS RANGERS"- WALTER PRESCOTT WEBB. The High Priest, Supreme Apologist, or Ultimate Groupie, depending on your intellectual/racial bias. In Webb's eyes the Rangers could do no wrong; is it History or Hero Worship? Only Time will tell...

"FOREIGNERS IN THEIR NATIVE LAND"- DAVID WEBER; "OCCUPIED AMERICA"- RODOLFO ACUÑA. Currently making the rounds on the college level as "Chicano Studies" texts. The former noteworthy for its choice racial slur quotes, the latter for its militant, vaguely revolutionist "Brown Power" stance.

"THE KING RANCH"- TOM LEA. The "Authorized Version" of the King/Kleberg clan, masterfully written and beautifully illustrated in two volumes. Depicts Captain King as the two-fisted benefactor of La Raza, not as the red-handed gringo Robber Baron that others whisper he was. Whitewash, or artistic Public Relations?

"A VAQUERO OF THE BRUSH COUNTRY"- J. FRANK DOBIE. One gets the feeling that he, if ANYBODY, knew the truth but chose to stop at "Rocky times in Texas" when his evidence struck too close to home. A pity.

"AFTER SAN JACINTO"; "ATTACK AND COUNTERATTACK"- J. MILTON NANCE THE monumental reference work covering the years 1836-42. Hefty.

"A JOURNEY THROUGH TEXAS" (1857)- FREDERICK L. OLMSTED. One of the best peeks into pre-Civil War Texas, if you remember that the author was a rabid Yankee "free-soiler," who thought that Slavery made brutes of master and slave alike.

"MY CONFESSION"- SAMUEL CHAMBERLAIN. A relaxed account of the Mexican War by a cocky young U.S. Dragoon — with watercolors. Chilling.

"WITH SANTA ANNA IN TEXAS"- JOSÉ E. de la PEÑA. The Revolution as seen by an observant Mexican soldier. Excellent.

"AN AMERICAN-MEXICAN FRONTIER"- PAUL S. TAYLOR. Written in 1934; still stands as the best scholarly study of the Anglo takeover of South Texas.

"THE TEXANS"- DAVID NEVIN. From media "Big Bucks" Time-Life Books. Lots of pictures at least. See also their "The Mexican War." Better than nothing...

IF YOU COME AWAY WONDERING WHY JUAN SEGUIN RECEIVES SO LITTLE MENTION IN THESE STUDIES, CONSIDER HIS OWN ASSESSMENT, GIVEN IN 1858:

"My enemies had accomplished their object; they had killed me politically in Texas, and the less they spoke of me, the less risk they incurred of being exposed in the infamous means they had used to accomplish my ruin."

WHATEVER THE REASONS FOR SEGUIN'S NEGLECT, SOONER OR LATER, THE TRUTH FINDS US ALL; "LA MENTIRA DURA HASTA QUE LA VERDAD LLEGA."

LOST CAUSE

JOHN WESLEY HARDIN,
THE TAYLOR-SUTTON FEUD,
AND RECONSTRUCTION TEXAS

BY JACK JACKSON

P R E F A C E

Texas reaped a bitter harvest from the War Between the States. Part of this dark legacy was the great civil unrest that plagued the beaten but unbowed populace during Reconstruction times. Although much of the violence was racially motivated, in certain localities it produced bloody feuds among kinsmen that deepened family rifts caused by the war. None of these was more devastating than the Taylor-Sutton Feud that raged in South Texas, embracing two generations and causing untold grief.

Most chroniclers of the feud have not approached their subject without bias, and I am no exception. My great-grandfather Ancil Jackson and his siblings were sheltered by Creed Taylor, one of the feud's crustiest participants. I was born and raised within "hollerin' distance" of Creed's log cabin on Ecleto Creek, Wilson County, where Federal men ambushed and killed his son, Hays. As a child I engaged in frolicsome chinaberry fights with neighboring kids at the old Taylor homeplace, never suspecting the tragic events that had unfolded there a century before.

In time I learned the stories passed down through the generations, stories that have enriched our heritage though they are now scorned for their factual frailty and often dismissed as fanciful folklore. Being a suspicious sort, I also learned to subject these stories to documentary scrutiny, under the fond illusion that the human spirit can be measured or understood by such impersonal means. Finally I realized that "facts" are just as frail and flimsy as "folklore," for their validity depends on who is using them and to what purpose.

Thus, in defense, I can only say that my ancestors are buried in the feuding ground, and I am a product of what they were. This is the story of their struggle for survival in hard times, as best I can tell it (warts and all).

Jack Jackson
Austin, Texas

LONGHORNS
IN THE BRUSH

CREED TAYLOR'S RANCH ON THE ECLETO. THE YEAR IS 1857.

I GOT ONE! I GOT ONE!!

HIYA, HIYA..

BAWWLL..

QUICK— BRING TH' BRANDIN' IRON SOMEBODY!

HERE IT IS!!

OKAY, STICK HIM ON TH' BACK— HURRY!

SSIZZZ..

THERE! NOW TH' WHOLE WORLD KNOWS THAT THIS HERE IS A TAYLOR DOGIE!!

IN THE AFTERMATH OF THE TEXAS REVOLUTION AND THE MEXICAN WAR, MANY HISPANIC RANCHERS ABANDONED THE COUNTRY, LEAVING THEIR HERDS BEHIND. THESE WILD CATTLE HAVE BECOME "PUBLIC PROPERTY."

WHERE'D THEY COME FROM THIS TIME, MR. TAYLOR?

SAME PLACE AS ALWAYS... WE JUS' RODE RIGHT IN TH' PEARLY GATES AND THERE THEY WUZ, CHEWIN' THEIR CUDS!

HUMPH! THEN HOW COME YALL'S REEKING OF FIRE AND BRIMSTONE?

NOW YOU BOYS MAKE YERSELF USEFUL! THEM COWS BE THIRSTY AND SO'S TH' HOSSES!!

THERE'S A BITE TO EAT, WHEN YOU'RE SO INCLINED, MR. BIRD.

WHY, THANK YE, MRS. TAYLOR.

LIKE I WUZ SAYING DAN—THAT BLACK HEIFFER IS YOURN' IFFIN' YOU WANT HER. WHAT SAY YE?

CREED AND DANIEL BIRD ARE MARRIED TO SISTERS, THE DAUGHTERS OF OLD PHILLIP GOODBREAD.

SHE'S TH' PICK OF TH' LOT, ALRIGHT.

THEN TAKE HER—MAKES ME NO DIFFERENCE A'TALL..

THE REST OF THE "CROWD" SOON FOLLOWS, DUMPING SADDLES IN THE DOGTROT AND SHUCKING SPURS AND PISTOLS.

IFFIN' WE DON'T GIT SOME RAIN SOON, TH' BIZNESS IS DONE PLAYED OUT.

YEP, IT'S AWFUL DRY.. THAT'S A FACT.

THESE ARE THE SECOND GENERATION — MOST IN THEIR LATE TEENS OR EARLY TWENTIES. THEY ARE THE "COW BOYS," SOON TO MAKE TEXAS FAMOUS AS A KINGDOM HELD TOGETHER WITH RAWHIDE.

GIT TO IT, BOYS — BLACK-EYED PEAS 'N SALTBACK. CORNPONE'S A'COMIN'...

THEY ARE CLAN MEMBERS, ALL RELATED BY BLOOD OR MARRIAGE — LIKE MOST RANCHING ENCLAVES ON THE RAW FRONTIER, WHETHER ANGLO OR HISPANIC.

HOW'S PAPA DOIN' THESE DAYS?

OH, FAIR TO MIDDLIN'. HE'S STAYIN' WITH TH' WESTS FER A SPELL...

CONSTANTLY IN THE SADDLE, THEY HAVE LITTLE USE FOR MEN WHO LEAVE THE TENDING OF THEIR STOCK TO OTHERS.

NOW DANIEL, I FIGGER TO GIT SOME MIGHTY FINE CALVES OUTTA THET RED BULL WITH TH' TWISTED HORN.

YEP, I RECKON THAT'S ONE MISTER MAVERICK WILL NEVER MISS!

PHILLIP GOODBREAD TAYLOR — CREED'S YOUNGEST SON, KNOWN AS "DOBOY," AGED FOURTEEN — ASKS A DUMB QUESTION.

PA, WHO EXACTLY IS THIS MR. MAVERICK?

WHY SON HE'S A BIG LAND SPECULATOR UP AT SAN ANTONE.

YESSIR. TOO BUSY SHUFFLIN' PAPERS TO FOOL WITH HIS COWS, BUT HAS TH' GALL TO CLAIM EVER DOGIE IN TEXAS AS HIS OWN..

THET'S WHY EVERY TIME FOLKS SEE AN UN-BRANDED CRITTER THEY SAY "YONDER GOES A MAVERICK."

YEAH— JUST BEFORE THEY SLAP THEIR OWN BRAND ON IT!!

UNCLE CREED, CAN ME AND JAMES SET ON YOR' MESKIN SADDLE?

YEAH, CAN WE?

WAHL, I RECKON SO, BUT DON'T MESS NONE WITH MY LARIAT, YOU HEAR?

NAW SIR WE WON'T.

OBOY, C'MON!!

IT SURE IS FANCY— LOOK AT ALL TH' SILVER DO-DADS!

YEAH, HE GOT IT OFF A DEAD MESKIN IN TH' LAST BIG WAR.. HIYA HIYAHH

HAULING FREIGHT CHEAPER THAN ANGLO TEAMSTERS, MEXICAN DRIVERS HAVE A VIRTUAL MONOPOLY ON THE BUSTLING TRADE ROUTE THAT LINKS SAN ANTONIO TO INDIANOLA ON THE COAST.

THEIR CONSTANT PRESENCE LEADS TO DIFFICULTIES WITH ANGLO PROPERTY OWNERS ALONG THE ROAD, ESPECIALLY IN TIMES OF DROUGHT.

NOT A BLADE OF GRASS LEFT... AND I'M MISSING SOME STOCK.

IT'S THEM NO-ACCOUNT MESKINS!

UNEMPLOYED WAGONERS ATTEMPT TO BREAK THEIR MONOPOLY WITH ATTACKS ON THE CART TRAINS NEAR GOLIAD IN JULY.

THESE "OUTRAGES" THREATEN DIRE CONSEQUENCES FOR THE MERCHANTS DEPENDENT ON CHEAP LABOR TO KEEP THEIR GOODS MOVING—AND FOR THE CITIZENS DEPENDENT ON THOSE GOODS.

HAVEN'T RECEIVED A SHIPMENT IN OVER A MONTH!

RUINING MY BUSINESS.

IN SEPTEMBER ANOTHER ATTACK OCCURS NEAR HELENA, KARNES COUNTY, NOT FAR FROM CREED'S RANCH. IT PUTS THE COUNTRY IN AN UPROAR.

BURN 'EM, AND LET'S HIGH-TAIL IT!

CONVINCED THAT THE CIVIL AUTHORITIES IN KARNES COUNTY SYMPATHIZE WITH THE ATTACKS, CITIZENS IN SAN ANTONIO TAKE MATTERS INTO THEIR OWN HANDS. A VIGILANCE COMMITTEE IS FORMED.

IF THEY WON'T EN-FORCE THE LAW DOWN THERE THEN *WE WILL!*

COL. JOHN WILCOX, A VOCAL MEMBER OF THE "KNOW-NOTHING" PARTY,* TAKES HIS COMPANY OF ALAMO RIFLES DOWN THE CIBOLO VALLEY.

LET'S HAVE US SOME FUN, FELLERS.

I'LL DRINK TO THAT!

THE LIQUOR FLOWS, AND WILCOX'S PARTY GOES ON A RAMPAGE, RUNNING ROUGHSHOD OVER SOME OF THE OLD CITIZENS OF THE AREA.

STRING 'EM UP, BOYS!

(144)* A PRODUCT OF RACIAL AND RELIGIOUS ANTAGONISM WHICH SWEPT THE U.S. IN THE 1850s, DIRECTED AT "FOREIGNERS."

THEY RIDE TO HELENA AND LAY DOWN THE LAW.

IF ANOTHER CART IS MOLESTED ON TH' ROAD WE'LL REDUCE THIS PLACE TO ASHES!

IN RESPONSE TO THE RISING TIDE OF MERCHANT INDIGNATION, GOV. PEASE OFFERS A $500 REWARD FOR THE ARREST OF THE CART RAIDERS.

THAT'LL GET SOME ACTION!

BUT NO ONE COMES FORTH TO COLLECT, AND GEN. TWIGGS MUST PROVIDE ARMED ESCORTS FOR MILITARY SUPPLY TRAINS THAT TRAVEL ALONG THE OLD GOLIAD ROAD.

DUE TO THE EXCESSES OF WILCOX'S "VIGILANTS," THESE ESCORTS ARE MET WITH PUBLIC HOSTILITY AS THEY PASS THROUGH THE TOWN OF HELENA.

BUT CERTAIN LOCAL CITIZENS, STIRRED TO ACTION BY THE EXAMPLE OF BEXAR COUNTY, FORM THEIR OWN VIGILANCE COMMITTEE.

GENTLEMEN, WE'VE GOT TO CLEAN HOUSE AROUND HERE OR WE'LL FIND OURSELVES UNDER MARTIAL LAW!

(145)

JOHN LITTLETON IS APPOINTED SHERIFF AND A NEW COUNTY JUDGE IS INSTALLED. THEY HASTEN TO REASSURE THE MERCHANTS OF SAN ANTONIO THAT THE ROAD IS SAFE.

NO PROBLEM. WE GOT THE SITUATION UNDER CONTROL.

THE BUSINESSMEN ARE NOT CONVINCED. WHEN GOV. PEASE VISITS TO INVESTIGATE THE TROUBLE, THEY ASK HIM TO CALL OUT THE STATE MILITIA.

VERY WELL, GENTLEMEN. IF THAT'S WHAT IT TAKES...

WELCOME GOV. PEASE

BY MID-OCTOBER "PEASE'S ARMY" INVADES THE COUNTIES LYING ASTRIDE THE CART ROAD.

ARMED TROOPS, OCCUPYING US IN A TIME OF PEACE.

AND ALL FOR TH' BENEFIT OF A PACK OF THIEVIN' MESKINS!

HELENA SALOON

ONE GROUP IS STATIONED AT HELENA, WORKING CLOSELY WITH LITTLETON'S VIGILANTES.

THESE PEOPLE AROUND HERE ARE IN-BRED AND TIGHT-LIPPED!

A TUFF NUT TO CRACK.

IT IS NOT LONG BEFORE LITTLETON'S CROWD EXPANDS ITS AVOWED PURPOSE.

ALL THIS HORSE STEALIN' AND MAVERICKIN' HAS GOT TO STOP.

YEAH, THEY'RE CUTTIN' IN ON OUR FREE CATTLE!

SO THE KARNES COUNTY FACTION TURNS ITS ATTENTION FROM THE CART TRAFFIC TO ROUNDUPS AND BRANDING ACTIVITIES.

I RECKON WE CAUGHT YOU FELLERS AT IT RED-HANDED!

I GOT A ROPE — LET'S FIND A TREE!

DAMN YOU, JIM COX. WE AIN'T DOING NOTHIN' YOU AIN'T DONE A THOUSAND TIMES.

THESE HERE ARE RANGE CRITTERS—NOT A BRANDED ANIMAL AMONGST 'UM!

MOST "VIOLATORS" ARE MERELY THREATENED AND TOLD TO LEAVE THE COUNTRY.

WE'LL LET YOU GO THIS TIME, BUT YOU GOT ONE WEEK TO PACK UP AND GIT OUT—TH' WHOLE BUNCH OF YOU!!

LITTLETON'S MORAL BRIGADE SOON HAS OLD-TIME STOCKMEN LIKE THE TAYLORS UP IN ARMS. CREED'S BROTHER-IN-LAW SPREADS THE ALARM TO ECLETO CREEK.

WHO'S THAT COMIN' YONDER?

WHY, IT'S MART WEST, AND HE'S RIDIN' LIKE TH' DEVIL HISSELF!

MART, WHAT'S TH' RUSH??

JACK LITTLETON'S GANG IS ON A TEAR. THEY COME CLOSE TO HANGIN' MY BOYS YESTERDAY — AND HAVE PUT THEIR EDICT ON OUR WHOLE FAMILY!

CREED, THEY AIM TO SHUT DOWN MAVERICKIN' TO ALL BUT THEMSELVES.

DO THEY NOW? WE'LL JUS' SEE ABOUT THAT!

A MEETING IS CALLED AT CREED'S RANCH. IT IS WELL ATTENDED.

MEN, THE OPPRESSION OF THIS GENTRY HAS PLUMB GOT OUT OF HAND! IT'S TIME FOR A SHOWDOWN!!

WE'RE WITH YOU!

COUNT US IN!

CREED SENDS A LETTER TO THE HELENA VIGILANCE COMMITTEE.

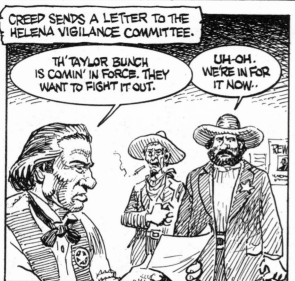

TH' TAYLOR BUNCH IS COMIN' IN FORCE. THEY WANT TO FIGHT IT OUT.

UH-OH. WE'RE IN FOR IT NOW..

ON THE APPOINTED DATE, EIGHTY RESOLUTE MEN RIDE TO KARNES COUNTY, ARMED TO THE TEETH.

BUT THEIR ADVERSARIES FAIL TO SHOW..

TOM, WHAT ARE YOU DOIN' HERE?

THEY SENT ME TO SET UP A TALK, CREED. WE CAN WORK OUT ALL OUR DIFFERENCES — NO NEED FOR BLOODSHED.

A MEETING AT THE HELENA MASONIC LODGE IS AGREED UPON, WHERE BOTH SIDES WILL AIR THEIR GRIEVANCES AND ABIDE BY THE MASONS' DECISION.

TELL JACK'S BOYS THEY'D BETTER BE THERE THIS TIME, OR WE'LL COME LOOKIN' FOR THEM!

MEANWHILE, THE LAME-DUCK GOVERNOR DELIVERS A MESSAGE TO A JOINT SESSION OF THE LEGISLATURE, DEFENDING HIS POLICY ON THE RECENT CART WAR.

OUR MEXICAN POPULATION HAS JUST CAUSE FOR REPRISALS. UNLESS WE STOP THESE BRUTAL ATTACKS, I FORESEE A CIVIL WAR OF THE RACES!

BUT LEADING CITIZENS OF THE OCCUPIED AREA DENOUNCE HIS DRACONIAN MEASURES.

PEASE HAS DEFEATED HIS OWN PURPOSE AND ADDED STRENGTH TO THE WAVE WHICH SOON WILL SWEEP PEON MEXICUNS OUT OF TEXAS!

STAR PRINTING

SOUTHERN RESTAURANT

H. RUNGE GENERAL STORE

(149)

THESE CRITICS ARGUE THAT BY CLOAKING THE ACTIVITIES OF THE VIGILANTS UNDER EXECUTIVE AUTHORITY, MANY MEN — INDIFFERENT TO THE CART TRAFFIC — HAVE BEEN DRAWN INTO THE CONFLICT.

THAT'S TH' GOSPEL TRUTH.

YEAH, I DON'T GIVE A HOOT ABOUT TH' DANG MESKINS, BUT CLOSIN' OFF TH' OPEN RANGE IS SOMETHING ELSE!

A PUBLIC MEETING IS HELD AT HELENA IN WHICH THE CITIZENS DEFEND THEMSELVES FROM PEASE'S ACCUSATIONS AND VENT THEIR FEELINGS ON THE CART DISTURBANCES.

WE REGARD THE PEON TEAMSTERS AS AN INTOLERABLE NUISANCE AND ASK THE SAN ANTONIO SHIPPERS TO WITHDRAW THEM!

HEAR!

HEAR!

LATER THE TAYLOR CROWD FACE LITTLETON'S VIGILANTS AT THE MASONIC HALL.

BY GOD, YOUR OUTRAGES AGAINST US HAVE GOT TO STOP!! WE FOUGHT TO MAKE TEXAS FREE OF TYRANNY, AND WILL NOT STAND STILL FOR SUCH HIGH-HANDEDNESS!

LITTLETON REPLIES..

WE ARE TRYING, UNDER THE GOVERNOR'S DIRECTION, TO BRING ORDER TO THE FRONTIER. HONEST MEN SHOULD APPLAUD US..

JACK, THAT'S A DAMN' LIE, AND YOU KNOW IT! I WILL HOLD YOU PERSONALLY RESPONSIBLE IF YOUR ROWDIES HARM ANOTHER COW CREW IN THIS DISTRICT!!

IS THAT UNDERSTOOD?

SO "PEACE" IS MADE AT HELENA IN THE WANING DAYS OF 1857, BUT IT IS A PEACE THAT SUITS NO ONE.

WE HAVEN'T HEARD THE LAST OF THIS, I'LL WAGER.

FROM THIS EPISODE MAY BE TRACED THE BEGINNINGS OF THE TAYLOR-SUTTON FEUD, BUT THE DARK WAR CLOUDS LOOMING ON THE HORIZON PUT ALL SUCH LOCAL GRUMBLINGS TO REST.

THE FALLEN BANNER

THE ELECTION OF ABRAHAM LINCOLN TELLS SOUTHERNERS THAT THEIR INTERESTS IN THE UNION WILL GO UNATTENDED.

THIS NATION CAN- NOT EXIST, HALF SLAVE AND HALF FREE!

TEXAS, LIKE OTHER SLAVE-HOLDING STATES, SEES THE WRITING ON THE WALL.

GIVE ABE HALF A CHANCE AND HE'LL TURN TH' NIGRAHS LOOSE ON US.

AT A CONVENTION CALLED IN AUSTIN IN JAN. 1861 THE ASSEMBLED DELEGATES DECLARE FOR SECESSION. ONE OF THEIR MEMBERS IS JOHN LITTLETON OF KARNES COUNTY.

THE 1845 ANNEXATION ORDINANCE IS NULL AND VOID, TEXAS IS AGAIN A SOVEREIGN ENTITY, OWING ALLEGIANCE TO NO ONE!

ORAN ROBERTS, PRES.   LITTLETON ⟨153⟩

GOV. SAM HOUSTON AND OTHER MEN WHO HAD FORGED THE REPUBLIC OF TEXAS, AND GUIDED IT INTO THE UNION, OPPOSE SECESSION—BUT THE TIDE IS AGAINST THEM.

WHEN THE ACTIONS OF THE CONVENTION ARE PUT TO A VOTE, MANY OLD TEXIANS LIKE CREED TAYLOR REFUSE TO RATIFY "DISUNION."

NONETHELESS, THE MEASURE PASSES BY A FOUR TO ONE MAJORITY, AND ON MARCH 23rd TEXAS BECOMES PART OF THE CONFEDERACY.

MANY OF HER YOUNG MEN MARCH OFF TO WAR, FULL OF ENTHUSIASM.

ONCE THE DIE IS CAST, SOME WHO HAD OPPOSED SECESSION VOLUNTEER FOR FRONTIER DUTY.

IF WE GOTTA' FIGHT, BETTER AGAINST REDSKINS THAN WHITEMEN.

OTHERS, LIKE CREED'S COWBOYS, SEEK REBEL SERVICE CLOSER TO THE HOME FRONT, WHERE THEY CAN PROTECT THEIR FAMILIES.

I GOT A BAD BACK DOC...

THEN WE'LL PUT YOU IN THE QUARTER-MASTERS DEPT.

THEIR DUTIES ARE MUCH AS BEFORE THE WAR: ROUNDING UP WILD CATTLE, EXCEPT NOW FOR THE BENEFIT OF THE CONFEDERACY.

HIYAA

HOME GUARDS ARE FORMED AT VARIOUS PLACES, LIKE THE ONE AT HELENA BY "CAPTAIN" JOHN LITTLETON.

MEN, OUR HELPLESS WIMMEN AND INNOCENT BABES LOOK TO US FOR SAFETY.

MANY SUCH "HEEL FLY" UNITS HAVE LITTLE TO DO EXCEPT ACT IMPORTANT AND HARRASS SUSPECTED UNIONISTS.

WHERE YOU GOIN' STRANGER?

HOW COME YOU AIN'T IN TH' ARMY, LIKE US??

WE NEED THAT GUN YOU'RE PACKING..

<155>

TEXAS, SPARED THE BRUNT OF MAJOR FIGHTING, SETTLES INTO A DULL ROUTINE.

BELTS TIGHTEN AS THE WAR DRAGS ON.

LET'S HAVE A PARTY!

WITH WHO? NOBODY LEFT TO INVITE EXCEPT OLD MEN AND LITTLE BOYS

WHAT I WOULDN'T GIVE FOR A REAL CUP OF COFFEE.

WOUNDED OR MAIMED, AN OCCASIONAL VETERAN RETURNS HOME. THEY BEAR DISCOURAGING PROSPECTS FOR THE SUCCESS OF THE REBEL BANNER.

OUR WHOLE OUTFIT WUZ WIPED OUT, EXCEPT FOR ME AND BODE..

WHEN NEWS OF LEE'S SURRENDER REACHES TEXAS IN LATE APRIL 1865 IT IS DENIED AS JUST ANOTHER YANKEE RUMOR, MEANT TO DEMORALIZE THE SOUTH'S FIGHTING SPIRIT.

BUT IT SEZ HERE—

DON'T BELIEVE A WORD OF IT—ALL LIES!

MASSIVE LOSS

LEDGER

CRUSHED!!

BAD WOR

ONCE THE SOLDIERS START STRAGGLING BACK, HOWEVER, GLOOM AND ANXIETY GRIP THE STATE.

WE'RE BEAT MAUDE.. THEY GIVE US A LICKIN'

BUT AT LEAST I GOT YOU BACK ALIVE—SOB

GEN. GRANT DEMANDS THE SURRENDER OF THE TRANS-MISSISSIPPI DEPARTMENT, AND TEXAS TRIES TO GAIN MORE FAVORABLE TERMS THAN AGREED TO BY GEN. LEE.

ASK FOR IMMUNITY FROM PROSECUTION

AND THE RIGHT TO RETAIN ARMS!

THINK THEY'LL LET US KEEP OUR SLAVES??

I WOULDN'T COUNT ON IT..

THE APPEAL FALLS ON DEAF EARS.

TELL THEM I CAN DISCUSS NOTHING BUT TOTAL SURRENDER!

ON JUNE 2nd GEN. EDMUND KIRBY-SMITH WALKS ABOARD A U.S. WARSHIP IN GALVESTON HARBOR AND SIGNS THE FORMAL PAPERS. WITH THIS GESTURE, THE LAST VESTIGE OF CONFEDERATE AUTHORITY IN TEXAS VANISHES.

THEN COMMENCES THE "BREAK UP." LOOTING TAKES PLACE THROUGHOUT THE STATE AS DISILLUSIONED SOLDIERS PILLAGE GOVERNMENT WAREHOUSES AND DEPOSITORIES.

YOU MEN DISPERSE! THIS IS PUBLIC PROPERTY.

THE HELL YOU SAY! THESE SUPPLIES WERE GATHERED FOR US!!

WHO'S GOT A BETTER RIGHT TO THEM?

CSA XB205 142807

(157)

PUBLIC OPINION SELDOM DENIES THEIR RIGHT.

BUT THESE GOODS BELONG TO THE PEOPLE OF TEXAS..

WE'RE TH' PEOPLE, FOOL!

YOU STAID HERE, LIVING HIGH, WHILE WE WERE RISKIN' OUR BUTTS IN TH' WAR.

NOW STEP ASIDE!

WHEN SUBSEQUENT GROUPS OF DISBANDED SOLDIERS FIND THE BOOTY GONE, THEY BECOME VIOLENT.

STAY CALM MEN. WE'LL FIND SOME FOOD FOR YOU.

JUST DON'T BURN TH' TOWN!

GEN. JO SHELBY PASSES THROUGH TEXAS THAT SUMMER WITH HIS DIE-HARD MISSOURIANS, BOUND FOR MEXICO. THEY LIVE OFF THE LAND..

GOD BLESS YOU JOE, BUT SPARE ME THIS MILK COW.

SORRY FRIEND. WE GOT TO EAT.

BURYING THEIR TATTERED BANNERS IN THE RIO GRANDE, THEY CROSS TO SELL THEIR SWORDS TO EMPEROR MAXIMILIAN.

SINK OL' DIXIE OUT DEEP, WHERE TH' DAMN YANKEES WILL NEVER FIND HER.

GOV. MURRAH TRIES TO SAVE SOME STATE PROPERTY FOR THE REBUILDING THAT LIES AHEAD, BUT HIS ADMONITIONS ARE SWEPT ASIDE. LAWLESSNESS AND CHAOS REIGN.

RUMORS ABOUND THAT THE VICTORIOUS YANKEES MEAN TO CONFISCATE THE PROPERTY OF LEADING REBELS AND TRY THEM FOR TREASON.

ALL BY MILITARY COURTS, MIND YOU.

IT IS NOT LONG BEFORE THE GOVERNOR AND OTHER HIGH-RANKING OFFICIALS JOIN THE EXODUS TO MEXICO.

DAMN' THEIR HIDES! LEAVING US HERE TO HOLD TH' BAG.

AND AN EMPTY ONE AT THAT!

ON JUNE 19th GEN. GRANGER LANDS AT GALVESTON. HE DECLARES AUTHORITY RESTORED AND FREES THE SLAVES, A DAY THAT BECOMES CELEBRATED BY BLACKS AS "JUNETEENTH!"

BY THE POWER VESTED IN ME..

IN THE TURMOIL AND CONFUSION OF THE "BREAK UP" THE SLAVES HAD ALMOST BEEN FORGOTTEN. BUT NOW THE MOST SERIOUS CONSEQUENCE OF THE LOST CAUSE HAS TO BE DEALT WITH: WHAT'S TO BE DONE WITH THE NEGRO?

HALALEW-YAAH!! WE'S FREE AT LAST!

AS WORD OF EMANCIPATION SPREADS, THE BLACKS DRIFT AWAY FROM THEIR PLANTATION HOMES — SOME JOYFULLY, SOME RELUCTANTLY.

C'MON CASSIUS, 'FORE HE CHANGES HIS MIND!

WAHL, I RECKON WE BE LEAVIN' NOW, MASSA JOHN..

OTHER OWNERS HAVE NO INTENTION OF FREEING THEIR SLAVES, AND THE DASH FOR FREEDOM IS A RISKY AFFAIR.

TH' DAWGS IS GETTIN' CLOSE!

KEEP GOING. WE'LL MAKE IT!!

THEY CONGREGATE IN SHANTY-TOWNS NEAR CITIES OR MILITARY POSTS, OFTEN FALLING PREY TO VICE AND MISERY.

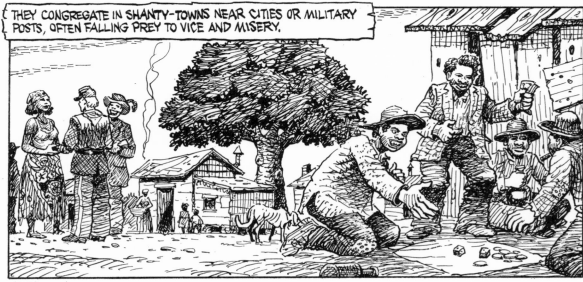

IDLE, WITHOUT MEANS OF SUPPORT, THEIR PRESENCE IS SALT IN THE WOUNDS OF THEIR FORMER MASTERS.

I GOT A FIELD FULL OF COTTON AND *NO* PICKERS.

WE NEED SOME NEW KIND OF LABOR CONTRACTS OR THIS WHOLE COUNTRY WILL PERISH.

IT IS HOPED THAT WHEN A.J. "JACK" HAMILTON ARRIVES AS INTERIM GOVERNOR A SYSTEM OF STATE-REGULATED LABOR WILL BE DEVISED.

JACK'S A UNION MAN, BUT HE'S A TEXAN AND UNDERSTANDS OUR PROBLEMS...

ALL BUT RABID UNIONISTS ARE DISAPPOINTED.

SLAVERY IS *WHOLLY DEAD* AND CANNOT BE REVISED IN ANY FORM. THE NORTH WILL NOT ALLOW IT!

INSTEAD, HAMILTON ADDRESSES THE SUBJECT OF WHO SHALL HAVE A VOICE IN RULING POST-WAR TEXAS.

ALL VOTERS MUST FIRST PASS A TEST OF LOYALTY TO THE UNITED STATES BY TAKING AN OATH OF AMNESTY.

OATH

IN THE MEANTIME, THE EX-SLAVES ARE LEFT TO THEIR OWN DEVICES, AND CROPS *ROT* IN THE FIELDS.

YOU BOYS WANT A JOB?

NAWSAH, COME CRIS'MAS WE'S GONNA' GET US FORTY ACRES AND A MULE!

DURING THE LATE SUMMER AND FALL, NEGRO TROOPS ARE BROUGHT TO TEXAS TO REPLACE DISCHARGED WHITE VOLUNTEER REGIMENTS.

OH LORD, IT'S FINALLY HAPPENED.

THE TROOPERS SPARE NO PAINS TO HUMILIATE THEIR FORMER FOES.

THIS HERE'S MY ONLY SET OF CLOTHES..

WELL, YOU'LL JUS' HAVE TO WEAR IT WITHOUT THESE PURTY CONFEDERATE BUTTONS, GREYBACK.

JUST AS FEARED, THE BLACK SOLDIERS INCITE THEIR HAPLESS BRETHREN TO A GREATER APPRECIATION OF THEIR RIGHTS.

LOOKY HERE, YOU'RE A FREE MAN NOW.

YOU DON'T HAVE TO STEP OFF THIS SIDEWALK FOR NO WHITE WOMAN, ESPECIALLY NO RAG-TAG REBEL GAL!!

THERE ARE NOT LACKING THOSE EX-SLAVES WHO TAKE TO THEIR NEW ROLE WITH SATISFACTION. MOST WHITES CANNOT ACCUSTOM THEMSELVES TO THE ALTERED STATE OF AFFAIRS; FEW EVEN TRY.

WE'S TH' COCK OF TH' WALK, LUTHER.

WE SHO' IS.. DE BOTTOM RAIL BE ON TOP NOW.

THESE NIGGERS DONE FORGOT THEIR PLACE, SETH.

RECKON WE'D BETTER REMIND 'UM.

HOWDEE, AUNT MARY.

SIMP DIXON!! WHY, BLESS YOU CHILD.. GET OFF THET NAG AND GIVE ME A HUG!

...STORIES OF YANKEE BRUTALITIES DURING THE WAR, IN OTHER SOUTHERN STATES, THAT CAUSE HATRED TO LINGER ON.

THEY TORTURED MA AND TH' GURLS, WITH PA LYING THERE DEAD. THEN THEY SET FIRE TO TH' HOUSE. I WUZ ONLY ONE GOT OUT..

HEAVENS SAKES!

THAT WINTER IS AN UNEASY ONE, AS NEGRO SOLDIERS ROAM ABOUT THE COUNTRYSIDE, KEEPING PEOPLE IN CONSTANT TERROR.

HEY GAL, WHUT YOU GOT IN THET BASKET?

SWEET TATERS, I BET! MMMM..

JACKSON COUNTY SENDS THE GOVERNOR A PETITION FOR RELIEF FROM THE ABUSES BEING COMMITTED BY 300 COLORED TROOPS STATIONED IN THEIR MIDST.

JUST SEND TH' BILL TO GENERAL GRANT.

YEAH, UP IN WASHINGTON, D.C.!

〈163〉

WHITE GARRISONS ALSO PROVE UNRULY (SUCH AS THE ONE AT GALVESTON), AND ASSAULTS UPON THE DIGNITY OF WOMEN CRY OUT FOR SOUTHERN VENGEANCE.

WHAT'S TH' MATTER MISSY? THINK YOU'RE TOO GUD FOR US, HUH?

BUT RACE IS AT THE CORE OF THE PROBLEM, SO WHEN THE FREEDMEN'S BUREAU SETS UP SHOP, RACIAL DIFFICULTIES INTENSIFY.

ANY TIME A WHITE MAN ABUSES YOU, JUST COME TO ME AND I'LL HAVE HIM THROWN IN THE MILITARY STOCKADE!

FOLLOWING CLOSELY ON THEIR HEELS ARE YANKEE "CARPETBAGGERS," COME TO TEXAS FROM THE NORTH TO EXPLOIT THE NEW ORDER OF THINGS.

TH' LAND OF MILK AND HONEY.

⟨164⟩

ADDED TO THESE TROUBLES ARE RENEWED COMANCHE RAIDS, NOW THAT CONFEDERATE TROOPS ON THE FRONTIER HAVE BEEN DISBANDED, AND THE UNION SOLDIERS ARE BUSY BEING POLICEMEN.

THE GRAYCOATS ARE WEAK, BROKEN FROM THEIR BATTLES WITH THE BLUECOATS. *NOW* IS THE TIME TO TAKE BACK OUR HUNTING GROUNDS!

THESE RAIDS DEVASTATE THE ENTIRE FRONTIER, AND THE SETTLEMENT LINE IS PUSHED BACK 100 MILES.

BESET BY HOSTILE INDIANS, OVERBEARING U.S. TROOPS, GANGS OF LAWLESS RUFFIANS, AND THE CARPETBAGGER PLAGUE, OLD TEXAN FAMILIES PULL TOGETHER FOR SURVIVAL. THE TAYLOR CLAN IS NO EXCEPTION.

LOOKS LIKE TH' McALISTERS STAYED TOO LONG...

A GATHERING OF THE CLAN

AT THE "BREAK UP" THE TAYLORS SUFFERED SEVERE LOSSES TO THEIR HERDS. LARGE NUMBERS OF CATTLE WERE CARRIED OFF BY DESERTERS, HEEL-FLIES, AND OTHERS WHO FELT THEY HAD A RIGHT TO ANY STOCK FOUND ON THE OPEN RANGE.

THE WILD HERDS IN SOUTH TEXAS HAVE MULTIPLIED PROLIFICALLY DURING THE WAR, AND EVERY RETURNING SOLDIER IS ANXIOUS TO MAKE UP FOR LOST TIME. MAVERICKING ATTAINS A SCALE UNKNOWN BEFORE THE WAR YEARS.

KEEP THOSE IRONS HOT, BOYS. WE GOT AN-OTHER HERD COMING.

STOCKMEN LIKE CREED TAYLOR ARE AGAIN FORCED TO TAKE THE LAW INTO THEIR HANDS. OLD RIVALRIES ARE REBORN AND NEW ONES SPRING INTO BEING.

ALRIGHT, BOYS, POUR IT ON 'UM!

TO COMBAT THE SITUATION VARIOUS RANCHERS MEET IN MARCH, 1866, AT RANCHO, GONZALES COUNTY, AND DRAW UP RESOLUTIONS TO PROTECT THEIR INTERESTS AS STOCK RAISERS.

RUSTLERS FOUND ON OUR RANGE WILL RECEIVE PROMPT JUSTICE!

SEVERAL HERDS WERE TRAILED NORTH IN THE FALL OF 1865, DESPITE HAVING TO PASS THROUGH THE YANKEE GAUNTLET IN EAST TEXAS.

NICE OF YOU TO BRING US SOME FRESH BEEF, REB.

MORE HERDS GO THE FOLLOWING SPRING, TAKEN BY HARDY MEN LIKE MONROE CHOATE OF KARNES COUNTY, THORNTON CHISHOLM OF DEWITT COUNTY, AND CAPT. EUGENE MILLETT OF GUADALUPE COUNTY.

IT IS ONE OF THE FEW WAYS THAT SONS OF THE SHATTERED CONFEDERACY CAN MAKE A LIVING IN THESE HARD TIMES.

TYPICAL OF THE PROBLEMS THEY ENCOUNTER IS THE HERD BOSSED BY 16-YEAR-OLD JIM DAUGHERTY. HE IS MET AT THE KANSAS-MISSOURI BORDER BY IRATE JAYHAWKERS, SPOILING FOR A FIGHT.

AFTER HIS HERD IS STAMPEDED, THE YOUNG TEXAN RECEIVES A LASHING.

THIS'LL TEACH YOU TO BRING DISEASED COWS TO KANSAS, BOY!

HE BARELY ESCAPES A WORSE FATE.

HANG HIM I SAY..

AW, LET HIM GO, JETHRO. HE'S JUST A DUMB KID.

OTHER GANGS, SUPPOSEDLY CONCERNED WITH "TICK FEVER," ATTACK DROVES OF TEXAS CATTLE — APPROPRIATING THE HERDS FOR THEMSELVES!

LET 'UM GET A LITTLE CLOSER. THEN YOU KNOW WHAT TO DO.

DESPITE THESE DANGERS, 250,000 LONGHORNS CROSS THE RED RIVER IN 1866, BRINGING MUCH-NEEDED CASH TO THE TEXAS ECONOMY.

AT HOME THINGS HAVE BEEN HEATING UP BETWEEN THE SEMI-VANQUISHED REBELS AND THE U.S. MILITARY.

THE QUICKER THESE REBS LEARN WHO WON TH' WAR, THE QUICKER WE CAN GO HOME.

DUE TO THE "BAD CONDUCT" OF CERTAIN CITIZENS, A SQUAD OF 18 SOLDIERS IS SENT TO CLINTON, IN DEWITT COUNTY, TO REPRESS INSURRECTIONIST TENDENCIES.

WAHL, LOOKY HERE—NEW YAWK 18th CAVALRY!

THIS WON'T HELP MATTERS.

THEY CRASH A WEDDING PARTY, LOOKING FOR A WANTED MAN.

PORTER! COME WITH US!!

IN THE ENSUING SCUFFLE SEVERAL SOLDIERS ARE ROUGHED UP AND THE FUGITIVE, BEFORE DYING, MORTALLY WOUNDS CAPTAIN NOLAN.

TWENTY-ONE CELEBRANTS ARE ARRESTED AND MARCHED OFF TO JAIL. MANY ARE TAYLOR RELATIVES OR SYMPATHIZERS.

IN KARNES COUNTY A DESPERADO NAMED CHARLEY TAYLOR SHOOTS THE SON OF A PROMINENT HOTELKEEPER AT HELENA.

NOBODY CALLS ME A HORSE-THIEF AND LIVES!!

THE DYING BOY, JACK POLK, IS CARRIED TO THE HOUSE OF JOHN LITTLETON — ONE FORMER REBEL WHO IS ANXIOUS TO MEND HIS WAYS.

WHO DID IT, SON?

IT WUZ.. A..TAYLOR.

BUT TROUBLED TIMES DO NOT KEEP THE TAYLOR CLAN FROM MAKING FESTIVE. ONE SUCH GATHERING IS THE PARTY THROWN AT JOE TUMLINSON'S PLACE NEAR YORKTOWN IN LOWER DEWITT COUNTY.

JOE IS A ROUGH-AND-TUMBLE FRONTIERSMAN OF THE OLD SCHOOL. HIS FIRST WIFE WAS CREED'S SISTER, JOANNA, AND JOE'S SISTER ELIZABETH HAD MARRIED ONE OF CREED'S BROTHERS, WILLIAM RILEY TAYLOR, NOW DECEASED.

HOWDY CREED. SEE YOU BRUNG OL' DARBY..

YES, I WUZ THINKIN' WE MIGHT HAVE US A LITTLE SPORTING MATCH!

CREED — LIKE MOST OF THE CLAN — IS A LOVER OF FINE HORSES. HIS CHAMPION "DARBY" IS KNOWN AT DIRT TRACKS ALL OVER TEXAS.

GOOD! OLIVER WILL PUT HIM IN TH' SHED WITH TH' OTHER HAWSES.

Y'ALL COME JOIN TH' PARTY!

THE INTRODUCTIONS AT SUCH AFFAIRS ARE ELABORATE..

JOE, YOU REMEMBER THESE YOUNG FOLKS, DONCHA? ANCIL JACKSON... HIS WIFE SELETIA WEST..KIDS..

WHY YES, ANCE, I BELIEVE WE MET DURING ONE OF YOUR COW HUNTING TRIPS IN THE LATE AND NOT-SO-GREAT WAR.

YESSIR WE DID. ON TH' MEDIO AS I BEST RECALL..

..HIS BROTHERS NATHAN AND PONY — COME DOWN FROM TH' HILL COUNTRY.

BOYS — HOW'S STOCKRAISIN' UP THERE THESE DAYS?

NOT SO GOOD. INJUNS ARE CLEANIN' US OUT, SIR.

SORRY TO HEAR THAT.

NATHAN'S WIFE IS ONE OF TH' TINKLE GALS OVER ON TH' CLAYTO.

OH, J.P.'S GIRL? CHARMED, MY DEAR..

THIS HERE'S FREEMAN MYRES, MARRIED TO ANCE'S SISTER...AND TH' SIFFORD BOYS, JOSH AND JENK.

WHY, THESE ARE TH' KIDS YOU TOOK IN AFTER SOL JACKSON DIED OF TH' CHOLERA, AIN'T THEY?

TH' VERY ONES — TAUGHT 'EM HOW TO WORK COWS, DIDN'T I BOYS?

YOU SHOR' DID, MR. TAYLOR..

THEN THERE'S MY SONS, HAYS & DOBOY.

CREED, YOU NEEDN'T INTRODUCE ME TO MY VERY OWN NEPHEWS! I STILL RECOGNIZE 'EM

...AND DAUGHTER CAROLINE, NEWLY WED TO MAJOR WILL AD SPENCER OF KARNES COUNTY.

ADDISON..I KNEW YOUR FATHER WELL—AND I HEAR YOU'RE SOMETHING OF A WAR HERO.

A DISTINCTION I COULD DO WITHOUT AT THIS PARTICULAR TIME, SIR.

NONSENSE, SON. WE'RE ALL PROUD OF YOUR SERVICE HERE, ON THAT YOU CAN RELY. NOW, WHO'S THIS BUNCH?

AND SO IT GOES, AS ONE FAMILY AFTER ANOTHER ARRIVES AT THE TUMLINSON RANCH.

THE WOMENFOLK TEND THEIR BROOD OF CHILDREN AND PREPARE THE OUTDOOR TABLES.

I DECLARE, SUSAN, THAT LITTLE ONE HAS GOT A VORACIOUS APPETITE.

TAKES AFTER HIS PA, BEST I CAN TELL..

CACKLE

THE MEN CONGREGATE TO SPEAK OF THE RECENT CATTLE DRIVES AND DISCUSS FUTURE PROSPECTS.

I HEAR THEY'VE DANG' NEAR SEALED OFF KANSAS WITH THEIR QUARANTINE LAW.

YEP! CAN'T TAKE 'EM IN 'CEPT BETWEEN NOVEMBER AND FEBRUARY.

HELLS BELLS! A MAN CAN'T DRIVE COWS IN TH' WINTER.

NOTHIN' TO DO BUT PASTURE THEM IN INJUN TERRITORY TILL THEY'LL LET 'EM CROSS. OR ELSE SWING 'EM FAR TO TH' NORTH, AROUND TH' QUARANTINE.

MILLETT, HOW'D YOU COME OUT ON YOUR HERD?

ARMED MOB MET ME AT TH' MISSOURI LINE, SO I HAD TO GO DOWN THRU ARKANSAS, COME BACK UP AND SWIM 'EM CROSS TH' MISSISIP AT OL' ST. LOUIE..

BY THAT TIME THEY WAS WORE OUT, SO I TOOK 'EM TO ILLINOIS AND FATTENED THEM UP ON CORN.

HOW'D YOU MAKE OUT ON TH' DEAL— IF YOU DON'T MIND SAYING?

WELL, MY SHARE WAS $2,600 BUT I'LL TELL YOU ONE THING: IT WEREN'T WORTH TH' GRIEF! NO SIR, I'M STAYIN' HOME NEXT YEAR!

THORNTON CHISHOLM — WHOSE MOTHER WAS A TAYLOR — RECOUNTS HIS EXPERIENCE TO THE GROUP.

WE WERE LUCKIER THAN MOST. TOOK 1,800 HEAD UP THRU' TH' INDIAN NATION. NO TROUBLE IN KANSAS AND SOLD TH' HERD AT ST. JOE'S, MISSOURI — SEVEN MONTHS AND TEN DAYS ON TH' TRAIL!!

SEVEN MONTHS?! HOW COME IT TOOK YOU SO LONG?

HELL, WE DIDN'T KNOW WHERE WE WUZ GOIN' MOST OF TH' TIME!

HA HA

JOE'S WIFE ENDS THE GAB SESSION.

DINNER'S READY. Y'ALL COME ON!

RATTLE RATTLE

THE MULTITUDE IS SEATED BY SOME PROTOCOL KNOWN ONLY TO THE MISTRESS OF THE HOUSE.

BIGFOOT — YOU'RE RIGHT HERE.

TUMLINSON, NOT A CHURCH-GOING MAN, YIELDS THE HONORS TO A VISITING CIRCUIT PREACHER.

REVEREND HARDIN, WOULD YOU ASK TH' BLESSING?

HE IS JAMES GIPSON HARDIN, HERE WITH HIS RELATIVES, THE CLEMENTS FAMILY.

OUR HEAVENLY FATHER..

AS CUSTOMARY, CONVERSATION AT THE TABLE IS LIMITED TO FAMILY TALK AND SOCIAL AFFAIRS.

HOW'S YOUR PA DOIN' SALLY? STILL HUNTIN' BEARS UP IN TH' CEDAR BRAKES AROUND KERRVILLE?

I RECKON SO- AND WILL BE TILL THERE AIN'T NONE LEFT..

AFTERWARDS, THE MEN DIGEST THEIR MEAL WHILE THE WOMEN CLEAR THE TABLES.

THAT SHOR' WUZ GOOD BERRY COBBLER MISS LOUISA.

WHY, THANK YOU, MR. CHOATE.

ONCE THE LADIES HAVE DRIFTED AWAY, POLITICS DOMINATE THE TALK.

HOW'S THINGS IN Y'ALL'S NEW COUNTY, CREED? I HEAR OL' LONGWORTH HAS OPENED UP A FREEDMEN'S BUREAU AT SULPHUR SPRINGS..

YES, THAT DAMNED SCALLYWAG HAS GOT TWELVE UNION SOLDIERS OVER THERE AND IS RAISIN' HELL AMONGST DIAL'S AND POLLEY'S NIGRAHS!

WILLIAM LONGWORTH, A CANADIAN BY BIRTH AND POST-MASTER AT RANCHO BEFORE THE WAR, HAS BENEFITTED FROM THE CHANGING OF THE GUARD.

BUT WE GOT RID OF TH' RASCAL ON THE COUNTY LEVEL.

DAN BIRD'S A COMMISSIONER AND PROSPECTS LOOK REAL GOOD FOR WALKER BAYLOR AS CHIEF JUSTICE.

YEAH, BUT HOW DO YOU KNOW LONGWORTH WON'T GIT A MILITARY WRIT & OVERTURN TH' WHOLE BUSINESS?

CAN'T SAY.. LEASTWISE, SOME OF OUR CROWD HAS TAKEN THE OATH OF ALLEGIANCE.

THE "AMNESTY OATH," NECESSARY FOR FORMER REBELS TO PARTICIPATE IN CIVIL AFFAIRS.

YES, I HEAR QUITE A FEW HAS TAKEN IT — SUCH AS CAPT. JOHN LITTLETON OVER AT HELENA.

JACK TOOK IT?!? DAMN HIS HIDE — HE WUZ ONE OF TH' LOUDEST SECESSION-ISTS AROUND!!

YEAH. NO SOONER WAS HE BACK FROM TH' BIG CONVENTION THAN HE STARTED RAISIN' COMPANIES OF FIGHTIN' MEN!

OLD JOE TUMLINSON PUTS IT SUCCINCTLY...

WAHL BOYS, THESE IS STRANGE TIMES, WHAT MAKES PEOPLE DO SOME STRANGE THINGS.

I SEE IT THIS WAY: BETTER TO TAKE TH' BLASTED OATH AND STAY ON IN TH' SADDLE THAN LET TH' SCALAWAGS AND NIGRAHS RUN THINGS, DONCHA' THINK? AIN'T THAT SO??

A MURMUR OF AGREEMENT GOES UP, BUT THE OATH REMAINS A DEGRADING REMINDER OF CONQUEST FOR MOST SOUTHERNERS.

AWAY FROM THE MAIN HOUSE, THE YOUNGER CROWD ENTERTAINS ITSELF IN A DIFFERENT WAY.

YALL WANT TO HAVE A SHOOTING MATCH?

RECKON SO.. AIN'T NOTHING ELSE TO DO..

IT IS ORGANIZED BY HAYS AND DOBOY, ALONG WITH THEIR TAYLOR COUSINS FROM DEWITT COUNTY.

DICK — YOU CALL FAIR OR FOUL. THREE SHOTS TO EACH ROUND.

BUCK, A SON OF WILLIAM RILEY TAYLOR AND JOE'S SISTER ELIZABETH TUMLINSON, IS THERE WITH HIS COUSINS, THE CHISHOLM BROTHERS — ONE OF WHICH IS DICK.

TOO EASY — LET'S GO IT MORE!

ALRIGHT. HOW DOES FIFTY PACES SOUND?

ANOTHER CLUSTER OF YOUNG MEN ASKS THE INEVITABLE QUESTION..

HOW MUCH WE SHOOTIN' FER?

WHY, 2 BITS A ROUND, IF IT'S NOT TOO STEEP FOR YOU.

IT IS, BUT THE PROUD SONS OF EMANUEL CLEMENTS WOULD BE THE LAST TO ADMIT IT.

SAY, WHO ARE YOU FELLERS ANYWAY?

WE'S TH' CLEMENTSES, FROM OVER NEAR RANCHO.

(179)

ARE YALL KIN TO US?

YOU'RE TH' PREACHER'S KID, AIN'T CHA?

I GUESS, SOMEHOW OR ANUTHER. THIS IS OUR COUSIN WES, FROM UP EAST TEXAS WAY.

FOR A 13 YEAR-OLD, WES HARDIN EYES DOBOY TAYLOR STERNLY.

I RECKON YOU COULD CALL ME THAT..

MANNING CLEMENTS KNOWS HIS COUSIN'S FIESTY NATURE AND IS QUICK TO DEFUSE THE SITUATION.

WES HERE IS LEARNIN' US TO WRITE OUR NAMES AND WE'RE LEARNIN' HIM TO ROPE AND RIDE!

THE SHOOTISTS LOOK TO THEIR PISTOLS, A MOTLEY COLLECTION OF BROKEN DOWN RELICS FROM THE PRE-WAR YEARS.

"SNAPPING" IS AS COMMON WITH THESE WEAPONS AS AN ACTUAL SHOT IS.

BLAST IT!!

SNAP

THAT'S TWO—A HIT AND A MISS. JIM GETS TO RELOAD FOR ANOTHER GO!

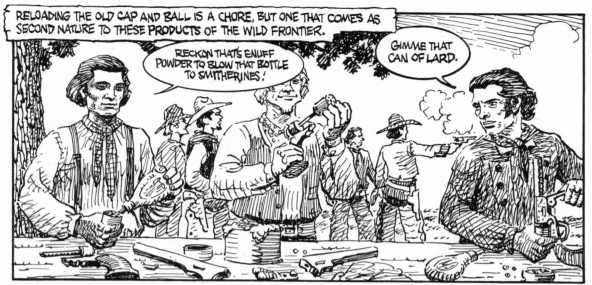

RELOADING THE OLD CAP AND BALL IS A CHORE, BUT ONE THAT COMES AS SECOND NATURE TO THESE **PRODUCTS OF THE WILD FRONTIER.**

RECKON THAT'S ENUFF POWDER TO BLOW THAT BOTTLE TO SMITHERINES!

GIMME THAT CAN OF LARD.

ALRIGHT!

WOO-HA!

BLAM

AS THE CONTEST NEARS THE BOTTOM OF THE PECKING ORDER, WESLEY HARDIN WHISPERS TO HIS COUSIN...

JOE, LEMME BORROW YOUR GUN.

IT IS A DECREPIT OLD COLT DRAGOON, ALMOST AS BIG AS THE BOY HIMSELF.

BLOOM

THE RESULTS ARE HOLLERED OUT.

TWO DEAD CENTER, AND NECK'S OFF TH' THIRD!

SAY, THAT'S PURTY FANCY SHOOTIN' FER A KID STILL WET BEHIND THE EARS.

HARDIN BRISTLES. AGAIN MANNING IS THERE.

AW, HE'S JUST JOKIN' WES. YOU DONE GOOD AS ANYBODY— THREE OUT OF THREE!

THE SECOND ROUND BEGINS, THOSE ELIMINATED PLACING SIDE BETS ON FAVORED CONTENDERS.

WE GOT US A PILE, BOYS—WINNER TAKE ALL!

FINALLY IT COMES DOWN TO LITTLE WES HARDIN AND BUCK TAYLOR (WHO IS TWICE WES' AGE).

WATCH 'EM CLOSE, DICK. I DON'T WANT ANY FOOLISHNESS..

(182)

THIS TIME BUCK IS NOT SO LUCKY. HE HITS ONE BOTTLE, MISSES ONE, AND GRAZES THE THIRD.

IS IT BUSTED?

NAW, JUST KNOCKED OFF.

THE PRESSURE IS ON. WES LICKS HIS LIPS AND TAKES CAREFUL AIM.

HE MISSES THE FIRST BUT NAILS THE SECOND.

THE EXCITEMENT GROWS.

ALRIGHT, WES... SHOW HIM TH' FAMILY TOUCH!

C'MON WES!

NAH—HE CAN'T DO IT.

HIS FINAL SHOT HITS THE POST BELOW HIS MARK..

THUD

BUT THE FIRST BOTTLE SWAYS AND FALLS!

THE CLEMENTS BOYS ARE JUBILANT.

WA-HOO!

THE TAYLOR COUSINS ARE ADAMANT.

HOLD ON! THAT'S NO GOOD.

HE WEREN'T EVEN SHOOTIN' AT TH' FIRST ONE!

DON'T MATTER— ONE'S BUSTED AND ONE'S ON TH' GROUND!

SAME DIFFERENCE, BY GOD!

CREED STOMPS OUT TOWARD THE RUCKUS.

HEY. YOU BOYS STOP ALL THAT INFERNAL RACKET! IT'S ALMOST RACE TIME AND YOU'RE MAKIN' MY HOSS SKITTERISH!

THEY EXPLAIN THE POINT OF DISSENTION TO THEIR ELDER AND HE PRONOUNCES HIS VERDICT.

ANY FOOL KNOWS IT'S A TIE. DON'T MATTER HOW TH' BOTTLE HITS TH' GROUND, LONG AS IT'S THERE WHEN TH' SMOKE CLEARS!

NOW IF YOU BOYS AIN'T WILLIN' TO CALL IT EVEN, THEN GO ON DOWN TO TH' CRICK AND SHOOT IT OUT! MY OLD DARBY IS HIGHSTRUNG AND DON'T TAKE TO CANNONFIRE!

FACE IS SAVED ALL AROUND, MUCH TO YOUNG HARDIN'S DELIGHT.

I'LL CALL IT A TIE IF YOU WILL, WES..

SUITS ME. I'M READY FOR TH' RACES ANYHOW...

(184)

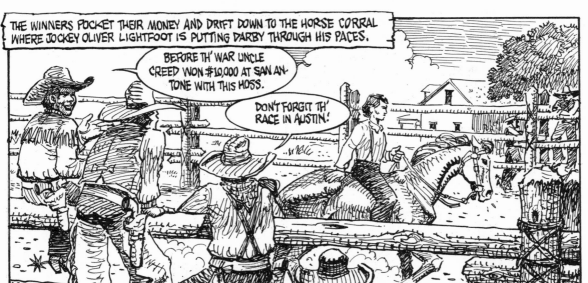

THE WINNERS POCKET THEIR MONEY AND DRIFT DOWN TO THE HORSE CORRAL WHERE JOCKEY OLIVER LIGHTFOOT IS PUTTING DARBY THROUGH HIS PACES.

BEFORE TH' WAR UNCLE CREED WON $10,000 AT SAN AN-TONE WITH THIS HOSS.

DON'T FORGIT TH' RACE IN AUSTIN!

YEAH, HE WON BIG THERE TOO..

BUT PA'S GOT HIM OUT TO STUD NOW — $50 A WHACK!

Y'ALL KEEP BACK NOW! DARBY DON'T LIKE TO BE CROWDED...

WHOA BOY, EASY..

JOE TUMLINSON LEADS OUT *HIS* PRIZED STEELDUST STALLION.

CREED, RECKON THAT OL' NAG HAS GOT ANYTHANG LEFT IN HIM? I'M THINKIN' MY GRAY EAGLE CAN PUT DIRT IN HIS EYES!

TAYLOR, AN EXPERT AT CONNING EASY MARKS, BEGINS ON HIS BROTHER-IN-LAW.

MOST LIKELY, JOE.. THIS OL' SAWBONES AIN'T BEEN ON A TRACK IN YEARS.

YEAH, SEEMS A SHAME TO RUN HIM ANYMORE. MIGHT BE FATAL! GUESS MY STEEL-DUST IS TOP-DOG NOW.

FROM WHAT I HEAR HE'S A DANDY PONY—ON ANY KIND OF GROUND.

I THINK SO — AND HAVE $50 TO BACK IT UP!!

CHOMP

FIFTY IS IT? WAHL, LET'S PUT ON A LITTLE PRIVATE SHOW FOR TH' FOLKS — SAY, FOR AN EVEN HUNDRED??

JOE GRINS.

OKAY, BUT JUS' YOU AND ME — LIKE IN TH' OLD DAYS.

US RIDE? AT YOUR AGE?? YOU SURE?

NOW CREED, YOU DIDN'T MIND RACIN' ME WHEN WE WUZ TOGETHER IN TH' BIG RUNAWAY SCRAPE, WITH OL' SANTY ANNY ON OUR TAIL..

YEAH, BUT YOU CAME OUT AHEAD OF ME BACK THEN! HAHAHAA

SO THE CROWD GATHERS AT A CLEARING BEHIND THE TUMLINSON HOUSE TO WATCH THE "OLD TIMERS" HAVE A GO AT IT...CREED IS 46 AND JOE 55.

'ROUND THAT MOTTE YONDER, ALONG THE GULLY AND BACK HERE — JUST ABOUT A MILE..

(186)

CREED STRIPS FOR ACTION WHILE JOE VIEWS THE SCENE WITH BEMUSED INDIFFERENCE..

BETTING AMONG THE CLAN IS HOT AND HEAVY.

MY SADDLE AGAINST YOR' SPENCER RIFLE, ANCE!

TWO BUCKS ON OL' JOE!

AT THE SOUND OF THE GUN THEY STREAK OFF, ADVANCING YEARS FORGOTTEN.

WHO'S AHEAD NOW?

CAN'T SEE FOR TH' DUST.

CREED'S TACTICS REFLECT HIS EXPERIENCE IN THE PROFESSION.

WATCH IT, CREED!! YOU'RE CROWDIN' ME!

IT'S A FRIENDLY RACE, AIN'T IT?

JOE BARELY AVOIDS A LOW BRANCH, BUT GRAY EAGLE THUNDERS ON.

AS THEY NEAR THE FINISH LINE, CREED DIGS IN HIS BARE HEELS AND TURNS OLD DARBY LOOSE.

RELATIVES RESPOND AND REV. HARDIN'S EXORTATIONS REND HEAVEN'S VEIL.

BY JEHOVAH!! PUT TH' LASH TO HIM!

C'MON JOE!

CREED! CREED!!

DARBY EDGES THE CONTENDER BY A NOSE — ALMOST TOO CLOSE TO CALL.

TUMLINSON IS GRACEFUL ABOUT IT. SURLY, BUT GRACEFUL.

WILL YOU ACCEPT CONFEDERATE MONEY, CREED?

DIDN'T THINK SO..

FIVE $20 GOLD PIECES COME OUT OF OL' JOE'S MORRAL.

WAHL, WE'VE HAD OUR FUN. LET'S LET TH' YOUNG'UNS SHOW OFF FOR AWHILE..

AND SO THEY DO, EXCEPT THIS TIME THE FIELD IS CROWDED.

KICK HIM BUCK!

FOUL! FOUL!!

FINALLY, AS THE SUN SINKS BELOW THE RUGGED HORIZON, THINGS QUIETEN AND THE MEN TALK OF RANCHING IN MUTED VOICES.

CREED, DID YALL SETTLE ANYTHANG WITH YOR' STOCKMEN'S MEETING AT RANCHO?

NOT MUCH. IT'LL TAKE HOT LEAD, NOT HOT AIR, TO SOLVE OUR PROBLEM.

THE "PROBLEM" BEGAN AFTER THE BREAK-UP, WHEN EVERYTHING REMOTELY CONSIDERED GOVERNMENT PROPERTY WAS POUNCED UPON. ANCIL JACKSON EXPLAINS.

ME AND PONY BIRD WAS HOLDING A HERD DOWN IN LAVACA COUNTY. WE'D ROUNDED THEM UP FOR TH' CONFEDERACY BUT HADN'T TURNED 'EM OVER YET.

A GANG OF POLECATS HIT OUR CAMP AND TOOK ALL 500 HEAD AT GUNPOINT. SAID THEY WUZ OWED BACK-PAY. HELL, I HADN'T BEEN PAID MYSELF FOR TWO YEARS!

FROM THAT SORT OF THIEVERY THESE SO-CALLED SOLDIERS STARTED FORMING INTO PACKS, CARRYING IRONS WITH THEM AN' BRANDIN' EVERYTHING IN SIGHT—ALTERING BRANDS, TOO.

HERD AFTER HERD IS DRIVEN OUT AND NOBODY KNOWS TH' RIGHTFUL OWNER.

AND MONEY PASSIN' HANDS!

THAT'S WHY WE APPOINTED INSPECTORS FOR OUR RANGE, AND YOU CAN BE DAMN' SURE NO COWS ARE GONNA LEAVE WILSON & GONZALES COUNTIES WITHOUT TH' BRANDS BEING RECORDED.

IT'S BAD DOWN HERE TOO, MAYBE WORSE. DURING TH' WAR I LOST 1,300 HEAD OVER AT FT. CLARK. WE'RE TALKIN' ABOUT OUR OWN ASSOCIATION AT HELENA.

SOONER OR LATER, BOYS, WE GOT TO CLEAN UP THIS COUNTRY AND SEPARATE TH' SHEEP FROM TH' GOATS!

MULLING JOE'S WORDS OVER, THE SOMBER RANCHERS HEAR THE BAND TUNING UP ON THE FRONT PORCH. LIKE MOST SOUTHERN CLANS, THIS ONE HAS ITS SHARE OF MUSICIANS.

ALRIGHT KIDS OF ALL AGES, IT'S TIME FOR SOME HIGH-STEPPIN'.

LANTERNS GO UP IN THE TREES, JUGS ARE OPENED, AND THE PARTY IS SOON UNDERWAY.

♪ SWING YOUR PARTNER-DOCE DOE ♪

BUT THIS TRIBAL STOMP HAS NOT ESCAPED THE NOTICE OF A CERTAIN SQUAD OF YANKEE SOLDIERS, ALWAYS ON THE LOOKOUT FOR DENS OF INSURRECTION.

KEEP YOUR WEAPONS READY.

WORD HAS SPREAD THAT BUCK TAYLOR WILL BE IN ATTENDANCE, AND BUCK IS WANTED ON SOME MINOR OFFENSE AGAINST A STAUNCH "UNION MAN."

STEP ASIDE! MAKE WAY YOU REBS!

IT IS AN UNFORTUNATE CIRCUMSTANCE THAT THE BLACK SERGEANT ATTACHED TO THIS PATROL HAS KEEN EYES AND A LOUD MOUTH.

DERE BE DAT' BUCK TAYLOR!

THOSE ARE HIS LAST WORDS..

BLAM!

IN THE CONFUSION THAT FOLLOWS, BUCK RUNS INTO THE HOUSE AND ESCAPES THROUGH A BACK DOOR.

BACK, DAMN' YOU — OR WE'LL OPEN FIRE!

JOE STEPS FORWARD AND CALLS FOR QUIET.

THIS IS AN ORDERLY GATHERING, SIR. AS YOU CAN SEE, WE ARE UNARMED.

JOHNSON, YAGER, SEARCH THE HOUSE FOR WEAPONS!

(191)

IT IS A LONG-STANDING CUSTOM AT FRONTIER SHINDIGS FOR THE MENFOLK TO SHUCK THEIR PISTOLS (MOST OF THEM ANYWAY). JOE'S DAUGHTER ANN DEMURELY SPREADS HER HOOPED SKIRT OVER THE CACHE OF ARTILLERY.

DON'T SEE NUTHIN' IN HERE — 'CEPT A REAL PRETTY GIRL!

NONETHELESS, ALL THE MEN WHO HAVE NOT SCATTERED INTO THE BRUSH ARE ROUNDED UP AND TAKEN TO SAN ANTONIO IN CHAINS.

DAMNED YANKEES..

AFTER QUESTIONING, THEY ARE RELEASED. JOE TUMLINSON MAKES HIS WAY HOME WITH A WORRIED MIND.

THAT HOT-HEADED BUCK DANG NEAR GOT US ALL KILLED.- MUMBLE..MUTTER

PA, WUDN'T THAT YANKEE *NICE*, NOT ASKIN' ME TO MOVE OFF TH' BED?

YES—BUT IT WOULD HAVE GONE BAD WITH US IF THEY'D FOUND THOSE GUNS!

SEGUIN MERCURY

HIS NEPHEW BUCK TAYLOR HAS TO GO "ON THE DODGE". HE BECOMES KNOWN AS THE LEADER OF THE TAYLOR PARTY.

THE TAYLOR PARTY

SHORTLY AFTER THIS NEAR DISASTER, HAYS TAYLOR TAKES A HERD FROM WILSON COUNTY TO THE BUSTLING PORT OF INDIANOLA.

Chas. MORGAN

REUSS DRUG STORE

HE GOES INTO A SALOON WITH SOME OTHER COWBOYS TO WASH THE DUST FROM HIS THROAT.

AHH..THAT FEELS GOOD.

WHILE THEY ARE DRINKING, SEVERAL NEGRO SOLDIERS ENTER AND PUSH THEIR WAY TO THE BAR.

WHISKEY, BARKEEP!

HAYS REACTS WITH PREDICTABLE SOUTHERN DISDAIN.

YOU FELLERS STAND ASIDE! I'M NOT IN TH' HABIT OF DRINKIN' WITH NIGRAS.

YOU SMART-ASSED REBEL WHELP! I'LL SHOW YOU WHO DRINKS AT THIS BAR AND WHO DON'T!!

AGAIN THE REACTION IS PREDICTABLE..

HAYS, THIS ONE IS DEADER THAN A DOORNAIL. YOU BETTER HIGHTAIL IT FOR HOME!

SEE YOU BOYS NEXT TRIP!

FIFTEEN MILES OUTSIDE OF INDIANOLA, HAYS RUNS INTO A MILITARY PATROL.

HOLD UP THERE! WHAT'S YOUR BIG HURRY?

HE NOTICES THAT THE SERGEANT'S MULE IS FRESHLY BRANDED. IT IS A DEAD RINGER FOR ONE BELONGING TO A FRIEND AT HALLETSVILLE.

WHERE'D YOU GET THAT THERE MULE, SARGE?

I'LL ASK TH' QUESTIONS. NOW YOU COME WITH US!!

AFRAID NOT, BOYS..

BLAM BLAM

GIT, YOU RASCALS!

COME ON, MULE. I'M TAKIN' YOU BACK TO MR. WALTON.

AT HELENA HAYS MEETS HIS FATHER AND TELLS HIM WHAT HAPPENED.

DAMMIT SON — GEORGE WALTON FOUND HIS MULE LAST WEEK. YOU'RE IN A PACK OF TROUBLE!

(195)

WE GOT TO GET RID OF TH' EVIDENCE. THEY FIND YOU WITH THAT MULE, THERE'LL BE HELL TO PAY!

GRUDGINGLY HAYS TAKES HIS PRIZE TO A REMOTE SPOT AND DOES AS CREED ADVISES.

CRYIN' SHAME TO KILL A FINE MULE LIKE THIS..

CREED SENDS BOTH HAYS AND DOBOY TO THE HILL COUNTRY, WHERE HE KEEPS SOME OF HIS CATTLE.

GO ON UP TO MASON AND LAY LOW TILL THIS THING BLOWS OVER.

THE OCCUPATION FORCES NOW HAVE TWO TAYLORS ON THEIR LIST. RADICAL SPOKESMEN CITE THEIR ACTIONS AS PROOF THAT TEXAS IS UNBOWED.

TH' WAR'S NOT OVER YET!

MEANWHILE, THE OLD GUARD TRIES TO REGAIN CONTROL OF ITS POLITICAL FUTURE. THROCKMORTON, A "CONSERVATIVE," BEATS THE "RADICAL" UNION CANDIDATE, PEASE, IN THE ELECTION FOR GOVERNOR.

I ATTENDED THE SECESSION CONVENTION AND WAS ONE OF THE FEW TO VOTE AGAINST IT!

IN AUGUST 1866 PRESIDENT JOHNSON DECLARES THE REBELLION AT AN END IN THE STATE OF TEXAS.

WE'LL SOON BE ONE BIG HAPPY FAMILY, JUST LIKE BEFORE.

THROCKMORTON, IN HIS ATTEMPT TO WREST CIVIL AUTHORITY FROM THE MILITARY ESTABLISHMENT, RUNS INTO STIFF OPPOSITION.

THESE LABOR CODES THEY'VE PASSED AMOUNT TO SLAVERY IN DISGUISE.

THE DEFEATED RADICALS RAIL AGAINST THROCKMORTON'S CONSERVATIVE FACTION, CONVINCED THAT IT INTENDS TO HOLD THE NEGRO IN BONDAGE, DENY HIM HIS CIVIL RIGHTS — AND REMOVE *THEM* FROM LUCRATIVE OFFICES ACROSS THE STATE.

ARE WE GONNA' SIT STILL FOR REBEL RULE ?!?

NO!

AGENTS OF THE FREEDMEN'S BUREAU KEEP THE POT BOILING, AS IN BOSQUE COUNTY WHERE A YOUNG NEGRO IS INDICTED FOR THE RAPE OF A WHITE GIRL.

RELEASE HIM TO ME, SHERIFF, OR I'LL HAVE TH' ARMY ARREST YOU!

THE GUILTY MAN IS DELIVERED UP — BUT NOT BEFORE THE GIRL'S FATHER HAS HIM CASTRATED!

IF IT'S ANY CONSOLATION, WE'LL MAKE THEM PAY FOR THIS.*

* THE PERPETRATORS WERE ACQUITTED.

IN MATAGORDA COUNTY ANOTHER AGENT FORCIBLY TAKES FROM CUSTODY A FREEDMAN CHARGED WITH MURDEROUS ASSAULT. THE MILITARY UPHOLDS IT.

WE WILL NOT BE DETERRED FROM ESTABLISHING A NEW SOCIAL ORDER IN TEXAS!

AT VICTORIA NEGRO TROOPS STORM THE JAIL AND SET FREE A HORSETHIEF AND A UNION SOLDIER CONVICTED OF ROBBERY, BOTH OF THEM BLACK.

CIVIL COURTS HAVE NO JURISDICTION OVER THE MILITARY.

THEN THEY LYNCH A WHITE MAN AWAITING TRIAL FOR KILLING A NEGRO.

OTHERWISE HE'D HAVE GONE FREE.

CITIZENS ARE ROUTINELY JAILED AND MONEY DEMANDED FROM THEM TO DROP THE CHARGES.

BUT, I'M INNOCENT!

THEN IT'LL COST YOU MORE..

UNITED STATES ARMY

IN A FEW INSTANCES COUNTY JUDGES, LAWMEN, AND EVEN NEWSPAPER EDITORS ARE JAILED FOR ACTS DISAGREEABLE TO THE MILITARY AND THEIR TOADIES.

WHAT ABOUT FREE SPEECH?

NOTHING'S FREE, AS YOU'LL SOON FIND OUT..

FLAKE'S BULLETIN

AT LOCKHART AND SEGUIN CERTAIN COURT RECORDS ARE SEIZED AND DESTROYED TO MAKE SURE "JUSTICE" IS DONE.

NO RECORDS, NO CASE.

THE WORST INCIDENT— SOME CALL IT AN ATROCITY— OCCURS AT BRENHAM, WHERE DRUNKEN SOLDIERS LOOT AND BURN THE TOWN.

DRY GOODS CLOTHING

A JUDGEMENT AGAINST THE PERPETRATORS IS THROWN OUT BY A MILITARY TRIBUNAL.

MAJOR SMITH WAS MERELY DOING HIS DUTY, AND THE CHARGES AGAINST HIM STEM SOLELY FROM DISLOYAL SENTIMENTS!!

BASED ON REPORTS FROM HIS FIELD COMMANDERS, GEN. SHERIDAN CONCLUDES THAT FREEDMEN IN TEXAS CANNOT RECEIVE JUSTICE AT THE HANDS OF WHITE JURORS.

REBS KILL MORE BLACKS AND UNION MEN IN THE INTERIOR OF THE STATE THAN INDIANS DO OUT ON THE FRONTIER!

MATTERS WORSEN WHEN THE 11th LEGISLATURE SELECTS TWO UNCOMPROMISING SECESSIONISTS AS U.S. SENATORS.

ORAN ROBERTS AND OL' BURNET GOT PICKED.

HELL, NEITHER ONE CAN PASS TH' OATH TEST!

JUST IN!! U.S. SENATORS CHOSEN

THE "IRON-CLAD OATH," REQUIRED OF ALL FEDERAL OFFICIALS, REJECTS ANY MAN WHO HAD PREVIOUSLY SERVED THE CONFEDERACY.

THAT LEAVES OUT JUST ABOUT EVERYBODY IN TEXAS 'CEPT NIGGERS, MESKINS AND DUTCHMEN!

ONCE THEY ARRIVE IN WASHINGTON THE SENATORS-ELECT ARE REFUSED THEIR SEATS AND HAVE TO WATCH THE CONGRESSIONAL PROCEEDINGS FROM THE GALLERIES.

HELL WITH IT— I'M GOING HOME...

ALL THIS POLITICAL BICKERING BECOMES IRRELEVANT WHEN THE U.S. CONGRESS PASSES THE FIRST RECONSTRUCTION ACT IN MARCH OF 1867 — DECLARING THE NEW REGIMES ILLEGAL AND DIVIDING THE SOUTH INTO 5 MILITARY ZONES.

PRES. JOHNSON USED HIS VETO, BUT IT DIDN'T DO NO GOOD.

GEN. PHIL SHERIDAN, STATIONED AT NEW ORLEANS, HEADS THE FIFTH MILITARY DISTRICT CONSISTING OF LOUISIANA AND TEXAS.

WHAT DO I THINK OF TEXAS? IF I OWNED TEXAS AND HELL, I'D LIVE IN HELL AND RENT OUT TEXAS!

(199)

SHERIDAN'S HAND-PICKED SUBORDINATE, GEN. CHARLES GRIFFIN, IMPOSES THE NORTHERN CONCENSUS ON HIS TEXAS SUBJECTS FROM HEADQUARTERS AT GALVESTON.

FIRST THING WE GOTTA DO IS GET RID OF THE GOVERNOR. HE'S NOTHING BUT A PAIN..

IN JULY SHERIDAN, ON THE BASIS OF GRIFFIN'S REPORTS, DECLARES THROCKMORTON AN "IMPEDIMENT" TO RECONSTRUCTION. HE IS REPLACED BY THE RADICAL PEASE.

GENTLEMEN, OUR TRIP TO WASHINGTON HAS BORNE FRUIT. NOW WE'RE GONNA' SEE SOME CHANGES!

UNDER THE NEW SETUP, THE MILITARY HAS THE POWER TO REMOVE ANY PUBLIC OFFICIAL, AND THE IRON-CLAD OATH IS EXTENDED TO CIVIL JURIES.

WE'RE WIPED OUT HORACE. NOT A THING WE CAN DO..

ARMED WITH MILITARY ORDERS, RADICALS, SCALAWAGS, AND CARPETBAGGERS FLOCK TO WELL-PAID POSITIONS. WILLIAM LONGWORTH IN WILSON COUNTY IS ONE OF THEM.

YOU'RE OUT, BOYS, AND I'M IN!!

IN SEPT. '67 GEN. GRIFFIN DIES OF YELLOW FEVER AND IS REPLACED BY THE EVEN LESS SCRUPULOUS J.J. REYNOLDS.

AND THAT'S SAYIN' SOMETHING, CAUSE GRIFFIN WAS THE MEANEST RADICAL REPUBLICAN TEXAS HAS EVER SEEN!

SUNDRIES

CREED TAYLOR, DURING THIS CHAOTIC PERIOD, FEARS FOR THE SAFETY OF HIS SONS WHO ARE CONSTANTLY IN TROUBLE WITH THE YANKEE OVERLORDS.

JOE, I'M WORRIED ABOUT DOBOY. HAYS CAN TAKE CARE OF HISSELF, BUT DOBOY'S GOT A CHIP ON HIS SHOULDER.

JOE TUMLINSON AGREES TO ACCOMPANY HIS FIRST WIFE'S BROTHER AND HIS NEPHEW, DOBOY, TO MEXICO.

WAHL, THERE'S OL' MONTE REY!

HADN'T CHANGED MUCH SINCE TH' WAR HAS IT??

BUT THEY SOON LEARN THAT MONTERREY IS A DANGEROUS PLACE FOR GRINGOS.

MAXIMILIAN HAS JUST BEEN EXECUTED AT QUERETARO, AND NOT ONLY THE FORMER REBS WHO COURTED HIS FAVOR BUT ALL REBS (FOREIGNERS) ARE UNWELCOME GUESTS.

THINGS ARE GETTIN' CRAZY DOWN HERE.

ME AND TH' REST OF TH' BOYS ARE THINKIN' OF GOING HOME TO FACE TH' MUSIC.

OUT ON A CRUISE OF THE CANTINAS, DOBOY GETS INTO BIG TROUBLE.

DAMN' GREASER! TRY TO CUT ME WILL YOU?!

HE IS TOSSED IN THE CALABOOSE, AND IT TAKES SOME DOING TO GET HIM OUT.

JOE TUMLINSON HAS ABOUT HAD IT WITH HIS NEPHEW.

DOBOY YOU'RE TOO COCKY FOR YOUR OWN GOOD!

NOW JOE, DON'T BE HARD ON TH' BOY. TH' MEX WUZ OUT TO STICK HIM.

DON'T CARE. HE'S NUTHIN' BUT A TROUBLEMAKER AND YOU'RE TOO EASY ON HIM, CREED — YOU DAMN' WELL KNOW IT!

IT'S TH' SAME HERE AS EVERWHERE ELSE — GUNPLAY, FIRST & LAST!

WAHL, IF YOU FEEL THAT WAY ABOUT IT, WHY DON'T YOU JUST GO ON HOME?

LIFE IN MEXICO HAS NOT SUITED OL' JOE.

I BELIEVE I WILL — AND I'LL TELL YOU SOMETHIN' ELSE: WHEN YOU COME LIMPIN' BACK, KEEP YOUR COWHANDS WHERE THEY BELONG.

WHAT'S THAT SUPPOSED TO MEAN?

I DON'T WANT YOUR BOYS MESSIN' WITH MAVERICKS ON MY RANGE, THAT'S WHAT!

NOW WAIT A MINUTE, JOE.. MAVERICKS IS MAVERICKS — WE ALL GOT A RIGHT TO 'EM.

YEAH, BUT SOME GOT MORE RIGHT THAN OTHERS, LIKE YOU FELLERS DECIDED AT RANCHO, EH?

⟨202⟩

THAT'S CRAZY TALK. WE WERE JUS' TRYIN' TO PROTECT OURSELVES, AND YOU TOO!

WAHL, CREED, I RIGHT MY OWN WRONGS, AN' I GOT SOME GOOD MEN WHAT FEELS TH' SAME WAY.

TAYLOR WATCHES OL' JOE RIDE AWAY.

DAMMIT TO HELL! THAT'S ALL WE NEED AT A TIME LIKE THIS — FUSSIN' IN TH' FAMILY!

JOE TUMLINSON IS A MAN OF HIS WORD. IMMEDIATELY FOLLOWING HIS RETURN TO DEWITT COUNTY, A BAND OF "REGULATORS" IS FORMED.

MEN, LIKE YOURSELVES I AM A SOUTHERN MAN, BORN N' BRED. BUT WE GOT TO HAVE SOME LAW AND ORDER AROUND HERE!

THEY RANGE FAR AND WIDE. THEIR AIM IS TO GIVE MAVERICKING SOME RESPECTABILITY.

WHERE YOU BOYS FROM?

NOWHERE IN PARTICULAR.

WAHL, YOU BETTER GIT BACK THERE, RAT QUICK LIKE!!

JOE HOLDS MEETINGS WITH OTHER RANCHERS WHO HAVE BECOME PROSPEROUS ON MAVERICKING BUT WHO NOW FEEL THREATENED BY THE PRACTICE.

SHANG'S MY NAME, GENTS, AND COWS ARE MY GAME!

ABEL HEAD "SHANGHAI" PIERCE IS ONE SUCH MAN. HE RETURNED FROM THE WAR WITH NOTHING BUT A TEAM OF OXEN. NOW VAST NUMBERS OF CATTLE WEAR HIS BRAND.

YEP, I OWE IT ALL TO TH' REMARKABLE REPRODUCTIVE POWERS OF THEM 2 OXEN.

HA HA

ONE OF PIERCE'S RANGE "ENFORCERS" IS A MAN NAMED JACK HELM, A CONFEDERATE DESERTER AND A BRAGGART WITH A MURKY PAST.

I'M GLAD WE SEE EYE-TO-EYE ON THIS THIEVERY, MR. TUMLINSON — MIGHTY GLAD!

UNATTACHED YOUNG MEN WHO FREQUENT PIERCE'S COW CAMPS — LIKE THE LUNN BROTHERS AND "ALL JAW" SMITH — ARE VIEWED WITH SUSPICION.

MY GUESS IS THESE FELLERS IS SCOUTIN' OUR OPERATIONS FER TH' TAYLORS, FIXIN' TO HORN IN ON US!

WE'LL SEE..

ALTHOUGH THE 11th LEGISLATURE ENACTS A LAW TO PROTECT STOCKMEN'S INTERESTS, MEN LIKE HELM AND TUMLINSON DO THE ENFORCING.

COUSIN BOB, I THINK WE BETTER FIND US A NEW LINE OF WORK!

THAT FALL, BY JOSEPH McCOY'S VISIONARY PLANNING, ABILENE KANSAS IS OPENED TO TEXAS DROVERS, STILL STRAPPED FOR CASH.

BRING THEM COWS ON UP, BOYS. WE'LL ALL MAKE A KILLING!

QUICK TO TAKE ADVANTAGE OF McCOY'S COW TOWN, TEXANS MOVE MORE HERDS NORTH. COMPETITION FOR WILD CATTLE BECOMES FIERCE.

JOE TUMLINSON'S REGULATORS ARE KEPT BUSY, RIGHTING A MULTITUDE OF WRONGS.

IT'S A DIRTY JOB, BUT SOMEBODY'S GOT TO DO IT..

MEANWHILE, GEN. REYNOLDS PLACES THE TAYLOR BOYS UNDER MILITARY EDICT, FORCING THEM TO KEEP ON THE MOVE.

WE'LL MAKE AN EXAMPLE OF THEM. THIS RANDOM KILLING OF SOLDIERS HAS GOT TO STOP!

IN OCT. 1867 DOBOY TAYLOR AND ELIZABETH STEPHENS ARE MARRIED ON THE OPEN PRAIRIE, READY TO MAKE A DASH IF NEED BE.

LORD, BLESS THESE YOUNG FOLKS IN THIS TIME OF TYRANNY.

THE FOLLOWING MONTH CREED TAKES BOTH BOYS BACK TO MASON, WHERE HE HAS MATCHED A RACE.

TH' TRACK'S IN FAIR SHAPE. Y'ALL GO ON OVER TO RANCK'S STORE, AND I'LL MEET YOU THERE LATER.

⟨205⟩

A GROUP OF SOLDIERS FROM THE NEARBY POST ARE AT RANCK'S STORE. THE LIQUOR IS FLOWING.

HADN'T WE BETTER LEAVE?

NAW. THEY'LL SUSPECT SOMETHING IF WE DO.

SETTLING DOWN OUTSIDE UNDER AN OAK TREE, HAYS READS THE LATEST ISSUE OF THE *HERALD*, A SAN ANTONIO NEWSPAPER CRITICAL OF THE RADICAL REGIME.

SEEING THIS, A DRUNKEN SOLDIER TAKES OFFENSE.

WHO AROUND HERE SUBSCRIBES TO THAT DAMNED RAG?

I DON'T KNOW, AS I'M A STRANGER TO THIS NECK OF TH' WOODS.

THE BLUECOAT MAKES THE MISTAKE OF FOOLING WITH A TEXAN'S HAT.

THAT'S A DAMN LIE! I'VE SEEN YOU AROUND HERE OFTEN ENUFF.

I'LL GIVE YOU A CHANCE TO TAKE BACK THOSE WORDS.

DOBOY AND RAN SPENCER KEEP THE DOGS OFF.

HEY, WHAT'S GOIN'ON HERE?

ONE MOVE OUTTA YOU FELLERS AND LEAD WILL FLY.

THE SOLDIER STILL TRYING TO DRAW HIS PISTOL ON HAYS IS DEALT WITH BY DOBOY.

THAT'LL COOL HIM OFF..

WHACK

FEELING THE WARM GLOW OF HIS LIQUOR, MAJOR THOMPSON, THE BUREAU AGENT ATTACHED TO THE POST, INTERCEDES.

SURRENDER YOUR ARMS, IN THE NAME OF THE UNITED STATES ARMY!

HOLD ON CAP'T. WE AIN'T HURT NOBODY, AND WHUT WE DONE WUZ IN SELF-DEFENSE.

IN THAT CASE GIVE ME YOUR GUNS AND I'LL SEE YOU'RE TREATED FAIRLY.

THE BOYS, ALREADY DODGING ARREST WARRANTS, KNOW THAT THIS IS OUT OF THE QUESTION.

'FRAID NOT..

THEN, BY GOD, I'LL TAKE THEM!

MRS. THOMPSON, IN A BUGGY, RIDES UP JUST IN TIME TO SEE HER HUSBAND SHOT BETWEEN THE EYES.

ALEX!!

BLAM

A SERGEANT PULLS HIS GUN AND FALLS AS WELL, THE VICTIM OF DOBOY'S BLAZING REVOLVER.

I WARNED YA!

BLAM BLAM

COVERING THE OTHERS, THE BOYS CALMLY MOUNT UP AND RIDE OFF.

STAY PUT, GENTS.

RANCK

REMEMBERING THAT THEY HAD STASHED THEIR GRUB SACKS ON A TREE LIMB OUTSIDE THE STORE, HAYS RETURNS TO GET THEM. IT IS DEATHLY QUIET.

BUT NOT FOR LONG! SOON THE NEIGHBORHOOD IS SWARMING WITH SOLDIERS FROM FT. MASON.

THE TAYLORS RIDE HARD TO THE MILLIGAN PLACE WHERE THEY ARE STAYING WITH THEIR COUSIN GEORGE BIRD, WHO IS MARRIED TO MRS. MILLIGAN'S DAUGHTER MARY JANE.

PA, WE HAD TO SHOOT SOME MORE YANKEE SOLDIERS IN TOWN.

AND THEY WUZN'T NIGRAHS NEITHER!

CREED KNOWS THE FAT IS IN THE FIRE BAD THIS TIME.

MAKE FER HONEY CREEK BOYS. THEY WON'T BE FAR BEHIND!!

HAYS AND DOBOY ARE BARELY OUT OF SIGHT BEFORE A TROOP OF SOLDIERS GALLOP UP.

WHERE'S THOSE KIDS OF YOURS, OLD MAN?

GEORGE BIRD, WHO HAS BEEN BUTCHERING A HOG, WANDERS OUT OF THE BARN.

HAVEN'T SEEN 'EM SINCE THIS MORNING..

YOU! HOW'D YOU GET THAT BLOOD ON YOUR SHIRT?!

CREED AND FOUR OTHER MEN AT THE HOUSE ARE ARRESTED AND MARCHED AFOOT TO THE POST.

COME ON— STEP SMARTLY!

ALL ARE LATER RELEASED EXCEPT BIRD, WHO IS PLACED IN THE GUARDHOUSE.

A HOG, EH? LIKELY STORY..

THAT'S YANKEE BLOOD. ADMIT IT!

MEANWHILE CREED HAS MADE PLANS TO DEPART MASON COUNTY. HE HIRES GEORGE GAMEL TO GUIDE HIM AND THE BOYS OUT OF THE HILL COUNTRY BY REMOTE TRAILS.

WELL THAT HE DOES, FOR THE ALARM HAS BEEN SOUNDED, AND THE COUNTRY IS CRAWLING WITH BANDS OF ARMED MEN OUT FOR TAYLOR BLOOD!

ACTING ON THIS SUSPICION ONE MILITARY PARTY RAIDS THE ECLETO HOMEPLACE BEFORE CREED, HAYS, AND DOBOY ARRIVE, FINDING ONLY THE WOMEN THERE.

THEN *DO IT!* THIS IS MY HOUSE, BUILT WITH THE HONEST LABOR OF MY HUSBAND AND MY SONS, AND I'LL NOT TURN IT OVER TO A PASSEL OF DAMNED YANKEES!

YOUR HUSBAND HAS BEEN HUNG, AND YOUR SONS WILL SOON RECEIVE THE SAME! NOW COME OUT, I TELL YOU!!

IF SO, THEY'RE BOUND FOR A BETTER PLACE THAN THIS OLD WORLD.

I HEAR YOU YANKEES ARE EXPERTS AT BURNING OUT HELPLESS WOMEN AND CHILDREN, SO GIT TO IT, AND QUIT IDLING ABOUT!

REALIZING THEY CANNOT INTIMIDATE MRS. TAYLOR, THE SOLDIERS DEMAND FOOD AND FRESH HORSES.

OUR HORSES ARE IN TH' PAST-URE. AS I'M POWERLESS TO DEFEND THEM, TAKE WHAT YOU WANT!

BUT DARBY, CREED'S PRIDE AND JOY, IS NOT OUT TO PASTURE.

CAP'TN, LOOKY HERE!

WELL, WELL — SO THIS IS THE FAMOUS $7,000 FLYER!!

BLAST YER MANGY HIDES! YOU LEAVE THAT HORSE BE!!

CREED NEVER SEES DARBY AGAIN. HE HEARS THAT THE YANKEES RODE HIM TO DEATH OUT OF SHEER SPITE.

MILITARY RULE

AFTER THE RAID ON CREED'S HOUSE THE EXPEDITION GOES AFTER BUCK TAYLOR IN DEWITT COUNTY. AGAIN THE SOLDIERS DRAW A BLANK.

AT THIS POINT ANY TAYLOR WOULD SATISFY US.

THE MASON KILLING PROMPTS GEN. REYNOLDS TO PUT A $500 PRICE ON EACH OF THE TAYLOR BROTHERS' HEADS. MRS. THOMPSON MATCHES IT.

WHEW — THAT'S A LOT OF MONEY THESE DAYS!

JOHN LITTLETON OF HELENA, WHO SERVED AS A SENATOR IN THE 11th LEGISLATURE, PROMISES — IN THE "PUBLIC INTEREST" — TO COLLECT THE REWARD.

THE TAYLORS HAVE KILLED ONE TOO MANY GOOD MEN!

OTHERS TRY, WITH THE RESULT THAT CREED'S RANCH HOUSE BECOMES AN ARMED FORTRESS.

KEEP AWAY FROM THEM WINDOWS ELIZA.

HUNTED RELENTLESSLY AND DEPRIVED OF MAKING AN HONEST LIVING, SOME YOUNG MEN TURN TO SHIFTY OR UNLAWFUL MEANS. CHARLES TAYLOR, STILL ON THE LAM FOR KILLING JACK POLK AND NOW IN TROUBLE WITH THE UNION LEAGUE IN ATASCOSA COUNTY, MAKES A HABIT OF TRAILING STOLEN HORSES NORTH.

MORE MONEY IN IT THAN FOOLIN' WITH COWS..

IN MAR. 1868 A POSSE SETS OUT FROM CLINTON TO CATCH HIS GANG. ONE OF THE POSSE MEMBERS IS 22 YEAR OLD BILLY SUTTON.

BILLY, ONE OF THEM CROOKS IS RIDIN' A FANCY SILVER-MOUNTED SADDLE.

YOU WATCH. WHEN WE GET BACK, I'LL BE RIDING ON IT!

GENERAL MERCHANDISE

NEAR BASTROP SEVERAL OF THE HORSETHIEVES ARE CORNERED AND CHARLEY TAYLOR IS KILLED.

ANOTHER MAN, JAMES SHARPE, IS TAKEN INTO CUSTODY.

THERE'S A NOOSE WAITING FOR YOU BACK IN CLINTON, JIM.

HIS BODY IS LATER FOUND BESIDE THE ROAD, RIDDLED WITH BULLETS.

When the news reaches Jack Littleton, he approves.

An election is called to pick delegates to the new constitutional convention in Austin.

Formation of such organizations as the "Loyal Union League" to exploit the new negro vote gives rise to rival groups, like the Ku Klux Klan.

MANY OLD-LINE SOUTHERNERS (ESPECIALLY THOSE WITH ANY CONFEDERATE CONNECTION) FIND THEMSELVES DISENFRANCHISED AT THE POLLS.

NEGRO SUFFRAGE — LONG CONSIDERED A REMOTE POSSIBILITY BY ALL WHITE TEXANS—IS AT LAST A REALITY.

THE RETURNS ARE SENT DIRECTLY TO GEN. HANCOCK, THE COMMANDER WHO HAS TAKEN SHERIDAN'S PLACE AT FIFTH MILITARY HEADQUARTERS IN NEW ORLEANS.

DESPITE THE DEMOCRATIC SLOGAN "BETTER YANKEE THAN NIGGER RULE," REPUBLICAN CANDIDATES TRIUMPH.

THE MOST RADICAL OF THESE DELEGATES SOON GAIN CONTROL OF THE CONVENTION. THEIR SCHEMES ARE ENDLESS.

ONE THING THAT THE REPUBLICAN DELEGATES ARE AGREED UPON IS THE NEED TO SUPPRESS VIOLENCE, WHICH HAS BECOME ENDEMIC THROUGHOUT TEXAS.

WHILE THIS "MONGREL" CONVENTION SLOPS AT THE PUBLIC TROUGH — ADDRESSING SUBJECTS FAR REMOVED FROM THE WRITING OF A CONSTITUTION — RACIAL TROUBLES PROLIFERATE.

AT PLACES LIKE THE TOWN OF MILLICAN THERE ARE PITCHED BATTLES FOUGHT.

BUT USUALLY THE THREATS COME IN MORE SINISTER WAYS.

WHUT IS IT DAHLIN?

UH WAHNIN' FROM DUH KLUCKERS..

TYPICAL OF THE DAILY CONFRONTATIONS IN REMOTE CORNERS OF TEXAS IS THE ONE INVOLVING 15 YEAR OLD WES HARDIN. VISITING HIS UNCLE BARNETT IN POLK COUNTY, WES AND A COUSIN GET INTO A WRESTLING MATCH WITH AN EX-SLAVE NAMED MAGE.

C'MON BOYS! YOU CAN THROW TH' BLACK OX!

GRAB HIS LEG!

THEY THROW HIM ONCE BUT ON THEIR SECOND GO, MAGE'S FACE GETS SCRATCHED.

NO WHITE BOY DRAWS MY BLOOD AN' LIVES— NOT NO MORE!

THE NEGRO STORMS OFF IN A RAGE.

YOU'LL DIE FOR DIS'— SOON AS MAGE GETS A GUN!

LEARNING OF THE INCIDENT, BARNETT HARDIN ORDERS MAGE OFF HIS PLANTATION.

YOU GIT ON OUTTA HERE. AIN'T GOT NO ROOM FOR CRAZY NIGRAHS ON THIS PLACE!

RETURNING HOME THE NEXT MORNING, WES ENCOUNTERS THE FREEDMAN ON THE ROAD.

SO DERE YOU IS, YOU LITTL' COWARD!

WES TRIES TO GET AWAY, BUT HIS HORSE IS VERY POOR AND THE NEGRO VERY PERSISTENT.

AH'L KILL YOU NOW, YOU WHITE TRASH— SICCIN' YO' FOLKS ON ME!

LET MY HORSE GO! I'M WARNING YOU!!

YOU THINKS YOU IS AWFUL BIG WID DAT OL' GUN, DONCHA?

BACK, DAMN' YOU!

BLAM

MAGE KEEPS COMING AND WESLEY KEEPS PUMPING SLUGS INTO HIM.

BLAM BLAM

SCARED OUT OF HIS WITS YOUNG HARDIN RIDES TO THE FARM OF HIS UNCLE CLABE HOULSHOUSEN, MAGE'S FORMER OWNER.

IS HE DEAD??

I DON'T THINK SO. HE WUZ STILL CUSSIN' ME WHEN I RODE OFF.

THEY GO BACK AND FIND MAGE STILL ALIVE AND FULL OF FIGHT.

DAT BOY'S A LIAR! AH' NEVER TOUCHED HIS HOSS!

DON'T, WES. HE CAN'T LIVE LONG CARRYIN' THAT MUCH LEAD.

HERE, TAKE MY $20 GOLD PIECE AND SKEDADDLE FOR HOME—THE BUREAU AGENTS WILL BE AFTER YOU!!

WES TELLS HIS HORRIFIED PARENTS THE STORY.

..AND I WOULD HAVE FINISHED HIM OFF FOR CALLIN' ME A LIAR IF UNCLE CLABE HADN'T STOPPED ME.

AFTER QUIETLY CONSIDERING THE OPTIONS, REV. HARDIN SPEAKS...

SON, TO BE TRIED NOWA-DAYS FOR KILLIN' A NIGRAH MEANS YOU'LL BE EXECUTED, NO TWO WAYS ABOUT IT!

YOU MUST GO INTO HIDING TILL JUSTICE IS SERVED OTHER THAN AT THE POINT OF A YANKEE BAYONET.

GOD WILLING, THAT TIME WILL NOT BE LONG!

SO JOHN WESLEY HARDIN — LIKE MANY OTHER YOUNG TEXANS — GOES ON THE DODGE, HIS HATRED FOR THE OPPRESSOR BURNING WHITE-HOT.

A MAN OUGHTA' HAVE TH' RIGHT TO DEFEND HISSELF!

BACK ON THE COASTAL PLAINS, JOHN LITTLETON'S DETERMINATION TO HAVE THE $2,000 REWARD FOR THE TAYLOR BOYS ALSO BURNS BRIGHT. BUT LITTLETON, A STICKLER FOR LEGAL NICETIES, WANTS EVERYTHING ON THE UP-AND-UP.

GENERAL, IF YOU'LL DRAW UP THE OFFICIAL WRITS, I'LL BRING YOU THE TAYLORS ON A PLATTER!

IN EARLY DECEMBER HE AND A COMPANION, BILL STANNARD, LEAVE SAN ANTONIO WITH MILITARY ORDERS FOR THE ARREST OF THE BOYS, DEAD OR ALIVE.

NOW IT'S ALL LEGAL AND PROPER.

THEY TAKE THE OLD GONZALES ROAD, UNAWARE THAT THE TAYLOR BROTHERS HAVE LEARNED OF THEIR ERRAND

THIS OL' DEEP SAND MAKES FOR SLOW GOIN' DON'T IT, BILL ??

IT'S A GOD-FORSAKEN STRETCH, ALRIGHT..

...AND AWAIT THEM AT BLACK JACK SPRING, NEAR THE TINY COMMUNITY OF NOCKENUT !

THAT'S THEM FER SURE.. I'D RECOGNIZE THAT LARD-ASS STANNARD ANYWHERE !

HOWDY JACK. WHERE YOU FELLERS OFF TO ?

NOT LOOKIN' FER US BY ANY CHANCE, ARE YOU ??

THEIR GUNS ARE STASHED UNDER THE BUGGY SEAT. LITTLETON AND STANNARD BOTH GO FOR THEM AT THE SAME TIME, KNOCKING HEADS.

KLONK

BEFORE THEY REACH THEIR PISTOLS, BOTH MEN ARE SHOT FULL OF HOLES.

WHEN THE SPOOKED HORSE FINALLY COMES TO A HALT, HAYS GOES THROUGH LITTLETON'S COAT POCKET.

I'LL JUST TAKE THESE HERE PAPERS, CAPTN. DON'T RECKON YOU'LL BE NEEDEN THEM.

WITH THE KILLING OF THESE TWO FORMER REBELS, NOW IN THE PAY OF THE RECONSTRUCTIONISTS, THE TAYLOR BOYS BRING THE WRATH OF THE MILITARY DOWN UPON THE HEADS OF ALL THEIR KINSMEN.

CREED'S DEWITT COUNTY RELATIVES ARE SOON DRAWN INTO THE RING OF FIRE.

CLINTON TEXAS

BAD BLOOD HAS BEEN BREWING BETWEEN THEM AND BILLY SUTTON'S CROWD SINCE THE KILLING OF BLACK-SHEEP CHARLEY TAYLOR.

LOOK HOW HE *STRUTS* AROUND WITH CHARLEY'S GOLD BUTTONS SEWED ON HIS VEST.

BUT THE DEAD HORSETHIEF WAS NOT THE ONLY MAN ON THE FRONTIER TO DEAL IN HORSES OF DUBIOUS OWNERSHIP — AS BUCK TAYLOR SOON LEARNS.

BUCK, THEM HORSES THAT SUTTON PUT IN WITH YOUR LAST DRIVE — THEY WASN'T *HIS*.

IS THAT SO?

CONFRONTED WITH THIS ACCUSATION, BILLY DENIES THAT THE HORSES WERE STOLEN, AND THERE THE MATTER RESTS...

I'M STILL WONDER-ING HOW HE CAME BY THOSE ANIMALS..

WELL, HE DIDN'T RAISE THEM, NOR BUY THEM, SO YOU FIGURE IT OUT!!

...UNTIL CHRISTMAS EVE, WHEN BUCK AND HIS COUSIN DICK CHISHOLM SPOT BILLY SUTTON IN A CLINTON SALOON.

RAISE YA TWO BITS!

LET'S TELL OL' HOT-SHOT WHAT WE THINK OF HIM!

BILLY, DON'T LET TH' SUN GO DOWN ON YOU AGAIN IN DEWITT COUNTY!

WITH SUTTON IS DOC WHITE, ANOTHER MAN WHO RODE ON THE POSSE.

IF YOU'RE LOOKIN' TO START SOMETHING, WHY WAIT TILL SUNDOWN?!

THE ROOM EXPLODES WITH GUNFIRE, AND BUCK TAYLOR SLUMPS TO THE FLOOR.

(223)

DICK CHISHOLM STUMBLES OUTSIDE AND IS FINISHED OFF.

OUTRAGED OVER THESE DEATHS, THE TAYLOR CLAN TRIES TO BRING BILLY SUTTON TO TRIAL BUT FAILS.

THEN, BY GOD, WE'LL SEND MR. SUTTON BEFORE A HIGHER COURT!

YOUNG BILLY SUTTON THUS BECOMES ENSNARED IN THE FEUD, AND HIS SUPPORTERS ARE SOON KNOWN AS "THE SUTTON PARTY."

LET 'EM GRIPE.. IT WUZ A FAIR FIGHT!

YEP.

PERHAPS SENSING THE VOLATILE SITUATION, THE FIFTH MILITARY DISTRICT SETS UP A POST AT HELENA THE FOLLOWING MONTH, WITH JURISDICTION OVER ALL OF KARNES, DEWITT, GONZALES, GOLIAD, AND BEE COUNTIES.

GEN. J.J. REYNOLDS, THE TOP AUTHORITY IN TEXAS, RECRUITS MEN TO DISPOSE OF THE OFFENDING TAYLORS AND OTHER UNRECONSTRUCTED REBS LIKE THEM. TWO WHO OFFER THEIR SERVICES ARE CAPT. C.S. BELL, A FORMER UNION SPY, AND JACK HELM, THE HIRED THUG WHO RODE SHANGHAI PIERCE'S RANGE LOOKING FOR "RUSTLERS."

REMEMBER— THE ELEMENT OF SURPRISE IS A POWERFUL WEAPON.

WE GET YOUR DRIFT, GENERAL.

THEY BOTCH THEIR FIRST ATTEMPT, MERELY WOUNDING CREED'S SON-IN-LAW, WILL AD SPENCER.

BLAST! WE'LL NEVER CATCH THEM OUT THERE! THEY KNOW EVERY NOOK AND CRANNY OF THIS NEIGHBORHOOD!

HELM GOES TO AUSTIN FOR SPECIFIC ORDERS AND MAKES A BIG HIT WITH THE SCUM IN CHARGE.

MR. HELM, YOU'RE JUS' TH' MAN WE NEED! GO BACK DOWN THERE AND PRESS TH' LOYAL CITIZENS INTO SERVICE

SPARE NO EXPENSE, LEAVE NO ROCK UN-TURNED!

GOOD PAYING JOBS ARE HARD TO FIND, AND JACK IS NOT MODEST ABOUT HIS DIPLOMATIC COUP AT THE CAPITAL.

BY GOD, I'M THE MAN, AIN'T I ??

DRINKS ARE ON ME, BOYS!

DURING THE SUMMER MONTHS OF 1869 HELM'S REGULATORS BRING TERROR TO THE PASTURE-LANDS BETWEEN DEWITT COUNTY AND THE COAST.

THEY'RE MEXES THIS TIME.

HUMPH! CAN'T NOTCH MY GUN ON BEANERS!

THIS SYSTEMATIC ONSLAUGHT CLAIMS OVER TWENTY LIVES AND FORCES MOST RESIDENTS OF THE REGION TO CHOOSE SIDES — OR BE CONSIDERED ENEMIES BY BOTH! RANCHER JOHN CHOATE'S CHOICE IS TYPICAL.

HOWDY JOHN WHAT BRINGS YOU CALLIN'?

BIG TROUBLE, JOE. TH' PEACES JUS' SHOWED UP ON MY DOOR-STEP. VIGILANTS IS AFTER THEM.

DON'T SURPRISE ME.. THEY'RE TH' ONES WHAT KILLED SHERIFF JACOBS OVER IN GOLIAD COUNTY.

JOE, WE WANT YOU TO JOIN US. TOGETHER WE CAN WHIP THAT DAMNED RASCAL HELM AND PUT THIS COUNTRY BACK ON ITS FEET!

NOW JOHN, HELM IS A GOOD MAN, ACTING UNDER LEGITIMATE AUTHORITY. I'VE SUPPORTED HIM IN THE PAST, AND WILL DO SO AGAIN.

CONVINCED THAT TUMLINSON IS A HOPELESS CASE, CHOATE RIDES TO THE TAYLOR RANCH.

CREED, YOUR TUMLINSON BROTHER-IN-LAW IS A HELM'S MAN.

YES, I HAVE SUSPECTED IT WOULD COME TO THAT.

TURNS OUT STAPP WAS KILLED BY HIM WHEN TH' PEACE BOYS FLED TO MY HOUSE!

YOU'D BETTER FORT UP, JOHN. TH' VIGILANTS WILL BE ON YOU NOW THAT THEY KNOW WHERE YOU STAND.

SO THE CHOATE RANCH IN SAN PATRICIO COUNTY PREPARES FOR WAR. FIFTY MEN, ALL ON HELM'S BLACKLIST, GATHER SUPPLIES AND PUT THE HOUSE IN FIGHTING TRIM.

LET 'EM COME. WE GOT ENOUGH AMMO TO HOLD OUT FER MONTHS!

ABOUT DAYBREAK ONE MORNING, HELM, COX, TUMLINSON, AND 125 MEN STORM THE HOUSE.

CHOATE MEAT FOR BREAKFAST!

THIS RASH RECRUIT IS DRILLED, AND THE CHOATES BARRICADE THE DOOR.

THE ASSAULT DEGENERATES INTO A STAND-OFF. MRS. CHOATE CALLS FOR A PARLEY.

MY HUSBAND WILL SURRENDER, IF YOU POSSESS LAWFUL AUTHORITY FOR HIS ARREST.

MADAME, I HAVE THE HIGHEST AUTHORITY IN THE LAND!

JOHN CHOATE, ACCOMPANIED BY SEVERAL OTHERS, STEPS OUT WITH HANDS HELD HIGH..

COME ON OUT, GENTS— YOU WON'T BE MOLESTED!

BUT A TRIGGER-HAPPY VIGILANT FILLS A YOUNG MAN NAMED SKIDMORE WITH BUCKSHOT, AND ALL HELL BREAKS LOOSE IN SOUTH TEXAS.

BLOOM!

⟨227⟩

JOHN CHOATE IS KILLED, AND HIS SON CROCKETT BOLTS FROM THE HOUSE, SIX-SHOOTER IN HAND.

THE ENTIRE POSSE RUSHES AFTER HIM.

QUITE SATISFIED WITH THE MORNING WORK, HELM'S MEN RIFLE THE PREMISES AND COMPELL THE DISTRAUGHT WIDOW TO FIX THEM BREAKFAST.

MAY YOU ROT IN HELL FOR THIS, JOE TUMLINSON — AND YOU TOO, JIM COX!

BLAME US NOT FOR THE FOLLY OF YOUR MENFOLKS, MA'M.

SHORTLY AFTER THIS RAID, HELM DECIDES TO FINISH OFF THE TAYLORS, HAYS AND DOBOY.

IF THEY'RE NOT THERE, SECURE THE HOUSE AND SET UP AN AMBUSH.

HE SENDS A SQUAD UNDER CAPT. BELL DIRECTLY TO THE ECLETO RANCH, WHILE TAKING A LEISURELY ROUTE HIMSELF TO DIVERT ATTENTION FROM BELL'S OPERATION.

CAN'T BE TOO CAREFUL WITH THESE VARMITS.

BELL'S MEN MOVE IN AT NIGHT.

WHERE'S YOUR BOYS, MR. TAYLOR?

THEY AIN'T HERE. GONE TO LOUISIANA WITH SOME HORSES.

THEY MAKE HOSTAGES OF CREED AND THE WOMEN AND SETTLE DOWN TO WAIT.

YOU MEN FAN OUT. WE'LL SEE WHAT DAYLIGHT BRINGS.

AS USUAL, HAYS, DOBOY, AND A FRIEND NAMED WESTFALL HAVE BEEN SLEEPING OUT TO AVOID CAPTURE.

HOPE ELIZA'S GOT BREAKFAST READY— I'M STARVED!!

ME TOO.

DOBOY ALREADY HAS ONE FOOT ON THE GROUND WHEN HIS WIFE SCREAMS A WARNING.

RUN PHILLIP! YANKEES!!

WESTFALL IS HIT BY THE HAIL OF BULLETS.

DOBOY TAKES A SLUG IN THE ARM, AND HIS MARE—SHOT IN THE VITALS—COLLAPSES AFTER A 300-YARD DASH.

HE MAKES HIS ESCAPE THROUGH A CORN PATCH.

BUT NOT HAYS. SEEING HIS FATHER HELD IN THE GALLERY, HE DETERMINES TO RESCUE HIM—

HAYS, GO! GET AWAY FROM HERE!

— OR DIE TRYING!

BELL'S MEN DUMP HIS MANGLED CORPSE IN THE DOGTROT AND REFUSE TO ALLOW THE GRIEVING PARENTS TO TOUCH HIM.

IF YOU'D RAISED YOUR BOYS PROPERLY, NONE OF THIS WOULD HAVE HAPPENED.

CREED IS TAKEN TO HELENA AND HELD FOR A MONTH IN THE "BULL PEN" BEFORE BEING RELEASED ON $10,000 BOND.

DAMN' YANKEES..

RETURNING HOME HE VISITS HIS SON'S UNMARKED GRAVE ON THE ECLETO.

BELL GOT TH' BLOOD MONEY FOR YOU SON, BUT IT'LL BURN HIS HANDS BAD — I PROMISE YOU THAT!

BUT THE BLOODY SPOT ON THE DOGTROT'S ROUGH TIMBERS WON'T WASH OUT. IT IS NOT LONG BEFORE CREED MOVES TO THE HILL COUNTRY, FAR FROM SUCH GRIM REMINDERS.

DOBOY LEAVES THE STATE, AS DO OTHERS IN THE WAKE OF HELM'S BRUTAL SUMMER CAMPAIGN.

IN SEPT. 1869 JACK HELM PUBLISHES AN ACCOUNT OF HIS ACTIONS, DEFENDING HIMSELF OF ANY WRONG-DOING.

LIKE IT SEZ, "THE LAW-ABIDING CITIZEN IS MY FRIEND, THE DESPERADO MY ENEMY"— AND THAT IS DEFENSE ENOUGH!

VICTORIA ADV
SEPTEMBER 23, 1869

TO THE PEOPLE OF TEXAS—
LUCKY TO HAVE STATE OFFI-CER HELM.

HIS ACTIVITIES ARE WIDELY HAILED IN THE REPUBLICAN NEWS-PAPERS AND DENOUNCED IN THOSE PUBLISHED BY DEMOCRATS.

LISSEN AT THIS: "FOR REYNOLDS TO CONVEY THIS SORT OF POWER TO AN IRRE-SPONSIBLE MAN IS BEYOND THE PALE!"

HAVING DISPOSED OF CREED'S UNRULY SONS, THE REGULATORS SEEK OTHER CULPRITS.

BOYS, MARTIN TAYLOR IS HIDIN' OUT DOWN IN McMULLEN COUNTY.

COME NOVEMBER TUMLINSON'S PARTY RIDES TO DAVE MORRIS' RANCH JUST NORTH OF THE FRIO RIVER.

WE'RE TAKIN' YOU TO OAKVILLE, MART. COME QUIETLY..

OLD MAN MORRIS OFFERS TO ACCOMPANY THEM AS BONDSMAN FOR HIS DAUGHTER'S HUSBAND.

CHANCES OF THEM TRYIN' SOMETHING ARE LESS WITH WITNESSES.

COWHANDS FROM THE NEIGHBORING DILWORTH RANCH LATER FIND THEIR BODIES IN A REMOTE GULLY.

THEY'LL CALL IT "ANOTHER ATTEMPTED ESCAPE!"

MARTIN'S YOUNGER BROTHER RUFAS "SCRAP" TAYLOR VOWS VENGEANCE.

HE WHO SHEDS A TAYLOR'S BLOOD, BY A TAYLOR'S HAND MUST FALL.

THE STATE POLICE!

THAT SAME MONTH THE RADICAL ELEMENT AIMS TO COMPLETE ITS STRANGLEHOLD ON TEXAS POLITICS BY "ELECTING" E.J. DAVIS AS GOVERNOR.

HAMILTON'S SO-CALLED "CONSERVATIVES" MEAN TO SUBVERT THE GOALS OF RECONSTRUCTION.

HELL, THEY'RE ALL EX-REBS.

GEN. REYNOLDS, CRAVING POLITICAL FAME, TRIES TO GET HIMSELF NOMINATED AS A CANDIDATE FOR THE U·S· SENATE. REBUFFED BY MODERATES, HE THROWS HIS WEIGHT BEHIND THE DAVIS FACTION.

I'LL TEACH THEM TO BITE THE HAND THAT FEEDS 'EM.

PRESIDENT GRANT ALSO ENDORSES THE DAVIS TICKET, VIRTUALLY GUARANTEEING THE RESULT.

THINGS ARE MOVING TOO SLOW DOWN THERE TO SUIT ME!!

No. 5
Events in TEXAS

THE POLLS ARE GUARDED BY YANKEE SOLDIERS; THE REGISTRARS USE HIGHLY RESTRICTIVE VOTING LISTS.

BY CHOICE OR BY EXCLUSION, MANY WHITES STAY AWAY FROM THE FARCE.

LET'S GO FISHING INSTEAD.

REYNOLDS ANNOUNCES THE FINAL TALLY: 39,901 FOR DAVIS, 39,092 FOR HAMILTON.

ONE WONDERS WHY HE EVEN BOTHERED TO CALL IT SO CLOSE.

ELECTION RESULTS!

DAVIS WINS

IN APRIL 1870, GEN. REYNOLDS RELINQUISHES MILITARY AUTHORITY TO THE DAVIS REGIME. ONE OF THE GOVERNOR'S FIRST ACTS IS TO PUSH THE "POLICE AND MILITIA" BILL THROUGH THE LEGISLATURE.

DUE TO THE LAWLESS-NESS IN MANY PARTS OF TEXAS, WE MUST TAKE APPROPRIATE AND TIMELY MEASURES!

TO DO SO, HE HAS TO ARREST AND HOLD CAPTIVE EIGHT OPPOSING SENATORS.

TEXAS WILL RUE THE DAY THIS INFERNAL MACHINE WAS CREATED!!

THUS BEGINS THE INFAMOUS STATE POLICE, AN ORGANIZATION THAT TAKES UP WHERE THE U.S. MILITARY-SANCTIONED REGULATORS LEAVE OFF.

ARE YOU FELLOWS LOYAL MEN?

YAS'SUH!

WAHL, MAKE ME YOUR MARK RAT' HERE!

JAMES DAVIDSON IS NAMED ADJ. GENERAL OF THE FORCE AND JACK HELM, RECENTLY ELECTED AS SHERIFF OF DEWITT COUNTY, IS APPOINTED ONE OF THE FOUR CAPTAINS UNDER HIM.

YESSIR, I'M THE MAN, AIN'T I?

HELM RECRUITS HIS OLD GANG — JIM COX, JOE TUMLINSON, AND BILL SUTTON — TO SERVE HIS DISTRICT.

BOYS, WE'RE GONNA' KICK ASS AND TAKE NAMES AND IT'S ALL LEGAL.

STATE POLICE

SUTTON QUICKLY ASSUMES A LEADERSHIP ROLE.

ME, I GOT JUST TWO CHOICES: TO GRAB THE BULL BY THE HORNS, OR GET OUT OF THE COUNTRY.

ONE OF THEIR FIRST MOVES IS AGAINST THE LUNNS AND "ALL JAW" SMITH, WHO HAVE SET UP A GREASE KETTLE ON SHANGHAI PIERCE'S RANGE.

SHANG, YOU SON-OF-A-BITCH! YOU TAUGHT ME HOW TO STEAL TH' FIRST COW I EVER STOLE!

THAT TAKES CARE OF THEM PESTS!

BUT ONE OF THE LUNN BROTHERS, WILBORN, ESCAPES THE LYNCHING AND VOWS TO MAKE THINGS HOT FOR THE CATTLEBARON CROWD.

YOU'LL PAY FOR THIS WORK MR. PIERCE.

(235)

NEXT THE POLICEMEN RIDE TO PITKIN TAYLOR'S NEIGHBORHOOD JUST SOUTH OF CUERO WHERE HE (CREED'S BROTHER) LIVES WITH HIS KELLY SONS-IN-LAW.

IF THERE'S ANY TROUBLE, YOU KNOW WHAT TO DO..

WILLIAM KELLY IS ARRESTED AT HIS HOUSE AND LEFT WITH BILLY SUTTON.

KEEP HIM ON ICE. WE'LL STOP BACK BY AFTER WE GET HENRY.

HENRY'S WIFE, AMANDA TAYLOR, SEES THEM RIDE UP.

HONEY, THERE'S SOME MEN AT TH' GATE..

A FEW DAYS SINCE, THE KELLY FAMILIES ATTENDED A "CIRCUS" IN SWEET HOME, FOUND THE ENTERTAINMENT LEWD, AND SHOT THE LIGHTS OUT IN DISGUST.

WE WANT YOU TO COME WITH US TO HALLETSVILLE.

OH, ABOUT THAT CIRCUS DEAL?

THINKING THE MATTER INCONSEQUENTIAL, HE GOES IN THE HOUSE FOR HIS HAT AND GUNBELT.

YOU WON'T NEED THAT PISTOL, HENRY. CONSIDER YOURSELF UNDER ARREST.

WAHL OKAY, BUT I GOT TO GO CATCH MY HORSE..

PITKIN IS UP BY NOW AND COMES OUT TO MAKE CONVERSATION.

HOW'S THINGS OVER IN LAVACA COUNTY, DOC?

BAD. WE GOT MARTIAL LAW AND PEOPLE IS BEIN' BLACKLISTED.

AMANDA, GROWING ALARMED, HITCHES UP THE BUGGY AND DRIVES TO THE HOUSE OF WILLIAM DAY, HER HALF-BROTHER, TO WAIT FOR THE POSSE TO COME BY.

WHAT'S TH' MATTER, AMANDA?

SOME POLICE HAS GOT HENRY AND BILL. I'M SCAIRT ABOUT IT..

DELILAH KELLY CLIMBS INTO THE BUGGY.

WELL, LET'S GO ALONG. THEY WON'T TRY NUTHIN' WITH WOMEN PRESENT.

THEY RETRACE THEIR ROUTE AND MEET THE POSSE, STRUNG OUT ALONG THE ROAD.

WELL, YALL TOOK SO LONG WE GOT UNEASY.

AMANDA, WHAT'S YOU AND MA DOIN' OUT HERE?

THEIR UNEASINESS INCREASES WHEN THE POSSE INSISTS ON TAKING THEIR PRISONERS BY A NARROW, OUT-OF-THE-WAY TRAIL.

BUT TH' MAIN ROAD IS CLOSER.

NO, THIS WAY IS CLOSER—AND WE WILL USE IT!

MOTHER KELLY, I DON'T LIKE THE LOOKS OF THEM MEN. THEY IS UP TO NO GOOD.

AMANDA HEADS OUT ON FOOT THROUGH THE BRUSH.

FROM THE BROW OF A HILL SHE SEES THE POSSE, STOPPED IN A LITTLE CLEARING BELOW.

HER BROTHER-IN-LAW DISMOUNTS TO FILL HIS PIPE. AS HE KNEELS, BILLY SUTTON SHOOTS HIM DOWN.

BLAM

DOC WHITE THEN BLASTS HER HUSBAND OUT OF THE SADDLE.

MY GOD, MY GOD!!

SOMEONE'S COMIN'!

LET'S GET OUTTA HERE!

PITKIN TAYLOR RESOLVES TO BRING THE MURDERERS OF HIS SONS-IN-LAW TO JUSTICE. AFFIDAVITS ON THE KILLING ARE SWORN OUT AND PRINTED IN THE PAPERS.

WHAT HAPPENED THEN?

SUTTON DREW HIS PISTOL..

TELEGRAPH & TEXAS REGISTER

STATE SENATOR BOLIVAR PRIDGEN DENOUNCES DAVIS' STATE POLICE AND THE "INFAMOUS WRETCHES" WHO FILL ITS RANKS.

HELM IS AN UNSCRUPULOUS LIAR, IGNORANT, RECKLESS, AND INDISCREET!

THIS, OF COURSE, EARNS HIM THE SYMPATHY OF THE TAYLOR PARTY, AND THE UNDYING HATRED OF HELM'S CROWD.

SENATOR, YOU KNOW NOT THE MURDEROUS BAND THAT STANDS READY TO DO HIS BIDDING! THEY'LL KILL YOU TOO!

THEN LET THEM— BUT IN SO DOING, THEY WILL BRING THEIR OWN HOUSE DOWN.

HELM HAS OVERPLAYED HIS HAND THIS TIME. BECAUSE OF THE PUBLIC OUTCRY, HE IS FIRED FROM THE STATE POLICE.

THAT'S ALRIGHT.. I'M STILL SHERIFF OF DE-WITT COUNTY, BY GOD!

WANTED

WANTED

REWARD

WANTED

DEA

(239)

MEANWHILE, THE YOUNG FUGITIVE JOHN WESLEY HARDIN HAS BEEN CONSTANTLY ON THE RUN FROM THE YANKEE OVERLORDS.

HE HAS BECOME A COWBOY AND ADOPTED SOME BAD HABITS. DRINKING, GAMBLING, AND GUNPLAY ARE HIS WAY OF LIFE.

THIS IS A SQUARE HOUSE

THERE'S ONLY FOUR ACES IN A DECK OF CARDS, MISTER.

EACH TIME HE KILLS, HE FINDS HIS FATHER FORGIVING.

WELL, IF IT WAS FORCED UPON YOU SON, IT'S NOT YOUR FAULT. IT'S TH' TIMES..

HIDING AT HIS UNCLE BOB HARDIN'S FARM AT BRENHAM, WES TAKES IN THE SIGHTS AT NEARBY EVERGREEN.

THERE HE MEETS BILL LONGLEY, A TEXAS BADMAN IN ALMOST AS MUCH TROUBLE WITH THE YANKEES AS HIMSELF.

I CALL YOU.. WHATCHA' GOT?

"ACES OVER!"

"HOLD ON — I GOT TWO PAIR!"

"HA! TWO PAIR AIN'T WORTH A DAMN' AGAINST A FULL HOUSE!"

"YES, BUT NOT IF THEY'RE TWO PAIR OF JACKS!"

WES MOVES FREQUENTLY ONCE THE STATE POLICE IS ESTABLISHED. NONETHELESS, HE IS ARRESTED AT LONGVIEW ON A CASE OF MISTAKEN IDENTITY.

"WAHL, THERE'S A MAN WANTED DOWN AT WACO ON A BARBERSHOP KILLIN' AND YOU FIT TH' DESCRIPTION!"

HE PLANS TO ESCAPE DURING THE TRIP TO WACO.

"I'M GETTIN' OUT SOON. I GOT THIS OL' COLT I'LL SELL YOU.."

WES WHINES AND WHIMPERS UNTIL HIS GUARDS ARE LULLED INTO COMPLACENCY.

"PLEASE DON'T HURT ME, MR. SMOLLY. I WON'T DO NUTHIN'."

"HA! WHAT A WIMP!"

WHEN CAPT. STOKES GOES OFF TO GET THE HORSES SOME FODDER, HARDIN MAKES HIS MOVE.

"HANDS UP, DAMN' YOU!"

JIM SMOLLY DIES BECAUSE "HE DID NOT HAVE SENSE ENOUGH TO THROW UP HIS HANDS AT THE POINT OF A PISTOL".

AFTER ANOTHER HARROWING ESCAPE—AND THE DEATH OF THREE MORE "POLICEMEN"—REV. HARDIN REALIZES THAT HIS SON MUST QUIT THE COUNTRY.

GO TO MEXICO, SON, THE CLEMENTS BOYS WILL HELP YOU FIND YOUR WAY.

God bless our home

SO JOHN WESLEY, AGE 18, RIDES SOUTH—LEAVING A TRAIL OF TWELVE DEAD MEN BEHIND HIM.

THERE'D BEEN MORE, IF I'D HAD MY DRUTHERS..

HIS CLEMENTS COUSINS CAUSE HIM TO CHANGE HIS PLANS.

HELL, COME WITH US—WE'RE FIXIN' TO TRAIL A HERD TO KANSAS.

THEY DON'T SERVE TEXAS PAPERS UP THERE!

BY THE END OF FEBRUARY 1871, THE HERD IS FORMED AND READY TO GO. WES AND COUSIN JIM ARE HIRED TO BOSS IT, WITH ANOTHER HERD UNDER MANNING, GIP, AND JOE FOLLOWING CLOSE BEHIND.

ABERLINE,* HERE WE COME!

* THE TEXANS CALLED ABILENE "ABERLINE".

SEVERAL WEEKS LATER THEY CROSS INTO INDIAN TERRITORY AT RED RIVER STATION; THE TRAIL NORTH IS CLOGGED WITH CATTLE

THEIR PASSAGE THROUGH INDIAN COUNTRY IS FULL OF NEW EXPERIENCES FOR THE BOYS.

GOD ALMIGHTY! LISTEN TO THEM WOLVES HOWLIN'..

THEY SMELL OUR BEEF!

NEARING KANSAS THEY ARE SUBJECTED TO A CUSTOM LOATHED BY ALL TEXAS DROVERS.

CATTLE TAX, FOR US CROSSIN' THEIR LAND..

IT'S STRAIGHT-OUT ROBBERY, IF YOU ASK ME!

〈243〉

FINALLY WEARYING OF THE EXTORTION, WES WHACKS AN OSAGE WITH HIS PISTOL.

KLUNK

NO MORE I SAID!

YOU LET ME CUT OUT FAT WHOA-HA OR I KILL ONE!

SHOOT THAT STEER AND I'LL SHOOT YOU!

BOTH MEN FOLLOW THROUGH ON THEIR THREATS. THE DEAD INDIAN IS TIED TO HIS HARD-WON BEEF.

..MAYBE HIS BUDDIES WILL GET TH' MESSAGE!

NOT LONG AFTER THEIR HERD PASSES INTO KANSAS, MORE TROUBLE DEVELOPS.

THEM MESKINS BEHIND US IS CROWDIN' OUR STEERS AND GETTIN' ALL MIXED IN..

ONE THING LEADS TO ANOTHER UNTIL A PITCHED BATTLE ERRUPTS BETWEEN THE TWO CAMPS.

⟨244⟩

AFTERWARDS, THE RED-NECKED VICTORS CONDUCT A BODY COUNT OF THEIR FALLEN FOES.

OUT OF THE SIX, I FIGURE WES NAILED FIVE.

REACHING ABILENE WITHOUT FURTHER MAYHEM, THEY DELIVER THE HERD AND GO INTO TOWN TO COLLECT THEIR PAY.

WAHL HERE IT IS BOYS—TH' FASTEST TOWN THIS SIDE OF SODOM.

ABILENE IS A FAST TOWN INDEED, FILLED WITH YOUNG TEXANS EAGER TO BLOW OFF A LITTLE STEAM AFTER THE LONG DRIVE. PRESIDING OVER THE FESTIVITIES IS JAMES B. HICKOK, BETTER KNOWN AS "WILD BILL".

A MAN'S GOTTA' MAKE A LIVING SOMEHOW..

ONE OF THE COWBOYS' FAVORITE HANGOUTS IN THE "TEXAS SECTION" IS THE BULL'S HEAD SALOON, RUN BY A COUPLE OF GAMBLERS FROM THE LONE STAR STATE NAMED BEN THOMPSON AND PHIL COE.

HAW! LOOK AT TH' BALLS ON THAT BULL, WILL YA?

THAT SIGN IS TH' DANGEST THING I EVER SAW!

THOMPSON THINKS THAT HICKOK IS PREJUDICED AGAINST SOUTHERNERS — TEXANS ESPECIALLY— AND TRIES TO GET WES TO DO HIS DIRTY WORK.

IF HE NEEDS KILLIN' WHY DON'T YOU DO IT YOURSELF?

I'D RATHER GET SOMEBODY ELSE TO DO IT..

WHEN HICKOK SENDS A CREW OF PAINTERS OVER TO ALTER THE OFFENDING BOVINE, RELATIONS WITH THE TEXAN PROPRIETORS SINK TO AN ALL-TIME LOW.

THERE'LL BE TROUBLE OVER THIS, BILL.

THAT'S WHAT I'M COUNTIN' ON!

BULLS HEAD SALOON

WILD BILL HAS A STRICT RULE AGAINST FIREARMS IN TOWN AND HE TRIES TO ENFORCE IT ON HARDIN.

TAKE THOSE PISTOLS OFF AND BE QUICK ABOUT IT!

LENE

WES PRESENTS HIS HARDWARE, BUTTS FIRST.

ALRIGHT, IF THAT'S THE WAY YOU FEEL ABOUT IT..

REACHING FOR THE SHOOTING IRONS, HICKOK FINDS HIMSELF STARING INTO THEIR COLD MUZZLES. ONCE HE HAS THE UPPER HAND, WES SPEAKS HIS MIND.

ZIP

WHAT'S TH' MATTER, BILL? AIN'T A FANCY GUNSLINGER LIKE YERSELF NEVER HEARD OF TH' BORDER ROLL?

HA HA

YOU LONG-HAIRED SCOUNDREL, WHAT'S THIS I HEAR ABOUT YOU PLANNIN' TO BACK-SHOOT ME?

THE ABILENE MARSHAL CHANGES HIS TACTICS.

NOW, LITTLE ARKANSAW, YOU HAVE BEEN WRONGLY INFORMED. LET'S HAVE US A DRINK AND BE FRIENDS.

THEY DO, AND WES CONTINUES TO WEAR HIS PISTOLS.

UNDER CONDITION THAT YOUR CROWD PULLS THEIRS OFF.

IN THAT CASE WE CAN BE FRIENDS.

BUT TROUBLE IS HARD TO AVOID IN A TOWN AS WILD AS ABILENE...

TEXANS IS TH' SCUM OF TH' EARTH! TH' LOWEST VERMIN THAT EVER SLITHERED BELLY OUT OF TH' SLIME!

WES TURNS FROM HIS PLATE OF STEAK AND EGGS.

I'M A TEXAN..

WHEN THE OBNOXIOUS DRUNK BEGINS TO CURSE HIM, THINGS GET OUT OF HAND.

BLAM!

AFTER THIS INCIDENT HARDIN WISELY LEAVES TOWN TO TRACK DOWN A MEXICAN NAMED BIDEÑO WHO HAS KILLED BILLY CORAN, A COWMAN UP FROM TEXAS.

SURRENDER AND I'LL TAKE YOU BACK IN SAFETY.

BIDEÑO, KNOWING THE CERTAIN FATE THAT AWAITS HIM IN ABILENE, MAKES HIS LAST PLAY.

UPON HIS RETURN WES IS WINED AND DINED BY CATTLEMEN GRATEFUL FOR THE AVENGING OF CORAN'S DEATH.

HERE'S A LITTLE COLLECTION WE TOOK UP FOR YOUR TROUBLE..

WE HAVE TO KEEP TH' MESKINS IN LINE.

HE IS SOUGHT OUT BY MANNING AND GIP CLEMENTS, WHO HAVE JUST ARRIVED WITH DOC BURNETT'S HERD.

WES, WE'RE IN A HEAP OF BAD TROUBLE! WE HAD TO KILL TWO OF THEM DAT-GUMED SHADDENS ON TH' TRAIL LAST NIGHT..

BUT WE WUZ JUSTIFIED, IF A MAN EVER WUZ.

WES SURRENDERS HIS KINSMEN AND, THROUGH MANEUVERINGS WITH HICKOK, SPRINGS THEM FROM JAIL.

MANNING, YOU GIT HOME FAST AS YOU CAN, AND I'LL BRING GIP WITH ME.

BILENE JAIL

HARDIN RETURNS TO ABILENE BUT SOON FEELS THE HEAT OF WILD BILL'S WRATH AND DECIDES TO HEAD FOR HOME HIMSELF, DOUBLE-QUICK.

MEET ME AT CAMP, GIP. WE DONE OVERSTAYED OUR WELCOME!

HOTEL

IN NEARBY KANSAS CITY, NEWS OF HIS DEPARTURE BRINGS RELIEF TO SHANGHAI PIERCE, WHO STANDS ACCUSED OF LYNCHING THE LUNN BROTHERS BACK IN TEXAS.

THE LUNN BOYS WUZ FRIENDS OF TH' TAYLORS, SHANG, AND HARDIN IS A FRIEND OF THEIRS.

LORD HAVE MERCY, AND I HEAR HE'S GOT OL' WILD BILL HICKOK DANCIN' ON A STRING!

PIERCE HAS SOLD HIS CATTLE BUSINESS FOR $100,000 AND LEFT TEXAS BECAUSE THE "CLIMATE WAS GETTING TOO OPPRESSIVE," AS HE IS FOND OF SAYING.

GENTS, I'M HERE TO LOOK FOR SOCIETY!

WHEN THE LUNN AFFAIR WENT BEFORE A GRAND JURY, PIERCE WAS RELUCTANT TO STAY AND TESTIFY.

THE SOCIETY IS NOT GOOD IN TEXAS RIGHT NOW. THERE'S TOO MUCH INTEREST IN THE HUMAN FRUIT BORNE BY DEAD TREES...

LATER THAT YEAR THINGS COME TO A HEAD BETWEEN WILD BILL AND PHIL COE IN ABILENE. THE TROUBLE IS OVER CROOKED CARDS AND SOFT WOMEN...

IF YOU TEXES WANT THE REST OF THESE PILLS COME AND GET 'EM!

THE CATTLE SEASON OVER, ABILENE SOON GIVES WILD BILL HIS WALKING PAPERS.

I HOPE I NEVER SEE ANOTHER TEXAS COWBOY!

MEANWHILE THE DAVIS ADMINISTRATION IS BUSY MAKING ITSELF ANATHEMA TO TEXANS. THE LEGISLATURE'S EXTRAVAGANT POLICY OF RAILROAD SUBSIDIES CREATES A SCANDAL.

DAMN' POLITICIANS ARE LINING THEIR OWN POCKETS!

SO WHAT'S NEW?

WORSE IS THE STATE POLICE, WHICH PLACES MANY COUNTIES UNDER MARTIAL LAW AND THEN BRAZENLY EXTORTS TRIBUTE FROM THE CITIZENS.

PAY UP AND WE'LL LEAVE.

POLICE FUND DONATIONS

AS A RULE, EX-CONFEDERATES REFUSE TO ENLIST IN THE POLICE (EVEN IF ELIGIBLE) AND THE ADJ. GEN. MUST FILL HIS RANKS FROM THE DREGS OF SOCIETY.

YOU BOYS WANT A GOOD JOB?

LONG AS WE DON'T HAVE TA' WORK!

MANY ARE "UPPITY" FREEDMEN, SUCH AS THE DUO THAT CORNER WES HARDIN IN A GONZALES COUNTY GROCERY STORE SOON AFTER HIS RETURN TO TEXAS.

THROW UP YOR' HANDS OR DIE!

WES USES THE "BORDER ROLL"—THIS TIME WITH DEADLY RESULTS.

THE OTHER POLICEMAN IS KNOCKED OFF HIS MULE..

..BUT LIVES TO BEAR WITNESS.

I KNOW I WINGED HIM..

RECKON HE CRAWLED OFF SOMEWHERES.

NEWS OF THIS OUTRAGE AGAINST THE STATE POLICE SPREADS LIKE WILDFIRE. POSSES RIDE TO GONZALES COUNTY FROM AS FAR AWAY AS AUSTIN.

WE'LL TORCH TH' ENTIRE AREA!

HARDIN AND HIS SUPPORTERS MEET THEM HEAD-ON, ENDING THE ROLE OF THE NEGRO POLICE IN THIS BASTION OF REBEL SUPREMACY.

BUT NOT BEFORE LOCAL CEMETERIES SPROUT TOMBSTONES TO REMIND US OF THE ERA'S *BITTER RACIAL HATRED...*

IN MEMORY OF PHILLIP GOODBREAD WEST
Born Jan. 5, 1846
Died Aug. 2, 1870
Killed by W.W. Davis and His Nigger Police

HARDIN'S KINSHIP WITH THE CLEMENTS BOYS SOON DRAWS HIM INTO THEIR FEUD WITH *WHITE* POLICEMEN AS WELL.

SUTTON, COX, AND OL' JOE TUMLINSON IS AS BAD AS TH' NIGRAHS.

WORSE, IF YOU ASK ME, FOR THEY MURDERS THEIR OWN KIND!

WES SPARKS A NEIGHBORING GIRL FROM COON HOLLOW NAMED JANE BOWEN. WHEN JIM CLEMENTS AND ANNIE TENNILLE TALK OF MARRIAGE, HIS THOUGHTS TURN TO THE SAME SUBJECT.

IF THEY CAN TIE TH' KNOT IN THESE PERILOUS TIMES THEN SO CAN WE.

I THOUGHT YOU'D *NEVER* ASK!

THE DAVIS FACTION, MORE PARANOID THAN EVER, STANDS GUARD OVER THE FALL ELECTIONS. RESULTS FROM MANY DISTRICTS ARE THROWN OUT.

THE ENDS JUSTIFY THE MEANS!

VOTE HERE

DURING THE SAME MONTH, NOV. OF 1871, DOBOY TAYLOR IS INVOLVED IN A DISPUTE AT KERRVILLE OVER A NEW YORK CATTLE CONTRACT.

SIM, I WANT TH' JOB, SO YOU BETTER BACK OFF.

IN THE RUCKUS THAT FOLLOWS, HOLSTEIN WRESTLES DOBOY'S PISTOL AWAY AND KILLS HIM WITH IT!

CREED, WHO HAS SETTLED IN THE HILL COUNTRY WITH OTHER FAMILIES FROM THE WAR-TORN COUNTIES, RECEIVES THE NEWS AT A CEDAR-BRAKE COW CAMP.

IS IT DOBOY?

'FRAID SO..

HE DENIES THAT THE DEATH OF HIS SECOND SON IS FEUD-RELATED.

JUST A FRIENDLY MISUNDERSTANDIN', THAT'S ALL IT WUZ.

THE FOLLOWING MARCH, WES AND JANE GET HITCHED AT RIDDLEVILLE AND SETTLE INTO MARRIED LIFE IN FRED DUDERSTADT'S RENT HOUSE ON THE SANDIES.

WHAT IS IT, WESLEY?

THOUGHT I HEARD RIDERS..

DOMESTIC LIFE APPEALS TO HARDIN — SO MUCH SO THAT HE "RIDES DOWN" A FAVORITE PINTO PONY TO REACH THE ARMS OF HIS SWEET YOUNG WIFE.

TOO BAD ABOUT OLD BOB, SUGAR, BUT I'M REAL GLAD YOU'RE HOME.

HE AND HIS CLEMENTS COUSINS TRAIL HORSES TO LOUISIANA, DODGING STATE POLICEMEN ALL ALONG THE ROUTE.

VISITING RELATIVES IN POLK AND TRINITY COUNTIES ON THE WAY BACK, HE GETS INTO A DISTURBANCE OVER A GAME OF TEN PINS.

WES CATCHES SOME BUCKSHOT IN THE BELLY AND IS CARRIED TO A DOCTOR BY COUSIN BARNETT JONES— THE SAME WHO HAD WRESTLED MAGE THE EX-SLAVE.

BARNETT, IF I *DIE*, YOU MAKE SURE JANE GETS THE $2,000 IN MY MONEY BELT.

WHEN A LOCAL MOB GATHERS, HE SURRENDERS TO A FRIENDLY LAWMAN AND IS TRANSPORTED BACK TO GONZALES DESPITE HIS WOUNDS.

HE'S STARTED BLEEDIN' AGAIN..

UHH..

HE MAKES HIS ESCAPE FROM JAIL AS SHERIFF JONES LOOKS THE OTHER WAY.

PITKIN TAYLOR HAS NEVER CEASED RAISING HELL ABOUT THE MURDER OF HIS KELLY SONS-IN-LAW, AND THE SUTTON GANG FINALLY DECIDES TO SHUT HIM UP.

GET THAT BELL OFF HIS COW.

THE RATTLING OF THE COWBELL AWAKENS PITKIN.

SOUNDS LIKE THAT DANG OL' OX IS IN TH' CORNPATCH AGAIN.. MUTTER

COMING OUTSIDE HALF DRESSED, TAYLOR IS STOPPED IN HIS TRACKS BY HIDDEN ASSASSINS.

THE OLD MAN LINGERS FOR SIX MONTHS TILL HE DIES.

IT WUZ THEM SUTTONS FOR SHOR'.

AS IF TO CONFIRM IT, DURING HIS FUNERAL THE SUTTON GANG HOLDS A *BOISTEROUS* VICTORY CELEBRATION ACROSS THE RIVER FROM THE TAYLOR BURYING GROUND.

AMONG THE MOURNERS ARE SON JIM TAYLOR AND FIVE OTHER YOUTHFUL RELATIVES OF THE DECEASED.

DON'T CRY, MA .. I WILL WASH MY HANDS IN BILL SUTTON'S BLOOD.

AND SO A NEW GENERATION OF TAYLORS TAKES OVER THE FEUD — BAD NEWS FOR THE THINNING RANKS OF THEIR ADVERSARIES.

WE PLEDGE OURSELVES NEVER TO REST UNTIL...

SHORTLY THEREAFTER, JIM, BILL, AND SCRAP TAYLOR, ALONG WITH COUSIN ALF DAY, STICK A SHOTGUN THROUGH THE DOOR OF BANKS SALOON IN CUERO.

THEIR AIM IS *BAD*, BILL SUTTON ONLY BEING WOUNDED.

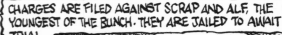

CHARGES ARE FILED AGAINST SCRAP AND ALF, THE YOUNGEST OF THE BUNCH. THEY ARE JAILED TO AWAIT TRIAL.

WHO WUZ IT BILLY? TAYLORS?

DON'T KNOW, BUT THEY WAS KIDS 'CAUSE TH' RECOIL KNOCKED ONE DOWN.

YOU CAN'T PROVE NUTHIN'!

YOU'RE GUILTY LESS YOU CAN PROVE OTHERWISE, FAR AS I'M CONCERNED..

WES HARDIN AND TWELVE OTHER MEN CUT THEM LOOSE.

JAIL IS NO PLACE FOR KIDS—'SPECIALLY NOT TAYLOR KIDS.

GONZALES COUNTY JAIL

MERCHANT HARDWARE

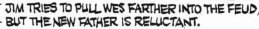
JIM TRIES TO PULL WES FARTHER INTO THE FEUD, BUT THE NEW FATHER IS RELUCTANT.

IT AIN'T JUST ME ANYMORE — I'M A FAMILY MAN NOW..

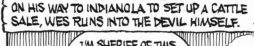
ON HIS WAY TO INDIANOLA TO SET UP A CATTLE SALE, WES RUNS INTO THE DEVIL HIMSELF.

I'M SHERIFF OF THIS COUNTY — JACK HELM'S TH' NAME!

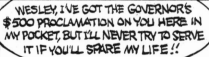
WES TELLS HELM WHO HE IS.

OH, ARE YOU WESLEY? WELL LET ME SHAKE YOUR HAND.

HE REFUSES HELM'S OUT-THRUST HAND AND DARES THE SHERIFF TO BACK UP HIS LOOSE TALK.

YOU'VE HAD YOUR DOGS ON ME, SAYIN' I WUZ A MURDERER AND A COWARD. HERE WE ARE, MAN TO MAN. NOW TAKE ME IF YOU CAN!!

WESLEY, I'VE GOT THE GOVERNOR'S $500 PROCLAMATION ON YOU HERE IN MY POCKET, BUT I'LL NEVER TRY TO SERVE IT IF YOU'LL SPARE MY LIFE!!

WARILY THE TWO MEN RIDE ON TO CUERO.

LET'S SET UP A MEETING AND WORK THINGS OUT BETWEEN US, ALRIGHT?

WHILE IN A LOCAL BARROOM HARDIN IS APPROACHED BY J.B. MORGAN, ONE OF HELM'S HENCHMEN WITH AN ITCH FOR REWARD MONEY.

SO YOU'RE TH' NOTORIOUS HARDIN BOY. I WANT TO BUY YOU A BOTTLE OF CHAMPAGNE!

WES REFUSES TO DRINK WITH MORGAN, AND HE USES IT AS AN EXCUSE TO PULL HIS PISTOL.

BLAM BLAM

THE KILLING, THOUGH A FAIR FIGHT, OCCURS ON HELM'S TURF.

PAPER SEZ MORGAN WUZ TH' "AGGRESSOR"

WE CAN'T LET IT PASS JACK, OR TH' CHANGIN' TIDE WILL SWEEP US AWAY!

THE TIDE IS INDEED CHANGING. ADJ. GEN. DAVIDSON HAS ABSCONDED WITH $37,000 OF PUBLIC MONEY AND, BECAUSE OF ITS RECORD OF BRUTALITY THROUGHOUT TEXAS, HIS POLICE ORGANIZATION IS IN *BIG TROUBLE*.

I HEAR THAT TH' CLIMATE IN CANADA IS NICE AN' COOL.

TYPICAL OF WHAT HIS UNDERLINGS HAVE BEEN PULLIN' ALL ALONG!

LAW AND ORDER

IN APRIL OF 1873 AN INDIGNANT LEGISLATURE ABOLISHES THE STATE POLICE OVER GOV. DAVIS' VETO. TEXAS REJOICES, BUT NOT THE SUTTON PARTY! NOW THE COMING MEETING WITH HARDIN TAKES ON ADDED SIGNIFICANCE.

BOYS, WE GOT TO..TO NEUTRALIZE THAT GUNSLINGER OR OUR GOOSE IS COOKED.

WES, ACCOMPANIED BY MANNING CLEMENTS AND GEORGE TENNILLE, SHOWS UP AT JIM COX'S HOUSE AS PROMISED.

GLAD YOU COULD COME BOYS, GLAD TO SEE YOU!

STEERING WES ASIDE, HELM AND COX PROPOSE A DEAL.

JOIN US AND WE'LL SQUASH ALL CHARGES AGAINST YOU — IT'LL BE A CLEAN SLATE!

THERE'S ONLY TWO WAYS TO GO, WESLEY: EITHER YOU'RE FOR US OR AGAINST US!

WES PLAYS ALONG AND HEARS THEIR PLAN: TO ELIMINATE ALL WHO OPPOSE THEIR RULE.

WELL, WHAT DO YOU SAY?

MANNING, GEORGE, AND ME WANT PEACE, BUT WE WON'T SWAP WORK WITH YOU..

SEEING THEY CANNOT SWAY THEIR GUESTS, A TRUCE OF SORTS IS AGREED TO.

ALRIGHT, WE'LL STAY CLEAR OF ONE ANOTHER. BUT THAT TAYLOR BUNCH HAS GOT TO GO!

MANNING EXPRESSES HIS DOUBTS ABOUT THE PACT.

THEY'LL BE ON US WITHIN A WEEK!

SURE ENOUGH, HELM AND A POSSE OF FIFTY MEN SOON COME VISITING BUT FIND THE MENFOLK GONE.

WHERE ARE THEY??

I DUNNO..OUT ON A ROUNDUP I SUPPOSE.

WHEN JANE OFFERS NO INFORMATION ON THE WHEREABOUTS OF THE TAYLOR BOYS, HELM GROWS ABUSIVE.

YOU'RE COVERING FOR THOSE DAMNED RASCALS MISSY..

..YOU AND THEM IS ONE OF A KIND!

LEARNING OF THE INSULTS TO THEIR WOMEN, WES AND THE CLEMENTS CLAN DECIDE TO JOIN THE TAYLORS OPENLY.

THIS WAY OF DOIN' HAS GOT TO STOP!

A MEETING IS CALLED AT MUSTANG MOTTE.

BOYS, OUR FAMILIES IS ENDANGERED AND THAT'S WHERE I DRAW TH' LINE.

THEY MOVE SWIFTLY. IN MAY, JIM COX IS FILLED WITH BUCKSHOT...

...AND HIS THROAT SLIT FROM EAR TO EAR.

JOE TUMLINSON, ASTRIDE HIS FAST GRAY EAGLE, NARROWLY ESCAPES DEATH AT THE SAME TIME.

I KNEW SOME- THIN' DIDN'T SMELL RIGHT BACK THERE..

SUTTON IS BUSHWHACKED IN JUNE BUT AGAIN THE TAYLOR KIDS ARE TOO HASTY AND HE GETS AWAY.

DAMMIT BILL, YOU FIRED TOO SOON!

JULY FINDS JACK HELM IN A BLACKSMITH SHOP ON THE WILSON-GONZALES COUNTY LINE.

THIS COTTON-CHOPPER IDEA OF MINE WILL MAKE ME A RICH MAN··

BLAND'S BLACKSMITH

BY STRANGE COINCIDENCE WES HARDIN AND JIM TAYLOR COME RIDING INTO LITTLE ALBUQUERQUE THAT VERY DAY!

THAT THERE HOSS BELONGS TO THET LOW-DOWN SHERIFF.

YOU KEEP TH' DOGS OFF, WES— HE'S MINE!

BLAND'S BLACKSMITH

NOT EXPECTING ANY TROUBLE IN THIS REMOTE AREA, HELM HAS LEFT HIS GUNBELT ON HIS SADDLEHORN.

HELM! TURN AROUND!!

〈262〉

UNARMED AND SEEING HIS DANGER, HELM PULLS A KNIFE OUT OF HIS BOOT.

SOMEBODY SHOOT TH' SCOUNDREL!

IGNORING THE FACT THAT THE REMARK WAS INTENDED FOR *HIM*, WES FIRES A LOAD OF BUCKSHOT INTO THE "ONLY SCOUNDREL PRESENT" AND THEN TURNS HIS SIX-SHOOTERS ON THE BYSTANDERS.

STAY QUIET, FOLKS, AND YOU'LL LIVE TO TELL TH' TALE.

JIM TAYLOR FINISHES OFF THE SCOURGE OF HIS KINSMEN.

THAT'S FOR BUCK AND HAYS AND MART AND TH' KELLYS AND *MY PA!*

BAM BAM

THIS BOLD KILLING GREATLY AGITATES OL' JOE TUMLINSON, WHO FEELS THE NOOSE TIGHTENING.

MEN, THEY'LL GET US NEXT— IF WE DON'T GET THEM FIRST!

ANTICIPATING JOE'S VENGEANCE, WES MOVES AGAINST THE TUMLINSON HOUSE.

HIS GANG IS SLEEPIN' OUT ON TH' FRONT PORCH.

WE'LL WAIT TILL SUNUP.

BUT JOE'S COON DOGS SOUND THE ALARM.

TAKE COVER BOYS! TH' TAYLORS IS LURKIN' ABOUT!

THE SIEGE IS FINALLY LIFTED WHEN NEUTRAL CITIZENS INTERVENE.

WES, THEY'S WILLIN' TO CALL IT QUITS IF YALL ARE..

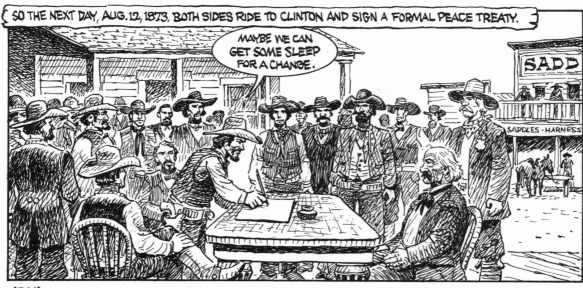

SO THE NEXT DAY, AUG. 12, 1873, BOTH SIDES RIDE TO CLINTON AND SIGN A FORMAL PEACE TREATY.

MAYBE WE CAN GET SOME SLEEP FOR A CHANGE.

SADD

SADDLES · HARNESS

⟨264⟩

TRANQUILLITY DESCENDS ON THE GUADALUPE VALLEY, BUT IT CANNOT LAST LONG BECAUSE BILL SUTTON'S NAME IS NOT ON THE CEASE-FIRE AGREEMENT...

--AND HE'S THE ONE WE WANT MOST OF ALL!

ENCOURAGED BY THE DEFEAT OF THE POLICE BILL, DEMOCRATS RALLY TO BEAT GOV. DAVIS AT THE POLLS.

GUADALUPE COUNTY BOX 42

THE INCUMBENT TRIES TO HAVE THE RESULTS OVERTURNED AND THE CAPITAL DIVIDES INTO TWO ARMED CAMPS.

TIL BAKERY

PAL SUE

BUT PRESIDENT GRANT WILL NOT SEND FEDERAL TROOPS TO SUSTAIN DAVIS, AND THE "LOYAL" LOCAL MILITIA GOES OVER TO THE OPPOSITION.

TH' JIG IS UP, EDMUND. WE'RE HERE TO SEE TEXAS RETURNED TO ITS PEOPLE!

EMBITTERED BY THE FAILURE OF HIS NORTHERN FRIENDS TO SUPPORT HIM, DAVIS BOWS OUT TO COKE IN MID-JANUARY.

THIS IS TH' THANKS I GET!

♫ SHE'S TH' YELLOW ROSE OF TEXAS ♫

THE EBULLIENT TEXANS, REFUSED THE KEY TO THE SENATE, BREAK THE DOOR DOWN AND OUST ITS DIE-HARD OCCUPANTS.

OUT YOU RASCALS! SCALAWAG AND CARPET-BAGGER RULE IS DEAD!

THE DEMOCRATS' JOYOUS SPIRITS ARE SOON DAMPENED.

TH' STATE IS IN HOCK UP TO ITS EARS—LOOK AT THESE FIGURES!

DURING THIS CHANGING OF THE GUARD, WILEY PRIDGEN, BROTHER OF THE OUTSPOKEN SENATOR, IS SHOT DOWN IN THOMASTON, DEWITT COUNTY.

IT'S THEM CON-SARNED SUTTONS!

THE FEUD FLARES UP AGAIN, BECOMING OPEN WAR IN CLINTON AND CUERO.

LOCAL "PROTECTION CLUBS" ARE FORMED BY CITIZENS WEARY OF THE UNENDING VIOLENCE.

YOU FELLERS ARE WRONG TO ENDANGER INNOCENT FOLKS WITH YOUR SHOOTIN' MATCHES.

GO TAKE YOUR QUARREL ELSEWHERE. ENUFF IS ENUF!

MEAT MARKET

ANOTHER PEACE TREATY IS SIGNED AT CUERO, JAN. 3, 1874.

STABLE

J.I. CONE

THE KILLING CONTINUES, BUT NOT SO OPENLY.

WHAR'S THET POMPOUS OL' LIAR BOLIVAR PRIDGEN AT, BOY?

I DOESN'T KNOW SAHR..

PRIDGEN, IN HIS ROLE AS SENATOR IN THE STATE LEGISLATURE, HAS BEEN ONE OF THE MOST VOCAL OPPONENTS OF RADICAL RULE AND THE STATE POLICE.

REGARDLESS OF THE COST, A MAN'S GOT TO STAND UP FOR WHAT HE BELIEVES IN..

COME HOME ENATOR

IN HIS ABSENCE THE SENATOR'S FAITHFUL EX-SLAVE IS MURDERED, BY SUTTON'S PARTY, HIS GUTS REPLACED WITH ROCKS.

THAT'LL KEEP TH' BASTARD ON TH' BOTTOM!

BILL SUTTON DECIDES THE FRYING PAN HAS BECOME TOO HOT TO HANDLE. HE PREPARES TO LEAVE TEXAS.

WES HARDIN SENDS HIS BROTHER JOE TO KEEP TABS ON SUTTON'S MOVEMENTS. ALSO, A BANKER IN VICTORIA MAKES REPORTS TO BOLIVAR PRIDGEN, WHO IN TURN KEEPS THE TAYLOR BOYS INFORMED.

IT'S JUST A MATTER OF TIME TILL THEY GET ME IF I STAY..

LET'S LEAVE FOR AWHILE, AT LEAST TILL TH' BABY COMES.

HE'S GOT A HERD TOGETHER AND IS PLANNING TO CATCH A BOAT TO NEW ORLEANS NEXT WEEK.

I'LL PASS IT ON..

AT THE APPOINTED TIME THE TAYLORS ARRANGE TO BE IN INDIANOLA WITH A HERD OF THEIR OWN.

BILLY, HIS WIFE, AND GABE SLAUGHTER ARE GETTIN' READY TO BOARD..

THAT'S ALL WE NEED TO KNOW..

JIM AND HIS COUSIN BILL TAYLOR, BUCK'S NEPHEW, DO THE SHOOTING.

TICKETS

JIM CALMLY REACHES DOWN AND REMOVES SUTTON'S IVORY-HANDLED PISTOL, WHICH HAD BELONGED TO HIS COUSIN BUCK.

YOU WON'T HAVE NO MORE USE FOR THIS, YOU MURDERIN' SCALLYWAG.

THEY HEAD FOR THE CATTLE PENS, LEAVING THE PREGNANT, HYSTERICAL LAURA SUTTON BEHIND.

SOMEBODY DO SOMETHING — OH MY GOD! >SOB<

ON THEIR WAY BACK TO CUERO, THE BOYS STOP AT SEN. PRIDGEN'S HOUSE AND ARE TREATED TO A TURKEY DINNER.

YOU YOUNG MEN HAVE RIGHTED A CONSIDERABLE NUMBER OF WRONGS TODAY. LET'S DRINK TO BETTER TIMES IN TEXAS!

AFTER MANY TOASTS JIM TAYLOR MAKES HIS WAY TO A GONZALES COUNTY COW CAMP WHERE WES IS PUTTING TOGETHER ANOTHER KANSAS HERD.

BETTER COME WITH US, JIM, TILL THINGS SETTLE DOWN.

(269)

BILL IS FOOLISH ENOUGH TO STAY AROUND CUERO. WHILE TRYING ON A NEW PAIR OF BOOTS AT A LOCAL SHOP, HE IS NABBED BY THE TOWN MARSHAL.

GOTCHA!

LEMME GO DAMN' YOU!

THEY SEND HIM TO GALVESTON, WHERE CHANCES OF HIS RESCUE ARE SLIM.

I SHOULD OF LISTENED TO MY COUSIN JIM...

THE FOLLOWING MONTH GOV. COKE RE-ESTABLISHES THE TEXAS RANGERS WITH A THREE-FOLD MISSION: TO FIGHT HOSTILE INDIANS, CATCH MEXICAN RUSTLERS, AND RID THE STATE OF OUTLAWS.

IT'S A BIG JOB BOYS, BUT TH' CITIZENS OF TEXAS WANT LAW AND ORDER.

THIS ACTION ROUSES THE OPPRESSED PEOPLE OF THE STATE TO TAKE JUSTICE INTO THEIR OWN HANDS, BELIEVING THAT THE RANGERS WILL BACK THEM UP.

TH' TIMES THEY ARE A CHANGIN'.

I'LL DRINK TO THAT!!

GABRIEL SLAUGHTER'S KILLER NOW BEHIND BARS, LAURA SUTTON OFFERS A $1,000 REWARD FOR HER HUSBAND'S EXECUTIONER.

MIGHTY TEMPTIN'..

NOTICE!

$1,000 REWARD

BUT JIM TAYLOR IS WITH WES HARDIN UP IN THE FRONTIER TOWN OF COMANCHE. WES' PARENTS HAVE MOVED THERE, WHERE JANE IS STAYING AND OTHER KINFOLKS AS WELL.

WHILE AWAITING NEWS OF THE HERD FROM DOC BOCKIUS, THEY MATCH A HORSE RACE AND WIN BIG. IT IS WES' 21st BIRTHDAY.

WE'RE SAFE WAY OUT HERE.

YEAH—EXCEPT FROM TH' INJUNS!

TONIGHT TH' DRINKS ARE ON ME—LET'S GO WHOOP IT UP!

CHARLES WEBB, A DEPUTY FROM NEIGHBORING BROWN COUNTY, HAPPENS TO BE IN TOWN. THERE IS BAD BLOOD BETWEEN HIM AND SOME OF WES' CROWD — INCLUDING JOHN CARNES, THE SHERIFF OF COMANCHE COUNTY.

DON'T DRINK SO MUCH.. THERE MIGHT BE SOMETHING WITH WEBB.

DON'T WORRY, I'M.. ≷HIC≷ ON SECOND THOUGHT, BETTER ≷HIC≷ SEND JEFF FER TH' BUGGY..

LEAVING JACK WRIGHT'S SALOON THEY RUN INTO DEPUTY WEBB.

YES, I KNOW WHO YOU ARE, BUT I HAVE NO PAPERS ON YOU.

THEN WHATCHA GOT BEHIND YOUR BACK, DAMMIT?!

JUST A SEEGAR..

OH—WELL, C'MON INSIDE AND WE'LL HAVE ANOTHER ROUND!

(271)

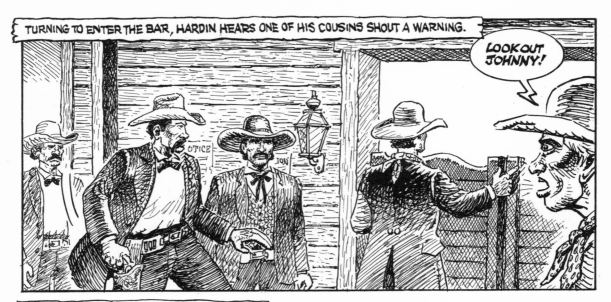

TURNING TO ENTER THE BAR, HARDIN HEARS ONE OF HIS COUSINS SHOUT A WARNING.

LOOK OUT JOHNNY!

HE SPINS AND FIRES, HITTING WEBB IN THE FACE, WHILE A BULLET GRAZES HIS RIBS.

JIM TAYLOR AND BUD DIXON, UNAWARE THAT WEBB IS DEAD ON HIS FEET, BLAST HIM WITH MORE LEAD.

MANGY SKUNK!

SUSPECTING THAT HARDIN'S GANG WOULD MAKE TROUBLE, AN ANGRY CROWD RUSHES UP.

HARDIN'S SHOT CHARLEY WEBB!

LET'S HANG HIM!

GET A ROPE!

WRIGHT'S SALOON

LIQUORS WINES CIGARS
RNES & WILSON, PROPS.

WES' BROTHER JOE AND SHERIFF CARNES KEEP THE LYNCH MOB AT BAY LONG ENOUGH FOR EVERYONE TO RIDE OUT.

WEBB PULLED FIRST..

YOU'RE ON TH' WRONG SIDE SHERIFF.

WE'RE FED UP

LATER CARNES VISITS THE HARDIN PLACE.

LOOK, WE'LL SURRENDER IF YOU CAN PROTECT US

SORRY, BOYS. TH' TOWN'S OUT OF CONTROL... YALL BETTER GO HIDE IN TH' HILLS!!

OUT OF CONTROL INDEED — ENOUGH FOR THE IRATE CITIZENS TO TAKE JOE HARDIN AND TWO COUSINS, TOM AND BUD DIXON, OUT AND HANG THEM!

THAT'LL TEACH 'UM TO BRING A PACK OF GUNSLINGERS INTO OUR COUNTY!

ARRESTED AT THE SAME TIME ARE REV. HARDIN AND DOC BOCKIUS, WHO HAS WANDERED INTO THE HORNET'S NEST.

GEE REVEREND, WHAT'S EVERBODY SO STEAMED UP ABOUT?

DOC'S CREW IS HOLDING WES' KANSAS-BOUND HERD AT NEARBY HAMILTON. IT IS NOT LONG BEFORE RANGERS GO LOOKING FOR THE MEN WHO ESCAPED EARLIER.

BUT WE AIN'T DONE NUTHIN' 'CEPT DRIVE THESE COWS.

COME WITH US ANYWAY!

TWO ESCAPEES WHO TAKE THE SITUATION LIGHTLY, HAM ANDERSON AND ALEX BAREKMAN, ARE LATER FOUND *SHOT DEAD* IN THEIR BEDROLLS.

WES AND JIM HAVE SEVERAL CLOSE SCRAPES WITH SCOURING POSSES. THEY MAKE THEIR WAY TO COUSIN "FANCY JIM" TAYLOR'S PLACE OUTSIDE AUSTIN.

WES, I'M TIRED OF RUNNING. I WANNA' GO BACK HOME TO GONZALES.

OKAY, WE'LL SPLIT UP...

ALF DAY BRINGS THEM NEWS OF THE FAMILY DISASTER AT COMANCHE.

MY BROTHER JOE.. GOD, I DON'T BELIEVE IT. NOT JOE!!

SLIPPING BACK TO SEE HIS FATHER, WES HEARS THE WORST.

SON, TH' COUNTRY'S CHANGIN' ON US. IF YOU'RE SEEN HERE, THEY'LL KILL US ALL. FLEE I TELL YOU!

MEANWHILE WES' COWHANDS ARE TAKEN BACK TO CLINTON AND JAILED — AFTER RANGER CAPT. WALLER SENDS HARDIN A WARNING.

HE SEZ THE SAFETY OF MY FAMILY DEPENDS ON THEM REACHIN' DEWITT COUNTY WITHOUT INTERFERENCE.

ON A RAINY NIGHT IN JUNE, JOE TUMLINSON'S MOB BREAKS INTO THE CLINTON COURTHOUSE. KUTE TUGGLE, JIM WHITE AND SCRAP TAYLOR ARE TAKEN OUT AND STRUNG UP.

WITH THE HELP OF A FELLOW MASON (WHO HIDES HIM UNDER HIS SLICKER), DOC BOCKIUS ESCAPES THE MOB.

A WEEK LATER A SHERIFF'S POSSE CORNERS GEORGE TENNILLE, TWO OF WHOSE DAUGHTERS ARE MARRIED TO THE CLEMENTS BOYS.

I'M GONNA' MAKE A RUN FOR IT.

GEORGE WAS SET ON GOING TO MEXICO, BUT HE WENT ABOUT IT TOO SLOW..

WES HARDIN, FRIGHTENED BY THE QUICK SHIFT OF PUBLIC OPINION, LEAVES TEXAS FOR FLORIDA. HIS FEUDING DAYS ARE OVER.

MOB LAW RULES SUPREME — AND MOBS MAKE ME NERVOUS.

PENSACOLA DEPOT

THREE YEARS LATER HE IS APPREHENDED BY RANGERS, BROUGHT BACK TO TEXAS, AND SENT TO PRISON FOR KILLING DEPUTY WEBB.

(275)

GOV. COKE SOON SENDS RANGER CAPTAIN MCNELLY TO QUIET THE RECENT DISTURBANCES IN DEWITT COUNTY.

ABOUT TIME.

IT IS WELL THAT HE DOES. COURT IS IN SESSION AT CLINTON AND A NUMBER OF CASES PENDING COULD BE BAD FOR THE "WRATHY" SUTTON PARTY, NOW LED BY OL' JOE TUMLINSON.

BOYS, THINGS ARE GOIN' OUR WAY FOR A CHANGE, AN' I AIM TO KEEP THEM GOIN' THAT WAY!

TUMLINSON'S GANG GOES AFTER HOSTILE WITNESSES — EVEN THOSE HELD BY THE RANGERS IN PROTECTIVE CUSTODY!

SORRY FELLERS. WE THOUGHT Y'ALL WUZ TAYLORS.

MCNELLY SUMS UP THE SITUATION IN A DISPATCH TO HIS SUPERIOR.

"THEY'RE ALL ALIKE, TAYLOR AND SUTTON, EQUALLY TURBULENT, TREACHEROUS, AND RECKLESS."

BUT JOE'S TACTICS WORK..

YOUR HONOR, TH' PROSECUTION CAN'T LOCATE ANY OF ITS WITNESSES.

THE CASE AGAINST HIM IS LAID OVER UNTIL NEXT SESSION.

CHUCKLE

EMBOLDENED BY THIS, THE "TUMLINSON ORGANIZATION" PLANS TO ATTEND BILL TAYLOR'S TRIAL IN INDIANOLA.

WE'LL MAKE SURE HE GITS JUSTICE — JUST IN CASE TH' COURT FOULS UP.

BUT THE TRIAL IS POSTPONED. IN THE MEANTIME OL' JOE "GETS RELIGION."

YOU BOYS STAND GUARD TILL I GET TH' WATER OUTTA' MY EYES.

SOON AFTER, HE DIES A NATURAL DEATH IN BED, HIS BOOTS OFF.

WITH THE PASSING OF THIS FIESTY OLD PARTICIPANT, THE FEUD GRADUALLY WINDS DOWN — MUCH TO THE RELIEF OF ALL CONCERNED.

THINGS WON'T BE TH' SAME AROUND HERE WITHOUT OL' JOE.

YOU CAN SAY THAT AGAIN!

THE LULL LASTS UNTIL SEPT. 1875 WHEN A STORM DESTROYS INDIANOLA. DURING THE DISASTER BILL TAYLOR MAKES HIS GETAWAY.

THE MAN WHO CAPTURED HIM IN A CUERO BOOT SHOP, MARSHAL RUBE BROWN, IS SOON GUNNED DOWN BY "UNKNOWN ASSAILANTS."

NOT LONG AFTER, JIM TAYLOR IS KILLED IN A BIG SHOOTOUT AT CLINTON. HE DIES AT AGE 23, WITH A $1,500 PRICE ON HIS HEAD.

M. KING & SONS
BLACKSMITH ~ LIVERY

WOFFOR.
NOTIONS

AUTUMN OF 1876 WITNESSES THE BRUTAL MURDER OF DR. BRASSELL AND HIS SON BY SUTTON SYMPATHIZERS, BUT THE DRAMA OF THE FEUD HAS MOSTLY PLAYED OUT.

THE BOLD STANCE OF JUDGE CLAY PLEASANTS AND THE TEXAS RANGERS SEES TO THAT.

YOU MURDERERS, BUSH-WHACKERS, AND MIDNIGHT ASSASSINS BEWARE. YOUR LAWLESS REIGN IN DEWITT COUNTY IS AT AN END!

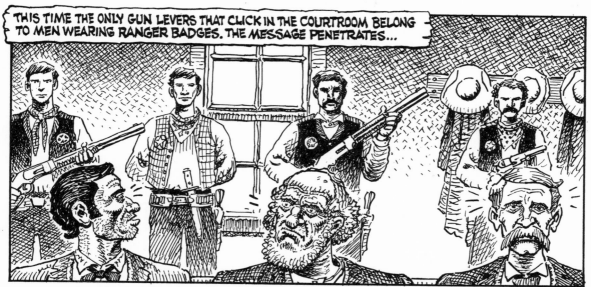

MEANWHILE, JOHN WESLEY HARDIN IS AT THE HUNTSVILLE PENITENTIARY, SERVING A SENTENCE OF 25 YEARS AT HARD LABOR. FREQUENT ESCAPE ATTEMPTS AND GENERAL INSUBORDINATION LAND HIM IN SOLITARY CONFINEMENT, HIS BACK RAW FROM DISCIPLINARY LASHINGS.

I GOTTA *BUST OUT* OF HERE..

HIS LETTERS HOME TO JANE HELP HIM KEEP HIS SANITY.

"JANE DEAREST, YOU KNOW THAT I KILLED WEBB IN SELF DEFENSE AND DID NOT GET A FAIR TRIAL.."

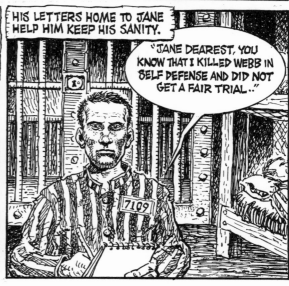

EVENTUALLY HARDIN BECOMES RECONCILED TO LIFE BEHIND BARS. HE TEACHES SUNDAY SCHOOL AND JOINS THE PRISON DEBATING TEAM.

MY OPPONENT WOULD HAVE YOU BELIEVE THAT WOMEN SHOULD ENJOY THE SAME RIGHTS AS MEN.. *HOW RIDICULOUS!*

IN THE 1880s HIS LETTERS TO JANE AND THEIR THREE CHILDREN BECOME RAMBLING DISCOURSES, REFLECTING HIS STUDY OF LAW, HISTORY, THEOLOGY, AND THE CLASSICS BUT LACED WITH RUSTIC PROVERBS.

"EMBRACE EACH OF OUR DEAR, PRECIOUS CHILDREN JANE AND QUOTE THEM THAT OLD SAYING: LET EVERY TUB STAND ON ITS OWN BOTTOM.."

WHAT DOES *THAT* MEAN, MOMMA?

(279)

AT THE END OF 1892 HARDIN'S SPIRITS, ELEVATED BY HOPES OF AN EARLY RELEASE, ARE CRUSHED BY NEWS OF JANE'S DEATH.

SHE'S GONE ≥ SOB ≤

BUT GOV. HOGG GRANTS HIM A PARDON, AND IN FEBRUARY 1894 HARDIN WALKS OUT OF THE STATE PEN A FREE MAN HAVING SERVED ALMOST 16 YEARS OF HIS SENTENCE.

YOU'LL BE BACK, HARDIN.

YOUR TYPE ALWAYS IS!

HUNTS STATE PE

HE FINDS HIMSELF A STRANGER TO HIS CHILDREN, WHO HAVE GROWN UP WITH THE DUDERSTADT FAMILY DURING HIS LONG ABSENCE IN PRISON.

..AND YOU MUST BE JENNIE, THE BABY..

I'M NOT A BABY ANYMORE, I'M GOIN' ON SIXTEEN!

IS THIS THE FATHER WE'VE HEARD SO MUCH ABOUT?

HIS ELDEST, MOLLIE, AGE 21, HAS ALREADY DECIDED ON HER FUTURE.

CHARLEY AND ME ARE GETTIN' MARRIED, PA— WITH OR WITHOUT YOUR BLESSING.

HARDIN IS CERTIFIED TO PRACTICE LAW, BUT SOON LEAVES GONZALES COUNTY AND HEADS WEST.

I'LL MAKE A FRESH START SOMEWHERE ELSE. MY KIDS DON'T NEED ME HANGING AROUND TO COMPLICATE THEIR LIVES.

⟨280⟩

HE STOPS IN KIMBLE COUNTY AND VISITS CREED TAYLOR, WHO HAS REMARRIED SINCE THE FEUD AND PRODUCED A SECOND CROP OF CHILDREN. ONE OF THEM, MARY, WILL SOON WED WES' YOUNGER BROTHER JEFF.

FIND YOURSELF A YOUNG GAL WES AND GET HITCHED. PUT TH' PAST BEHIND YOU, LIKE I DID..IT'S GONE!

FIFTEEN YEAR OLD CALLIE LEWIS, THE WILD, RECKLESS, BEAUTIFUL DAUGHTER OF CAPT. LEN LEWIS, BECOMES FASCINATED WITH WES, NOW 41.

BUT HE'S SO OLD!

HE'S SWEET ON YOU, THAT'S FOR SURE.

NOT REALLY— AND I'VE NEVER MET ANYONE AS IMPORTANT AS HE IS.

THEY MARRY, BUT IT IS OVER AS SOON AS THEIR HONEYMOON. WES TAKES CALLIE BACK TO HER FOLKS AND DRIFTS WEST.

LET ME KNOW IF SHE CHANGES HER MIND.

ME AND TH' MISSUS SURE FEEL TERRIBLE ABOUT THIS, WES..

HE WINDS UP IN EL PASO — STILL A WILD FRONTIER TOWN — WHERE HE IS TO REPRESENT KINSMAN-BY-MARRIAGE "KILLIN' JIM" MILLER IN HIS COURT CASE WITH A PECOS LAWMAN, BUD FRAZER.

NOW THIS IS MORE LIKE IT.

THOUGH HARDIN TRIES TO WALK THE STRAIGHT AND NARROW, HIS REPUTATION AS A GUNMAN HAS PRECEDED HIM AND HE FINDS IT HARD TO RESIST EXPLOITING IT.

BY GOD— JOHN WESLEY HARDIN! LET ME BUY YOU A DRINK.

SAY, IS IT TRUE YOU'VE KILLED FORTY MEN?

SOON HE IS SPENDING MORE TIME IN BAR ROOMS THAN COURTROOMS.

LOOK WHAT HE GAVE ME! MAN, WHAT SHOOTIN'!

NO TELLING WHAT HE CAN DO SOBER.

HARDIN'S POPULARITY IS RESENTED BY TWO LOCAL LAWMEN, JOHN SELMAN (A TOUGH OLD GUNFIGHTER) AND HIS SON JOHN JR.

LOOK HOW THEY FAWN OVER HIM— DISGUSTING!

HE'S NOTHING BUT A DRUNKEN JAILBIRD, PAST HIS PRIME...

WES TAKES UP WITH A FORMER PROSTITUTE WHOSE HUSBAND IS IN JAIL ACROSS THE RIVER. SHE HELPS HIM FINISH HIS AUTOBIOGRAPHY.

SO THEN THE MEXICAN WENT FOR HIS GUN—

WAIT! WAIT! YOU'RE GOING TOO FAST!!

WHEN HER HUSBAND IS KILLED CROSSING BACK TO EL PASO, BEULAH COMES INTO A CONSIDERABLE AMOUNT OF CASH.

LOAN ME $1,000 HONEY. I WANT TO BUY HALF INTEREST IN THE WIGWAM SALOON.

WITH WES GONE FOR A FEW DAYS, BEULAH *TIES ONE ON* AND IS ARRESTED BY OFFICER SELMAN THE YOUNGER.

YOU DIRTY ROTTEN SKUNK! GET YER PAWS OFF ME OR I'LL BLOW YOU TO KINGDOM COME!

SHUT UP, YOU OL' WHORE.

HARDIN IS NOT HAPPY WITH JOHN JR.'S TREATMENT OF "HIS" WOMAN.

HE'D NEVER HAVE DARED TO ARREST HER WHILE I WAS IN TOWN, I CAN TELL YOU THAT!

CONVINCED THAT HARDIN MEANS TO KILL BOTH HIM AND HIS SON, CONSTABLE SELMAN SNEAKS UP BEHIND WES IN THE ACME SALOON ON AUG. 19, 1895, AND, IN COWARDLY FASHION, SENDS HIM TO HIS MAKER.

YOU HAVE FOUR SIXES TO BEAT...

WES IS BURIED IN AN UNMARKED GRAVE, AND HIS SON REQUIRES A LAWYER'S SERVICES TO OBTAIN THE EFFECTS OF HIS FATHER — INCLUDING WES' AUTOBIOGRAPHY.

YOUR HONOR, THIS MANUSCRIPT IS HARDIN'S LEGACY TO HIS CHILDREN AND BY RIGHTS BELONGS TO THEM..

IT IS PRINTED AT SEGUIN THE NEXT YEAR, ONE OF THE RARE ACCOUNTS WRITTEN BY A FAMOUS GUNFIGHTER OF HIS LIFE.

JOHNNY, I'M AFRAID PEOPLE ARE GONNA THINK BADLY OF OUR FAMILY WHEN THEY READ THIS.

LET 'EM THINK WHAT THEY WANT, MOLLIE... LIKE PA USED TO SAY: EVERY TUB'S GOT TO STAND ON ITS OWN BOTTOM!

SO ENDS THE LONGEST AND BLOODIEST FEUD THAT EVER MARRED THE GREAT STATE OF TEXAS. FOR MANY FEUDISTS, VIOLENCE DOGGED THEIR TRAIL TO THE END. SEVERAL OF THE CLEMENTS BOYS DIED IN GUNPLAY, AS DID WES' KID BROTHER JEFF DAVIS HARDIN.

THEIR KILLERS USUALLY MET SIMILAR FATES.

BY CONTRAST, WES JR. LED A PEACEFUL LIFE IN GONZALES COUNTY AND WAS RESPECTED BY ALL HIS NEIGHBORS.

MANY SONS OF THE OPPOSING FEUDISTS JOINED THE RANGERS AND WORKED TOWARD A COMMON GOAL IN THE 20TH CENTURY— KEEPING TEXAS SAFE.

REGARDLESS OF WHICH SIDE THE PARTICIPANTS TOOK, THEY WERE TEXAN TO THE CORE. THEIR DESCENDANTS STILL ARE, A COMMON PRIDE IN THEIR ANCESTORS BINDING THEM TOGETHER WHERE MUTUAL CALAMITIES ONCE TORE THEM APART.

jaxon·97

END

SOURCES

Those readers who have finished *Lost Cause* have realized by now that my telling of the Reconstruction Era is not "politically correct." I believe that there is no point in trying to explain this era if you're not going to do it truthfully, with all its racism, violence, and other dark aspects that are repugnant to modern social theorists and every ethnic group involved.

In my earlier Texas historical graphic novels I told the story of Quanah Parker from the Comanche perspective (*Comanche Moon*) and the story of Juan Seguin from the Mexican (Tejano) perspective, so I figure I am obliged to tell Hardin's story from the point of view of Hardin and his partisans (*Los Tejanos*) — without sanitizing it or even changing the language used during this racially volatile period. I am a stickler for authenticity in my work, regardless of the consequences. Why? Because old tintypes — scratched, crusty, fading and flaking with age — have a ring of truth about them that I find irresistible. My experience with *Comanche Moon* and *Los Tejanos* has taught me that, as an artist, you can never please everybody and it's a waste of time to try. We can judge past events by present standards, I suppose, but we should not rewrite history to conform to our "enlightened" notions of morality. To attempt it produces bad history as well as a dull story.

My readers have also figured out that the "Taylor-Sutton Feud" or "Sutton-Taylor Feud" is a misnomer and that it should have more properly been called the Taylor-Tumlinson Feud. Billy Sutton was actually a minor player in the trouble and his death did little toward ending it. Joe Tumlinson, on the other hand, figured into practically all the violence directed against the Taylor Party and only with his death did the feud quiet down. Considering Joe's many ties with the Taylors, this is a rather amazing twist.

What caused the Taylors and Tumlinsons to start shooting at each other? Despite the considerable amount of literature that the feud has generated over the past century, no one has satisfactorily explained the cause of the feud or identified the specific event that triggered the fighting.

On the origin of the feud I have followed Creed Taylor's unpublished account at the Texas State Archives, "Life of Creed Taylor or Eighty-Three Years on the Frontiers of Texas. . . To Which is Appended an Account of the Great Taylor-Sutton Feud in DeWitt and Adjoining Counties," along with that of Victor Rose (published in 1880). Both cite the practice of mavericking, as do most others who've sorted through the matter in later years. Creed's account is particularly important because he was one of the few participants to set forth the reasons for the feud and to describe many of its bloody episodes.

As is well known to all old Texans, at the close of the War there was a long period in which there were no local officers in authority and every man became, as it were, a law unto himself. In the vast expanse of country extending from the Brazos [River] to the Rio Grande, thousands of cattle and horses roamed at will. The fall of the Confederacy precipitated a great number of ex-confederate soldiers upon this section — men who had fought through four long years without pay, while, as they claimed, those who remained at home had grown wealthy at the expense of the men in the ranks. Seeing their opportunity to make up for lost time and knowing the impotency of the law, wholesale cattle stealing became the rage and this was one of the first causes that led to the Taylor-Sutton Feud. ... It must be remembered further that nearly or quite all of these [victimized} stockmen were ardent supporters of the Southern Cause, and during Reconstruction days, when the state was under carpetbag rule, these men were the objects of special hatred by the satraps in power. When a feud sprang up in any community, the lawless element had but to declare their present and previous loyalty to the federal government, report their grievances against this or that "rebel," and though their intended victim may have been a patriot, pure and noble as Travis or Fannin, he soon found himself imprisoned in a federal stockade — "Bull Pens" we called them — guarded by Yankee bayonets.

Creed Taylor's memoirs were dictated to John Warren Hunter of Mason, Texas, in 1891 when Taylor was seventy-one years old. Hunter evidently planned to publish the account, polishing it for a decade, but instead sold it to James DeShields. The latter culled out the Revolution-era sections (with considerable rewriting) and published it as *Tall Men With Long Rifles* (1935) to capitalize on the state's first centennial celebration. Prior to its publication, DeShields sold the original manuscript to the Texas State Archives for four hundred dollars.

Apart from Creed's "reminiscences," few other first-hand accounts exist and none from the Sutton point of view. The earliest and most extensive telling of the feud is Victor M. Rose's *The Texas Vendetta: or, The Sutton-Taylor Feud* (New York: J.J. Little & Co., 1880). Rose was a Confederate vet, had legal training, and worked as a newspaper editor and writer. More importantly, he was a native of the feud area and wrote his account soon after the events took place. Considering that emotions still ran deep on both sides in 1880, this was a fairly brave thing to do.

After Rose — whose account no doubt influenced other writers' perceptions of the feud — we have a look at Creed's sons, Hays and Doboy, by J. B. Policy in several 1908 issues of the *San Antomo Express*. These articles were reprinted as "The Taylor Boys" in a 1928 edition of *Frontier Times*. Policy had been raised in Wilson County, was a wounded Civil War veteran and later attorney in Floresville, and knew the Taylors well. In 1937 Jack Hays Day published *The Sutton-Taylor feud*, giving the Taylor side as his mother married Josiah Taylor after the death of her first husband, John Day. Some feud information also appears in Lewis S. Delony's *Forty Years a Peace Officer* (1937), in Louise and Fullen Artrip's *Memoirs of Daniel Fore (Jim) Chisholm* (1949), and in Walter Dixson's *Richland Crossing* (1994).

The best modern summary of the feud appeared in *The History of DeWitt County, Texas* (1991) and is titled "The DeWitt County Feud." Its author, Chuck Parsons, has written many other feud-related books and articles over the years. Earlier studies include C. L. Douglas's *Famous Texas Feuds* (1936) and C. L. Sonnichsen's *I'll Die Before I'll Run* (1962). Dwain Browning did "Texas' Bloody Taylor-Sutton Feud" in *Best of the West Annual* for 1973, followed in 1974 by Robert C. Sutton Jr.'s *The Sutton-Taylor Feud*. The latter, as one might expect, is heavily slanted to the Sutton side. In the 1980s Marjorie B. Hyatt of Smiley, Texas, began publishing material on feud participants, and her interest quickly moved from genealogy to history. Her latest is *Fuel for a Feud* (1989), self-published. Another book of this type is *The Taylor Party* by Eddie Day Truitt (1992).

John Wesley Hardin has enjoyed coverage in just about every collection on gunfighters, and articles about him in magazines are too numerous to mention. His autobiography was published in 1896, shortly after his death, and it is one of the few detailed accounts actually penned by a notorious gunman of the Old West. *The Life of John Wesley Hardin from the Original Manuscript as Written by Himself* has naturally served as the basis for most subsequent literature about Hardin. These articles, anthologies, books, etc. vary a great deal in quality — as do the novels written about his exploits. In the fictional-but-based-on-fact category we have Lewis Nordyke's excellent *John Wesley Hardin: Texas Gunman* (1957), along with J.H. Plenn and C.J. LaRoche's *The Fastest Gun in Texas* (1956) and Lee Floren's *John Wesley Hardin: Texas Gunfighter* (1962). The first-mentioned, though sprinkled with imaginary dialogue, approaches a biography while the latter two were intended for the pulp market. They all contrast favorably with James Carlos Blake's absolutely dreadful *The Pistoleer* (1995) and the horrendously concocted "literary" effort, *Reflections in Dark Glass* (1996) by Bruce McGinnis.

Various aspects of Hardin's life are also treated in Eugene Cunningham's *Triggernometry: A Gallery of Gunfighters* (1934); Thomas Ripley's *They Died With Their Boots On* (1935); J. Marvin Hunter and Noah Rose's *The Album of Gunfighters* (1951); Ed Bartholomew's *Kill or Be Killed* (1953); Web Maddox's *The Black Sheep* (1975); James D. Horan's *The Authentic Wild West: The Gunfighters* (1976); and Sonnichsen's off-beat *The Grave of John Wesley Hardin* (1979), a topic currently much in the news as Hardin descendants attempt to have his remains moved from El Paso to South Texas, where his wife and children are buried.

The most extensive biographies of Hardin to date are Richard C. Marohn's *The Last Gunfighter* (1995) and Leon C. Metz's *Dark Angel of Texas* (1996). These two studies should satisfy most Hardin buffs for a while, although Marohn's book is poorly written and Metz's effort suffers from a noticeable anti-Hardin bias.

To understand phenomena like the feud and the careers of gunmen like Hardin, one must know about the times and social situations in which they flourished. Concerning subjects like Reconstruction and race relations in Texas, there has lately been considerable revision of earlier studies. Charles William Ramsdell's classic *Reconstruction in Texas* (1910) and W.C. Nunn's *Texas Under the Carpetbaggers* (1962) are often challenged nowadays, with scholars like Randolph B. Campbell arguing that Carpetbaggers hardly existed in post-war Texas and that southern-born Scalawags — men like Jack Helm and Joe Tumlinson who cooperated with the Reconstruction regime — were the real culprits. However, because it was more convenient to blame greedy outsiders than local opportunists for the ills of Texas during this period, the myth of the Yankee Carpetbagger was born.

Readers who wish to sample the latest thinking on post-war Texas should consult the works of Campbell, Barry A. Crouch, Alwyn Barr, James M. Smallwood, and Carl H. Moneyhon. For the Army's role, William L. Richter is my favorite authority, and he did me the favor of critically reading the script for *Lost Cause*; he has also written on the Freedmens Bureau. So has Crouch, along with a new study in progress on the State Police, which he assures me will make these long-maligned officers look as heroic as the Texas Rangers. I have my doubts, although from a Mexican perspective the Rangers were not always heroic themselves.

And what about Hardin? Some may say that his violent, murderous streak should not appeal to modern sensibilities even though most writers have treated him sympathetically and continue to do so. Despite his professed code of honor, he tried to solve life's problems, large and small, with a gun. Such behavior is not acceptable nowadays, we are told. But is it really? A survey of our popular culture suggests otherwise — that Hardin would be right at home on the silver screen, blowing away enemy spies, terrorists, predatory aliens, and other social undesirables with a technologically advanced version of his Colt .45. Like our nation's leaders from Teddy Roosevelt to Ronald Reagan, Hardin believed in walking softly and carrying a big stick. This "stick" — his myriad collection of firearms — he would not hesitate to use when his life and value system was threatened. Was he a paranoid personality who enjoyed killing, or just like us if we had the nerve to act on our convictions? Whichever, Hardin was an American icon, and interest in his exploits is not likely to slacken.

Jack Jackson

JACK JACKSON TALKS ABOUT *LOST CAUSE*

The following interview with Jack Jackson appeared in *The Comics Journal* #213 (1998). The main impetus of the interview was a scathing review of *Lost Cause* by Michael Ventura that appeared in Jackson's hometown alternative newspaper, *The Austin Chronicle.*

I wanted to give Jackson an opportunity to respond to the review and discuss the broader issues it brought up. Jackson was angry over the review, which he thought was intellectually and morally dunderheaded, but he was angrier and personally hurt that the paper to which he had contributed for many years wouldn't give him space to reply.

In 2001, Jackson compiled a series of extensive comments about the review and a chronicle of his two-year correspondence with the editors of the paper, appropriately titled "Jaxon's Rant." In it, he reprinted my interview with him, which is reproduced in the following pages. He also wrote a preface to the interview, providing background on the controversy, his affiliation with *The Comics Journal*, his friendship with me, and insight into his own career as a cartoonist.

I include Jackson's preface because I want readers to have a sense of Jackson's informal, colloquial, no-nonsense voice. Jackson, who I was privileged to know from the late 1970s until his death in 2006, was mercifully free of intellectual guile and sophistry; he tackled intense and complex subjects head-on.

Following Jackson's preface is my own introduction, as it appeared in *The Comics Journal*, which provides a more extensive context to the interview.

— *Gary Groth*

PREFACE, 2001

by Jack Jackson

Hi Folks,

Here's the interview that Gary Groth ran in his house organ, *The Comics Journal*, concerning *Lost Cause* and the *Chron's* censorship.

I've known Groth — a personable comics nut with brains & a fellow who does his homework before opening his mouth — practically ever since he started *The Comics Journal (TCJ)* 25 years ago. I think we first met when some guys were throwing an annual comics convention up in Dallas in the late '70s-early '80s. His pub is the leading intellectual format in the known universe on the comics/comix profession, past and present. Somehow, month after month, year after year, *TCJ* keeps cranking out top-notch issues that cover the wide spectrum of the comics world.

Gary liked my work, recognizing it (perhaps) as a worthy successor to the Harvey Kurtzman historical strips done for EC Comics in the Fifties. He published my Seguín book, *Los Tejanos*, in 1982, after Last Gasp had published parts of it as *Recuerden El Alamo* and *Tejano Exile*. I added another 32 pages to Fantagraphics's edition, and Juke Garrett did the cover. Thanks, guys!

In Issue 61, 1981 Winter Special, *TCJ* ran an interview with me called "Tejano Cartoonist," by Bill Sherman. A photo shows me as the handsome stud I then was but will never be again; another pic shows me with the Rip Off Press gang & my foxy girlfriend, Beatrice Bonini. Seems like there were several other issues of *TCJ* where I was profiled and my latest work mentioned, but I can't locate them.

In addition to such feature treatment, *TCJ* also published a couple of articles I wrote as a contributor to the mag. My "Learning Texas History the Painless Way" (#119, Jan 1988) was about the little comic book, *Texas History Movies*, that some of us old-timers studied in grade school — and our recent efforts to sanitize its objectionable ethnic/racial stereotypes. This was the same booklet that my landlord on Bellvue Street later

gave me his 1st edition copy of. I still have my own revised copy from the Fifties, with "Jackie Jackson" on the cover.

A Hispanic lady friend of mine down in Cuero was horrified to learn that this nasty, racist little comic book had launched my career as a distinguished Texas historian recognized for my attention of the Latino contribution. Hmmm; must be a meaning there somewhere... If so, the dear girl is too politically correct to grasp it.

Another piece I did for *TCJ* (Issue 144, Sept 1991) was called "The Good, the Bad, and the Foreign" — a short history on Western comics here and abroad. In it, I pondered the question of why Europeans seem to do better Western comics than us home-growners. Señor Ventura should have read it before he accused me of using dialogue from the Gabby Hayes/Hopalong Cassidy era.

Then Gary got the bright idea to republish my old stuff in two volumes, so it would be available in a classy format. He's done this for lots of other artists whose work is scattered hither & yon in comix and now yellowing, chipping, and crumbling into dust.

In 1991 Fantagraphics released *Optimism of Youth*, a collection of my underground rank & racy stuff. Included was a not-before-published fuck story called "Sleeping Beauty & the Beast" that I had drawn in 1970 for one of Wally Wood's X-rated anthologies that Ron Turner's Last Gasp was gonna publish. WW, one of the great EC artists, died before getting it out. I dedicated *Optimism of Youth* to Greg Irons and Dave Sheridan, "Gone but Not Forgotten." *God's Bosom* came in 1995, and I LOVE the color job that Gary's crew did on my cover — best thing ever put out with my name on it.

My intro for the book ranted about how screwed-up Texas was becoming. Ranting & raving is not exactly a new characteristic of mine. This book collected my miscellaneous "historical" strips, including those done after I moved back to Austin; some were published in the *Sun*, others never published anywhere.

Thus it is safe to say that Gary Groth was "sympathetic" to me on the *Chron's* review. He was also sensitive to the slander/libel angle — the same thing that it had taken him years and megabucks to clear his name from on Señor Fleischer's charges. Though he was on the other side of the fence, the one accused of libel, knew first-hand how messy & complicated things can get when the right to free speech is at stake. Well, I wasn't suing the *Chron*, editor Black, or critic Ventura,

This sequence from "Grant!" in *Two-Fisted Tales* #31 (Jan.-Feb. 1953) was written by Harvey Kurtzman and drawn by John Severin. ©2012 William M. Gaines Agent, Inc.

and Gary was in my corner for sure on the free speech question — as he always has been. His questions took the discussion above & beyond V's review to greater issues, asking if the goals of "art" are compatible with "humanizing" oppressors and whether or not this presents a moral conflict to artists like myself.

Hope you enjoy...

INTRODUCTION
by Gary Groth

Upon publication of Jack Jackson's graphic history, *Lost Cause*, Jackson's hometown alternative paper, *The Austin Chronicle*, ran a double-barreled hatchet job in its September 21, 1998 edition: a review of the book by pop critic Michael Ventura and an accompanying essay condemning the book's main character, John Wesley Hardin by Jesse Sublett. The book itself is a dramatic account of one of the most volatile periods in American history — how white Texans dealt with post-Civil War Reconstruction.

Ventura attacked the book from several angles. His first devastating strategy was to sneer at the book's designation as a "graphic novel" ("Well, it's graphic enough — without pictures, the 148 page story would shrink to maybe 25 pages, if that"), which is a little like saying that if you took the images away from a movie, the experience would shrink to staring at a blank screen in a dark room for two hours. He went on to question Jackson's historical accuracy — falsely, as it turned out — and finally called the author and his work racist.

I thought it was a boneheaded review by someone who evinced no awareness, much less sympathy, with the comics medium in general and Jackson's work in particular — which is the least you should expect from a review of a respected artist's work.

This didn't outrage me, though; after all, shoddy reviews are published every day, and it was more or less par for the course. What really pissed me off was the *Chronicle*'s refusal to give Jackson space to rebut the review on the specious grounds that "if we allowed everyone... who disagreed with a review of their art to rebut it, we would have room for little else."

This is obvious bullshit. Every restaurant owner, musician, filmmaker, and theatre director who's criticized in the pages of the *Austin Chronicle* would not choose to rebut a negative review and in the unlikely eventuality that the paper was overwhelmed by such rebuttals it could establish parameters accordingly. The *Chronicle* was clearly taking advantage of its privileged position of owning the local press. This is unjust on the face of it, and gives the victim of a bad review no recourse to have his say. So, this interview with Jackson is my way of helping even up the odds.

I've been an admirer of Jackson's satirical and historical comics, which he began drawing in the late '60s, and I published his *Los Tejanos* graphic novel in 1982. *Lost Cause* is a major work by one of the most important artists currently working in the medium, and if the *Chronicle* refused to behave decently and give him space to address Ventura's charges, I felt the least I could do is show him the respect the *Chronicle* didn't, and provide a forum to do just that in the pages of the *Journal*. We discuss not only the review that started a firestorm on net chat rooms, but the book more generally and the delicate position of writing politically charged historical drama.

From *Lost Cause*

THE INTERVIEW

GARY GROTH: *Let's talk about* Lost Cause *and the controversy created by the review by Michael Ventura in the* Austin Chronicle.

JACK JACKSON: I was pretty upset about it, and didn't really have any way to deal with it, except appeal to the *Chronicle* to let me defend myself, which they wouldn't do. And that was even more aggravating than the review itself.

GROTH: *That they wouldn't give you the same kind of space that they gave him I found to be pretty contemptible. The review ran in the* Austin Chronicle *on Sept. 18, 1998. Was there any backlash towards you, as far as you could tell, after he called you and your work racist?*

JACKSON: No. On the contrary, people were rising to my defense — calling me, writing me, and trying to e-mail me — but I'm not on the internet so a friend of mine who was, passed these things along. I was amazed at the issues that were being discussed on these posts, you know? They were going to the nitty gritty, and half of them hadn't even read the book yet. They were just looking at the review itself, and the ignorance that it manifested.

GROTH: *So you didn't catch any more flak because of the review?*

JACKSON: Oh, absolutely not. No, it was very supportive, and that's what finally made me realize that hey, there's no point in trying to dodge this, you might as well grab the bull by the horns, you know? I don't want to use the term "milk it," but controversy sells books. So if this guy wants to label me a racist, sure, let's talk about it.

Consequently, I was going to book signings and discussing the racial aspects of my book. For example, the governor's wife every year throws a thing down at the state capitol called the Texas Book Festival, and I was an invited speaker on a panel on John Wesley Hardin — and guess what came up? The review.

So I figure there's black people sitting in the audience, and you just have to deal with it, once somebody decides that your work is racist garbage. That's basically what the guy was saying, that *Lost Cause* is going to pervert and twist the minds of innocent young children, and he sees himself as their savior, as it were, by denouncing my work. To say it blindsided me would be an understatement, because as you know, all my previous work had done just the opposite. It had tried to tell the story of "the neglected historical others," as Rusty Witek would call them. And simply because I wanted to do a book and tell the story from the perspective of the white Southerners who John Wesley Hardin was representing, as it were.

Then all of a sudden, I get this kind of reaction. At my age, I just don't need it, you know?

GROTH: *Tell me a little about this panel you were on, and what the reaction there was, and what the discussion was.*

JACKSON: Well, I was simply trying to say that you're talking about a very, very difficult historical period here, Reconstruction. And this is one of the few instances in which the white folks, particularly those in the South, found themselves the oppressed, as opposed to being the oppressor. They were just not ready for it, and could not make the transition to a subjugated people.

They could not accept the standards that were being imposed on them, the way people were coming down from the North and saying, OK, I want you to act this way and that way, I want you to think this way, and these people are now going to be your social equals. So you had these pockets of resistance, which I think is natural in any similar situation: even worse here. And violence, of course, was a necessary aspect of this transitional period before the kinks were worked out. Hell, they're still not worked out. But you can imagine in those days what the situation was like.

The difficulty came mainly with the young men, the youngbloods, those who weren't old enough to have taken part in the Civil War. They had not experienced all of the obscene things that go on during war. They're sitting around listening to their older brothers, cousins, and uncles talk about them, and they kind of saw themselves as the champions of this lifestyle which all of a sudden is gone. "Don't worry, Pa. I'll make things right."

This was why you had the violence that occurred in that period so much, and their elders provided them with a support network that prolonged the ordeal.

From *Lost Cause*

From *Lost Cause*

GROTH: *Let me quote from Ventura's review and ask you to respond to this accusation. He said, referring to the white Texan population in Reconstruction Texas, "Jackson's heroes have courage in the face of danger, fierceness, determination, flair, and a kind of flat-out pedal-to-the-metal madness that is very American —"*

JACKSON: [*Laughs.*] This guy's great. He's a gonzo journalist by trade, I believe, always talking in his column about the major book he's about to do.

GROTH: *He goes on to say, and I think this is the central accusation, "Jackson is a racist because he finds these qualities only in white people. Almost without exception, he presents blacks as oafs, exactly as blacks were represented in the old-type movies that are the model for his dialogue." And then he goes on to say "Every drawing of a black man is the same drawing, same bone structure, same expression, same lips. His whites, by contrast, are differentiated. This is more than a simple gap, this is how Jackson sees."*

JACKSON: Well, the guy needs glasses very badly, and several of the people whose letters the *Chronicle* did publish pointed this out, that there is as much differentiation in the black people in the book — because I'm working from photographs, for heaven's sake — as there is with white people. But the reviewer evidently did not notice these. He thinks that because my blacks have flatter noses and larger lips than my whites, that these anatomical differences are somehow an insidious plot on my part to dehumanize these people. Gary, he's saying that I'm operating on exactly the same level as the Nazi artists in Germany.

GROTH: *Right, right.*

JACKSON: Those artists/cartoonists who depicted the Jews as squat, fat, little hooked-nose subhumans to prepare the German population for the idea that they should be exterminated. He's saying that I'm doing the same thing, and that by depicting my blacks in this fashion, I make the white violence against them more acceptable. Hey, man, that's a heavy charge. And it is not justified by the artwork. If you look at it, you will see these people come in different shapes and flavors like the white folks.

GROTH: *I didn't detect that the blacks were any more caricatured within your style than the whites.*

JACKSON: This is what is happening: I've never seen a single bit of artwork that Michael Ventura's ever produced, yet he claims to be an artist in his review, and he is not even perceptive enough to note the differences in the people that I'm drawing. And I was just floored by that and many of his other accusations.

I'm not an ignoramus. This was not kind of a happy-go-lucky, "Let's try to draw these subhuman Negroes so that everybody will think that they got what was coming to them," sort of thing. Ventura's write-up was just a litany of putdowns — everybody who read it said that it was the most bitter kind of so-called review they had ever read in their life and that it really amounted to a personal attack, a smear. I certainly wasn't prepared for it.

So like I said, it put me in a state of mind where for like a couple of weeks, I didn't even want to do anything, you know? Why bother? If this is the kind of response that you get to something that you slaved on for a couple of years — It really did take the wind out of my sails, I must say. And he later defended himself, because evidently he had been getting a lot of letters and feedback from people himself.

GROTH: *Now where did he defend himself?*

JACKSON: He has a weekly column called "After 3 A.M.," or "Midnight Hour," or something like that. I don't know if he lives here in Austin or in L.A. I know that he bounced back and forth for a while, trying to become a screenwriter out there, and had no luck at it. One of his projects, as it turns out, was a screenplay dealing with John Wesley Hardin, which nobody wanted. I think that when he saw my book, a lot of something — antagonism — came into play. I just don't know. I've never met the gentleman, who, I understand, hails from the Bronx.

GROTH: *How do you respond to his charge that you imbued the whites with certain qualities that you did not imbue the blacks with?*

JACKSON: Well, it's horseshit. But my point is this: you have to, when you do a book, take a perspective, OK? My perspective in this case was from the side of the white Southerners during the Reconstruction period. Basically, I saw the book, because it is about a feud, as dealing with white-on-white violence, none of which Ventura even mentioned in the review. He only saw the white-on-black aspect of it, which in fact is a very minor part of the book.

I am not trying to tell the story of John Wesley Hardin from the black point of view. And I'm not even interested in what happened to the blacks except insofar as it was a contributing factor to the overall violence of the era in terms of military rule and Reconstruction. So I am taking probably the most unpopular perspective for the book imaginable. And that is the politically incorrect idea that you can tell a story about racists sympathetically.

You see what I'm saying? Because they were racists, as Ventura points out, but they were also human beings. In other words, racism was just part of the mindset of that day and time. So it just seems mindblowing to me that you cannot take any perspective you deem appropriate in the story you're telling. I think that an artist should have that latitude, in terms of putting together his story, and deciding on a perspective that is key to all that follows. And I say, hey, I'm not telling this story like Alex Haley would tell it. I understand and appreciate his approach, but it's not my cup of tea. Roots come in different colors.

GROTH: *When you decided to tell the story from the point of view of the white Texas population, you must have known that you were treading a real razor's edge between sympathizing with their historical moment, with them as people caught up in an historical moment, and sympathizing with racism per se.*

JACKSON: Well, of course I did. This is why the project sat on my back burner for a decade. During this agonizing period of time, I'm sending Xeroxes of the script out to people who specialize on the Reconstruction era, as well as historians in South Texas. In other words, I'm soliciting response on different levels here.

I'm going to the chronistas of those counties concerned, and I'm going to authorities on a national level, and I'm saying, "Tell me if I've got my facts straight here. Tell me if this is the way it happened." And so I got a lot of feedback over a period of time, and I finally felt pretty confident about it, except, of course, for the powder keg that it represents in telling the story from a point of view that most people do not find sympathetic.

GROTH: *I think that one of the things that seems to come through his review, is that there seems to be an implicit accusation that you didn't condemn the racism from an authorial point of view, and yet —*

JACKSON: Oh, yeah. That was a major problem with Ventura.

GROTH: *But you did not feel the need to do that?*

JACKSON: No, I didn't. In this case, I figured that what I needed to do was to make the story more up close and personal, and to show what was motivating these people to act the way they did, to reinforce, in my narrative voice, what you saw below, as opposed to qualifying it. There's a couple ways you can go in this voice. You can say, folks, what you're going to see in the panel below is horrible, an atrocity, a real stain against humanity, but, sad to say, this is the way it happened. And then show the artwork. I would argue that that is not effective storytelling because it strips away whatever power the artwork would have. By that kind of a qualifying voice, you work against and negate the visual side of the equation — and visuals are integral to the comics medium, aren't they?

GROTH: *You're making a distinction between propagating racism — which is what Ventura accused you of, I think — and depicting racism — which is what you're claiming to have done. But would you agree with the proposition that an author could assert racism by the way he depicts it, that this is a matter of interpretation?*

JACKSON: Yes, it's all in the interpretive realm, and this is exactly why our society has tied itself in knots concerning what's racist and what isn't. Today, many Chinese-Americans would find *The Yellow Kid* an objectionable symbol of past racism. That's also why humorous classics like *Amos 'n' Andy* have fallen into the racist category. Funny, bust-your-gut-laughing stuff, but black intellectuals think it's the worst depiction of their society imaginable. I, a

LI HUNG CHANG VISITS HOGAN'S ALLEY.

R. F. Outcault's *Hogan's Alley* strip, Sept. 6, 1886. The Yellow Kid reacts to a visit from Li Hung Chang.

young country hick who'd never even seen a black person, much less a big-city slum, thought it was a riot — every bit as good as Red Skelton's "Freddy the Freeloader" bum character. [It's] All in how you interpret it and who's doing the interpreting. What a white person might find amusing, a black person might see just the opposite. This is a given, and seldom can you please everyone — especially if your "interpretation" deals with a period as troubled as post-war Reconstruction in the South.

Ventura, so it seems, thinks that I must be a racist for even trying to tackle this subject, for even wasting my time with people he denounces as all racists themselves. "Why bother with such scumbags?" he asks. "Better that they and their evil ways remain forgotten."

So I was doomed, in his estimation, from the git-go.

GROTH: *One thing he objected to was your narration, and your use of the word "Negro" in the narration, and he said that's "Jackson talking, not his characters," but it was my impression that it was an omniscient narration, circa 1870 or so.*

JACKSON: Are you talking about the use of the words "Colored" and "Negro" in my narrative banners?

GROTH: *Yeah, in the captions. And it seems to me like what you were trying to do was to narrate it from the point of view of someone in 1870.*

JACKSON: Yes, precisely! Now, Ventura makes some sort of a snide remark about that, saying regardless of "what the politically correct crowd thinks," and my argument is. "Hey, you're one of *them* yourself." What is a politically correct person? Has

the reviewer never heard of a national organization that advances the rights of who? — Colored people. Has he never heard of the [United] Negro College Fund, whose motto in TV commercials is "A mind is a terrible thing to waste"? And yet he is condemning me for using "Colored" and "Negro" as a narrator.

What is a politically correct person except somebody who hustles to make sure they're using the latest term that a minority group decides to call itself? "African-American" didn't exist as a term in that era. And yet that's how he would have me refer to black people in my captions, for to do otherwise is a slap in the face to modern readers and especially to blacks. So I'm just at a total loss as to how to deal with that kind of criticism.

They were "Colored" people back in the 1860s and 1870s. They were "Negroes," which comes from the Spanish word for "black" [negro]. So I really don't know what to say to such bullshit charges that my work is racist and unfit for younger readers.

GROTH: *He claimed to have caught you on a historical mistake, with the Winchester rifle...*

JACKSON: Right. And he cited that one example, I might add, to say that my entire work was historically inaccurate and not to be trusted as a legitimate history of the era.

GROTH: *Right. But he was in fact wrong, wasn't he?*

JACKSON: He was, in fact, wrong. After letters started coming to the *Chronicle*, Ventura wrote a little blurb at the end of one of his columns. He said, "It was an honest mistake, which needs no apology." I loved that. He calls me a shoddy historian, but all he's doing is displaying his own ignorance and pretending it's okay to do so.

GROTH: *And he based his diatribe virtually on that one mistake, which he later conceded wasn't a mistake.*

JACKSON: On that one damn thing: that a Winchester couldn't have been in a scene in 1857. And I'm not even drawing a Winchester. You know, a Winchester on the right side of the plate has a slot where you slide a bullet in? You look at the picture and tell me if you see one of those things on the side of the plate. No! It's a Henry rifle, and it's the same kind that Blondie used to save old Tuco's neck from the noose in *The Good, the Bad, and the Ugly.* They were rare pre-Civil War weapons, but people down in Texas got the latest in military technology available. Old Sam Colt himself said that the Texans had basically made his arms, and, without them, he would have stayed in bankruptcy. So when these types of repeating rifles came out, you know who was buying them first? Texans.

Anyway, that was just another example of the review's misdirected criticism of me, and Ventura

From *Lost Cause*

From Lost Cause

used it to make a mountain out of a molehill.

GROTH: *In the book itself, you talk about your various historical sources, but can you tell me what you used for the visual sources? How do you dig up that stuff?*

JACKSON: Oh, there's quite a bit of it: for example, Hardin himself. All of his papers and photographic collection have been preserved. He wrote scores and scores of letters while he was in prison, and his relatives down there at Nixon gave all this stuff to the university in San Marcos, which is about 30 miles south of Austin. All that material is there, including pictures of the children, his wife, himself, and other relatives. Much of it has been published, by the way, because he's one of the more notable gunfighters who actually left an autobiography behind. So in one sense, you've got a

store of visual materials available for a project of this kind, cameras having been invented by the Civil War era. You've got no problem with weapons, costumes, houses — the whole shebang. Photographs of many of the main characters. They exist.

GROTH: *What's always struck me about your historical work is just how authentic all the visuals look; I'm talking about the scenery, the carriages, the wagons, the houses, and so forth. Is all that, in fact, accurate?*

JACKSON: Absolutely. I pride myself on it. In fact, one of the leading authorities on the Reconstruction period and the military's role in it is a man named William Richter. He lives out in Tucson. He not only read the script for historical accuracy, but he's now a big fan, and when I sent him the finished book, he wrote back and he said, "I can't believe it. I can recognize every general in your panels. Is this a comic book? I didn't know comics were so sophisticated." And stuff like that. So it's edifying when somebody who has combed the archives for these types of documents thinks that you're doing a halfway decent job.

But of course I'm not trying to cater to academic "specialists." I'm trying to get the general readership to feel the mood and the tempo of the time, and understand what it was like. This is my whole thing. When I create these books, what I'm trying to do is take people back in a time machine to that day and time and let them see events as they occurred *through these people's eyes.*

Well, some people don't like the view.

GROTH: [Laughs.] *Right.*

JACKSON: I notice that Alex Haley didn't beat around the bush with *Roots*, even when the thing was filmed. I mean, there was a lot of very objectionable

From Lost Cause

issues that he met head-on. The white owner's abuse of the attractive black women. Did he skirt the issue? Hell, no. Chuck Connors is crowded right on top of her telling her to relax and enjoy herself. And so I figure if a black man can tell the story and do it well, from his side — his racist, if you would, point of view — why the hell can't a white man do the same thing? But that's just not the way it works. We have a double standard about such things. Now people are even shy about naming a high school after somebody if they owned slaves. In an era when it was socially acceptable to do so! It's just mindblowing. Jim Bowie, for example. There was a great stink when they tried to name a high school here in Austin "Bowie High School," because he had been a slave runner and owned slaves before dying at the Alamo.

It gets a little bit bizarre. Everybody in the South owned slaves in those days if they could afford to. It was a mark of one's social standing.

GROTH: *As someone who has drawn some of the most virulent anti-racist comics in the history of comics, are you conflicted about that kind of political correctness?*

JACKSON: It's not a matter of being politically correct to me at all, Gary. My creative mandate is to try to tell the story truthfully.

GROTH: *No, no, I mean, when decent people lobby not to have schools named after people they consider to be oppressive people. I mean, do you feel conflicted about your feelings toward that?*

JACKSON: Do I feel conflicted?

GROTH: *Yeah, do you have some sympathy for that point of view?*

JACKSON: Not really. I don't, because once you start hauling skeletons out of the closest, we won't have anybody worthy of naming *anything* after. For example, there's all of that hullabaloo about Thomas Jefferson and his children by a mulatto slave girl, or whatever, and then the family came up with DNA results that proved it. But earlier, when Nick Nolte made that movie about Jefferson in Paris, scholars were outraged. "Oh, you're showing Jefferson doing something that the historical record doesn't definitely say he did." So when the DNA thing hit the media, I got a chuckle out of it, needless to say.

No, I don't lose any sleep at night over what my ancestors may or may not have done. Trying to guilt-trip an entire culture is — I don't know, it's a little sick. We're not responsible for our ancestors' failings. It's not a problem with me. My problem in telling a story like *Lost Cause*, is to try and tell it as well as possible, from whatever perspective is most effective. In other words, with the *Los Tejanos* book, I certainly didn't want to tell that story from the white Texan point of view. Am I a racist for using the Mexican

Jackson's take on *Texas History Movies* ©PJM

perspective? Most readers didn't think so. In fact they patted me on the back and said I was breaking new ground. I think it's a little ironic that the same approach to a different subject has now caused me to be branded a racist.

So it's not a matter of being politically correct. As a storyteller — once you take a focal character — as a storyteller, I think you're obliged to try to tell the story from that person's point of view, and his culture's as well.

GROTH: *You mentioned Haley's* Roots, *which is the history of slavery as seen through the eyes of a slave. Do you think that seeing history through the eyes of the victims gives the author a leg up, morally speaking, whereas seeing history through the eyes of the oppressor — whether its the racist South during Reconstruction or Nazis or Guatemalan death squads — could be intrinsically morally questionable? Does one of the goals of art — to humanize its subjects — run into moral conflict with such an approach?*

JACKSON: An interesting point. Obviously we "civilized" folk [who are] about to step into the 21st century identify with and see sympathetically the plight of victims of oppression. Thus, the success of Haley's *Roots*. White people the world over could appreciate the struggle for human dignity that his characters represented. Not only did Haley have a leg up, morally, but as a writer he obeyed the creative imperative that I just mentioned: to tell his story as well and as truthfully as possible, whatever the cost.

Imagine the reaction he'd have gotten if his book and TV series hit the market in 1910! Now, is it "intrinsically morally questionable" to attempt a story from the oppressor's perspective? I don't know. People are just people, and few are perfect. Yes, white Texans of Reconstruction times were racists — as we now define the term — but they also had the same hopes and dreams of any era. Their lives had some redeeming qualities, and I don't think it's right to sweep them into the historical dustbin because they did politically incorrect things by current moral standards. True, there's a thin line between "glorifying" their misdeeds — evidently what Ventura thinks I've done — and sympathizing with their human condition in rough times. They were my ancestors, but I don't see how I've "fallen under their spell" — as the self-righteous reviewer claimed — by attempting to recapture the spirit of the Reconstruction era from their perspective. I don't even see them as the oppressor but rather as the victim. Maybe that's what annoyed Ventura. Anyway, it's not like I tried to hide their blemishes in *Lost Cause*. I put them right out there for everyone to see, "warts and all." How is this glorifying my ancestors any more than Haley did his?

I guess, by extension, what I'm saying is that, yes, some death camp guard's son or daughter could do a book/film/comic about their father's "struggle" against the Jews or the Mayan Indians in whatever historical period. It probably wouldn't win the acclaim of *The Pawnbroker* or *Maus*, that's safe to say! But their father, whether a brutal fucker or a hapless soul merely caught in an institutionalized web of violence, was still human, and if the work "humanized" him, then it would qualify as art, wouldn't it? Objectionable to those whose parents/ancestors were gassed or hacked to death? Certainly. But such things are history. They happened, and we're still trying to understand why. I had never thought much about life from the Nazi point of view until I saw Marlon Brando in *The Young Lions*. Though he was on the "wrong side," his role made me realize that he was a human being, too, his inner workings worthy of attention just like the good guys.

So to me there's no "moral conflict" in humanizing your subjects, be they scumbags or saints, and I don't think the goals of art are incompatible with such an approach. If the story has a compelling ring of truth, it's art, and political correctness can take the hindmost.

GROTH: *Now, you have been criticized for* Lost Cause *as being a bit all over the map, because it's not only about John Wesley Hardin, it's also about the Taylor-Sutton Feud, and there's no one central character in this book like*

there is in, say, Los Tejanos. Did you feel that scattered?

JACKSON: No, not really. Part of the problem comes from the fact that the editor there at Kitchen Sink wanted to use a different subtitle on the cover. Something about "the story of famous gunfighter John Wesley Hardin." So a lot of people saw that and bought the thing, thinking that they were getting a full-fledged book about the life of John Wesley Hardin. Actually, I'm not interested in him except in terms of this feud that I'm writing about, and the era itself. So I think some people were disappointed, because the "main character" doesn't show up until deep into the book. But if you look on the title page itself, you will see what the book is really about.

GROTH: *I noticed that.*

JACKSON: That's misleading hype, but I don't feel like I should be blamed for that. I understand that when a publishing company does a book, they want to market it on the basis of name recognition, via the Bob Dylan song, and the *Time-Life* blurb about him being so mean that he shot a man for snoring, blah, blah, blah. True, the book has sort of a "cast of thousands." And I guess that that's discombobulating if you're expecting a very focused story told just from one individual's experiences throughout. But I didn't really see any other way I could deal with it, because this one person is not there all the time.

GROTH: *I gather that focusing on John Wesley Hardin would not have told the whole story.*

Original *Lost Cause* cover ©1998 Samuel Yeates

JACKSON: No, it wouldn't have. He's in there, but right beside Creed Taylor and Joe Tumlinson, both brothers-in-law, who are the two main feudists. It's kind of like the Hatfields and the McCoys. And they are actually as large, if not larger, characters in the book than John Wesley Hardin is. If I wanted to do a biography of Hardin, believe me, it would have been completely different than this. But as I say, I was only interested in him insofar as he related to the feud, which was basically white-on-white violence. It wasn't white-on-black, except just once in a while when black people crossed them either as soldiers or policemen. I think if you'll look in the book at the number of people that are shot down, you'll see more of them are white folks than anything else.

GROTH: *Can I ask you why someone else painted the cover?*

JACKSON: Because I don't paint very much. I'm basically a practitioner of black-on-white, you know? [Taking] the old crow quill to a blank piece of paper and getting something to arise from it is completely different from color work. I have no color vision or talent for it. My experiences in the past, when I've tried to do color separations for my own art, have been dismal. About the only thing that I've really done is the *Comanche Moon* cover. And to me, this guy, Sam Yeates, is just incredible. I didn't think that Sam really captured the facial features of John Wesley Hardin. He's a little chubby there, and Hardin was more raw-boned and lean. But I think it works OK. And the other thing that probably put off Ventura, and possibly other readers, is you'll notice what's hanging behind him there on the cover.

GROTH: *Oh, yeah!* [Laughs]

JACKSON: A tattered Confederate flag. As you well know, there are a lot of states in the Union that no longer fly such a banner from the flagpole of their capitol. In a sense, maybe that is a red herring, or something, and might put off some people.

GROTH: *Well, it is provocative.*

JACKSON: I suppose so. I've tried to be like that most of my artistic career.

GROTH: *But it certainly reflects the tensions that you were portraying, so…*

JACKSON: Not only that, the book itself has those dynamics in the background. In other words, the legacy of the lost cause in terms of the Confederacy's stars and bars is the background for the entire book. But that's not the way I'm using the title. I'm not referring to the Confederacy or the Civil War, per se. I'm talking more about a passing lifestyle, of which slavery was only one aspect. I mean, here are people being told that they are going to have to live differently and think differently than they have in the past. Nobody wants to be subjected to that kind of domination, especially whenever it's done at the hands of the military.

GROTH: *I assume you were heavily influenced by Kurtzman's war material?*

JACKSON: Oh, definitely so. The funny thing about the Kurtzman war books is that the Kurtzman strips were my least favorite of all. I much preferred the stories that other artists drew. I assume that Kurtzman had a guiding hand in writing them all. Did he, or did he not?

GROTH: *Kurtzman wrote them all, except in the last few issues.*

JACKSON: But nonetheless, as a *visual* storyteller, I did not find Harvey near as effective as the rest of the guys. He was too impressionistic for my tastes.

GROTH: *I bet you liked Jack Davis.*

JACKSON: Oh, of course. Davis particularly, but most of the rest of the crowd were also outstanding. You know, Wally Wood, Reed Crandall, and —

GROTH: *John Severin.*

JACKSON: — the whole gang. Yeah. Severin especially. Those books were a real eye-opener to me, and some of the best that were ever done.

GROTH: *Has your drawing changed over the years from* Comanche Moon *and* Los Tejanos *to* Lost Cause?

JACKSON: Well, I was rushed on this book. I was given a year to produce a 140-page book, and I told them I simply couldn't do it, and they gave me a year and a half. But then I was rushed on the inking and everything, and felt like that I was doing a sloppy job.

GROTH: *Who is "they"?*

JACKSON: The editor that I had at Kitchen Sink, Chris Couch. But I can't blame him, because at this time Kitchen Sink had fallen under the wing of their West Coast investment firm. And they had, I believe, some guy there barking orders about what would be done, when, and on what schedule, and so on. It was extremely difficult to get a contract out of the boys at that time because it had to pass so many musters. There were so many hurdles that you had to clear before you could even get an OK on a book. [It was] not like in the old days — all very "corporate." And once, like I say, that they decided, yeah, they wanted to do it, then I'm put on this incredibly demanding schedule, and — so what I was trying to do was to simplify the art a little bit in the book to deliver it on time. I don't know if it's readily noticeable. The lettering, in particular, is not as carefully done as I did on *Los Tejanos*, for example.

GROTH: *I can see that.*

JACKSON: Yeah. I had a much more satisfying experience with this book that I've just finished, which should come out this summer. I believe that it

HE MOUNTS AND PARADES HIS INVULNERABILITY BEFORE THE GATHERED TROOPS.

HEY HEY, YOU POSSUM LOVERS, COME OUT AND FIGHT IRON JACKET!!

From *Comanche Moon* ©1979 Jack Jackson

BUT WHEN VASQUEZ AND HIS ARMY SUDDENLY APPEAR ON THE OUTSKIRTS OF TOWN, THE SURPRISED TEXIANS HASTILY FALL BACK AND BEAT THE DUST TOWARD THE LITTLE SETTLEMENT RENAMED IN HONOR OF JUAN SEGUIN.

LET'S MEET ON THE GUADALUPE, AT FLORES' RANCHO!

From *Los Tejanos*

THESE RAIDS DEVASTATE THE ENTIRE FRONTIER, AND THE SETTLEMENT LINE IS PUSHED BACK 100 MILES.

From *Lost Cause*

From *Indian Lover* ©1999 Jack Jackson

is the best artwork I've ever done.

GROTH: *Now what book is this, Jack?*

JACKSON: It's called *Indian Lover.* Sam Houston and the Cherokees.

GROTH: *Now how can you afford to do these books?*

JACKSON: How can I afford to do them?

GROTH: *Yeah. [Laughs.] Yes. I mean, they can't pay well.*

JACKSON: No, the pay is not very good. But you know, I decided a long time ago that life is short and you might as well be doing something you enjoy. Even if you have to kind of skimp along and starve in the process. This becomes more difficult once you have a wife and child.

GROTH: *I know.*

JACKSON: Yeah. But nonetheless, I've miraculously managed to pretty much do the types of things that I want to do, whether it is commercially viable or not. I mean, my sympathies are to my publishers, you being one of them, for going along with it, and helping my projects come to fruition.

GROTH: *I know the royalty you earned on Los Tejanos and I can't imagine that the amount of money that you were paid for Lost Cause could possibly have sustained a year and a half of living.*

JACKSON: Like I say, the only thing that makes it possible is usually people pay me as I work. So I've got a little bit coming in each month, just to cover the basics. And then I scramble for the rest.

GROTH: *Well, I'm glad you can do it.*

JACKSON: Well, yeah. I'm crazy for doing it. And that's why it hurts when some turkey calls me a racist for a labor of love. But it's what I enjoy, and I've seen so many dear friends not make it as long as I have, you know? Sheridan, Irons, Griffin — each time one of them kicks the bucket, it makes me realize that hey, our time here is not guaranteed. It's a day-by-day proposition. We'd better be doing something that we're getting some fulfillment out of. And I assume this is why you continue to do what you've been doing.

GROTH: *I think it is.*

JACKSON: Now for how long?

GROTH: *Twenty-three years.*

JACKSON: That's what I'm thinking. Hey, you're almost to retirement age.

GROTH: *Yeah, right. On what? But yeah, that makes all the difference in the world, you know?*

JACKSON: Like the old-timer musicians that were sitting around chewing the fat: "Hey, you're getting old enough to retire," and the other guy says, "Retire from what? I've never worked a day in my life." If you're enjoying it, it's not like work. I continue to do it, and I've found something that's even less rewarding, financially, than doing comic books.

GROTH: *Good God, like — let me guess — translating Croatian poetry?*

JACKSON: No, scholarly publications for the university press circuit. And I've been cranking them out, almost as many as my comic books.

GROTH: *I'd love to see some of that. How would I get a hold of it?*

JACKSON: Have you got four hundred bucks?

GROTH: *Four hundred bucks?*

JACKSON: The Book Club of Texas, which is a brainchild of Stanley Marcus, the guy who ran the big Nieman Marcus chain clothing store here in Texas. Back before the Second World War he started a thing called The Book Club of Texas that would issue quality reprints of rare and out-of-print books. It lapsed during the war, but it's been revived and they decided to publish new scholarship as well as these oldies but moldies. This summer, I hope, they're coming out with a deluxe two-volume boxed set of a book I wrote. The books are like 10-by-15, finely printed in an edition of 300 copies, and the book's called *Shooting the Sun.* It's a history of the mapping of early Texas. And you know, there is just no pay there, considering all the years of work I put into it. Because it's a worthy project, I basically forego my royalties, production costs being so high. But it will be so stunningly beautiful once it comes out.

———

GARY GROTH is the publisher of Fantagraphics Books.

James Bowie, painted from life by Benjamin West in New Orleans in 1834. Note the eagle-headed object in Bowie's right hand and compare it with the knife shown, known as "The Seguin Bowie" because Juan Seguin's name is engraved on the handle side of the quillon. It surfaced near Monterrey, Mexico, in the 1930's and the blade is inscribed, "Searles of Baton Rouge, Louisiana" (Daniel Searles made several other existing Bowies during the 1830-40's). Its blade is almost 14 inches long; overall the knife is over 17½" — an impressive weapon and one of the most elegant specimens known. (Texas State Archives, The Alamo-Office of the Curator)

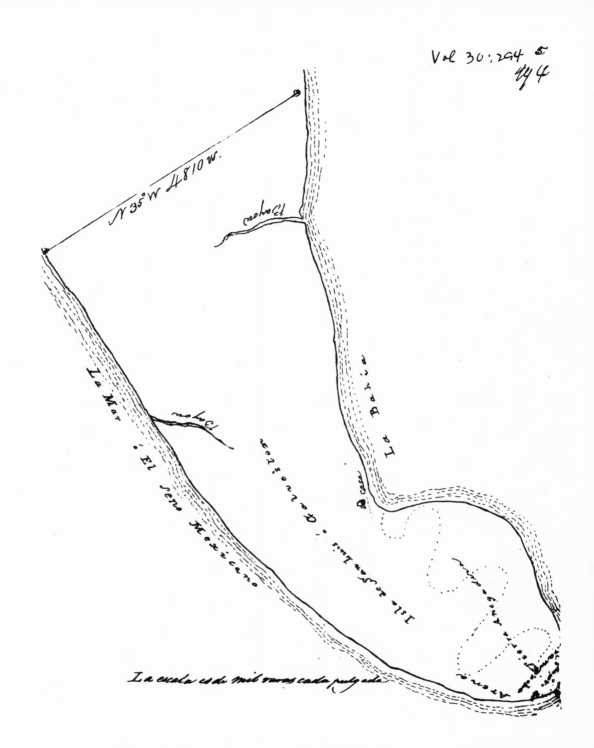

The plat map accompanying Seguin's grant of a league of land on "Isla de San Luis", or Galveston Island, issued BEFORE the Revolution, July 30, 1834. Oddly, the First Congress of the Republic then sold the island to a prominent group of businessmen led by Michel B. Menard — the same man who had located the grant for Juan under a power of attorney. Like many other early land "deals", this mysterious transaction was never fully explained, and caused some scandal in its day. Note the solitary "casa", probably the remains of Jean Lafitte's pirate stronghold, altho one surveyor noted: "No habitations... but the old Mexican custom-house." (General Land Office)

Comandancia de
Bejar. —

Al coronel. en Jefe de la armad. i
Tejas..

Señor

El día 4 del corriente tomé posesion de
esta plaza sin oposicion ninguna, se
hallava guarnecida por orden del genera
Andrade qe. mandava en esta en jefe.
por el Tente. D. Francisco Castañeda y dies
y ocho soldados, el oficial ya dicho a
contestarme la comunicacion que le hice
sobre que evacuase la plaza, me
podia entrar á ella sin oposicion y
que el se retiraba con los pocos soldados.
que tenia los qe. se hayan dispersos en la
ciudad y Castañeda salio de aqui el 6.
de este mes.
        En la ciudad corre la voz qe.
las tropas Mexicanas se han detenid
en el rio de las Nueces, camino para
Matamoros, y qe. muy pronto se rom
peran las ostilidades: en virtud de es
tar dicho punto mas inmediato de es
plaza qe. de esta, he omitido mana
espias á observar al enemigo;

The first "Texian" report to come out of San Antonio after the fall of the Alamo. Addressed to Gen. Rusk at Goliad and bearing the date of June 7, 1836, Seguin wrote: "I took possession of this place on the fourth day, instant, without any opposition whatsoever." He considered his situation with so few men (22) "very embarrassing" (muy comprometido), and asked that he be permitted to withdraw unless his promised reinforcements arrived. Local sentiment? "The majority of the citizens don't want to take up arms against the Mexican soldiers; they wish to remain neutral." "Many families are about to go to the Rio Grande and I do not know if I should detain them or let them go…" (Barker History Center, UT)

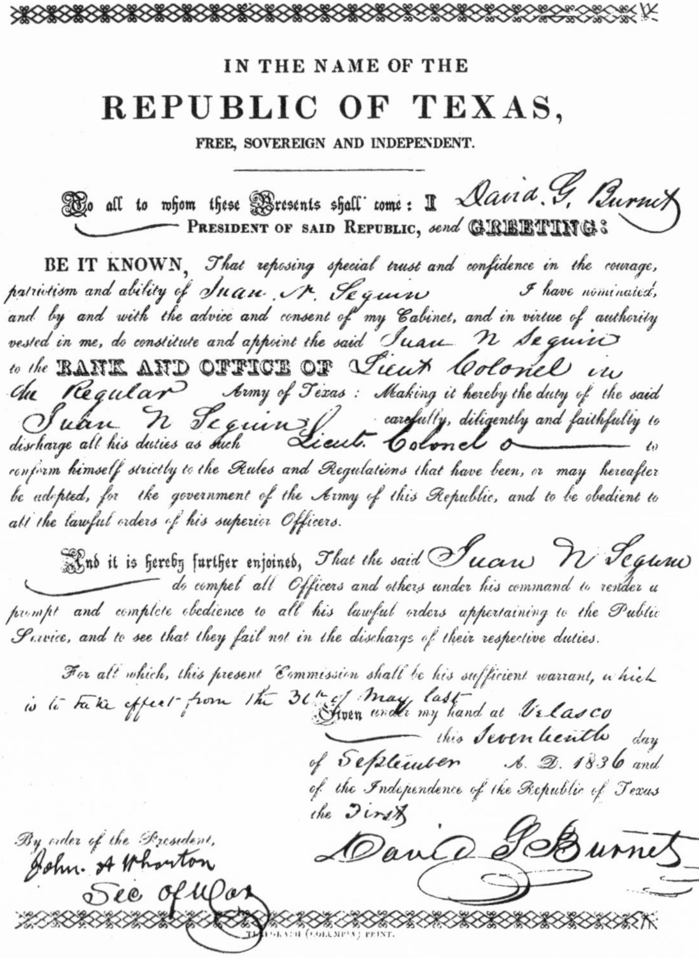

IN THE NAME OF THE

REPUBLIC OF TEXAS,

FREE, SOVEREIGN AND INDEPENDENT.

To all to whom these Presents shall come: I *David G. Burnet*, PRESIDENT OF SAID REPUBLIC, send GREETING:

BE IT KNOWN, That reposing special trust and confidence in the courage, patriotism and ability of *Juan N. Seguin* I have nominated, and by and with the advice and consent of my Cabinet, and in virtue of authority vested in me, do constitute and appoint the said *Juan N. Seguin* to the RANK AND OFFICE OF *Lieut Colonel* in the Regular Army of Texas: Making it hereby the duty of the said *Juan N Seguin* carefully, diligently and faithfully to discharge all his duties as such *Lieut. Colonel* to conform himself strictly to the Rules and Regulations that have been, or may hereafter be adopted, for the government of the Army of this Republic, and to be obedient to all the lawful orders of his superior Officers.

And it is hereby further enjoined, That the said *Juan N Seguin* do compel all Officers and others under his command to render a prompt and complete obedience to all his lawful orders appertaining to the Public Service, and to see that they fail not in the discharge of their respective duties.

For all which, this present Commission shall be his sufficient warrant, which is to take effect from the *30th of May last.*

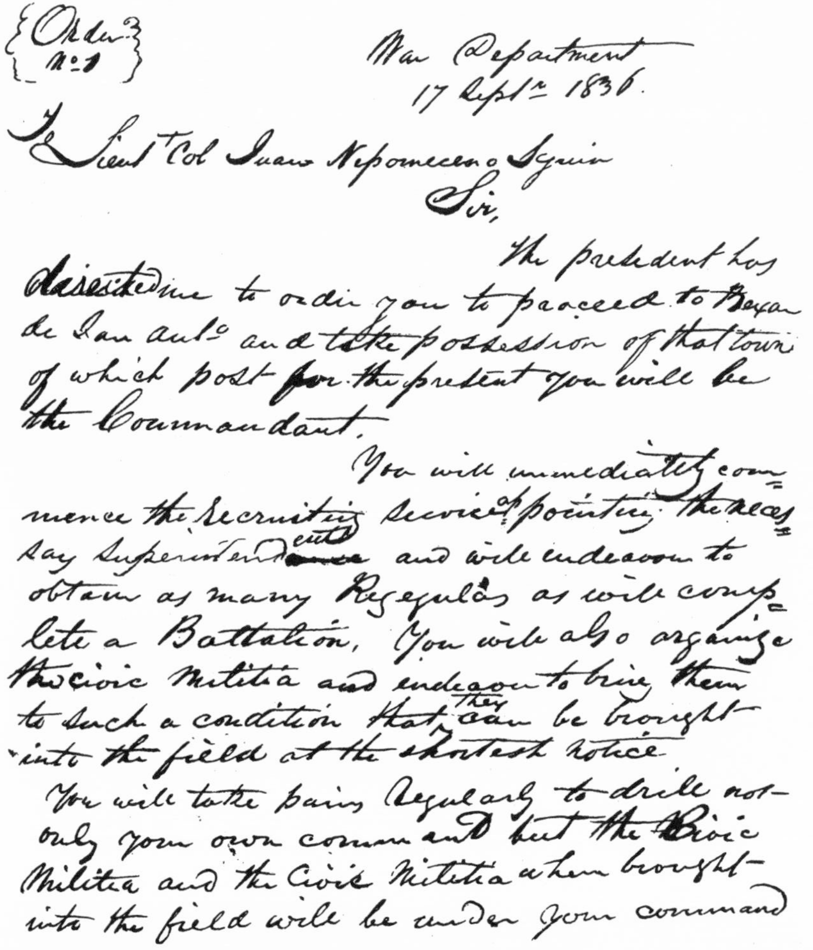

Given under my hand at Velasco this *Nineteenth* day of September A. D. 1836 and of the Independence of the Republic of Texas the First.

David G. Burnet

By order of the President,
John A Wharton
Sec of War

War Department
17 Sepr 1836.

Order
No. 1

Lieut Col Juan Nepomceno Seguin
Sir.

The President by me directs to order you to proceed to Bryan at San Antonio and take possession of that town which post for the present you will be the Commandant.

You will immediately commence the recruiting service pointing thereby more the Recruits...

[handwritten order — partially legible]

You will take being Auxiliary to drill not only your own command but the Bexar Militia and the Civic Militia when brought into the field will be under your command

---

collected, the procession halted, the coffin was placed upon the Spot, and three volleys of Musquetry wer discharged over it by one of the Companies, procceeding onwards to the Second Spot from whence the ashes were taken where the same honors were done and thence to the principal Spot and place of interment the Coffin was then placed upon the large heep of ashes when I addressed a few words to the Battalion and assemblage present in honor of the Occasion in the Castillian language as ~~to arnay proper the~~ English, Major Western then addressed the concourse in the latter tongue, the coffin and all the ashes were then interred and three volleys of Musquetry were fired over the grave by the whole Battallion with an accuracy that would do honor to the best disciplined troops. We then marched back to quarters in the City with Music and Colors flying. Half hour guns were not fired because I had no Powder for the purpose, but every honor was done within the reach of my scanty means. I hope as a whole my efforts may meet your approbation.

The cattle I alluded to in my former respects are on the March and you may expect them shortly, and more shall be collected as soon as possible circumstances permitting

I have the honor to be
Very Respectfy. &c.

John N. Seguin
Lieut. col commgr.

Seguin's translated account of the burial of the "Heroes of the Alamo" ashes, given to Gen. Albert Sidney Johnston, March 13, 1837. The actual burial site was soon lost, despite numerous efforts to relocate it, and the event itself has since become obscured by controversy. After Seguin's Fall from Grace, other Texans claimed to have performed the ceremony, and as late as 1935 Anglo writers were still trying to strip him of even this patriotic honor ("Tall Men with Long Rifles").
(Tulane)

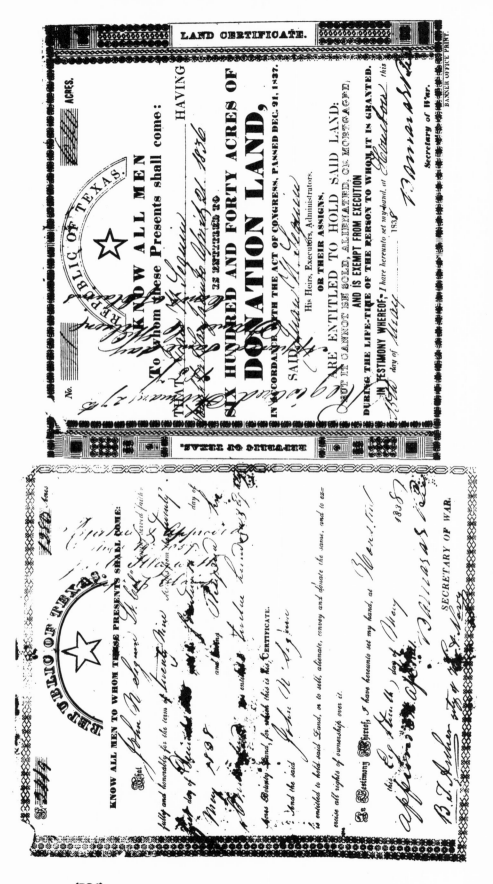

Two of Seguín's land certificates: Land Warrant No. 3449, good for 1,280 acres, awarded for "29 months service in the Army"; and Donation No. 81, 640 acres for having "fought at San Jacinto." He, like so many other soldiers, sold them for needed cash—the first in 1858 a week after it was issued; the second shortly after returning to Texas in 1848. (General Land Office)

San Antonio Octubre 14 de 1840.

Exmo. Señor Presidente dela Republica

Señor

El mal estado de Salud en que me encuentro, y la proximidad delas futuras Sesiones del Congreso, me obligan con bastante sentimiento mio a dar el indispensable paso. de renunciar el destino de Senador que obtengo por la confianza que les hé merecido á mis Constituyentes, lo que pongo en conocimiento de V.E. para que sesirba proveer en este caso conforme ala ley, desuerte que el condado que dejo de representar, no sufran algun perjuicio en las proximas Sesiones por falta del Senador que les señala ley. Al hacer a V.E. esta Comunicacion, ten el honor de ofrecerme de V.E. respetuosamente su mas adicto y obediente Servidor que atento b.S.M.

Juan N. Seguin.

Seguin's resignation as a Senator of the Fourth Congress of the Republic of Texas, dated Oct. 14, 1840. Reason given: "the poor health in which I find myself…" Actually he was organizing a 200 man volunteer outfit to fight in the Federalist War, an undertaking which he claimed that President Lamar not only "authorized", but also agreed to supply with weapons from the armories of Texas! (Texas State Archives)

(307)

country and erecting a barrier between us and our enemies

There is a difficulty as to the manner of approaching Arista but that I think can be obviated by the employment of John N. Seguin for that service, he is at present in bad odour among the Texians from which circumstance he could frame a good pretext for crossing the Rio Grande and asking an audience of Arista whether or not Seguin would accept of such a mission I cannot say, but I should think it would give him an opportunity to retreive his former standing that he would gladly embrace, for if he be successful it would redound to his credit in an eminent degree and establish his loyalty to Texas and if he be not successful he would be in none the worse condition Yourself are better acquainted than I of his fitness for such a mission.

I have understood that your Lady has been afflicted with ill health — Be pleased to present her my kind regards and my sincere wishes for her speedy recovery.

Accept the friendship
of Yours Truly

A Somervell

PERSONAL MEMOIRS

OF

JOHN N. SEGUIN,

FROM THE YEAR 1834

TO THE

RETREAT OF GENERAL WOLL

FROM

THE CITY OF SAN ANTONIO

1842.

PRINTED AT THE LEDGER BOOK AND JOB OFFICE.

1858.

PREFACE.

A native of the City of San Antonio de Bexar, I embraced the cause of Texas at the report of the first cannon which foretold her liberty; filled an honorable situation in the ranks of the conquerors of San Jacinto, and was a member of the legislative body of the Republic. I now find myself, in the very land, which in other times bestowed on me such bright and repeated evidences of trust and esteem, exposed to the attacks of scribblers and personal enemies, who, to serve *political purposes*, and engender strife, falsify historical facts, with which they are but imperfectly acquainted. I owe it to myself, my children and friends, to answer them with a short, but true exposition of my acts, from the beginning of my public career, to the time of the return of General Woll from the Rio Grande, with the Mexican forces, amongst which I was then serving.

I address myself to the American people; to that people impetuous, as the whirlwind, when aroused by the hypocritical clamors of designing men, but just, impartial and composed, whenever men and facts are submitted to their judgment.

I have been the object of the hatred and passionate attacks of some few disorganisers, who, for a time, ruled, as masters, over the poor and oppressed population of San Antonio. Harpy-like, ready to pounce on every thing that attracted the notice of their rapacious avarice, I was an obstacle to the execution of their vile designs. They, therefore, leagued together to exasperate and ruin me; spread against me malignant calumnies, and made use of odious

The title page of Seguin's 32 page pamphlet, published in 1858, the year after his father's death. Most Texans considered it a confession, not a defense, and used it as proof of his treachery—"by his own admission". (TSA)

Ranchos of the Nueces Strip

BASED ON THE OLD MAP COLLECTION, GENERAL LAND OFFICE, AUSTIN, TEXAS

THE BIGGEST OF THE BIG: (1.) San Juan de Carricitos, 601,657 acres, granted to Jose Narciso Cavazos, a consolation prize for disputing De la Garza's claim to #3. and losing ; (2.) San Salvador del Tule, 315,391 acres, granted to Juan Jose Balli. His momma Rosa was the first Texas "Cattle Queen" and brother Nicolas was the padre who owned an island; (3.) Espiritu Santo, 284,418 acres, granted to Jose Salvador de la Garza, who married a daughter of Capt. Blas Maria de la Garza Falcon, founder of Camargo. (Don Jose was also Juan N. Cortina's great-grandfather on his momma's side.); (4.) Hacienda de Dolores, 276,350 acres, granted to Juan Jose Vasquez Borrego, a big rancher from Coahuila who needed some elbow room so he founded the town of Dolores; (5.) Las Mesteñas, 146,670 acres, granted to Vicente Ynojosa (Hinajosa). He was Rosa's brother and a bachelor, so her kids inherited "The Mustangs" ranch; (6.) Joaquin Galan, grantee of Balconcitos, 159,482 acres, and Palafux, 66,975. His family was big in the military, which helped; (7.) Llano Grande, 127,625 acres, granted to Juan Jose Ynojosa de Balli, Rosa's pa. He and her husband, Jose Maria de Balli, made joint application for the "Big Plain" ranch but since both died before the paperwork came through, Rosa got it ; (8.) La Barreta, 124,297 acres, granted to Jose Francisco Balli, whose daddy Juan Antonio was a "primitive" (first) settler of Reinosa and gave land for a new townsite after a big flood wiped out the old one ; (9.) Rincon de los Laureles, 100,848 acres ; (10.) Santa Anita, 95,202 acres ; (11.) La Feria, 53,140 acres. This was her husband's 12 leagues out of the Llano Grande grant, but Rosa Maria Ynojosa had it put in her own name.

Spanish and Mexican grants in the Nueces Strip have always stood apart from other Texas lands because the Republic during its ten year existence did not exercise control over this contested area. Following the Mexican War, Gov. Bell of Texas sent the Bourland-Miller Commission to investigate all titles on the Rio Grande made prior to 1836. Bell assured the old Mexican settlers that this procedure was not meant to dispossess them (as they believed) but when all the gathered documents were lost on the steamboat Anson, which sank on the river between Rio Grande City and Brownsville, their consternation may be imagined. However, a list of the titles survived and was confirmed by the State Legislature on Feb. 10, 1852. Since then, litigation over many of these original titles — and others not on the list — has provided a rich harvest for generations of talented legal minds. Some questions remain unresolved, still tied up in the courts. Even now a group of grantee descendants called "Asociacion de Reclamantes" are engaged in a suit for compensation on lands lost during the "no-holds-barred" transition from "Mexican" to "American". The line forms to the rear...

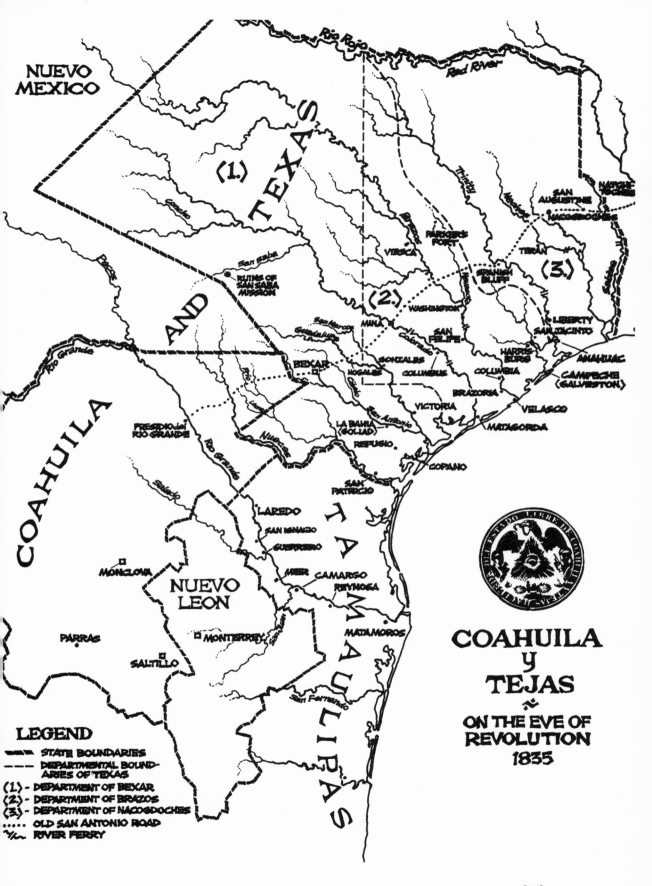

NUEVO MEXICO

TEXAS

(1.)

Rio Rojo

Red River

AND

NACOGDOCHES

SAN AUGUSTINE

NATCHITOCHES

TERAN

(3.)

PARKER'S FORT

YEGUA

SPANISH BLUFF

WASHINGTON

(2.)

MINA

LIBERTY

SAN JACINTO

SAN FELIPE

RUINS OF SAN SABA MISSION

BEXAR

NOGALES

GONZALES

COLUMBUS

COLUMBIA

HARRIS BURG

ANAHUAC

CAMPECHE (GALVESTON)

VICTORIA

BRAZORIA

VELASCO

MATAGORDA

COAHUILA

PRESIDIO del RIO GRANDE

Rio Grande

LA BAHIA (GOLIAD)

REFUGIO

COPANO

SAN PATRICIO

LAREDO

SAN IGNACIO

GUERRERO

MONCLOVA

NUEVO LEON

MIER

CAMARGO

REYNOSA

TAMAULIPAS

PARRAS

MONTERREY

MATAMOROS

SALTILLO

San Fernando

LEGEND

COAHUILA
Y
TEJAS

ON THE EVE OF
REVOLUTION
1835

JACK JACKSON

by Patrick Rosenkranz

Jack Jackson ©1972 Clay Geerdes

Jack Jackson had integrity and a personal blend of grit and persistence that compelled him to seek out the painful truth even when he knew a storm would follow. His life and his art were forged by the same hard-won lessons.

Magic happens. Freedom means acting free and helping to free others. Work with the hand you're dealt.

That's certainly the way Jackson, born May 15, 1941 in Pandora, Texas played out the hand life dealt him. His dad died when he was very young. His mom died when he was 10. He went to live with his uncle's family on a farm nearby. Ranching was a hardscrabble life to start, and young Jack was physically handicapped, to boot — heir to a genetic abnormality, Charcot-Marie-Tooth disease, which attacks the motor and sensory nerves, leading to muscular atrophy of the hands and feet and the of loss of fine motor skills.

After high school, Jackson attended nearby Texas Agricultural and Industrial College. Upon graduating in 1962 with a degree in accounting, he moved to Austin, where he got a job with the state comptroller doing "terribly boring work."

"It was a real straight job," he recalled. "If you did anything weird they'd bounce you out on your ear..."

He "started hanging around [the University of Texas] and seeing the interesting people there."

Three of those interesting people would later become his partners in founding Rip Off Press. Two of them, Dave Moriaty and Fred Todd, became Jackson's roommates.

The third, Gilbert Shelton, was editor of the school's humor magazine, *The Texas Ranger.* He recruited Jackson to be the exchange editor and a cartoonist, even though Jackson wasn't a student.

To protect his job, though, "it was imperative that I use a pen name to cover up my identity," Jackson said.

Shelton gave him that pen name — Jaxon, as in Jax Beer, a regional brand from New Orleans.

Jackson invented a cartoon character called God Nose, who used his magic sinus wand to right wrongs. When he had enough stories drawn, he decided to turn them into a comic book.

The printer in the basement of the state capitol building agreed to print them on the sly if Jackson supplied the paper.

"It was all very furtive and he got a real charge out of it. I can't say that he really thought it was a great book, but he obviously realized he was putting one over on the bigwigs," Jackson later recalled.

The 1,000 copies of *God Nose* comic books sold out locally within weeks. The proceeds allowed Jackson and Moriaty to take a trip to Europe, where they bought motorcycles and drove from England to Spain.

In 1966 he moved to California, where he got an accounting job at a clothing store on Market Street in San Francisco. Many fellow Texans were prominent in the emerging psychedelic music scene, including Janis Joplin, Boz Skaggs, and Steve Miller. Austin poet Chet Helms, head of The Family Dog, a tribal group that staged dances at the Avalon Ballroom, asked Jackson to set up a poster production and distribution department. Jackson revived the old exchange lists from *The Texas Ranger* and started a direct mail operation to sell the posters, quickly turning it into a cash cow that underwrote the dance hall end of things.

Two years later, when the poster scene was fading and underground comix were coming into their own, Jackson, Shelton, Todd, and Moriaty each plunked down $75 to buy a used printing press and start Rip Off Press. None of them knew how to run the thing, so they learned through trial and error by printing posters for Soundproof Productions. They switched to comic books, reprinting Jackson's *God Nose*, then publishing Robert

Crumb's *Big Ass* and *Motor City Comics*. Others titles followed, including *Radical America Komiks*, *The Furry Freak Brothers*, *Skull Comics*, and *Hydrogen Bomb Funnies*.

The partners soon discovered that expenses often exceeded income and their generous royalty structure was getting the best of them. As long as orders poured in from the hinterlands for everything in their catalog they could ignore the inevitable accounting. But when the triple whammy of federal crackdowns on head shops (which were their main retail outlets), a Supreme Court decision allowing obscenity to be defined by local standards, and the end of the cohesiveness of the anti-war movement, the boom turned to bust.

It was very quiet around Rip Off Press during the winter of 1973-74. Sometimes they burned comic books in the stove to keep warm.

Jackson moved back to Austin and turned to regional materials for new inspiration. He began work on his first historical comic book, *White Comanche*, which was published by Last Gasp Funnies in 1977. Within a year he had completed two more comic-book-length tales, *Red Raider* and *Blood on the Moon*.

In 1979 Rip Off and Last Gasp jointly published a trade paperback edition of his entire Native American epic, *Comanche Moon*, subtitled "the true story of Cynthia Ann Parker, her son Quanah, and the wild Comanches of Texas." It was universally hailed as an example of what would become known as a graphic novel. Jackson preferred the term pictorial fiction but had problems with that name, too. "They're not novels. They're non-fiction," he insisted.

By dint of long hours, concentration, and serious self-discipline, Jackson was able to produce more than a dozen books, ranging from graphic story histories to books of cartography to historical treatises. He also produced articles for academic journals, covers, comics for the *Austin Chronicle*, music promotions, and much more.

His 1986 book, *Los Mesteños, Spanish Ranching in Texas, 1721-1821* set new standards in historical documentation. Not only did he illustrate the characters, their livestock, brands, and tools, but he also wrote the text for the 700-page tome. It won every major history award in Texas, including the Coral Horton Tullis Memorial Prize, the Kate Broocks Bates Award, and a San Antonio Conservation Society Publication Award. (Jackson also won Kate Broocks Bates Awards in 1996, 1999, and 2003.)

Jack Jackson died the way he lived — on his own terms. At age 65, he put his affairs in order, made his own funeral arrangements, and left his home in Austin to visit his sister, Joanne, in Stockdale, Texas.

The next morning, June 8, 2006, he went to the cemetery in Stockdale where his parents were buried, knelt on their graves, and shot himself.

Poor health had a lot to do with that decision. His Charcot-Marie-Tooth disease had gradually atrophied his hands and feet, and in his last years he had developed type 2 diabetes and prostate cancer. But it may have been the death of his dream that finally led him to end his own life. He could no longer work because his hands were too unsteady to draw. His work was his life.

―――――――――

PATRICK ROSENKRANZ is a writer, educator, photojournalist, filmmaker, and noted scholar of the underground comix movement. He is the author of *Rebel Visions: The Underground Comix Revolution*, *You Call This Art?! A Greg Irons Retrospective*, and *The Artist Himself: A Rand Holmes Retrospective*.

Jack Jackson ©2006 Kathy Doyle